I0692317

Heavenly Realm Publishing Company
Houston, Texas

My Song of Solomon

a novel

Heavenly Realm Publishing Company
Houston, Texas

Stephanie Franklin

For information on how to order, re-order, bulk orders, or book signings and speaking engagements, please contact Heavenly Realm Publishing Company at 1-713-742-3405 or P.O. Box 547, Houston, Texas 77001-0547, or visit www.stephaniefranklin.org

Other Books by Stephanie Franklin

When Ramona Got Her Groove Back From God

My Song of Solomon Prayer Journal

I Believe God! *Prayer Journal*
Write Your Own Profession of Faith

He is my song. His words—His voice—His emotion. God, my infinity… I dedicate this to you.

*Dipper, I knew you were an
angel sent from dog Heaven...*

Acknowledgements

I am so grateful and thankful to my Lord and Savior Jesus Christ for allowing me to write another book. I pray that You are pleased Heavenly Father just as You were with the first best selling novel, *"When Ramona Got Her Groove Back From God"*. I also pray that so many lives will be changed and blessed through this novel just like they were with the first one.

To all of those who constantly pray and support me, thank you, you know who you are...

To all of those who played a part in any advice and towards the printing of this book, thank you.

To Heavenly Realm Publishing and to my editing staff, thank you and continue to let God use you.

Preface/Introduction

You may be someone who has made many mistakes and you are feeling as though God will never forgive you. But I'm here to tell you that God will. He is a forgiving and a merciful God. Once you have repented, asked Him for forgiveness, and have accepted Him as your Lord and Savior, He will began to change your life and turn your situation around. So many people have counted you out and have torn your reputation apart. Told you, you were not going to be anything; nobody will ever accept you because you're dumb and stupid, and that you will never amount to anything in this life. If this fits you, after reading this novel you will receive back everything that the devil has stolen from you: your life, your confidence, your mind, your dignity, your love, your heart, your future, and your blessings.

Just because you make a mistake in life does not mean that you still cannot and will not become successful. Look at Barina's life, a perfect example of another we fall down but we don't stay there, we get back up and try again.

Barina made a terrible choice early in her life that she had to pay for. But she did not give up, she proved to her family, friends, and to the entire world that single young mothers can still find their destiny and make something big out of themselves.

Remember, when God begin to bless you financially, spiritually, and emotionally, remember to stay humble and to give Him all the glory. Continue to live for Him because if not, it will all come crashing down just like it did in Barina's life. *(Proverbs 16:18)*

She succeeded despite her circumstances. She was a young fourteen-year old mother, homeless at one point, but God helped her because she did not give up. She hung in there with all of her strength and she made it. She regained her life, her mind, her confidence, her dignity, her freedom, her future, and the priceless love that was stripped from her: finding a new love—an everlasting love—a spiritual love song...

Many waters cannot quench love; neither can floods drown it..."
(Song of Solomon 8:7 KJV)

My Song of Solomon

May 2003

The sound of the ocean waves are gushing against the seashore like the sound of a forceful command. Strong tides are rushing over the wet sand like a roaring lion as they rush towards me and roll back into the ocean. Birds are squawking in the air as they watch their prey, make their final move, swoop down towards the watered sand, and grab their choice selection. The head of the sun is now peaking over the horizon, as the wind blows through my purple flowered spaghetti strapped sundress I bought at the thrift shop for $2. A good wash and dry makes it looks like it's well worth $200. I smiled at the thought. Every strand of my long, sandy colored, twisted kinky hair is stickin' straight up from the coolness of the wind, as it rests on top of my light cream-colored skin. My hair is molded on top of my narrow face and partially oriented eyes. I have to mention my thin lips; they're a little parched from the dampness of the moistened air.

Night's fallin' fast, I better hurry if I wanna' finish this book. I'm just about done, just a few more lines…

Night fell fast and God knows it's been such a beautiful day all day today. And this' been some relaxin' weather too. The rush of the wind is now blowing through the opened floor modeled windows of my oceanfront Santa Fe' style mansion. I love it because it's sitting right off the ocean and it's deep in the heart of Ocean Creek Estates—a place where everybody wants to put their dream home. The open front floor modeled windows start almost at the top of the ceiling and then run down not quite to the floor. There's plenty of life outside to see,

1

that's why I wanted em' so large. I love looking out of em' at night with the dark ocean view in the foreground, and the dark shadows of the town's night life, with glowing action lights shinning bright in the background. When I walk through the front door I'm surrounded by this two-story ceiling and cream tile that covers the entire downstairs floor. Not a carpet in sight. Just the way I like it. That's one thing I do not like is the feel of carpet rubbing through my toes. If anybody asks me why, I can't even tell em'. Just a few throw rugs do enough justice to satisfy the toes. I guess that's what I can say. My beautiful spotted, burgundy velvet cushioned couches in my formal room is the first thing I see when I walk in from a long day. I'm proud because I got em' at a garage sell for a little of nothin'. I have an ottoman sittin' in front of each one of my sofa's and recliner's. I love ottoman's, there's so many different designs and so many ways that they add to the outcome of the room and also to the furniture. I put my designers touch to use—I got the furniture surrounded by decorative floor modeled plants and contemporary cherry wood grained corner tables with fashionable vases sittin' on top, just right and not too cluttered. A bit retro? Yes indeed. The white sheer curtains do so much justice as they shower out of the upstairs windows like flying angels. I still can't believe this' all mine. It's a spanking brand new built from the ground up mansion with five bedrooms, along with the master bedroom being another room all by itself. It has a fireplace that can be seen in the bedroom and also in the bathroom. The bathtub is as large as the Jacuzzi in the backyard. My mansion also has a four car garage, four ½ baths, game room, a private room I made for my study and prayer, with a beautiful circular stair case that runs up to the ceiling like a funnel, wrapping itself around a huge antique formal sparkling chandelier. And out back there's a waterfall pool that sits off the rocks and a Jacuzzi that sits off the beach. It's a dream within itself. I can't complain none whatsoever. My privacy is so perfect! My neighbors live about a hundred yards away, and I'm taking advantage of all the peace and quiet I have around me. Every now and then I can hear the sound of children playing because my neighbors have children. They all come out and wade in the water and walk up and down the beach. The dad must be an actor because it seems like I've seen him in a movie before on the big Hollywood scene.

I'm puttin' the finishing touches on my eleventh book. I've been asked to do a book signing down at the Convention Center. I'm so grateful! God's been so good to me! I can remember when I didn't have anything. I was homeless and out on the street with a child I wasn't old enough to take care of. There were so many times I wanted to give up. Throwing my baby in the dumpsters would have been the easiest way to get rid of it. That way I could run away somewhere and kill myself and not have to hear the moans of her cries as she would plead for me to come back. But thank God I didn't go down like that. It was so hard being a fourteen-year old mother. I got pregnant thinkin' I could keep a boy that at first I thought loved me, and then who I thought that if I just have his baby, he wouldn't go nowhere. Not! Didn't work! Just the opposite happened. When I told him that I was pregnant, he threw me down on the ground denying that the baby was his. He kept runnin' til' I never saw him again. One of the hardest things I ever had to do in my entire life was to tell my saved, sanctified, and Holy Ghost filled parents that I was pregnant. Tears are falling from my eyes at the thought. Back then they were tears of shame, bitterness, guilt, and hate. But now I can say that today they're tears of healing, deliverance, joy, and gratefulness. It's somethin' about when a person thinks back to where God has brought em' from, and brought em' out of, they just gotta' give Him praise! And right now I just gotta' give Him praise and all the glory that is due to Him.

3

August 1989- Reagan High

I'm a fool in love. Wayne loves me I know it. He tells me everyday but he doesn't get that much time to show it by him being so popular and all. He's one of the captains on the football team and he's also very well known and highly respected by so many. As for me, well, I'm just the opposite. I'm not popular at all. I'm just an average fourteen-year old freshman that's scared to death of the upper classmen. They say if we join the cheerleading team or the pep squad, we'd become well known real fast. Whatever that means... I'm not a dancer, nor can my slim waist and big hips jump as high as they can. I don't have time to do all that borin' stuff no way. I wish I felt different though. My life is basically based around church. I mean my body is based around church, but my mind and my heart are so far away from the church and from God. *(Philippians 4:7)* My parents are devoted Christians. Minister Jerry Charles Grant and Missionary Clara Grant is what people call em' at church, but I refer to em' as mama and daddy. They're highly respected and very well known in the community and in church. Mama is over the usher board and the women's ministry. And she's been working at the Post Office for about fifteen years. And daddy is a faithful minister and he's over the finance committee. He's a very smart man. He also has his own small business doing taxes, which sometimes requires late hours. Anything that looks like mess, they run from it. I couldn't mess up even if I wanted too. It gets hard trying to please the way my parents want me to live. They want me to be so perfect. They know me better than I know my own self. Their expectations are so high for me. I guess because I'm the younger of

5

two children. I had an older brother who got killed several years ago in a car accident on his way to his senior prom. He died instantly. They used to show him so much favoritism over me. He couldn't do no wrong. Stayed out all night, half the night, or when ever he wanted to come home. Me on the other hand, had a strict curfew. I had to be in the house before dark, and still do to this day. My life is so boring. Besides my writing, one thing I am happy about is the fact that I have a boyfriend. Well I think He's my boyfriend. Sometimes he acts like it, and sometimes he don't. His name is Wayne Matthews, but everybody calls him B-Wayne, which stands for Big Wayne because he's the biggest guy on the football team. He looks to be about 6'5, 290 pounds, with a slight muscle tone. Some people say he's a little chubby, but he's not, he's just a big thick guy. I know he's ganna' get a scholarship one day. Colleges are already writing him left and right. He's so popular, all the girls like him and all the guys like hangin' around him. I can't believe he chose me to be with. He can be a little controlling at times, but I look over it because I realize it's just him. His parents spoil him. They give him everything he wants. And I guess he wants the same from me. I give him money all the time. Sometimes I even give his friends money too. I buy Wayne clothes and put gas in his car. I figure this is what a girlfriend is supposed to do, even though he doesn't nearly do the same for me. Since my parents pick me up right after school, the time I have to spend with Wayne is so short. He's always beggin' me to skip school to spend some time with him, like goin' to his house to watch some movies. He's got all my favorite movies so I just might consider the offer. Let me go and call em' and tell em' that I guess I'll go ahead and skip with him. "Hello?" His answering machine comes on. "Yo' dis' B-Wayne, leave dim' digits...." The answering machine beeped.

"Hey Wayne, this' Barina—I guess I'll come over your house tomorrow so you can stop beggin'. Meet me by the gym instead of in front of the school." Click. I hung up the phone. I'm sure he'll get the message and call me back tonight to confirm.

Wayne dresses so nice to be so big. All the guys have this crazy style about em'. They wear these big baggy jeans, with big baggy button-down shirts, with t-shirts underneath—with the middle of the shirt only tucked in—I guess it's supposed to show off their belt buckles. I don't know but it really doesn't serve their figures any

6

justice. These lil' ol' guys be takin' it to the extreme with their pants hangin' past their butts. That's somethin' I can't quite get with and I'm not nearly attracted too. But I'll have to say that it really looks good on Wayne cause' he's such a big guy.

I made it to school early considering how late I woke up. Sometimes I hate comin' to my locker cause' everybody likes to step all over me with the halls being so crowded and congested. The sounds of screaming and loud conversations of, "you better get ready for the big test in third period," or, "yo' man, I'm ready for football practice coach got me startin' in the next game," or, "girl that's cute what chu' got on I started to get somethin' like that." All the things that they're saying to one another makes me know that it's mid August and in a couple of weeks all of this excitement will all wear down. There's an excitement in the atmosphere considering the fact that it's the start of a new school year and new things like hot lookin' guys and who I'm gon' get with first. As for me it means I'm in the year of initiation, which means all freshmen—fish—for lack of better words have to go through this process of proving who we are and establishing our own identities. All the upper classmen already went through this so I guess I'm no different. Wayne just came from around the corner with some friends and I quickly walked up to him. I gotta' check him for not handlin' up on his business last night. "You must of got in late, cause' you never called me back?" I smiled up at him tryin' to cover up the fact that I'm so intimidated by him.

"Naw', what had happened was I was with moms and pops all night. We went over my cousin's house. Hey why you checkin' up on me anyway?" He towered over me with a huge frown on his face. "I'm good about mine?" He pointed to himself as if he was all that. "Hey you ready? We ridin' in my car." He walked off without waiting for me.

"Yea', I guess so." I hesitated.

He quickly turned around and rushed up to me like I said somethin' about his mama. "You guess so? What's up, do you wanna' do this or not?" He raised his voice and pointed his finger in my face. "I ain't wastin' no gas on you girl, there's more girls that wanna' come too!" He stepped back and slowly started backing up. "I'm not beggin'!" He waved a back hand in the air and started walking towards the double doors going to the student parking lot. His friends walked off in the opposite direction laughing like what he said was so funny.

"Alright, I guess I'll go!" I threw up my hands, caught up with him, brushed passed him, and walked on out of the double doors.

"Cool." He smiled as he followed me.

We walked to his car, got in, and left going towards his house. It took what seem like an hour considering all the traffic lights. The weather's pretty chilly so Wayne let me wear his lettermen jacket. His jacket has every award he's ever won in high school on it. It has his name on the back with football patches on the arms. He's such a great athlete. He's really not supposed to be going to our school cause' he doesn't live in the school zone, but somehow the coach and his daddy worked it all out. He lives in an average size brown two-story brick corner house with red wooden shutters around the windows, and a cream trim around the out line of the house. It's not what chu' call a knock out, but it'll do. As we drove up to the driveway, I notice that there's not a car in sight. Wayne hurried up and zipped in the driveway like somebody was after him.

"Yo' we here. Come on." He got out and I followed. We walked to the door, went inside, and he took me straight upstairs to the family room. He motioned for me to sit on the couch while he turned on the big screen TV.

"You have a nice house." I lied. My smile I can't hide, but he doesn't know what I'm smiling about so I still look innocent. His house is uglier on the inside than it is on the outside. It's decorated too plain. I thought as I watched him walk back over towards the TV.

"Thanks." He grabbed the remote, started turning the channels, and slowly walked over and sat down beside me. "So, what chu' wanna' watch? All these movies are about to come on?" He scrolled through the TV guide on the screen.

"Are your parents ok with us watching these movies on pay-per-view? You know they have to pay for these movies?"

"How many times do I have to tell you that I run thangs? Moms and pops don't care. I wish you would just trust me?" He looked at me with a smirk on his face.

"I do trust you. I just don't do things without my parent's permission, at least at home that is."

"Well that's what makes us different. I do what I wanna' do and I go and come like I want too. I clean up my room when I want too—actually I hardly ever cause' moms do it for me. I talk to my parents like I want too. It's like we're friends. They really don't care. My life is cool, I love it cause' they ain't breathin' down my back. As long as I'm playin' good football, I can get anything I want from my dad. And as long as I'm makin' A & B honor roll, I'm in total control of my mom. So I got it made. It's like I'm already an adult." He closed his eyes and smiled with confidence, threw his hands behind his head, and leaned back into the couch like he's the man.

"Is that why you always think you can have your own way?"

"And you know it." He smiled even harder.

"Wayne that's not right how you treat your parents, and how you sometimes treat me." I hesitated because I thought he was gon' slap me like he did before when I disagreed with him about something else the other day. He's not abusive though, although some may think.

"Whose side are you on?" He turned his entire body towards me.

"I'm on your side, I'm just sayin'."

"You better be. Look, c'mon and pick a movie before I take you back to the school girl." He started changing the channels.

"That movie's fine, we can watch that one." I pointed at the TV screen. I don't know what movie I just chose, I just wanna' keep peace and make him happy. To be honest, I don't want him to hit me again even though he's only hit me twice since we've been talkin'; most of the time I just agree so he won't start acting crazy. A couple of girls in my 3rd period class said that he's controlling. I don't think he's controlling, he just wants his way all the time. They're just jealous.

"Hey you can take my jacket off and get comfortable, I ain't gon' bite." I took it off. "Now you can scoot closer to me. I just wanna' hold you while we watch the movie." I did what he wanted. "Hey look, my parents won't be home til' bout' another six hours, do you wanna'?"

"Wanna' what?"

"Wanna'. You know? That?" His eyes moved up and down my body.

"That what?" I pretended not to know, hoping he would change the subject and watch the movie.

"Awe' girl now you playin' crazy."

9

"Wayne, I'm just gon' be honest with you. I don't believe in having sex before marriage. *(1 Thessalonians 4:3)* Its fornication and it's against what the bible says."

He jumped to his feet. "I don't care bout' what no bible says! I just wanna' have sex with you!" He stood there for a moment then sat back down. "How long you think you gon' last til' you give it up, everybody's doin' it? You gon' be the outcast." I stared at the floor as he scooted closer to me. "Don't you know we're too young to do exactly what the bible says? I think God understands. He knows there ain't no way we gon' be able to last til' we get married. I'm a tell you straight up, I might not ever get married." He said as I turned and looked up at him. "I mean if I do I would consider you. But you wanna' wait too long. If we gon' get married anyway, why wait?" I didn't answer. "O' so I guess you don't wanna' marry me now, huh'?"

"Yea' I wanna' marry you. But…"

"But nothin'. C'mon, you thinkin' too deep. Stay young and stop tryin' to act like an old woman. We gotta' enjoy ourselves now so when we get old, we won't say we should've did this, or we should've did that. So what's up girl? What chu' gon' do?" I didn't answer him again. "C'mon baby, you know I love you? I know I never said it before, but I do love you. And if you love somebody, these are the things they share. So what's up?"

"Umm', well, I really don't feel comfortable doing this. And I really don't feel comfortable doing this in your parent's house."

"Awe' girl thea' you go. Don't think like that." He reached over and started massaging my shoulders.

Ain't nobody ever massaged these shoulders before, what have I gotten myself into? He took his hand and slowly went up my blouse up to my chest. "Stop!" I jerked away.

"C'mon now." He started rubbing my inner thigh. He was determined to make me loose my virginity. And eventually he did….

Two hours later.

"Are you ready? Let me take you back to school. You know you're special right?" He smiled like he just won a bet.

"I guess." I answered in pain, never looking at him. In the back of my mind I know God's not pleased with me. And what would my parents think if they ever found out that I just had sex with somebody

I'm not even married to. *(Romans 1:29-32)* How could I ever forgive myself, let alone God forgiving me? We got in the car, quiet all the way back to the school. I didn't see or hear from B-Wayne for about two weeks. How could I have done what I did? Maybe it was the right thing? I mean I did make him happy? And all I wanna' do is make him happy. He said he loves me and one day we're ganna' get married...

November 1989

It's going on three months now. Two weeks before the Thanksgiving Holidays. Everybody's gettin' into the Thanksgiving spirit. It's funny because no matter what season comes our way, the styles will never change. With Thanksgiving on the way, every family in town's gon' be together eatin' barbeque, potato salad, and playing loud music while doing the Harlem Shuffle. I laughed to myself. O' I can't leave out the Whop, the Prep, and the Skate those are some of the hottest dances at Reagan High. Basketball season is in full effect. Everybody's pumped up and excited, and I have to admit I am too. Well maybe sort of. Lately I've been feeling sick to my stomach. It's been goin' on for about a week now—straight. I haven't been able to hold anything in my stomach, especially in the mornings. I won't mention the fact that I haven't seen or heard from B-Wayne. I've tried calling him but he never returns any of my calls. When I go to his locker, he's never there during the times I can go. He doesn't play basketball, so I can't go see if he's at practice. I guess he leaves right when school lets out. So maybe it's over between us? I guess he got what he wanted, and now he's satisfied and wants nothing to do with me. I thought as I sat on my bed and looked out the window. Mama and Daddy are down stairs preparing for dinner. Daddy's barbequing on the grill in the backyard, and Mama's cookin' something to go with the meat Daddy's got on the pit. They seem to be havin' a good time with one another.

There's a knock at the door. "Who is it?" I yelled, still looking out the window.

13

"Its mama, are you alright? Dinner's ready! Come and eat!" She shouted as her voice forcefully squeezed its way through the cracks of the door. "Do you still have that stomach virus? It's going on a week now? If so, then we might need to take you to the doctor tomorrow morning. I'll just have to take off from work!"

"No mam' my stomach's fine!"

"Alright good then come and eat!" I heard her foot steps walk away.

When I got downstairs and took one look at the food, my stomach turned and I threw up all over the floor.

Mama looked at the floor and threw her hand over her mouth. "Oh' my God, you said you were feeling better? I'm taking you to the emergency room tonight! Jerry!" She screamed for Daddy to come in. It wasn't a second and he came dashing through the patio door.

"What's goin' on?" He looked down at the floor, looked at me, and then looked at mama. "What's wrong with her? You still sick girl? That shouldn't be? Now don't no stomach virus last this long? We're takin' you to the hospital, baby go get her stuff." She went upstairs. "I don't know what's wrong with you, but we gon' soon find out. You not pregnant are you?"

"Daddy how could you? So now you don't trust me, is that what chu' tryin' to say?"

"It ain't that I don't trust you, I do trust you, I just don't trust that knucklehead boyfriend of yours! I know you got one!" He yelled like I couldn't hear him.

"You been goin' through my stuff Daddy?" I threw my arm in the air in frustration.

"No, I just been prayin'!" He put the tray of barbeque on the kitchen counter, wiped his hands on the towel that's hanging from around his waist, and walked over to me. "Now you know you can't come back in here with no baby?" He pointed his finger at me. "We always tried to instill in you what the Word of God says about having sex before marriage. Yo' mama and I have always believed that you would save yourself for your husband and obey the Bible. It's not just about saving yourself, but it's about stayin' pure before God."

"Yea' Daddy I know what it says." I said as Mama came back downstairs with my purse and sweater.

Daddy walked over to the pantry door and grabbed his keys from off the key holder. "I mean what I said about you not coming back in this house with no baby." Mama didn't say a word. "As active as me and your mother is in church, we can't afford to put that shame on us and you either. How'd that look anyway, we preachin' about stayin' holy and pure before God, and our own child walks in church with a big ol' belly talkin' bout' she pregnant. How would that look huh?" He looks at me then at mama. We both shrugged our shoulders as if to be confused and intimidated by the force of his words. "Let's go, I got things to do." He said as we all walked out the door.

Daddy has this very stern voice and personality about him. He's a very bold man and he can be real intimidating at times. Mama always seems so afraid of him. She never stands her ground for nothin'. Whatever he says goes no matter what it is, even if he's wrong and he knows he's wrong. It can be the simplest things, and he's gon' be right. She ain't got no backbone. I ain't gon' never let no man do me like that.

It was about a twenty-minute drive to the hospital.

We've already seen the doctor and now we're waiting in the waiting room for the results.

After about another ten minutes he finally comes out. "Mr. and Mrs. Grant, how're you doing?" He shakes both of their hands. "I'm doctor Simons and I have the results of Barina's illness… Barina is 3-months pregnant." Everything got so quiet you could hear a pin drop. My mind went blank and my heart went numb. "There are many programs that you can sign up for. I've attached the sheets to her charts." He tries to hand them to Daddy but he pushes them away.

"No, we won't be needing em'." He grabs mama's hand. "Come on let's go." They started walking off. Didn't even bother including me so I just followed in silence. I had to trot just to keep up.

It was a longer ride going home than coming. I can hear mama sniffing and blowing her nose. Daddy's eyes are blood shot red. They said nothing to me the entire ride home. My mind's racing. My thoughts have become a reality. What am I gon' do with a baby? I can barely take care of myself, with the help of my parents. Don't even have a job? What will they think at school? What will B-Wayne say when I tell him? We only did it once. How could this be? I guess that's all it takes.

We pulled up in the driveway not a minute too soon, and not a minute too late. Daddy parked all the way in the garage like he always does. But this time he left the garage door open, which he normally closes. We all got out and started walking towards the door leading into the house. I was the last one walking in with my boots clicking the cemented pavement. My head's down and I'm careful with every step I take. Before I could step into the house, Daddy quickly turned around and blocked the door. "Where you think you goin'? I told you, you couldn't come back up in this house with no baby, and I meant what I said!" Mama had already vanished around the corner. Daddy's eyes are even redder. Hurt and tears are all over his face. I started screaming. He tries to close the door but I grabbed it trying to keep it open. We struggled for a moment but his strength was much too great. He slammed the door in my face.

"Daddy, no!" I bammed on the door with my fist. "Where I'm gon' go Daddy huh'? Where I'm gon' go?" I cried out. I slid my back down the door until my bottom hit the ground. "I'm sorry! Please don't do me like this!" I hit the door with the back of my elbows. "Mama you gon' let Daddy do me like this? I need ya'll! You all I got!...."

It's the next morning. I cried all night in the hot sticky garage. Mosquito bites are all over my body, and I'm a nervous wreck. Mama and Daddy just walked all over me, got in their vehicles and drove off like I was a piece of trash. Who would've ever thought that two people who brought me into this world would ever do their only daughter like this? It's like they never knew me. I'm not gon' bother goin' to school this morning, this' just too much for me right now. I can't believe that Mama didn't say a word. Daddy has so much control over her. She's so afraid of him. All I can do is think about how in the world am I gon' get myself out of this one? This is all new to me. I've never experienced anything like this before. How can I get rid of this baby without anybody knowing it? Maybe I can take something and poison it, that way it'll die and nobody'll ever know I was pregnant. I can't do that to an innocent life and plus I'd be in deeper trouble with God. Fornication then murder? No, I can't and I won't do it. *(Galatians 5:21)*

16

I left that same day Mama and Daddy walked all over me in the garage. I broke in the house, got all I could stuff in my backpack, took some money, and left walking to nowhere. It's going on 3 ½ weeks and I have survived out in the city of cold-hearted reality. I tried getting into a shelter but they were all booked up, or there was a waiting list. Thanksgiving holidays are over. I can't say how I got through it. I sat on the cold bus stop bench, flashed back to the memories of my parents, and all my family coming together and eating the traditional turkey dinner. It was more than a turkey it was about the love, the sharing, and the caring that I really miss. My parents probably lied and told the family that I was out of town just to keep from tellin' em' the truth. I spent two days tryin' to figure out who I was cause' it felt like I was about to loose my mind. I was standing neck-deep in hurt, shame, pain, and disappointment. Then all of a sudden this overwhelming Spirit of peace came over me, and I knew then that the Lord still cared for me. And that's what's been keepin' me from killing myself and somebody else. All I got left now is this tiny fetus livin' inside of me and my pride. I'm sittin'on this bus stop bench thinkin', can't nobody tell that I'm pregnant yet cause' I'm not showing that much. I've been wearing these large t-shirts that I stole down at this clothing store about 2-blocks from here, so that makes it harder to tell—which is good. It gives me some time to think about what I'm gon' do. Maybe if I had a reliable friend, I could ask them to help me, but I don't. The world would consider me as a runaway, but I'm officially homeless. I've been beggin' for money, food, and constantly searching for a warm place to lay my head. The street life is what it is. Dope pushers everywhere tryin' to steal my life and my body. Alcohol's been a substitute for food. It takes the hunger pains away. I never thought in my life that I would become an alcoholic. As holy as my parents are, they would die if they saw me drinking. This crack-head turned me on to it. I was hungry and thirsty, he offered, so I tried it. So what, what do I have to loose anyway my life is over. I got a baby on the way, haven't finished school, no home to go too, no food, no reliable friends to call on, and no parents to love me. Whatever.

My morning sickness is gone. Can't say when or how, but it's gone. Worse things are happening now. I'm hungrier and I'm using the restroom a lot. I used to go up to restaurants and eat food from off of the plates left by previous customers. I did this til' the managers ran me off. I've been sleeping down at the washateria along with some other homeless people. I make a little change when the owner lets me wash some loads that people bring in. I add that up with some of the things I steal down at the clothing store. I'm sure I'm not the only one, people steal all the time. I sleep all day. I have no energy. I need to go and get a check up but I'm too scared they might try and take my baby. I haven't been back to the hospital since I found out that I was pregnant.

I finally got the courage to go back to school after being out for what seem like forever. It seems that way because of the extra days we had out for the holiday. I'm determined to finish school and make a better life for me and my baby. Nobody else is, so I better do it. I've stopped drinking and stealing from the corner store. *(Exodus 20:15)* It ain't even worth goin' to the pen for years and to have to give birth to my child up in there, and then watch them take my baby away never to see it again. If God still loves me, He'll help me....

I busted up the courage to go tell B-Wayne that I'm pregnant. I think walking to his house would be better. Maybe his parents will hear me telling him and just maybe they'll take me in. I'll catch the bus over there and walk up to his house. It's late, I know it, but it's gotta' be done either now or never. And furthermore, I could care less.

As soon as I knocked on the door, B-Wayne opened it as if he was expecting somebody. "What's up girl? What're you doin' here?" He stepped outside and closed the door behind him. "Are you crazy? Do you know how late it is?"

"Look I need to talk to you. It's very important."

"Why you wearin' that big ol' t-shirt?" He started laughing.

"Look this is why I came over here! Ok?" I pulled the shirt tight around my belly. "I'm pregnant Wayne, and you're the daddy!" I yelled hoping the entire neighborhood could hear me.

"Girl would you shut up?" He grabbed my shoulders and started squeezing them. "My parent's gon' come out here."

"Owt'! That hurt!" I broke loose from him. "You don't have to grab me like that Wayne!"

"Wayne what's going on out there?" His mom screamed from inside the house.

He opened the door and yelled inside. "Nothin' I'm alright! Everything's alright!" He shut the door back. "Look I can't do nothin' for you. That's not my baby. I'm about to go to college, maybe even pro. I don't have time to be packin' round no family. I don't believe it's mine no way. Probably one of those chumps you hang with." He looked away.

"O' it's yours B-Wayne and you know it! I didn't wanna' do it in the first place: And you know I was a virgin!—Look, I really need your help, my parents kicked me out and I don't have anywhere else to go! Please help me!"

"I can't help you. Go tell yo' baby's daddy to help you cause' I ain't the one."

"You're the daddy; don't even play me like that! Don't do me like this B-Wayne! I thought you said you love me and that you wanted to marry me?"

"Girl don't you get it? That was only to get the goods. I don't love you. I'm too young to love you, let alone marry you." He laughed and I started crying. "Now you gotta' go before moms and pops come out here." He tried to turn and open the door, but I grabbed him and tried to pull him towards me. "Let me go girl!" He broke loose, grabbed me, and pushed me on the ground. I screamed. His parents came running outside.

"What's goin' on out here Wayne?" His mother yelled.

"She showed up here sayin' all kinds of lies!" He pointed at me.

"I ain't lyin' I'm pregnant by him!" I got up off the ground and rubbed the bloody scrap on my elbow as if the sooth it.

"You're what?" She raised her voice and looked at Wayne for his answer.

"Mama don't listen to her, you know I'm bout' to go pro and you tol' me how these females gon' come up lyin' tryin' to trap me?"

"B-Wayne, how many times do I have to tell you to leave these trifling lazy girls alone? Huh'?" He starts pushing his mother back in the house as his daddy followed.

"Too many times mama. I know…" Their voices faded as he shut the door behind them.

"Just like that? I road the bus all the way over here just to get pushed on the ground and a door slammed in my face!" I yelled as I threw myself down on the ground and tried to cry every tear from my eyes.

He never came back to the door again, and I left walking towards the bus stop. When I looked back towards his house, I found him watching me from his room with the curtain pulled back. "Busta'! You'll never get away with this!" I yelled into the night's air as if he could hear me.

How could the guy I thought loved me, betray me? I just knew he would help me, but instead he abandoned me just like my parents did. I now know that's why you should never give up your body just to make somebody happy and just to keep em'. Because by you givin' it up, ain't gon' change things for the better, it'll only change things for the worse. I didn't think about all that at first. All I knew was that he said he loved me and I had to keep him loving me. Not realizing that it was all a set up. And now I have a tiny little body growing inside of me because I chose not to think.

May 1990

These have been some tryin' days that I have not looked forward too. Six months have passed and little Karina have just been born, all 8 pounds 6 ounces of her. They didn't keep us in the hospital very long. In fact, they let us out the very next day.

We struggled on the streets for what seemed like forever. Karina would cry at night and all I could do was cry with her hoping for a miracle. Thank God there was finally an opening at the shelter that's located in the heart of downtown. The woman didn't even ask my age she just took me in. She was real nice. Anybody else probably would've called the police especially if they knew I was under 18, but she didn't. I guess I do look way more mature for my age. Now I have a warm place to stay and food to eat. The first meal I ate at the shelter I ate it like it was my last meal and it all came out as fast as it all went in. I was in the bathroom for a long minute. I'm sure it has somethin' to do with the fact that I hadn't eaten a full course meal in a while. I know I look stupid, but I don't care cause' I'm all I got, just my baby and me: And that's all that matters.

The baby is breast-feeding so I don't have to worry about buying any milk for a while. She's a fat lil' ol' thang'! Looks just like me, light skinned, wide nose, chubby cheeks, fat legs, and a head full of coal black hair. She has some features of her daddy. If he seen her, he definitely couldn't deny her. One thing I didn't like about having to go back to school was, the students starring and laughing at me. They would say all kinds of nasty words to me. The boys would grab my body sayin' things like, "we know you easy cause' you gotta' big head

21

baby", or "we know not to mess with you cause' you probably got somethin". It was even worse on the city bus. They would trip me and make me fall as I fought back to keep them from over-powering me. Most of em' don't mess with me, but there's always some bully that just don't wanna' let me forget that I had messed up having a baby at fourteen. Crying is my personality now days. I have no friends, sisters, or brothers. Nobody to talk too, nobody understands. I don't go in the lunch room anymore because all they do is group up and laugh at me. B-Wayne just stares at me then laughs. When they laugh. I wonder if God's dealing with him like He's dealing me? He won't get away with this. He'll get his.

I caught the city bus downtown to the shelter. When the bus got to my stop, I jumped off the bottom step with this major headache thinking, I can't take it anymore I might as well kill myself. Nobody'll ever know, and I'm sure they could care less. Maybe I can still throw my baby in the dumpster like I thought about before and go somewhere and kill myself? I don't know, I just don't know. I think I'm about to loose my mind. "Help me!" I yelled into the air as I stood on the lonely corner on my way back to the shelter. "Help me Lord if You're still there, and if You find a little more mercy! Please forgive me for what I've done!" I dropped to my knees and lifted up my hands. "I slipped, I know it, but I heard that You're a forgiving God! If I confess my sins You're faithful and just to forgive me and then cleanse me from all my wrong! *(1 John 1:9)* Cleanse me Lord! I'm cryin' out to You! I need You Lord! I don't have nowhere else to go! I don't have nobody else to turn too but You! God I confess You as Father and Master! I do believe that You died on the cross for my sins, and then You rose again! Save me Lord from all this mess I put myself in!" *(Romans 10: 9)* I wiped the tears from my eyes, the sweat from my forehead, got up off the ground, and walked down the street to the shelter, not caring that people had stopped to listen to what I was sayin'. This old lady from the shelter's been watchin' my baby while I go to school. She said she doesn't want me to drop out, and that she would help me all she could. Which I thought was nice. She really doesn't look like she knows how to take care of a baby, but she's all I got. I gotta' trust her.

Being out on the streets you learn one thing, a don't care mentality. All you try to do is survive, even if you have to steal. Mr. and Mrs. Grant, my supposed to be parents, never came looking for me and I never went back over there either. I don't claim em' as my parents anymore. You don't do your child like the way they did me. They gon' have to give an account for their actions one day. *(Galatians 6:7)*

Karina's been crying all night long. I can't get her to be quiet. "Shut up! Shut up!" I yelled. "What's wrong with you?" She kept on crying as I shook her. "It's 3 o'clock in the morning and I'm about to go crazy! I can't do this!" I left her on her bed, dropped to the floor, scooted up against the wall by my bed, buried my hands in my face, and cried.

"What's wrong with her?" The old lady came up and quietly asked.

I looked up. "I've tried to breast feed her but she don't want it! I changed her pamper and she's still hollering like she's tryin' to make me loose my mind!" I yelled with tears streaming from my eyes. "I can't do this anymore!"

She picked her up like she was her own. Within ten minutes Karina was quiet and went back to sleep. It was almost like an angel had touched her. Old ladies have so much more wisdom than we do. I realize more and more each day that this thing is really real. She's not a doll she's a real baby...

The only thing I look forward to is writing. After gettin' the baby to sleep, finish my homework, I write til' I fall asleep. I don't get but about 2-3 hours of sleep before she's up hungry again or need to be changed. I can't afford to get her no pampers, the shelter helps me out somewhat, but they can't do it all. This is hard. I got bags under my eyes, my hair's a mess, and I'm just about on the verge of giving up. It's too hard goin' to school, comin' back here feedin' her, changing her, playing with her, making sure she's clothed right, doing my homework, waking up all through the night with her, gettin' up at 5 o'clock every morning to get her ready, myself ready, and beat everybody else in the bathroom that we all have to share. I'll tell anybody it ain't easy raisin' no baby at 14. I'm still a baby. I still wanna' hang out and have fun like a normal 14 year old. But I can't now because I'm forced to be an adult—I'm forced to be a 14-year-old woman. I'll say to anybody who's a teenager and thinkin' about having a baby should think twice about it. Not only is it morally and biblically wrong, but it's also a job that no teen is ready for. And that goes for the guys too. If they're teens out there that have made a mistake, I would tell em' to first repent and ask God for forgiveness, turn from fornication (sin) surrender their life to Christ through salvation *(Roman*

10: 9), begin to allow Him to heal them, and take care of their child with guidance from the Lord. *(Proverbs 22:6)* That's what I would tell em'.

I'm tryin' to wake up much earlier so I can be the first one in the bathroom. Everybody's walking around goin' in all different directions doin' what they do to get ready for their day.

"Hey mam' how ya' doin'? I'm Pam. The lady you met when you first came up in here. I don't mean to get in your business or nothin' but how you takin' care of your baby and yourself? I mean I watch you all the time and wonder, how does she do it?" She had a bit of a concern look on her face.

"I'm not tellin' you my business." I kept straightening up my bed.

"Ok, ok you don't have to come at me like that. I'm not tryin' to be nosey, I just wanna' help if I can?"

"I don't trust nobody up in here, I don't trust nobody period."

"Somebody must've hurt chu' bad?"

"They did and they still do everyday. Everybody's evil."

"No, that's not true, I'm not evil. Can I ask you your name?"

"Why you wanna' know, you tryin' to steal my identity?" I picked up my comb, brush, toothpaste, and started walkin' towards the bathroom be mean to her but ain't nobody gon' hurt me nor my baby anymore, she's all I got. And the way she looks doesn't help either. Her short fade, broad manly shoulders, stocky thick-boned, 5'7 in height and look like she weigh about 300 pounds. This would intimidate anybody, even a man.

I finally got in the restroom, did what I had to do, got Karina ready, and then left for school. It's Friday, thank God I get a rest from all the name-calling. They're not as bad as they were when I was pregnant. I'm sure it's because my stomach's not huge anymore. But they're still cruel though, constantly reminding me of my past. I don't have much longer. It's just about time for us to get out for the summer. Only two more days left. The line was already long.

"While you're waiting, please tell me your name." She insisted.

"Why are you following me? Go away and leave me alone!" I yelled. She left real quick so that I would shut up. I really didn't mean to Thank God.

24

The day came and went.

When I came back the lady that was askin' me all those questions this morning had my baby in her arms, while the old lady sat on my bed and watched. I ran over and snatched my baby from her. "Look!" I yelled at the old lady. "I told you don't be lettin' nobody hold my baby!"

"I'm not just anybody, I'm a nice person and I'm not here to hurt you. You don't have to be so mean." The woman boldly said.

"Look I admit that I'm wrong for screaming, but I'm not wrong for the way I feel...Ok I'm sorry." I shrugged my shoulders as I looked at them both.

"We accept your apology. So you never told us your name?" The old lady spoke up.

"Barina. Barina Grant."

"Nice to meet you Barina." She smiled. "We're all family around here. All we have is each other, so if you need anything let us know." They both smiled.

We all try to make our small spaces look as homely as possible. Makin' the best out of our own privacy is not hard to do cause' we ain't got nothin' else.

I finally got Karina ready for bed. Now I can start writing again. I love writing it relaxes me. I thought as I sat Indian-style on the end of my small twin size bed, which feels more like a bunk.

Pam came from out of nowhere. "What're you writing?"

"Huh'?" I looked up. "O' I'm just writing a story, nothin' major."

"School is almost out, whatcha' planning on doin' this summer?"

"Nothin'."

"Are you planning on working?"

"Yea'." I kept writing.

"I heard they're hiring down at the Warehouse about 3 blocks from here." I looked up at her. "My friend works there. I'll put in a good word for you, ok?" She said as she walked away.

"Thanks!" I raised my voice so she could hear me.

Pam did put in a good word for me like she said that she would. I did get the job. In fact, school is officially out and I've already started. Thank God. I got the job right on the spot with the same hours as if I was still in school. It works great, that way it won't interfere with my breastfeeding schedule for Karina. It's a cool job. Money's still funny but it's a job down at the Warehouse. All we do all day long is make comforters and bed quilts for various companies—Simple.

I'm sittin' on my bed puttin' the pen to the paper and havin' an urge to talk to the Lord because he's done so much for me.... "Lord, I haven't forgotten about You." I quietly whispered to myself. "I know You're here because I can't help but see all this favor and all these miraculous blessings You've brought my way. I acknowledge You. I know that old lady who's watching Karina for me is Heaven sent. And I know Pam is Heaven sent even though she was a little over-bearing and weird at first." I smiled to myself. "I know this is not all You have for me so I'll just continue to watch, pray, and wait..."

September 1990

It's goin' on 4 months and I finally have a routine going. Work. Karina. Write. Sleep, and work. Karina's a little over 2 month's now and she sleeps all night, with exceptions of a couple of nights. She's gettin' easier to handle because she's now on a routine. The people up here have truly put up with her all night cries. I can't remember a time when they have complained or tried to do some-thin' to her or myself. All they've ever tried to do is help. Lord, I know You sent me here. That was the first favor. If You had not sent me here, I probably would be in a dirty alley or dead somewhere along with Karina. Thank God. Somehow, I still feel that there's more for me to do and more for me to receive, I just don't know what it is.

It's a cool day at work. I made sure I bundled myself up before leaving this morning. This' certainly a warehouse atmosphere, open door, no luxuries, huge machines everywhere. All the offices are in a mobile home outside the warehouse. Kinda' reminds me of an old factory building.

They just moved a girl over by me. She's ganna' be working with my assembly line. Our line only makes bedspreads. Assembly line jobs are so inconsistent. You may start on one line today and then tomorrow if things are too slow you'll be on another one in no time. I'm sure it's because they wanna' see us working at all times. They ain't payin' us to sit around. Like mama use to say, shootin' the breeze. I laughed to myself. Kinda' makes me mad when I think about how the economy is. It's all about that mighty dollar. All of us except the CEO are under

27

paid. Not to mention the illegal immigrants. They get paid almost nothin'. And I do mean nothin'. But that's life and the devil's dream. But I believe one day all this is gon' change in a twinkling of an eye. Just like the bible says it will. For all of His people that is. *(Matthew 12: 1-44)*

The girl they just moved by me I heard she was good. She's been working here for a while, so she's used to moving. She looks to be a very humble girl around my age. Well maybe a little younger but looks to be much wiser. Kinda' puts me in the mind of an old lady; must've been through a lot, just like me.

"Excuse me? You mind if I sit next to your sowing machine?" She asked as she towered over me like some 7-foot basketball player, considering the fact that she's actually only about 5'6 or 5'7. I guess it looks like that because I'm sittin' down and she's standing over me.

"Sure go ahead." I moved my arm in that direction.

"Thank you. How you doin'?"

"I'm fine, still tryin' to get the hang of this."

"Well chi', I've been doin' this for a while now, so if you have any questions just ask. I'm not impatient or rude so don't hesitate. You know, some people get their jobs, make a lot of money, and forget where they came from." She grabbed a spread from off the counter. "But I haven't and I never will."

I'm a fast learner.

I took her at every word she said. Now I totally got the hang of it after an hour of listening and experimenting.

"I see you got the hang of it now?" She smiled.

"Yea', I finally do. Thanks for all your help." I smiled with her.

"O' you welcome. You seem like a really nice person. What church do you attend?"

"I, well I don't go to church."

"I'm shocked. I see the call of God all over you."

"What chu' mean?" I asked, pretending not to know what she's talking about. I always knew that there was something different about me, and that I was put on this earth to do something.

"I mean, I can tell that there's something different and special about you. I can see that the Lord is with you."

"Wow thanks, nobody's ever told me that."

28

"First time for everything."

She started sowing the spread she got from off the counter. Her smile lit up the room like a diamond in darkness. I laughed at the thought. It's definitely not because of her yellow bone Porto Rican color; and naturally golden colored hair with black highlights, it's gotta' be because the Spirit of God is all over her. She kinda' puts me in the mind of an old lady as much wisdom as she has. Like the Wisdom of Solomon. *(1 Kings 4:29-34)* I know this ain't no fake Christian. She looks like she don't do nothin' but read her bible all day and sing church songs. I started grinning.

"I know I don't know you that well to be asking you this but I'm just lead to ask you anyway. Would you like to come to church with me on Sunday? I'll pick you up?"

"Um, well…"

"Come on now, I believe you'll enjoy yourself." She stopped sowing, looked at me, and then grabbed another sheet and started sowing it together.

"Ok, I'll go." I scooted back in my chair as if to push it back but it didn't move.

"Good. So where do you live?" She pulled a pen from her apron.

"I live about 3 blocks from here."

"Ok so you stay in the downtown area?" She started writing on the blank inventory sheets on the table.

"Yea' I do."

"Where bout'?" She looked up at me before writing again.

"I, um', I live in a shelter." I said with shame hoping that she doesn't ask why.

"Look that's ok. I don't judge nobody. Been there, done that, and got the trophy."

"O' so you used to live in a shelter?"

"Yep, when my ex-husband kicked me out the house. See I got married at a very early age as you can see. Yep, I'm still young. My parents were crack-heads, so they didn't care what I did, so they signed the papers. I married a young guy whose mother felt the same way, the only difference was that she molested him when he was a kid and mine didn't. His mother was a dope-head who stayed out partying all night and half the mornin'. She could care less what he did and his attitude showed it. He's the baby out of twelve sisters and brothers who never stayed home long enough for him to know them. He never knew his daddy, he was a con-artist and a womanizer, so that right there was a missing link in his life. He never dealt with his past and girl his attitude showed it. But anyway moving on, that's another story within itself and I really don't wanna' bore you anymore."

"No you're not boring me, keep talkin'."

"Well, I've been out on my own since then. It ended when I got tired of him beating up on me. He would jump on me for every lil' thing. He was young and wanted to control my every move, and I was young too so I let him because I loved him. It was basically headed nowhere. But to sum it all up, he kicked me out of his mama's house and there I was in the streets. I had no family to turn too, they all turned their backs on me felt that I was wrong for leaving and plus they were all doin' their thing anyway and could care less about what I did. I stayed in a shelter until I got on my feet. I worked at a grocery store even though I was under age and saved my money. I had an older friend at the time that hooked me up with this job at the grocery store even though I was under age; she also helped me get this apartment that I'm livin' in right now. Tell me God ain't good?" She smiled. "Hey, I can help you get chu' an apartment by me?" She looked at me and then started back sowing. She quickly looked back at me and said as if to think about it for a moment, "I'll see what I can do... I'll let you know. Now what's your address?" She pressed the head of the pen to make the tip pop out.

"3256 Walden St. The name of the shelter is Hope for Tomorrow Living Center. You can't miss it. There's a large sign in front of the building."

"I'll be there about 8am. Is that alright?"

"That'll be fine."

I got up to start my lunch break. We get an hour for lunch, and I don't waste no time cause' that hour always go so fast.

I got me something to eat, ate it real quick, and went and checked on Karina since she's only 3 blocks away. I was glad to see that she was ok. All I can think about is what the lady from my job said about helping me get this apartment by her. I wonder if that's the open door that God has for me? We'll see. And truly I can't forget about her inviting me to church.

The girl from my job was not a minute too late and not a minute too early. She drove up and stopped in front of Karina and me.

"Good mornin'. O', so is this your baby?" She asked.

She looked so surprised. Her eyes are wide open. The way she's looking at me I almost feel like I should've told her when I first met her.

"Yea', this is Karina." I answered still holding her in my arms.

"I didn't know you had a baby?" She asked as we drove off.

"It never permitted itself."

"Yea', you're right. You know I never asked you your name. I thought about that all last night."

I turned and looked at her. "It's Barina. Barina Grant. And yours?"

"My name is Salva. Salva King." We drove a little further. "What's the baby's name?"

"It's Karina." I didn't bother sayin' her last name because I gave her my last name. Wayne didn't deserve to have her last name. "So how far is your church?" I looked out the window tryin' to change the subject.

"It's all the way across town. You know this' a huge city?"

"Yep I know."

This girl seems so nice. I always wanted a saved friend. Somebody I can talk too and tell what's on my mind; laugh and pray with. I guess God knows what we all need and when we all really need it. I still have this anger built up inside of me though. Most it comes from my parents and how they did me. It's like I'm in a shell and don't know how to get out of it. Inside I'm crying and wailing. My moans are moans of a desperate plea. I'm like a ship in a sea storm that's being tossed and driven by humongous wages—and any minute it's on its way down—down to the bottomless pit of sand that rest at the bottom of the sea. I need help and I need it right now. I can never tell this girl what I'm goin' through she'll never understand.

She started playing with Karina. "Hi little baby, I see you lookin' just like yo' mama." Karina started smiling and cooing. "Yea' your name is even close to yo' mama's name. Barina and Karina. Ain't that sweet? You a pretty lil' thang', yes you are, yes you are." She slightly pinches her cheeks as Karina starts laughing again. "So how old is she?"

"2 ½ months."

"O' she's young. O' oh' hold on, these traffic lights always turn red on you so fast." I braced Karina and she gripped the steering wheel, sternly slammed on the brakes as the tires made a screeching sound and we quickly came to a sudden stop. "That was a close one. I don't like runnin' no lights. Are you ok?"

"We're fine." I looked at Karina.

We finally made it to church, which ended up being a 30-minute drive. Along the way I had a chance to see the rest of the city that I had never seen before. All these years I've been livin' here; I've never seen these parts of the city. This place is huge and it's gorgeous. Of course I didn't get out much as a child, and still don't. It was awesome to see suburban areas mixed with all the residential communities, and the large buildings scattered all over the place. Not to mention the rural areas on the out skirts of town. It was so beautiful to watch the trees sway back and forth on a windy day. Kinda' reminds me of the country life even though Cali. is far from it.

Church is over. I enjoyed everything about it. I could tell it's been awhile. The hardest part was gettin' back into the worship. My arms felt so heavy, like somebody was pullin' em' down. And I know it couldn't have been God doin' it, He would never pull my arms down when I'm tryin' to worship Him. It had to be the devil, because he doesn't want me to worship God let alone live for Him. But he can't stop me. It's something about this church I know I need to come back too. Salva is conversing with some of her friends while Karina and I are sittin' in the back seats by the front door. This is a huge church. It probably holds about 10,000 people.

The ride home wasn't as long as coming. I guess because I remembered the path we took from this morning. We were completely quiet for about 10-minutes then Salva finally broke the ice. "So did you enjoy the service?" She smiled never looking my way.

"I enjoyed it. I can't complain."

"Good."

"It's been a long time. I could feel it. You know I grew up in the church right?"

"No I didn't know that."

"Yea' my parents were devoted Christians…"

She cut me off. "So are they still alive?"

"Yea' they are."

"So why aren't you stayin' with them?"

"Long story."

"Ok, well I'll leave that alone. So why did you say they were devoted Christians? Are they dead?"

Salva has a way of picking information out of a person. She would make a great lawyer. The only thing is I'm not her client so I hope she knows she's startin' to get a little too personal. "Like I just said, no they're not dead. It's just been a long time since I've talked to em'." Things got quiet again and I'm starting to get a little sad. I didn't realize that I still have feelings for them after all they've done to me. I'm sure Salva can see it written all over my face, even though she never looked my way.

"Did somethin' happen?"

I stared out the window as the tears began to roll down my face. "I really don't wanna' talk about it." I answered.

"That's fine we can drop the subject." Things got quiet again this time longer than 10-minutes. "So what're you and Karina ganna' eat?" She reached over and rubbed Karina's hair.

"I don't know. They probably'll have some plates at the shelter." I pulled Karina up over my shoulder and started patting her back.

"You guys wanna' go eat at a restaurant? My treat?" She smiled as if that would cheer me up.

"No that's alright you can just drop us off at the shelter. I'm just ganna' pick up somethin' there." She didn't say a word. In fact neither one of us said anything for the rest of the ride back to the shelter.

When we finally made it, something inside of me wants to tell Salva about the situation that happened between my parents and me. But somehow I can't, I'm too ashamed, I'm still mad at em' and everybody else. I kinda' feel like she already is. She has a keen since of discernment.

Salva whipped in a parking space right in front of the shelter. "Alright, we're here mam'." She said. I thanked her and started gettin' out of the car. "You know Barina, whatever you're goin' through, I want you to know that I'm your friend and I'm her for you. Just when you think that don't nobody care, they really do. I think I'm a very trust worthy person and you never know I probably can help you. Our pasts are more similar than you think. I told you where I came from, but I haven't heard from you that's all. And I want you to know that God is with you no matter what has happened to you in your past."

"Alright Salva, I appreciate that. I'll see you at work." I quickly closed the door as if what she just said really didn't matter. It's hard for me to open up to anybody. I've been hurt and I don't think that I can ever trust anybody anymore. When my own so-called parents threw me a way like a rag doll, I didn't have anybody else to turn too. The tears began to fall down my cheeks as Karina and I went inside and laid down on our bed.

I mean, it wasn't like they were never in my life. They raised me. They took care of me. They gave me everything I wanted and needed. And most of all they took me to church even though they were too hard on me. But all those years and memories don't mean nothin' when a person can just throw you a way in a night's time, especially when I needed them the most. I trusted, loved, and respected them. They were all I had. I was a child in need of real love, the love that two parents are supposed to give so naturally. They cared more about what the church thought instead of forgiving me like Jesus did and helping me cope with the mistake that I had made. They cared more about keeping me clean and holy that they forgot to ask me the simple things like; 'how was your day at school, or how do you feel today, or what do you wanna' be when you graduate from high school?'—In fact they never even told me they loved me, even though I knew they did, but I needed and wanted so badly to hear it. I was a child then and I'm still a child. Now I'm a child with experience. One thing I am proud of after being out on the streets is that I didn't stay on drugs and alcohol, and I never turned tricks for money just to take care of Karina. I know it had everything to do with Karina. She stopped me from doing a lot of things. I'm not proud that I'm a 14-year old mother, but I am grateful for Karina because I could've had complications with her. She turned out to be a very beautiful healthy baby.

The clouds are dark and it's pouring down raining. I'm supposed to be at work in 10-minutes, or I'm gon' be late. I'm never late. How in the world am I gon' get to work? Let me go and call Salva's cell phone and see if she'll swing by and pick me up. She gave me her number last week at work I hope I can find it in this old shoebox where I keep all my important papers—Here it is. I dialed her number. "Hello, Salva?"

"Yes this' Salva."

"Good morning how you doin'?" I walked away from the pay phone stretching the cord to try and see what time the clock around the corner said.

"I'm fine. Is everything alright?" She asked. Salva has this soft humble nurturing motherly type spirit about her, even though she's around my age.

"Yea' everything's fine with me. Are you close by or in the downtown area yet?"

"Almost. I'm drivin' down the ramp into the East downtown area, maybe about 5- minutes from you. What? What's up?"

"I need you to come scoop me up. I'm runin' late this morning and it's pouring down raining. If I walk I'm ganna' be late."

"Girl that's cool, you don't have to explain. It's ugly out here; the rain is comin' down like cats and dogs. Just watch out for me I'm only about 3-minutes away now."

"Ok, I'm on my way out there now. Thanks."

"No problem." We both hung up at the same time.

Salva hasn't asked me about my parents anymore. I'm sure it's because she's waiting on me to open up and tell her. If so it's working cause' it's some-thin' about when people don't pressure you to talk to them, it makes you wanna' just open up and tell everything, verses somebody naggin' you all the time about tellin' em' everything. Those are the one's I stay away from. But she's not like that. I have to admit that I have been rude to her at times and she's been real patient and supportive with me. Unlike others, they probably would've left me alone, but she hasn't. I think God sent this girl to me. In my heart I did ask for a sister and friend so maybe she's the one that God has chosen? I thought as I waited patiently under the wet ledge of the building as the rain poured off of the sides going into the drainage's and the gutters.

I stood back as Salva drove up in front of me as her tires splashed the water away from them. I ran up and jumped in the front seat as if the rain were darts. "Hey girl, you know I appreciate cha'?" I said shaking from the cold rain.

"I know." She said as we both started laughing. "That rain's cold isn't it?" She kept on laughing as she took off down the street.

"And you know it is…" We both laughed again. "I'm not lookin' forward to today. It's one of those dreary days: The kind that makes ya' wanna' sleep all day and night."

"Chi' I know what chu' mean." She said, as she made a turn into the parking-lot of the warehouse. Parking can be a mess but Salva has a pass so we're able to park right up front. Thank God! And it's drizzling too? "My hair ain't gon' be good for nothin'." I told her. She agreed as we both laughed.

"Ok, meet me right after work and I'll drop you off. Don't be late or you gon' see my skid marks." She burst out laughing and I joined her.

"Bye girl, I'll be here."

"Bye." She said.

We departed going in two different directions. I think she's makin' towels this month, and I got comforters again this whole month.

Another new years party for this huge city and another 10 months have past which seems like yesterday. Salva's on her way to pick up Karina and me, she invited us over just to get away from the shelter life, and we both are ready to G-O. Salva is truly God sent. She's been talking to me about God and my relationship with Him. I accepted Him as my Lord and Savior for real the other day on our break at work. I'm not playing church anymore like I was at my parent's church. I'm back involved in the church and I have a whole new perspective on life now.

Karina's walking all over the place. She took her first steps about a month ago. Everybody in the shelter cheered. Karina has so many God mama's and papa's around here. They all love her so much. Most of em' never had families to care and see about them. We've all been thrown away in some kind of way. And I guess that's why we all are as close as we are because we all know what the pain of rejection feels like. We're all we got. I finally realized that it's ok to let somebody in my circle without shutting them out, even though I still don't tell my personal business. That part I'm still working on. It would take a lot for me to open that part up. I feel as though I need too because I've been holding all this pain way too long. I need to talk to somebody. Salva and I have talked a little. She's shared but I haven't. I just listened to her. She finally broke down and told me that she has a daughter that's a little older than Karina name Precious. Salva and her ex-husband had her before they got married. She said that she didn't tell me because she didn't know how I would take it considering the fact that she was a Christian and all, and she didn't want me to judge her and get even more discouraged than what I already was. But she finally had to break down and tell the truth. I asked her how she could keep a secret like this from me this long. And where did she hide the baby? She told me that the daddy had her. They were fighting for custody and she finally won the case after a long battle. And now she has her back for good. I'm glad for her and I'm especially glad that Karina and Precious are around the same age, now Karina has a playmate.

Salva just came up to Karina's and my bed. "Hey girl, you ready?" She asked. She reached down and picked up Karina as Karina reached up for her. "Hey what's that on your bed?"

"What's what?"

"What chu' writin'?" She put Karina down on the bed and reached for the manuscript.

"Oh' that's just my book I just finished writing." She didn't say anything, she just kept reading as if to ignore me.

Five minutes went by after I took Karina to the restroom and came back only to find Salva sitting on my bed still reading. "You still reading the book?"

"No, I'm readin' one of your magazines you had lying on your bed. Hey you ready?" She jumped up as if to be in hurry. "I gotta' go by the store and get some stamps and a large envelope." She started walking towards the front entrance as Karina and I followed.

"What chu' need stamps and a large envelope for?"

"I have some important papers I need to send off as soon as possible." She smiled.

"Girl you stay busy."

"You right. Come on I gotta' pick up Precious from her daddy's."

37

July 1996

*F*ive years have come and gone. I just heard through the grapevine that my parents got killed in a car accident. Their picture was on the news and in all the newspapers. I mourned for a while not because I was sad, but because I wondered if they repented and made it to Heaven. We never got it right. They never came looking for me and I never went back to them. Nothing was ever resolved. They never got a chance to see Karina, their only grand child. I have a chance to repent, but I don't know if they did.

I finally graduated from high school. Many said I couldn't do it, but I proved em' all wrong. I not only graduated, but I graduated top half of my class. Can't nobody tell me you still can't reach your goal with a baby, because you can. Even though I still have a long ways to go, but at least I've accomplished one goal I thought I would never accomplish. At first it seemed impossible because I was looking at the big picture. But when I started takin' one day at a time, each day became shorter and shorter, better and better.

They gave me a party at the shelter. I was surprised and happy all at the same time. I know all these people and Salva have been sent to me. Everybody at the shelter was giving me a graduation party and a going away party all at the same time. Salva helped me get an apartment in the same complex, not too far from hers. We still spend a lot of time together considering the fact that she has a boyfriend named Salvester now. He's really a nice guy. I can see them gettin' married soon. Well actually, he's her ex-husband and the daddy of her child. She forgave

39

him for all those years of how he treated her and they've decided to give it another try. This time I think it's a keeper considering the time they had apart to get themselves together. So now they're more mature and they get along much better. I never would've known that they used to fight if she hadn't told me they did. I figure it has something to do with the fact that Salva's a born again Christian, and Salvester just gave his life to the Lord. I believe when the Lord is in the picture, its ganna' be a master piece. And their relationship is starting to be just that. I just hope and pray that one day I'll be as blessed as she is to find a man that loves the Lord and loves me like I should be loved. I want a fine, strong, good lookin', romantic, poetic, lovin' the Lord, gifted, financially stable, supportive, and giving man. I actually want more than that but my thoughts won't hold no more. I smiled to myself. Salva said one day we may have a double wedding. But she's already got her prince charming so I don't see that ever coming to past.

I'm finally done with my second book, and almost finished with my third one. I love writing. I don't know what I'm gon' do with all these books I keep writing, I'll just keep em' as souvenirs. I can't remember what I did with my first book, probably lost it when I moved. I hope I find it.

Right after I graduated from high school, I enrolled at UCLA. They accepted me right away because of my good grades and all. I've been goin' all year. I guess I'm what chu' call a freshman all over again. It's ok because this' a whole new level for me. It hasn't been easy trying to study and trying to take care of Karina all at the same time. Salva enrolled too and got accepted so we both are trying to work out a schedule for the girls and us. It helps that they're around the same age so they can help keep one another company. When I'm in night class Salva watches the girls, and when she's in class, I watch the girls so it's working out so far. I'm working full-time, going to school part-time, studying, gettin' Karina ready for the next day, and finding time to do what relaxes me—write. I love writing, and writing loves me. We work so well together. I smiled. I've been doin' it for so long that it comes natural. I know it's not a streak of luck, it's a gift from God and I count my blessings everyday. This is what saved me from goin' crazy when I was in the shelter. Maybe one day all this writing will pay off. I don't take it as serious as I should. Salva gets on me all the time about it. She always says I'm gon' be famous one day because of my writing.

It's kinda' hard to believe that some-thin' that comes so natural could make a person a lot of money. But I do remember in the Bible where it says that our gifts will make room for us and bring us before great men. *(Proverbs 18:16)* And just maybe one day it will...

Chapter One

I'll always remember my past. I won't dwell on it, but the thoughts will always rest in my heart from time to time until it's time for me to leave this earth. I can't change em'—they've become my testimony.

I'm so glad Salva and I finally graduated from college to round it all off. It was a lot of hard work, but we made it despite all the obstacles. And I'm proud to say that Salva and Salvester tied the knot not too long ago. They went to the courthouse and made it official. I'm happy for them. They belong together. He's perfect looking for her. It's funny because he towers over her 5'7 body with his 6'3 physique, showing a slight muscle tone, thin fade, and smooth dark colored skin. Basketball jersey's is his style of dress. He's real laid back and down to earth, that's what I love about him—sometimes. It's a long story of how I got to the place of where I'm at right now in my life. I'll start by saying that, that scripture about my gifts making room for me is so true. My gift has truly made me a rich woman. Come to find out, Salva snuck my first book from me and got it published and it's been hittin' the best sellers charts, the magazines, and earning all kinds of awards ever since. And I wondered why I couldn't find it all these years. Actually it was never lost, it was just in hiding. I smiled to myself. Now I live in this huge mansion that sits off the California beach. I made sure that Salva and Salvester were well taken care of, even though that wasn't her intentions to make money off of me. Her intent was to help me because she knew that I wouldn't have ever done it myself. Now that's what I call a true friend and sister. I smiled again.

It's a bit windy out here on the beach, but it feels great. I can't come out here all through the year cause' the weather is not always nice. I rarely come out and swim, cause' last year I almost drowned. My ex-boyfriend talked me into going out too far and the tides started takin' me under. Ask me how I got back to the shore, I'd tell anybody quick that it was all God. The closest I get to the water now is to just put my feet in it. I'll even go a little further by wavin' my hands through it. That's all!

Bothered by a phone ring, I quickly brushed off the sand from the phone and answered it. "Hello?"

"Hey chick what's up, don't chu' have somewhere to go tonight?" I kicked off the sand from between my toes, forced my feet into my sandals, grabbed my paper's and ran up through the sandy maze to get back to the inside of the house.

"As a matter of fact I do. I was just thinkin' about you. I was gon' ask you if you wanted to go with me to this convention tonight? They're having a Book Festival and I'm supposed to be the guest speaker and I'm supposed to be signing some of my books. So what's up? Are you in? You know I need your help? You know you're my favorite play sista'?"

"Girl shut up, you know I'm your only sista'!" We both laughed. "I don't think I'm ganna' be able too. Salvester wants some quality time. He claims we don't spend enough quality time together. You know how men can be? Well, husbands are worse. The good thing about it is that I want to give him that time. I love spending every moment with my baby. Please don't be upset." I can tell she smiled.

"Now you know I'm not upset. Disappointed, but not upset. You know you my right hand girl? But I understand that your husband comes first. Well, can you baby-sit Karina for me? I can't possibly keep up with that girl and sale books too." I said.

"Sure, you know Salvester loves that girl. I'll send her with Precious. She's goin' to her friend's house from school. They're havin' a little birthday party. I just love the relationship that Precious and Karina have. Kinda' reminds me of you and me. We're a year a part and they're a year a part. Precious is eleven so that makes Karina ten. Your twenty-four, so that makes me twenty-three. Isn't that special?"

"Yea' that's special. I've come a long way Salva and you know that. I remember when I had Karina at fourteen, I didn't think I was gon' be able to keep her. You remember I told you that year's ago?"

"Yea'."

"My mama and daddy were on my back. They were so upset and disappointment. They wouldn't have believed that I finished school. But I did. That goes to show that you can do anything that you set your mind too. And I didn't stop there; I went on to graduate from college at the top of my class with a baby to raise. You know all the obstacles that came my way, but I made it through em' all by the grace of God. Now I have a beautiful little girl that makes fabulous grades just like her mother did..." I smiled.

"Let me cut in cause' you know how you can get long winded. I'll pick up Karina in about an hour."

"Good, that gives me time to get her ready. Ok. Bye." I said as we both hung up the phone.

The phone rang again.

"Hey girl, I just wanted to tell you that I'm very proud of you and your accomplishments especially as a young single parent. As I look back on it, all I know is that your mama and daddy had to be proud of you even though they never told you before their car accident, somehow I know they were. You know you're the example of many young women who get pregnant at a young age and don't let their mistakes keep them from doing what God would want them to do. Thank God He's a forgiving God. And now you're a successful professional anointed Christian author and novelist. I love you Barina. I know I don't say it enough, but today I'm saying it. And you have truly been an inspiration to me."

"O' Salva, that's so sweet. I love you too my sista'. Now how much money you wanna' borrow?" We both laughed. "No I'm just kidding, thanks and you can't leave yourself out. You're also a successful black woman with a successful money makin' husband who's a teacher and an entrepreneur. I'm so proud of you two and I really admire your marriage. I think it's awesome when two people can get back together after a divorce. Grow up and work that thing out. And most of the time you'll find that the other party wasn't the only one who had the problem. That's right point your finger at your self. Sometimes we're too busy pointing our finger at everybody else, when we need to be pointing at ourselves. It starts in you... But anyway, too bad I didn't get my prince before you did. And too bad he's not here right now so we can double date. But to be honest I really don't wanna' get married after how Karina's daddy did me. I don't wanna' even be bothered with no man. Look, thanks for callin' me back; you made my day with those words. And you know what?"

"What?"

"I now realize that I really do miss my mama and daddy. It's been what? Six years since they've been dead? I know they would be proud of me now, just like you said. Last time they were alive I was still in school."

"Alright girl let me let chu' go so you and Karina'll be ready when I get there. We'll talk more when I see you." I agreed as we hung up the phone.

That was so sweet of my sista'. "Karina! Go get your things together, you're goin' over Aunt Salva's and Uncle Vester's house!" I yelled up the stairs.

"Ok mama! Am I stayin' the night? Please mama please! Can I please stay?" She yelled back down from the top of the stairs. The stairs go up in a round circular maze with a chandelier hangin' down from the middle of the ceiling. I couldn't resist buying it. It was the last one they had. It's sparkling like diamonds as the light reflects off it.

"I guess you can stay! It'll be too late when I get back home! You need something a little dressy cause' you're goin' to a birthday party with Precious!"

"Yeaaa'! I can't wait! I'll wear my mini skirt and my flowered purple shirt!"

"Bring it down so I can see it! I might need to see it anyway; you can get a little loose with your clothes sometimes!"

"Awa' mama! Here I come!" Karina's what you call a cream colored little girl. She took my Chinese eyes, skin color and thin lips. But her wide nose and chubby cheeks she took after her daddy's. She still looks like her daddy. She has this bushy ponytail that's so hard to comb because it's so thick and naturally curly. It's the only style she likes to wear. And I don't argue with her because I don't wanna' comb it no way. She's the cutest and the sweetest child that God could've ever blessed me with. She's just 10-years old and I have to protect her. I refuse to let her go down the same road that I went down. God has broken the generational curse off of my life and hers too. I just gotta' believe that.

She came rushing up to me. "Alright mama see? This skirt's not too short?"

"You let me be the judge of that mam'." I looked her up and down, then round and a round. "Ok, you're clear. Now go get your backpack together. And don't forget to put you some clean underwear in there. You know how you tend to forget for some odd reason. Raunchy would be the best words." I giggled to myself.

"I got chu' mama!"

"What did you say?"

"I mean yes mam'!" She yelled back as she ran up the stairs laughing. Karina has this somewhat undeveloped voice. It has this high-pitched infant type sound to it. It's so cute.

"That's my baby." Now let me see what I'm gon' wear, while tending to her needs I need to be tending to my own needs. I walked into my room and went straight to the walk-in closet. Its part of my two culture heritage that we look good and have some-thin' in life. And fortunately for me I'm just an average half Black, half Hispanic woman that loves a whole lot a' Jesus. And the rest comes after that.

It took Karina and me 30-minutes to get ready before we heard a knock at the front door. Karina just ran past me and opened it without asking 'who is it?'

"Karina what did I tell you about opening up the door without askin' who it is?" I pointed my finger at her.

"I already knew who it was mama. Ok, I'm sorry it won't happen again. I'm ganna' close the door and try it again." She closed the door as if no one was standing there. "Who is it?" She yelled.

"It's your beautiful Aunt Salva!"

"Are you sure you're my beautiful Aunt Salva? You're not some bad person are you?"

"No I'm not! I'm the Aunt who's ganna' take her favorite niece to a birthday party, to the movies, and then for some ice cream!"

Karina thrust open the door like it weighed a pound, and ran and jumped into Salva's arms. "Yes! I'm so excited!"

"Hey girl." I hugged her smushing Karina between us, and then planted a big kiss on her cheek. "You don't have to come in, I'm just gon' grab our things and set the alarm. I'll meet you by the truck." I turned and walked back towards the living room, and then back out towards Salva's candy apple Suburban.

"Bye mama!" Karina yelled from Salva's window.

"That's who we're missing—Precious. Where is she?"

"She stayed cause' she wasn't quite ready yet. We're ganna' pick her up on the way."

"Ok, well have fun and take care of my baby. I'll pick her up sometime tomorrow evening." I waved, turned, and walked towards my Excursion. I got in, and let down the passenger window.

"She's in good hands as you already know!" She yelled from her window as we both backed up out of the driveway and drove off.

Chapter Two

It was a rather long ride downtown to the Convention Center considering all the traffic and all. Must've been a basketball game goin' on I thought, as I drove into a parking space in the garage of the Convention Center. Parking spaces are always so hard to find. Then you gotta' pay an arm and a leg after having to walk ten miles just to get inside the place. I would complain to the owner, but it wouldn't do any good. I laughed.

The attendants are at the doors taking tickets. It must be over a couple thousand people here. "Where can I find Banquet Hall Six?" I asked.

"Can I have your ticket mam'?"

"I have a VIP tag. I'm the guest speaker. I'm Miss. Barina Grant."

"O' I'm so sorry Miss. Grant, right this way. I admire you so much. And I just love to read your books. You're such an anointed writer. Your first novel changed my life."

"Thank you, if you get a chance come in and check out the new book I'm releasing tonight. I pray that God will continue to bless you through reading all of my books." I smiled and walked away heading towards the escalators. There's another big time festival going on at the same time. They're celebrating some foreign holiday, so there's a lot of people dressed in costumes with banners and signs hanging on the walls, the ceilings, and from the windows. They must've rented out a large space down the hall because there's thousand's of people goin' in and out with souvenirs in their hands. As I passed by I could see

49

different booths set up with the sounds of a foreign band playin' in the background.

When I finally walked in the huge banquet hall of the Book Festival, I can see that they're only about 100-125 people sittin' in some seats, considering the fact that its 30-minutes til' the occasion starts, I'll have to say that's pretty good timing. People aren't ever on time no way.

It took me about thirty minutes to set up everything. It wouldn't have taken this long had Salva been able to come. I'm so glad Cal had my books shipped here so that I wouldn't have to bring all my books with me. All I had is my paraphernalia to bring in which ain't nothin' but some souvenirs, and that only took four boxes which I carried in with my dolly and suitcase. It wasn't as bad as I thought it would be but I still wish that Salva could've been here to help me, she helps me with all of my book signings. I normally get her to set up my table, the credit card machines, and help with taking the money while I sign books.

A band just walked in. I guess their ganna' play for the evening. They actually have time to do about ten songs considering how long it's taking the people to get here. Everybody's all dressed up in his and her suits and dress suits. Some people call it church attire. It's always a dressy occasion with all the loud colorful dresses with matching hats. Looks like a normal Sunday church day. I laughed to myself.

The book festival is on the way and the band has already played about ten songs just like I said earlier. They must be taking a break cause' they just stopped playing and left the stage. I gotta' admit, they did sound a little jazzy. I like their style. It has a contemporary—jazzy—gospel feel to it. In other words, they're just playin' some good ol' soothing music.

I've already spoke and now people are buying my books left and right. I'm glad Cal sent more than he thought I'd need because I'm almost out. I really wish Salva could've came, I really need help. I thought I could do this all by myself, but I can't. I'm tryin' to sign books, take the money, hand their items to them, and then hold conversations with them, this' just too much for one person to do. But I gotta' do what I gotta' do.

I've been here for about 3-hours. People are scarce because everything's almost over and I'm taking down my booth. I don't have very much to take back home because I almost sold everything I brought. 2-books left out of 300-books ain't half bad. I thought reaching for the left over books.

"How are you Miss. Barina? I really love your books. Do you have any books left? I'd like to buy one for my little boy. He's in the hospital and I know it would lift up his spirit if I gave him one of your books because he loves reading your novels."

She stood in front of the table with a tall slender built. She's a Caucasian woman with blond hair looking to be about 6-feet. She's wearing a long pony tail with side burns draping around her smooth slender face. Her long fingers are wrapped around a 20-dollar bill as she reached to hand it to me. I can't dare take her money knowing that her son is in the hospital. I'm not a greedy woman. This is just another chance for me to sow a seed. *(2 Corinthians 9:6-7)* "Don't worry bout' it." I pushed her hand away. "It's a gift from the Lord. Tell the lil' fella' to hang in there and that God loves him and He's ganna' heal him." I said as I handed her a couple of bookmarks, a huge poster, and one of the last 2-books I have left over. "I'll be praying for him. What's his name?" I asked as I opened the book. She could hardly speak, she just kept crying and thanking God and me.

"Gregory. Thank you so much you don't know what this means to me. God's gon' bless you even more because you're always giving things to people. I'm grateful for these and I know he's ganna' love em'. Bye! And I'll be praying for you too!" She turned and walked away as I thanked her and waved good-bye.

"Let me finish cleaning this stuff up so I can get out of here. I'm so tired." I said out loud to myself as if someone was standing there listening. I turned and bent down to gather the empty boxes beside the table when a voice broke the silence.

"Will you marry me?" His voice is that kind that would make anybody easily fall for, the kind that when he spoke, I could feel the drumming of it in the channels of my ears.

I rose up and turned around to match my eyes with this astonishing face. His skin is like a creamy caramel, with this thick mustache resting over these perfectly, well-put together thick full lips that impelled this luxuriously sleekly heavy voice. "What in the world? Look I don't have time for games." What came out of my mouth certainly don't

51

match what I'm feelin' in my emotions and in the palms of my sweaty hands. I'm lost for words but I don't want him to know it.

"This' not a game I mean it, will you marry me?" He smiled with only the top layer of his teeth showing. He has a beautiful warm smile, the smile that'll make you wanna' give him everything you have and ever owned.

"Look I don't know who you are, but I'm about to call security if you don't leave. Better yet, I'll leave." I grabbed what I had left, brushed by him, quickly started walking towards the escalators, then down a couple of halls. Every step I took, my head was dashing backwards just to see if he was following me. Fortunately he wasn't, even though my flesh wanted him too. I ran out of the convention hall and into my truck. I have to say, he was nice lookin'. But it really doesn't matter cause' his arrogance out weighed his looks. He was very bold. In fact to darn bold. I ain't never had no man come up to me with that much authority. O' well, too bad it didn't work. Will I marry him. Shoot I wonder what men be thinkin' these days? They just come up to you and say anything. I wonder how many women he done tried that line on. I laughed to myself. I can't wait to tell Salva about this.

The ride back home was quicker than what I expected, everybody's out on the town doin' their own thang'. Good, I have the entire house to myself. I mean I love my baby very much, but I still love my time alone. I can't stop thinkin' about that guy comin' up to me and askin' me that stupid question. The games that some men play is so tide and out dated.

I pulled up in the driveway, got out, walked through my flowered maze sidewalk, up to the front door, and went in. Shoot, I forgot to turn on the lights its pitch dark in here. I turned off the alarm and flipped on the lights, then walked to the kitchen to see how many messages I have. Lord I have five messages somebody ain't gon' get called back tonight, in fact, nobody's gon' get called back tonight. I'm just too tired to be talkin' to anybody right now. I'll call em' tomorrow, I'm goin' to bed....

It's the early hours of the morning and light is fighting its way through the sheer curtains that's hanging over my window. I smothered myself underneath my thick all black king size comforter.

I know Precious and Karina's probably up watchin' cartoons. My nights rest was so peaceful, in fact too peaceful. My baby would be all over me right now. Let me call over there and see what they're doin'—I dialed their number. Salva answered and I quickly said, "Hello, good morning." I sat up against the long thick pillows I have draped across my king size bed.

"Hey girl good morning and now good bye." She groggily said.

"Now why you gon' do your sista' like that I got some-thin' to tell you girl?"

"What is it? And it better be worth listening too at 6:30 on a Saturday morning."

"O' trust me, it is…"

"Wait before you start, how was the Book Festival?"

"Ok would you give me a chance to tell you?" I smiled, raising my voice.

"Go ahead. I won't break in anymore." She waited. "Come on any day now! You know I really wanna' know?" She laughed still sounding dazed and sleepy.

"Well as I was sayin', the Book Festival went great. I had only two out of three hundred books left over. This lady wanted a book to give to her little boy that's in the hospital. After I gave her the book…"

"I gotta' cut chu' off again. You gave that woman that book free huh'?"

"You know I did."

"I knew you did. You're always giving some-thin' away, that's why you're so blessed because you give so much."

"Well you know how I am. I just remember where I came from. But anyway, after I finished with the lady, I was gettin' ready to leave and I bent down to pick up one of the empty boxes from off the floor, and when I turned back around this man was standing in front of the table and you won't believe what he asked me?"

"What girl what?"

"Girl he asked me to marry him."

She screamed. "Ha'! O' my God! What did you say? Did you say yes?" She laughed.

"Now I know you got to be crazy, no I didn't say yes. Girl I was about to call security on him. But instead, I just walked off. I went and put my stuff in the truck and left. I didn't see em' again after that."

"Well, how'd he look?"

"What chu' mean how'd he look? I'm not thinkin' about that. I'm thinkin' about the crazy question he asked me." I wanna' tell her that I found him very attractive but I just can't. "Whata' you think?" I threw the question back on her.

"Girl he probably was playing with you. Maybe he didn't know what else to say? Now I'm ganna' ask you again, how'd he look?" I knew she would ask me that question again.

"He was very attractive, just arrogant. He looks a little younger than me. Like two years or so."

"So, what's wrong with him being a little younger than you? There's nothing wrong with that as long as you're not robbing the cradle. He probably wasn't arrogant, you're just too sensitive with men and you're way too hard on em'. I mean, you haven't gone out on a date in I don't know when. I'm really prayin' that God will deliver you from your past. Look Barina, you've gotta' get over what Karina's daddy did to you. You've gotta' let em' go and stop holding him in your heart and give him to the Lord. He's not worth it. I know he got you pregnant and just left you like Karina was never his, but you've gotta' get over it. See while you sittin' up mad, he's happy and enjoying his life. I wouldn't give him the satisfaction. He ain't worth all the bitterness, nor is he worth you missing out on a good thing one day. And to top it all off, nor is he worth you going to Hell either. Do you hear what I'm sayin'?"

"Yea' I hear ya'." I sniffed and wiped the tears as they slowly rolled down my face. "I understand what you're talkin' about, it's just ganna' take some more time. I'll be all right. Thanks for being real and honest with me. And most of all, that's for being there. I love you sis." I sniffed again.

"I love you too Barina. I know what you been through. I just don't wanna' see you single for the rest of your life all because of some idiot. And besides, Karina needs a man figure in her life."

"She's got Uncle Vester?" I snickered.

"You know what I mean."

"I know. But I've told you that I don't wanna' get married."

"You'll get married one day."

"What makes you say that?" I jerked my head back and smacked my lips like whatever.

"I don't know I just feel it. And I believe you'll know it when he comes into your life." She sighed.

"Look let's change the subject. Where's my lil' angel?"

"She's in the room with Precious. They're watchin' some-thin' on TV I think it's a carton, or a movie. I just checked on em' right before you called. Hold on..."

A few minutes later. Hello?" Karina jumped on the phone excited.

"Good morning mommy's little angel."

"Good mornin' mama. I love you. Where're you?"

"Mama loves you too. I'm at home I'll be over there to pick you up later on today, ok? You be good and don't give Aunt Salva and Uncle Vester a hard time you hear?"

"Yes mam'. Mama I'm not giving Aunt Salva and Uncle Vester a hard time."

"Good. Did you take a bath last night and change your undies?"

"Yes mam' I did. Mama you make me laugh."

I laughed. "You make me laugh too kido'. I'm ganna' get off the phone now, I'll be there later to get you. Now give the phone back to Aunt Salva."

"Ok mama bye! Precious here I come don't start it without me!" She yelled as her voice faded into the background.

Salva jump on the phone. "Ok my chick, what's the deal for the day?"

"I don't know yet. I'll probably start on another book today since the weather looks great outside." I got up with the cordless in my hand and looked out the window I had opened from last night. "The wind seems to be blowing off the water. It shouldn't be too windy to write out on the beach." After a moment of silence I said, "I'll call you guys if my plans change but they shouldn't." I walked away from the window, put on my favorite sundress, my brown slippers, and went to the kitchen with the cordless in one hand and my note pad in the other.

"Alright chick, we'll be here until this afternoon. I'm takin' Precious to the movies. If I don't see you before we leave, then I'll just take her with us. The phone beeps. "That's my line I know it's for Salvester, he's expecting a call. I'll talk to you later."

"Alright then bye." We both hung up the phone. I set the phone on the kitchen counter and went and sat at the table.

"Ok Lord what're we gon' do today? You know I don't go nowhere without You." I got up and poured me some old hot coffee I had sittin'

55

in the pot from yesterday, got my notepad, walked out to the patio, and sat down on the reclining chairs by the pool. I love the sound of the ocean waves as they roll back and forth into the sea. I'm so glad I finally found a landscaping company that did an excellent job on the backyard. The most important thing to me is having a backyard that I feel just as comfortable in as I would in my own house. My favorite is the waterfall and the maze that it makes as it flows from the top of the small rocky hill, wrapping around several short trees and bushes, and showering down into the pool. I can feel the mist slightly spotting my face, and I must say it feels like a dream come true. It puts me in the mind of Cancun. I smiled, sipped on my coffee, closed my eyes, and slightly moaned at the thought. The breeze is barely lifting my hair while the sun's blazing down on my body. I took my notepad and started writing for about 45-minutes.

The phone rings.

"I'll just let the answering machine pick it up." I said out loud to myself.

It rang again.

"Why don't they just leave a message?" I kept writing.

It rang again, this time it never stopped. I ran back into the kitchen and snatched the phone from off the kitchen counter. "Hello?" I answered out of breath.

"Barina! I've been tryin' to call you for the last 30-minutes! Karina's been hit by a car! You gotta' come quick they said she might not make it! We're at Bethlem Hospital!" I hung up in her face.

"What? No this can't be true! Not my baby Lord? Please don't take my baby! Please don't let her die!" I screamed into the air as I ran and grabbed my purse, ran out of the house, jumped into the Excursion, and raced to the hospital. I hope this' some kind of joke. Or could this be real?

I arrived at the hospital in what seemed like a second. There wasn't a cop in sight on my way here. I ran up to the information desk like I was runnin' a hundred yard dash. Out of breath I asked, "Um'... yes can you tell me where my baby is?"

"Calm down mam'. What is your baby's name?" She calmly asked.

"Her name is Karina Grant!" I screamed pounding my fist so hard on the counter that the clip board fell off.

"Mam' you do not have to hit the counter. Do I need to get a doctor for you?"

"Look apparently you ain't never had your child to get hit by a car and they said she was about to die! Now I'm askin' that you tell me where she is?"

"Ok mam', I understand. She's in ICU. You can't go up there right now, they're operating on her. You may go in the waiting room up on the next floor. As soon as you come off the..." Salva screams from down the hall as she came running up to me as we both hugged and burst into tears.

"Where's my baby?"

"She's upstairs! I'm so sorry Barina! I turned my head and the car came from out of nowhere! I'm so sorry, please forgive me!"

I grabbed her shoulders. "Look, get a hold of yourself! Take me where my child is!" I yelled. We ran up the stairs to the next floor not even waiting for the next elevator.

We waited in the waiting room for over three hours pacing and praying. They finally came out and said that she made it but there were some internal bleeding that they had trouble stopping but all of a sudden it all stopped. They called it luck, but I called it a miracle from Heaven. The doctor said that while they were operating Karina slipped into a coma. She could wake up at any time, but be ready for the worse. He also said that she might turn out to be a vegetable. Which I don't receive, that don't even line up with the Word of God.

The doctor took us to her bed. When I saw her all I could do was cry. I've never seen my baby like this before. Her head is as big as a basketball. Her eyes and her nose look like they have golf balls stuck in em'. And her lips are swollen shut. They cut half of her hair off because they had to do surgery on her skull. That's where the bleeding was that God stopped. She has bandages all over her little body. My baby, I don't know what to do, how to touch her or what to say to her. Lord help me. I told Salva, Salvester, and Precious to leave me alone with my baby. They walked out into the waiting room without questions.

I can't do nothin' but put my head down on her little chest and cry out to God. "Lord, I'm Your child and she's Your baby. Why have You allowed the devil to do this to her? Please don't let the enemy take her life. You said that we shall live and not die. *(Psalms 118:17)* I trust

57

in Your Word and I know it's true, and I trust in You." I struggled the words out of my mouth with tears falling hard from my eyes. "If it's Your will for her to die, then I'm willing to accept it. But if it's not, heal her body and wake her up with no defects from her wounds." Tears fell from my eyes onto the sheet covering her chest. "Just like Your Word says in *Isaiah 53:5 kjv.*, '....By Your stripes we are healed.' And You also said in *3 John 2 kjv.*, '....that You wish above all things that we may prosper and be in health even as our souls prosper.' Lord, I'm taking You at Your Word and I know that it will not return back to me void." *(Isaiah 55:11, Isaiah 43:26)*

I prayed myself to sleep right on Karina's chest.

The doctor's just came in and said that visiting hours are over. I went into the waiting room and told Salva and the rest of them to go on home. I was going to stay the night in the waiting room.

Chapter Three

*W*hat I thought was going to take a matter of minutes took an entire month. Karina finally woke up out of her coma. Thank you Jesus! I prayed and fasted everyday and God finally answered my request. She's back home and she has all of her full energy back. She's back to the normal energetic Karina with no defects, just like I asked God. I've learned that God don't always do things right away so that we would believe more in Him, just like He did with Lazarus' death. *(St. John 11:1-45)* When Jesus heard about the death of Lazarus, He didn't go right away to the place where Lazarus was because He wanted them (Mary, Martha, and the Jews), me and anybody else to believe. He had already planned to raise Lazarus from the dead, just like He (God) had already planned to bring Karina out of the coma. But He wanted me to trust Him and believe that He is and was more than able to heal and to deliver her; and that He's in total control. He's definitely a prayer answering God!

I'm thinkin' I better go get this girl ready. Salva, Salvester, and Precious are supposed to be coming over soon. We're all going to the park.

Six month's went by so fast. I've written another book and Karina's gotten stronger than ever. Nobody would ever know that she was once in a coma kissing the heart of death. She just had a birthday the other day. We all gave her a huge party. It was Salva's idea that we have it at Game City because that's Karina's favorite fun place. It has go-carts, bumper cars, miniature golf, and hundreds of different kinds of video

59

games. Before the kid's went on their own, I shared a few words but couldn't finish cause' the tears clouded my eyes and my tongue stopped working. All I could think about was how the Lord had healed my baby. Its funny cause' my tears had transferred on everybody as they all started crying.

After all the tears were shed, the kid's ran towards the games. They had an entire day of fun and so did we.

Salvester has to go on a trip with the school for the weekend so Salva and Precious are coming over for the weekend. I must say that since the incident happened with Karina, Salva and I have gotten even closer. Our bond has strengthened. It's a blessing.

Salva and Precious should be here any minute now. Karina and I went and bought some games for us to play and now we're tidying up the house.

The thought of the guy from the convention just flashed across my mind. Hum' that's weird… Let me hurry up, I hear em' pulling up in the driveway. "Karina! Your auntie and your cousins here! Come down!" I yelled from the bottom of the stairs.

"I'm comin' mama!" She yelled back as she raced down the stairs. I went and opened the door. "Hey, come on in." We all hugged. "Have you guys eatin'? I ordered some Chinese food and Karina made some lemonade. It's in the frig." They came in and went straight to the kitchen, must be hungry.

"Got any napkins?" Precious asked, walking over to the cabinet.

"Yea', they're in the cabinet right in front of you."

The phone rings. I answered it. "Hello?" I paused. "This' Barina… O' hi Cal… Thank you… Yes, it's my eleventh book." I smiled at everybody as I answered his questions. "To what?…. Go where?…. Did you say?…. Me, do a seminar?…. When, I'll be there?…. Ok…. I'll be lookin' to hear from you soon… That'll be great. Thanks Cal… Bye." I slammed the phone down, jumped up and ran out to the pool, screamed thank you Jesus into the air, ran back inside and went and dropped down on the three piece burnt sienna leather sofa in the living room.

"What's yo' problem?" Salva yelled with excitement from the kitchen, as she came running behind me and dropped down on the recliner across from me.

"That was Cal, you know, my P.R.?" She shook her head yes like O' I remember now. "Are you ready for this girl?" She smiled and

60

nodded her head like hurry up. "Well!" I shook my hands as if they were hot. "He's bookin' me a plane to the Bahamas!" We both screamed at the same time.

"So what's the occasion?"

"There's a big time Christian Book Festival happenin' there for three days! Isn't that awesome?"

"That is awesome! Got some room for one more?"

"Now you know I need you. What we gon' do with the girls?"

"I don't know, maybe Salvester'll watch em', or Precious friend's parents will?"

"No. I'm not lettin' nobody watch my child other than Salvester." I said.

"Ok fine, I'm sure he won't mind. I'll ask him."

"We gotta' go shoppin' so I can be lookin' like I got a million bucks in my pocket." We both burst out laughing as I got up and ran over and high-five her, then came back and dropped back down on the sofa.

"Ok?" She laughed again. "Girl what if you meet your husband?" She winked her eye.

"Then I just meet em'. Ain't no need of gettin' your hopes up cause it ain't gon' happen." I sarcastically winked back at her. "And anyway, I'm not lookin' no way. My mind is on Jesus." I smiled, rolled my eyes, and tried to keep from laughing as we both burst out laughing like yea' right. "Ok, ok, ok, I can't lie; being in the presence of a man wouldn't be half bad right about now." I smiled again. Salva's lookin' at me with this big huge grin on her face. "Look Salva, I'm a Christian yes, but my flesh still wants to do the opposite of what my Spirit tells me to do. Like fall and have some sex with a man all night long. But I know I can't do that because that's contrary to the Word of God."

"I hear ya'. I don't see how you've lasted this long, it's gotta' be God who's been keeping you. I gotta' give it to you, I am proud of you Miss. Thang."

"I'm proud of myself." I snickered and fanned myself like I was hot. "Being single and celibate for ten years would be impossible for a whole lot of folks, but for me it has been the fear of God, *(Ecclesiastes 12:13)* the fear of ever makin' the mistake of havin' another baby out of wed-lock. And to be honest, I guess I've been so busy keepin' up with Karina that I haven't had time to be in a relationship, let alone even thinkin' about gettin' married." My tone got serious as our conversation got personal.

"Are you sure that's the way it's been? Or have you been too hard on men that it's never gotten to a relationship?" She looked at me, and then pulled her legs underneath her bottom.

"You may be right. I always feared God, especially after I got pregnant with Karina at fourteen. And I just didn't want that to happen to me again as I said earlier. Let alone to Karina. I don't want people to look at me one way behind close doors, and another way in front of everybody. I know God wouldn't be pleased with me. I realize that I'm not where I need to be, but thank God I'm not where I used to be. I know God is with me and has always been."

"So Barina." She uncurled her legs and sat up in the recliner. "I always hear you talk about the Lord and your relationship with Him, so why don't you go to church?"

"You know what? I really don't have an answer for that. I'm just too busy, maybe one day I will." We both got quiet.

Precious broke the silence as she and Karina came running down the stairs screaming. She rushed up to me like she was about to tackle me. "Aunt Barina! Aunt Barina! Karina won't play fair! She keeps taking her dolls from me!"

"Look Karina do I have to take your dolls from you? You better share and stop being selfish. Do you hear me?" I looked up at her from the couch.

"Yes mam'." She said slowly as she walked off with tears wailing up in her eyes. Precious followed her as if she was sorry she ever told on her.

"You two are cousins and you have to love one another. You hear Precious?" Salva yelled as Karina and Precious nodded yes and slowly went back upstairs.

"So what'll you wanna' do first? Hey wanna' run down to the beach and put our feet in the water?" I asked.

"I can't believe you out of all people are askin' me that. You haven't wanted to do that in years. In fact, ever since your so-called boyfriend almost drowned ya'. You remember that?"

"I remember it like it was yesterday. But I really don't wanna' go back to the past Salva, I just wanna' live for today. I believe God got great things for me." *(Deuteronomy 28:1-14)*

"What more could God possibly have for you? I mean you're already a successful anointed book writer that's worldly known. You

62

make a nice piece of change from all of em' without havin' to go anywhere. You have a beautiful daughter, a beautiful mansion, beautiful sister." She pointed to herself and smiled. "What more do you need?"

"Yea' right, I have a beautiful nosey sister and somethin' somethin' somethin' more but I won't go there... Ha'! Thanks for all the compliments but I'm not talking about money and my surroundings, I'm talking about somethin' spiritual. You don't understand."

"I do understand."

"Well tell me what I'm talkin' about then." I said.

"You're talkin' about God doin' somethin' on the inside of you. Look Barina, I'm going to church and I have a relationship with the Lord, and you know that. Furthermore, don't forget that I'm the one who ministered salvation to you."

"How could I ever forget?"

"Well act like you got some home trainin'." She laughed.

"Whatever, you act like you got some home trainin'. Who's the oldest?" I laughed as I pointed towards myself.

"You are."

"Say it louder!"

"You are!" She yelled.

"Now tell the whole world who run thangs!"

"You...what? Now wait a minute, sho' not you." We burst out laughing as we got up and made our way to the patio.

"Karina and Precious! We're goin' out to the beach! Do not leave this house unless you're comin' with us!" I yelled towards the stairs.

Karina screamed from upstairs. "No mama, don't leave us we're comin'! Wait! We're puttin' on our sandals!... Please don't leave us!"

"Hurry up we'll be at the pool!" I yelled back. We walked on out to the pool. Salva couldn't wait to put her feet in the miniature waterfall as it ran from off the rocks in a maze on into the pool. Karina and Precious just came runnin' out with their tank tops, shorts, and flip-flops on.

"Everybody ready?" I asked as Salva came running over and splashed water on me. I guess it transferred on the girls because they started doing it too.

We all had somewhat of a water war for about five minutes laughing and screaming, and then we all started walking out towards the beach. Each grain of sand squeezed through my toes as it got more and more moist the closer we got to the water. The girls ran out and dove towards the slow waves. They look so cute playing together. "Ya'll don't go too far!" I yelled towards the water.

"Ok!" They both yelled back at the same time as they caught another wave.

Salva turned and looked at me. "Let's go back up and get the lawn chairs and look like divas." She yelled with this huge grin on her face as the waves came rushing in through our legs.

"Girl we already look like divas. We don't need no lawn chairs. What we can do is go back up to the house and grab some towels, you know we gon' need some with these girls?"

"Now that's the truth." We both laughed. "Precious and Karina we're goin' back up to the house, we'll be right back! You guys come with us or get out of the water til' we come back!"

"We'll get out of the water!" Karina yelled back.

"Alright!" I yelled back then started talking back to Salva. "Girl you remember when people used to mistake you for a Porto Rican girl on the job at the Warehouse?"

"How well do I remember. Anyway, I know you not tryin' to rank on nobody? Don't chu' forget how they used to rank on you too." She laughed as she squint her eyes at me. "They used to call you ghetto girl cause' you was always drinkin' kool-aid and eatin' syrup sandwiches." She burst out laughing.

"Look I had to do what I had to do." I didn't smile.

"I hear ya'. You know I know where you came from girl. Its funny cause' you always knew how to get em' off your back, the difference between you and me was that you were bolder than me then. I don't know why, I just couldn't say nothin' back to em'. I can't say that now though, but maybe then I was too busy letting the Lord fight my battles?" She smiled to herself.

"Now that you said that, that is so true I used to tell everybody else off but I was scared to talk about you cause' time I said somethin' about chu', somethin' bad happened to me. Either I stomped my toe on somethin', or nothin' good would work out for me until I apologized to you."

"Well you know the bible says: …Touch not my anointed… *(Psalms 105:15)kjv* and that goes for the saved and the unsaved. You can't mess with God's people and get away with it."

64

"Umm'. I'm a leave that subject alone. That gave me chills." We started walking towards the house. "You know? Thinkin' back to when they used to talk about me, I didn't have any problems tellin' em' all off. I think I used to fight back because of all the anger I had built up inside of me from what my parents did to me. Then I was angry because I had a child at a young age and they used to talk about me because of that." I walked inside the house and Salva waited by the patio. I went and grabbed some towels from the downstairs bathroom closet and walked back towards the patio where Salva was. "And another thing, in high school you know they used to call me old woman, a slut, and a nasty prostitute? My reputation was ruined before my freshman year could ever get started. I couldn't keep a boyfriend because they always felt like they were a daddy at fourteen, so they left me alone. They would lie on me sayin' that they had sex with me when they didn't." We walked back out towards the beach. "Nobody cared Salva, nobody. Nobody understood, not even my parents. They disowned me because they were so-called devoted Christians who just couldn't handle the fact that I had a baby out of wed-lock. I feel like this, if they had of encouraged me when I was young and instilled some self-esteem and self values inside of me, like tellin' me that I'm pretty, I'm somebody, I'm smart, and that I will be successful in life, that wouldn't have happened. I believe what a child will be, starts right in the home."

"I know that's right girl. But remember what you said earlier, let the past be the past and just live for today." She quietly added.

"All my parents did was tell me what I was doin' wrong, and never what I was doin' right, always negative before positive. And I know this is what destroys a child because it destroyed my life. Now they are dead and I never got the chance to make it right with them." A tear fell from my eyes.

"Don't cry Barina. I totally understand where you're comin' from girl. You know my parents weren't there for me either. They could care less what I did. So I fully understand even though I didn't grow up with you, I was there through your most difficult times. Remember you weren't alone?"

"I know. It just felt like I was for so long even after we became the best of friends. You know how they say you can be in a room with a whole lot of people and still be lonely?"

"Yea'."

"Well, that's how it was for me." I said. I laid the towels over the damped sand and laid on top of em'. Salva, Karina, and Precious ran and got back in the water.

We all ended up bathing in the hot sun until it disappeared behind the water...

Chapter Four

*H*urry up Salva! You gon' make me late for my plane!" I yelled from inside Salva's Suburban. She is the slowest person in the world.

"I'm comin' woman!" She yelled back from inside the house.

I'm so hurt Salva can't come. She forgot that Salvester's parents are havin' a family gathering. I'm sort of glad she's ganna' stay here with Salvester. I mean nothin's wrong with him, it's just that I'm still nervous from Karina's accident. It's hard for me to trust people with my child now. The only one I trust to keep her is Salva, and sometime that's even a challenge. I wish she could come though we would have so much fun and she's such a great help while I speak and sign books.

Salva jumped into the truck like somebody was after her. "Ok, I'm ready. So what terminal are you at?"

"You act like we're already there. What chu' tryin' to do, get rid of me?" I chuckled behind my breath.

"Girl you are so silly. Now you know I'm not tryin' to get rid of you. You know how I get when I'm around a bunch of cars and chaos—I panic."

"Alright let's go."

We drove what seemed like forever. Traffic's crowded as usual, typical for a huge city like this. The population is well over a billion people. My patience feels better because I can now see the airport in the near distance.

"So what cha' gon' do when you get there?"

"I already know what chu' gettin' at."

"What am I gettin' at?"

67

"You tryin' to see if I'm gon' go out and get a man."

"You said it not me." She smiled and then turned into a drop off parking space.

"You have 30-minutes mam'!" The police yelled into the window as Salva let her window down.

"Well, here we are Miss. Thang', and I haven't forgotten about what I just asked you either." She got out of the truck.

"Whata' you mean you haven't forgot?" I got out the truck, opened the back door, reached and grabbed my suitcase from the back seat, and then slammed the door shut.

"Don't worry bout' it." She gave me a quick hug. "I'll get cha' back when you get back. Have fun for me too. Love you." She got back in the truck, and drove off into the congested traffic.

The plane ride was at times shaky because of the moisture in the clouds. But for the most part, the ride was peaceful.

Everything that Cal set up for me is going perfect and according to plan. The Festival starts tonight, opening up with a huge concert with different well-known Christian artists and bands.

I'm all unpacked and gettin' ready to make my way to the concert. It's so lonely being way up here in the Bahamas without anybody to share all this fun with. I hope I brought the right clothes. I guess I'll wear this black one peace spaghetti strapped dress that's hittin' my knees. I still can't get over how much I paid for it. Somebody would steal it off of me if they knew it was only $10 dollars at the thrift shop. I wish my sista' was here she could help me dress it up better, she's always had an eye for puttin' cheap clothes together and makin' em' look more expensive than what they're really worth. I've learned that riches don't make me, I make the riches. I didn't always have money like this so I'm quick not to forget where I came from. I do have as many expensive clothes as cheap clothes but they all don't make who I am. When I tell people this they all laugh at me but I don't care. I thought. Now let me see what I'm gon' wear with this dress. I guess I'll go ahead and wear these all black strapless 6-inch heals with my silver diamond earrings. I'm lookin' at myself in the mirror and saying, "Girl you got it goin' on. You could never be mistaken for a go-go girl." I put my hands on my hips. "Just classy umph', umph', umph', just classy." I shook my head and giggled as if somebody was in the room and was giggling with me.

The night is fresh with a slight cool breeze comin' from off the ocean water. I didn't have to wait for a cab because Cal had a limo waiting at the hotel for me. He rented it for all three nights. I'm actually here in the Bahamas, I can't believe it. I feel like a movie star ridin' in her limo to the Red Carpet. I flattered myself.

As we pulled up to the Festival I can see that there are so many exciting things going on all at the same time. People are everywhere. They've even set up a huge carnival outside. The loud sound of gospel praises are flooding the air as it past through the cracks of the limo's window on into my ears and through my heart. I can't wait for him to stop the limo so I can jump out and get my groove on.

The limo came to a stop and I got out thinkin' about what Salva said before I got on the plane. She makes me laugh. Hum'... I wonder if my husbands out here? Yea' right next thought. Cal already has my bookstand set up. He hired somebody to work my booth when he heard that Salva wasn't gon' be able to make the trip. All I gotta' do is enjoy the Festival until it's time for me to do my seminar, which isn't until the last day. It starts bright and early in the morning, which is good then I have the rest of the day to enjoy the other speakers and get a chance to visit their booths and different other venders.

The music's jumpin', people are walking in and out, up and down, and across one another without any special order. There's so much food to choose from out here. Shrimp on a stick, barbeque turkey legs, funnel cakes, big juicy pickles, snow cones, and so much more that I'll hurt my brain tryin' to name em' all.

I'm walking through the crowd towards the concert area as the music's gettin' louder the closer I get. Lights are blinking on and off with different colors flashing everywhere, venders are moving about trying to negotiate their sales, and a view of the beach is sittin' in the far distance; kinda' like my view at home but my view ain't got nothin' on this view. The weather is just right, perfect to be with someone special. Like my husband with his arms wrapped around me just enjoying one another. What am I gon' do with all these nights by myself? Everywhere I look couples are hangin' on one another. I need to find me a group of women—Single women. I know I'll have some fun then. Single women are so much fun, some of em' are. Most of em' feel like they don't have nothin' to loose, so that's why it's so easy for them to have so much fun together. I'm thinkin', a married woman gotta' make sure her husband is taken care of. She has to submit and please him totally. I don't know if I'm ready for all that drama. It's hard enough to please the Lord at times, especially when I get in my flesh. I thought. *(Galatians 5:19) (Romans 8:1)*

A familiar voice broke in through the crowd. "Will you marry me?" He secretly asked, as his voice snuck through my ears along with the different conversations around us.

I quickly turned around to match the face only to find that it's the same man from the last Book Festival in Cali. I can't believe my eyes. "How'd you get here?" I asked. My eyes are wide open and my heart's beating by the second.

"Will you marry me?" He calmly asked again but this time with a smile that took my breath away.

I can't stand his attitude. He's just way too arrogant for me and looks way too young and oughta' my league. He's got a baby face and I'm not tryin' to raise no babies. I slightly smiled at the thought. "Who are you, and why are you following me?"

"I'm not following you." His smile got wider.

O' no it's somethin' about that smile that makes him look real crazy. He's probably some stalkin' serial killer. "Look just leave me alone!" I took off runnin' into the crowd and never looked back nor did I ever see him again for the rest of the night. Which is good, arrogant men and me don't mix so I don't feel bad at all about what I just did. Plus that's the best thing to do than to just sit there and make him think he stands a chance.

The rest of the night was awesome. I bumped into some single women from a church in Texas while at one of the vender's booths. We all had a blast until I got tired and was ready to crash for the night. I couldn't wait to get back to the room and relax in my Jamaican style king size bed. All my papers are scattered across the bed like some unarranged puzzle. I'm tryin' to figure out what subject I'm gon' speak on. I got so many different topics to choose from. I'll just wait and see what kind of audience I'm ganna' have.

I just can't stop thinkin' about that man and how bold he was. It was something different about him; I can't put my finger on it. This time I felt different while he stood in my presence, I just can't figure out what the feeling was. I thought myself to sleep.

The next morning.

There's a knock at the door. I quickly threw the covers from over my head, looked at the clock and yelled from the bed with all my strength, "Who is it?"

"Room service mam'." He quickly answered.

"Shoot, don't he know its six o'clock in the morning, people still sleep?" I threw the covers back over my head and thought about it for a moment... "I am hungry and everything is free so I better take advantage of it." I jumped out of the bed, threw on my pink satin rope I had lying on the sofa in the front room, and slowly staggered and opened the door. "Thank you." I tried to reach for the cart of food.

"I'll bring it in for you mam'." He pushed the cart in not waiting for my response.

"Hum', he's a lil' o' aggressive somethin'." I muffled underneath my breath so that he couldn't hear me and smiled to myself thinking, his short thick, slicked back blonde hair; catering suit, makes him look to be in between a diet, a weight schedule, and a make-over all at once, which could be a good thing. I laughed at the thought.

"Anything else I can do for you mam'?" He asked with his hand out as he looked around as if to be looking for someone.

"No that'll be fine. Thanks." I looked at his hand and laughed. "I know what that mean, I guess I better go get what you're lookin' for." I went and got a ten from my purse and came back and handed it to him and gave him a quick goodbye shove from the back. He frowned and walked out looking at the ten dollar bill like it was a dollar. I just laughed and closed the door, and thought to myself, those doormen be hustlin'.

It's kinda' good that he came, because I needed to get up so I can get down to the vender's before the crowd does. I went and took a shower, came back and ate a little of the food from off the cart, went and put on my clothes, and headed out goin' towards the lobby.

The lobby's already startin' to get crowded. It's a good thing I got ready when I did. I guess everybody was thinkin' like me. Security and the police are well awake this morning, they're on every corner of the hotel, which is good especially for hoodlums who wanna' steal instead of buying stuff the right way. I know I'm too ready to shop. I better get

71

somethin' for everybody at home, because if I don't, they gon' be fussin'.

I got my empty back-pack in one hand and my wallet in the other one. I can't get over how inviting this lobby is. There's a huge 50' ft. tall open ceiling waterfall that's showering up towards the ceiling. Its looks so refreshing as it rests in the center of the Hotel's lobby— singing all by itself. A lot of people are going around it throwing money in it like its gon' make their wish come true. I better get in where I fit in, even though I don't believe that a waterfall can make my dreams come true, only God can. I smiled as I walked over to it, closed my eyes, said my prayer, and sat down on the edge of it as if God was going to give me my answer right away. I closed my eyes again and pushed my chin in my hands as they rest on my thighs. I can't help but think about what Salva said about Karina needing a man figure in her life. I don't know maybe she's right? But I'm just not ready for no husband. It's too much drama for me right now. Anyway it doesn't matter cause' it ain't like I got em' runnin' up to me makin' my decision hard?

Out of nowhere a voice whispered in my ear,

> *"Your stature is like that of a palm...*
> *I will take hold of its fruit...*
> *And sniff the fragrance of your breath*
> *which smells like apples... inside of*
> *the tunnels of your mouth like the best*
> *choice of wine...*
> *(Song of Solomon 7:7-9)Amplified*

...Now will you marry me?" He said.

My eyes are still closed. I can't say a word. I'm totally numb and my body's frozen from the sound of those words. No man has ever said anything like that to me before. I'm lost for words. I can't make em' leave if I wanted too. But I better get a grip cause' when I open up my eyes and find that this' the same guy, I'm a have em' put in jail. I opened my eyes, turned and looked, and sure nuff' it's him grinning from ear-to-ear like he don' won my heart. No, see, he don' made me mad is what he's done. He got off his knees. "No um', um', see I'm tired of this." I got up and pointed my finger in his face. He kept smiling. "This don't make no sense! First you're a stalker, last night you were a serial killer, and now you a bootleg poet! I can't take this anymore! I'm callin' security! Security! Security!" I yelled until one of them came runnin' over to us.

"Look I didn't mean to cause you any harm." He tried walking away.

"Na' um', um', where you goin'? Naw' don't leave now, be a man and face up to what chu' were tryin' to do to me!" I yelled so that everybody could hear me.

He walked back towards me. "I'm not trying to do anything to you." He tried walking away again but the security guard stopped him. That smile that was on his face is totally gone.

"Mam' was he trying to hurt you?" The security guard asked as he grabbed his arm and called for some of the police to come and help. I've caused a huge scene, people are now gathering around us as the police came and joined in.

"Do you wanna' press charges?"

"Yea' I wanna' press charges."

The police jumped in. "What did he do mam'?"

"He tried to seduce me and he put his hands on me!" I yelled.

They all looked around at each other, then at the crowd that had gathered as some were shouting take him, take him to jail. "Ok let's go buddy, you can't be putting your hands on women." They grabbed him and took him through the crowded hotel, and out of the building. I took one last look at his face and he flashed an expression that I don't think I'll ever be able to forget. It was an expression of sadness as if to ask why did I just do what I did? And then the fact that I lied and made a big scene that shouldn't have ever been. "O well, shouldn't ov' came over here messin' with me with those tied lines. I don't even feel bad.

After the Festival was over, I took the first flight back home. I enjoyed myself considering the fact that I sold out of all my books with some reorders to fill, and sold all of my paraphernalia. Salva's supposed to be at the airport to pick me up I hope that girl's on time. I thought, taking my bags off the baggage claim ramp, and then walking out to the passenger pick up area.

"Barina!" Someone called me from a distance.

I looked as I met eyes with Salva. She's hanging out of the door and waving her hands. I ran over like thank God she's on time. She jumped out of the truck and gave me a big hug like she hasn't seen me in years.

"Girl we missed you so much! Karina and everybody else couldn't stop talkin' bout' how much we all miss you." She said. She's grinnin' from ear-to-ear as she took my bags and tossed em' in the back seat.

"Ya'll act like I've been gone for years? It's only been a 3-day weekend?" I said as we both got in the truck.

"Well you know how spoiled we all are behind you?" She kept smiling and I smiled too.

"Yea' I know. Hey where's my baby? What chu' do, tie her up somewhere?" We both look at each other and laughed like yea' right.

"No silly, they're at the movies with Salvester. The movie was still goin' on and I didn't want to disturb them so I just came by myself. We gotta' swing back and pick em' up."

"Ok let's hurry up cause' I wanna' see my baby. I wish you had of went on and brought her." I didn't smile and it showed on my face. The thought of her not being there to run in my arms didn't set right with me. I know Salva didn't mean anything by it, it's just that, that girl's my pride and joy and if anything happens to her… well I don't wanna' even think about it.

"Please don't be upset with me Barina. I lost track of time and it all happened so fast. Next time I promise to have her there when you get off the plane. Ok?"

"It's cool don't sweat it. I'll see her soon enough."

"So tell me about this trip mam'." She looked over at me and cracked a smile.

"Tell you what?" I'm trying to act as if nothing happened.   "Don't even try it. You know you got somethin' juicy to tell me? " She took her hand off the steering-wheel and shoved me in the shoulder while never looking my way.

"What chu' wanna' know Mrs. Nosey?"

"Mrs. Nosey? O' so you got jokes now? Somethin' must've really happened cause' you're really giving me a hard time. Why, I don't know but I wish you would spill the goods before I give up?" She quickly glanced over at me then back at the road. "Ok fine. I had a great time. Met some new people and saw some awesome sights. The water was so beautiful Salva. I know you would've had a great time."

"So when you say you met some new people, who are you referring to females or males?"

"What difference does it make?"

"It makes a lot of difference. You could've met up with some females to chase some males and had a boring time? Or you could've met up with some males and got free dinners and free gifts and had a marvelous time? Which one?"

"Well I definitely wouldn't have taken some boring females over some gift givin' males. But as a matter of fact, I did meet some single Christian women from Texas. We all had a blast! And it wasn't boring either. We didn't sit around talkin' bout' why we ain't got no man, why we lonely cause' we single, and why we saved, sanctified, lonely, and filled with the Holy Ghost." Salva burst out laughing. "I'm serious." I laughed too.

"You are so silly. So what did ya'll single women do?"

"We walked all over the festival with our heads held high, laughing at silly things, and talking about the Lord."

"No offense but I know ya'll weren't talkin' about the Lord in the middle of this great big ol' exciting festival where He was tryin' to help ya'll catch ya'll husbands? You know that scripture that talks about the ten virgins? Five was ready but the other five weren't?" *(Matthew 25:1-11)*

"Salva, didn't nobody ask you to get all philosophical. Look we enjoyed it for what it was. I ain't lookin' for no man to take care of me, and I ain't lookin' for no man to come and sweep me off my feet either. I don't care if he did whisper sweet tied ol' lines in my ear?"

"What did you say?" She quickly took a glance at me and then back at the road then back at me.

"You heard me."

"Say it again."

"I said I don't care if he did whisper some sweet tied ol' lines in my ear. That's what I said."

"What are you referring too?"

I put my hand on my heart. "I'm referring to this guy who came up behind me and whispered a breath taking, romantic poem in my ears. And you'll never guess the rest…"

"What girl, please tell me?"

"Remember the man I told you about at my last book signing, the one who came up to me and asked me to marry him?"

"Please don't tell me what I think you're about to tell me?" She pulled up in the parking lot of the movie theater.

"Yes mam' it was him Salva, and girl I was scared. The first night before I met those ladies, I was walkin' by myself and all of a sudden this voice appeared behind me and said will you marry me. And when I turned around, it was him. I couldn't believe it. I got scared, said some choice words, and ran off into the crowd thinkin' and hopin' that I wasn't gon' ever see em' again. But the next morning was a whole new experience for me Salva. I was in the lobby and was sittin' by the waterfall..." She cut me off.

"Why were you by the waterfall?"

"You would ask. I had just thrown my coin in and said a prayer."

"What prayer did you pray?"

"Look now. Ok. I prayed that God would send my husband if He was ready for me to have one. Ok? Now there take that." We both laughed.

"Ok then what happened after that?"

"You'll never believe what happened. As I was sittin' with my eyes closed, his voice came up behind me and whispered,

> *"Your stature is like that of a palm...*
> *I will take hold of its fruit...*
> *and sniff the fragrance of your breath*
> *which smells like apples...*
> *inside of the tunnels of your mouth like*
> *the best choice of wine...*
> *(Song of Solomon 7:7-9)Amplified*

"Girl no he didn't do that?" She looked at me like it took her breath away.

"Not only that, but at the end of the poem he asked me to marry him again." We got out of the truck and started walking towards the theater.

"I hate to tell you, but that's your husband. You know that right?"

"No I don't and I don't appreciate chu' sayin' that."

"O' well get over it, it's the truth."

"Salva I did something that was so mean. Right after he whispered in my ear, I called security on him, pressed charges on him, and had

76

him put in jail. I lied and told the security that he put his hands on me and they took him away."

"Why did you do that Barina that was mean? That don't even sound like somethin' you would do? I'm so disappointed in you."

"Look I got tired of him following me, this whole thing is weird anyway and I really don't wanna' talk about it anymore."

"Fine, but I want you to know that what chu' did was wrong and pay backs a heart breaka'. You reap what you sow mam'." *(Galatians 6:7)* She waved Karina, Precious, and Salvester down as they came out of the theater.

"Hey you ain't gotta' say it like that. It ain't like I killed em'?"

"But you put an innocent man in jail for somethin' he didn't do." I couldn't say a word after that statement.

Karina came running towards me, planted a big juicy wet kiss on my lips, and hugged me for what seemed like forever. "Mama's baby, I missed you so much! Did you miss mama?" I asked, never letting her go.

"Yes mam' I sure did! Mama, next time don't stay away so long?"

"Ok mama promise. So did you mind Aunt Salva and Uncle Vester?" I put her down.

"Yes mam'." I looked at them for assurance as they nodded yes.

"Well very good, mommy's proud of you." I said as I reached to give Salvester and Precious a hug.

Salva's squinting her eyes at me as if she's mad at me for what I told her about my trip, and I gave her this look like, what?

Chapter Five

I don't know when I strayed away from God. I haven't been to church in I don't know when. I'm just too busy and too tired. When I finally get a break, I'm restin' and I don't wanna' be bothered by nobody. Not even goin' to church nor by church folks. But I still love the Lord though.

I slept in my bed all day and all night for the past two days. Tired and rest are the only words that's functioning in my brain right now. That trip took more out of me than what I expected. I'm thinkin' about what Salva said about pay back being a heart breaker. Just the thought of it makes me cringe. I can't stand the thought of my heart being broken again, especially by another man. B-Wayne and all the other straggler's was enough. It took me years to get over B-Wayne. He was my first and only love. I gave him my whole heart without wavering, and he still hurt me and left me with a part of him to take care of for the rest of my life. I can't complain she's the most beautiful thing I could've ever asked for. It's not a day that goes by that I don't thank God for giving me such a beautiful blessing. She's healthy; she has activity of all her limbs, and has her little right mind. I smiled at the thought. But it's taken a long time for me to be able to feel the way that I feel today because at first I didn't want Karina. I wasn't capable of being a young mother let alone surviving out there on the streets with one. Then I had to realize that it wasn't her fault that she had to come into this world. How dare I take it out on her for the mistake that I had made in my life? The sin was between Wayne and me, not her. She had nothin' to do with it. God held us accountable, not her. The feelings I

79

had concerning her started tugging at my heart. When she was finally able to talk she would say the most astounding words that a two year old could ever say. She would say words that my own mama has never said to me. She would encourage me and tell me that everything was gon' be alright. She would hold me and tell me not to give up when things got so bad I thought I was gon' take my own life and hers. I couldn't stand the thought of leaving her here by herself. I know it was God speaking through her because her words were so real and true and they were the only reason why I never took our lives. Like the bible says: "Out of the mouth of a babe..." *(Psalms 8:2)* And that it was. I know the wisdom she has, has come straight from God. Somebody somewhere must've been prayin'.

I didn't think that the situation I had with that lunatic was as bad as Salva put it. I guess I was wrong. I do feel a little convicted. I'm not a bad person unless you rub me the wrong way. Now thinking about it, the way she put it, I didn't have to call security and have him put in jail. I just could've simply walked away. O' well it's over now. All and all I enjoyed my trip and the time I had alone. My mind just flashed back on somethin' Salva said that's making me think, she said that he was my husband. Well, I beg to differ. First of all he's way too young, insane, and he has a terrible arrogant attitude. And besides, I don't wanna' be married. I'm just gon' pray and who God has for me I believe He'll show me. In fact He'll even bring him right before my face.

It's a month later and Karina's gotten a month older. Salva and Salvester are having a Super Bowl party at their house. Karina and I are on our way over there. I'm glad they live only about fifteen minutes away because I don't think I could do this across town thing.

We finally arrived.

Karina is so excited, she jumped out of the car and Precious came running out of the house with the biggest grin on her face as she and Karina embraced, hit one another, and then wrestled they're way into the house. Salva and Salvester's gotta' nice size home. One thing I made sure of is that they got a spankin' brand new home built from the ground up. It's a four-bedroom home. Salva didn't want anything larger. I tried talking her into it, but she refused. That's one thing I love about that girl, she ain't greedy and she don't try to take advantage of me and my money. Even though she couldn't anyway. I laughed to myself.

Salva came running out yelling. "Come on girl, the game's already started!"

"Already? I just got here?" I yelled back.

"You're a minute too late. Hurry up Salvester's on the grill cookin' up some stuff."

"For real? What he got on the grill?"

She slapped me on the shoulder. "Girl he got some baby back ribs, some smoked sausage, some wieners for the girls, some chicken and turkey legs. Need I go on?"

"Lord help me Jesus." We both laughed. "Ya'll must be expecting a lot of people?" We went in the house.

"No but Salvester's friend was gon' come but he backed out at the last minute. He had another singing engagement."

"O' his friend sings?"

"Yea' girl and gospel at that. Nothin' else."

"Is he single?"

"You know what? As a matter-of-fact he is and he ain't got no kids either." She smiled. "But I don't think you're ready for him. He's a highly spiritual man and he don't play games."

"What chu' tryin' to say?" I squinted my eyes at her.

"I'm tryin' to say just what I'm sayin'. You said so yourself that your tryin' to get yourself together. And I'm not gon' hook him up with you actin' crazy—puttin' men in jail and thangs." She gave me this serious look.

"Salva you're supposed to be lookin' out for me, not goin' against me?"

"I'm not against you and you know that. I'm just protecting you and him from gettin' hurt and most of all from wasting both of your time. I wouldn't even wanna' date a man if I knew I wasn't ready cause' it'll only cause a bunch of drama."

"I hear ya'. And you're right I'm not ready no way. Hey you changin' on me. You used to encourage me to date, what happened to all the encouragement?"

"I thought about what I was doing to you especially after you came back and told me how you did that guy you met in the Bahamas. I was so disappointed in you. I was trying to entice you to go out and get a man and not thinkin' that you said that you weren't ready. So I prayed

81

about it, God dealt with me and delivered me, and now I'm fine. So you don't have to worry about me tryin' to hook you up anymore. I've learned my lesson."

"What if I want you to keep doin' it? I mean I kinda' liked it when you were pickin' at me about men. It made me think that maybe in some small way I just might be ready?" I said as we walked through the house on out to the backyard where everybody else was.

"You are so funny, now all of a sudden you ready to date? I get it, it's because I just told you about Salvester's friend huh'?" She burst out laughing so Salvester could hear her. "Salvester, is your friend still coming?" Salva and I sat down in the patio chairs.

"Who baby?" He answered.

"Your buddy that sings."

"O' naw' somethin' came up at the last minute. He just came from out of town I don't know where he went though. He travels all over the world with his music group. Why you asked I thought I already told you this Salva?" He kept pickin' at the meat on the pit as the smoke slowly swarmed his face.

"I know baby, I just wanted to make sure." She looked at me and smiled.

I whispered. "Salva girl you somethin' else."

"Next week we're havin' a fund raiser at the Westlin Hotel to help raise money for our cancer students. I'm tryin' to get him to come and sing." He yelled through the smoke as he grabbed the pan next to the pit, jabbed the ribs with a long pitch-fork; then put em' on the pan as the fire gazed towards them as if to pull em' back down, and then walked inside of the house.

"Did you hear that? I'll think about letting you meet him. Girl he's so amazing and so romantic. This' just between me and you, if I hadn't of met Salvester, I'd a had to jump on this chance. He's just that nice and good looking girl."

"Salva you'll tell me anything."

"Alright then forget it." She jumped up from her seat, grabbed the volleyball that's sittin' in the grass, and threw it out towards Karina and Precious.

"O' mama you wanna' play?" Precious screamed with laughter.

I jumped up and followed her like she had something I needed. "Salva, don't do me like that. I do believe you. Just let me meet him."

"Alright let's change the subject." She said as Precious picked up the ball and threw it back. "I forgot to ask you, how many books and paraphernalia did you sell?" She caught the ball and threw it to me.

"I don't know the exact amount but I sold all of my books and I sold some t-shirts and gave away a lot of bookmarks." I caught the ball and tossed it to Karina.

"You wanna' go back in the house? I think Salvester's almost done with the barbeque?"

"Yea' cause' its gettin' a little too smoky out here for me." I followed Salva into the living room. Her living room is so glamorous because Salva's glamorous. Her curtains swag down to the floor with rippling folds of different imprinted marooned colors. She has cherry-stained crown molding all around the ceiling and cherry wood grain all around the fire place with matching furniture, and I can't leave out the million-to-one candles she has all over the house either. When they invented candles, they invented them for her. "Salva, girl you bought some more candles?"

"You know I had too. Candles America had some on sale and a fragrance you know I just couldn't pass up."

"Yea' I know cause' you got the whole house smellin' like a sweet candle shop." We burst out laughing.

"Hey are you gon' come with us to church Sunday?"

"Where did that come from?"

"I'm just askin'."

"No mam'."

"Barina what's wrong with you? God is blessing you way too much for you to do Him like this. You know He can take it all away don't chu'?"

"Yea' I'm aware of that. Look Salva I have nothin' against God, I love Him, it's just that it's been so long since I've even been inside of a church."

"That don't matter. That's all the more reason why you need to go."

"Look I'm a go back one day, just not right now."

"I'm gon' be prayin' because you got too many gifts that's being wasted, and you need to know that your soul is at stake. God loves you and you can still come back to Him Barina."

"I know."

Karina and I stayed over Salva's until it was time for Precious to go to bed, which was about 8:30 that night. It's a week later and I'm nervous about today because Salvester's concert is tonight. Salva called me the other day and told me that Salvester's friend agreed to come and do the concert for the school. I'm kinda' excited but then I'm not because I don't know if I'm ready for all this. I'll just have to see how he looks. I hope he makes me smile and not frown. I laughed at the thought.

The phone rings. "Hello?"

"Barina hey, what time are you comin' to the concert?"

"What time does it start?"

"It starts at seven."

"About 6:45. Is that too late?"

"No that's ok if you get there at that time and not leave at that time."

"Ok Salva I'll make sure I'll get there at that time. What chu' tryin' to say that I'm a late bird?"

"Sometimes you can be, I'll cut chu' some slack this time. But tonight you can't be late because I want you to see him when the curtains open up."

"Alright I'll be there."

"I gotta' go. Precious got open house at school in about 20-minutes. I'm tryin' to get there early so we can leave early. Afterwards I'm dropping her off at her friend's house until after the concert, do you want me to swing by and get Karina too? Better yet, I'll be by there cause' you and Mr. Concert", she laughed, "might want a little time after the concert to get to know one another."

"You are so silly. I see you got jokes. Alright I'll have her ready. Bout' what time will you be here?"

"Right after I leave from there. It starts at four. I'll be there about an hour and then I'll be on my way. So say—5:30?"

"That's perfect I'll have her ready."

"What're you wearing? Look don't come oughta' there with anything on or I'm a have ta' turn you around and send you back home."

"It sounds like you care more about what he thinks than what I think?"

"I care about what the both of you think. Girl you know I care more about you? I just want you to be happy and I want him to be happy too."

"Don't act like you haven't known me longer. How long have you and Salvester been knowin' this guy?"

"It's been what, a year now? Yea' cause' Salvester's been doing this new fundraiser for the students for about a year. This'll be goin' into the second year. Solomon came last year and sang for us. It was such a huge success that Salvester and everybody else wanted him to come back and sing again. He and Salvester became good friends after that. So I guess you can say that they've been close for about a year now."

"So Solomon's his name?"

"Yea' did I say that?"

"Yea' you said it while you were talking."

"Well yes, that's his name. You like it?"

"It's ok, it sounds like a name for a dog."

"There you go."

"No, I'm not tryin' to be mean or anything but it does sound like somethin' I would name a dog. Don't get me wrong it's cute. Look Salva the name is cute ok?"

"Well trust me he don't look nothing like his name, and he sho' don't look nothing like no dog either. You don't need to be worrin' bout' his name, what you need to be worrin' bout' is what chu' gon' look like when you meet him. Cause' first impressions mean everything." She chuckled.

"Don't chu' worry about that, you know I can hold my own. And further more, why didn't you tell me about this Solomon guy before now?"

"Because I wasn't that close to him and plus Barina I knew how you felt about meeting new men. You weren't ready. I knew Wayne was still in your heart and you needed some more time to release him, am I right?"

"You right."

"So what're you gon' wear?"

"I'm gon' wear my pants suit and matchin' strapless four inch spike heals."

"That sounds good." Her phone clicks. "Hold on somebody's beepin' in." She clicked over. A minute later she clicks back. "Hey I'm back. I'm so sorry that was Salvester, he was tellin' me that Solomon had an incident when he was out of town that he had to finish taken care of."

"What chu' tryin' to say, he's not gon' be there?"

"Of course he's gon' be there. He's just gon' be runnin' a little late."

"Like how late?"

"Don't worry it's only about 15-minutes."

"O' that's not too bad people ain't gon' start comin' in until about 7:15 to 7:30pm anyway."

"Exactly. Ok. Remember to have Karina ready when we get there we'll be rushing. Do you wanna' ride with me? Salvester drove his own car cause' he had to be there early to set up."

"I'm glad you asked, yea' I'll ride with you."

"Alright then be ready when I get there, bye."

Salva wasn't a minute late and she definitely wasn't a minute too early. Karina and I were ready by the time she came to pick us up. We dropped the girls off at Salva's friend's house and rushed to the hotel for the concert. We made it there about 10-minutes before 7:00.

The concert hasn't started yet for whatever reason. I'm just ready to see this Solomon that Salva keeps bragging about. The ballroom is crowded to the max. I hope they know that there's a maximum law for over crowded places? Let me ask this girl what's taken them so long to start, it's now 7:30. "Salva, how long are they gon' be?"

"I don't know. I don't think he's made it yet." She looked around as if to be looking for him. "They may be waiting on him to get here. I haven't talked to Salvester."

"Do you have your cell phone? Just call em'?"

"Are you crazy? Girl I gotta' go home later with that man. I don't need him fussin' at me tellin' me not to page him in the middle of one of the most important times of his life? You wait til' you get married, you'll see what I'm talkin' about."

"I didn't mean it like that. He got chu' all nervous and thangs." I burst out laughing.

"Look I'm not nervous, I just love my husband and I'm submitted to him like I'm supposed to be."

"It's one thing to be submitted, and it's another thing to be scared half to death."

"No see that's the difference between me and you, I'm far from scared, I just know how to keep my man happy, and that's respecting and loving him especially when he's doing something that's very important to him."

"I hear ya'. I just wanted to give you a hard time."

"I know I ain't thinkin' about chu' no way." She put her finger over her mouth. "Hey shuuuwww'... They're about to start."

The lights went down but the curtains are still closed. Salvester just came out from the side of the stage, introduced himself and the occasion, gave all the thank yous', and introduced the man of the hour—Solomon himself. The audience applauded and cheered as we all jumped to our feet. The curtain opened up and my heart dropped. "O' my God I could just ball up and die right now." I whispered to Salva as Solomon stood in front of his band.

"I know girl isn't he gorgeous?" She screamed and cheered. "I could faint myself."

"No that's not what I'm talkin' about." I yelled as the band started playing and the people started cheering louder. Yellow, blue, and red stage lights are flashing on and off as they're shining over the band, setting off a concert's atmosphere. I can feel the mood, the motion, and the action all at once.

"Would you be quiet, I wanna' hear this first song?" She nudged me in the ribs as he started singing.

"Salva just listen to me!" I tried yelling over the music.

"What girl what, and this better be good?" She yelled back.

"Don't trip but that's the guy that asked me to marry him!" She screamed. "What? Stop playin' Barina, I don't have time to play with you!"

"I'm not playin'! He's the one that I saw again in the Bahamas! The one I had put in jail!"

"What I can't believe this, how could somethin' like this happen? How could he be the guy out of all the men in America? Huh? I just can't believe this! There's no way I'll let you meet him—no way!" She threw her hand up as if to brush me off. "No I take that back, yea' you gon' meet him and I'm gon' let you reap what you sowed!"

"I don't wanna' talk about him anymore lets just enjoy the concert before it's over!"

"Yea' I see somebody's gettin' scared now?" She burst out laughing.

"Who, I'm not scared?"

"Ok. Well, we'll see after the concert!" She yelled never looking my way.

I've gone into a daze. I can't take my eyes off of him. I could pass out at the sound of his deep intriquing voice. He's singing contemporary gospel with a suave touch. A saved Luther would be the best words to describe the sound of his voice. I don't know why I haven't noticed how good he sounds before now? And he looks better than the last time I seen him too. His thick, dark, goatee is running around his full moistened lips, his coal jet black wavy hair is sparkling from the concert lights and the oil he put on it. I can tell he takes good care of it. I'm thinking that his cologne was well picked. I'm dreaming that I can smell it from the stage as if he wore it just for me—a sweet musk aroma smell as if he just came straight out of the shower. I smiled, slowly closed my eyes, and slightly sniffed the air. His 6' foot something stature with great big ol'coconut shoulders and a cute little butt that would make a woman run and tell somebody. His smooth honey nut colored skin glowed as his caramel hazel eyes gleamed in the night's concert atmosphere. I know my mind's playing tricks on me, it's like he's lookin' straight at me—I know that can't be true. He's wearin' a fly emerald green suit with a fittin' black under shirt and some black K. Coles on his feet. His moves are even smooth and not the, I can't wait to get cha' home in the bed kinda' moves. I thought laughing to myself.

He sang about six songs without stopping. He sang with so much energy and emotion. I could feel it in every expression of each word that came out of his mouth. I knew that he meant every word he said. The concert is well over now and we're waiting for Salvester and Solomon to come from the back. Salva just went to the back to get em'. I'm thinkin', what will he say when he sees me? What will he do? Or how will he react? Here they come…

Salvester has this match making grin on his face as he introduced us. "Solomon this is Salva's play sister and best friend Barina Grant." I'm trying so hard to smile. "Barina this is Solomon Pierre." Solomon took one look at me, frowned, grabbed Salvester by the arm, and walked off going towards the front entrance.

"Salvester ya'll just gon' leave us?" Salva shouted at Salvester, then glanced over at me.

"We'll be right back baby!" He answered never looking back.

Salva looked at me. "I told you so. That man ain't got nothin' to say to you and I don't' blame him." She went and sat down in one of the empty chairs close by. I can't say a word. I'm wrong but they don't have to rub it in.

Salvester came back by himself with a frown on his face. "You ready baby?" He never looked my way.

"Barina and I road together."

"Well I'll see you at home then, I'm leaving." He walked off never saying a word to me.

"Salva if I knew I was gon' spoil things for you and Salvester I never would've came. What I did to Solomon I can't take back. I'm sorry for what I did but I'm not fixin' to sit here and let ya'll condemn me. You can go ahead on and leave, I'll catch a cab." I tried walking off towards the front entrance.

She ran up to me and grabbed my arm. "Barina don't you ever do me like that. I'm your sista' and nothin' and nobody'll ever change that. Yes I'm upset with you but I'm not gon' let no man come between us; we've been through way too much. You must be crazy if you think I'm gon' let chu' catch a cab instead of riding back with me? Don't play, come on." She walked off and I followed her like she was my mother.

Several weeks has gone by.

Salva called me yesterday and said that Salvester did raise all the money they needed at the concert. In fact, they raised more than what they expected. I was glad about that. She never brought up Solomon's name. Salvester finally started talking to me again. He never asked me what happened between Solomon and I, and I never offered.

Chapter Six

Years just come and go. Karina's already fifteen and hittin' the boy's hard and heavy. I can barely control her. She's nothin' like I was when I was young. I mean, I made one mistake that changed my life forever, but I wasn't boy crazy like she is. We get into it almost everyday about some boy calling and hanging up in my face. I'm not surprised because Karina turned out to be a very attractive young lady. She's more developed than I was. She's about 5'5 and has beautiful long curly coal black hair with caramel streaks layered down her back. Kinda' reminds me of a professional model. I have to keep up with her all the time because I refuse to let her go down the same path I did. I don't control her, I protect her. There's a difference.

After the night of the concert, I never saw Salvester's friend again. Not even at different Christian Expo's and events. He just kinda' disappeared from off the face of the earth. I can't get over that happening the way it did. I never would've thought I'd see the man I had put in jail behind a curtain singing to me, a spiritual song at that. I really felt bad then, but now I'm over that. I'm sure I'll never see him again anyway so it's really not worth staying hurt about it.

"I'm sittin' in this big ol' mansion all by myself. Karina, Precious, and some of her friends from school are gone out to the movies. I'm lyin' on the couch with my remote flippin' the channels trying to find something decent to watch on TV, which is almost impossible.

The phone rings. It's Salva as usual. "Hello?"

"Girl you got cho' TV on? Turn it on channel 33. Look whose out on the professional football field? Yes Wayne girl. They say he was the

91

first round pick. He's playing for the Raiders. This' his eighth season, he went pro straight out of high school."

"Good for him. What else did you call for?" I got up and walked over to the big 64' flat screen TV to get a closer look.

"Hey don't take it out on me. I thought you were over Wayne?"

"I am I just don't wanna' talk about him. I'm glad Karina's not here to see him she probably would get upset. She used to ask me where her daddy was all the time and why he isn't in her life. I hated it because I didn't have an answer for her." I said, still standing by the TV.

"You might as well get over that because she's ganna' see him one time or another. I'm sure her friends talk about it?"

"Well let em' talk about it, I'm not. What else's new?"

"Nothin' I just thought I'd show you that, I didn't know it was ganna' upset you?"

"I'm not upset Salva, I just don't wanna' talk about it." I went and plopped back down on the sofa. "If he really cared he would've called Karina for all her birthdays, went to all of her cheer-leading practices and games, fed her, encouraged her, loved her, and…"

"I understand Barina. But he didn't do all that. What about now? How long are you gon' hold him?"

"I'm not holding him. I have truly let him go. There is no unforgiveness in my heart. But just because I forgave him don't mean I have to cheer him on."

"Hey let me ask you something while I'm thinkin' about it. Why didn't you ever put child support on him?"

"I didn't think about no child support back then. Shoot, I was a child myself. I was still tryin' to decide whether or not I was gon' keep her myself; let alone thinkin' about no child support. When I made up in my mind that I was gon' do this, I didn't want any help from anybody because I didn't trust anybody—not even God. I've come a long ways huh'?"

"Yes mam' you sure have, and I'm very proud of you. Would you want Karina to be apart of Wayne's life right now?"

"I wouldn't stop it, Karina needs to know who her biological daddy is, and I wouldn't stop that."

"Good. Girl let me get off of this phone I just wanted to tell you that… Hold on Salvester's calling me." She got off the phone and then came back. "Salvester wanted me to ask you if you wanted to come with us to the Convention Center tomorrow. They're celebrating Black History month and they have a lot of festivities goin' on down there. Are you in?"

"Sounds good to me, what time are you guys gon' come pick me up?"

"Hold on let me ask Salvester..." She removed the phone from her mouth, yelled asking Salvester what I asked her, and then got back on the phone and said, "Be ready at six tomorrow evening."

"Alright, I'll be lookin' for ya'll tomorrow evening."

"Ok bye." She said as we both hung up the phone.

The night came and went quicker than I could say my name.

It's a little after six and I'm runnin' late. I got caught up trying to wash too many loads of clothes and I lost track of time. Let me put my clothes on. Salva and Salvester is pulling up in the driveway. Let me grab my purse and finish puttin' on my shoes.

They knocked on the door and I ran and answered it before they knocked twice. "Hey ya'll, come on in for a second I'm runnin' a little late."

They came in with this huge grin on her faces. Salvester kept grinnin' underneath his breath, while Salva looked me up and down and said, "Alright na', I see somebody's lookin' groovy tonight?" She shook her hips and smacked her lips and Salvester burst out laughing.

"What chu' laughin' at Salvester? What's wrong with what I got on?" I looked myself up and down.

"Girl nothin' Salvester so silly. We're laughin' cause' you look like a winner—Girl you got it goin' on. I ain't never seen you dress like that, huh' Salvester?" She said, elbowing Salvester in the side.

"Yea', who you tryin' to catch?" He said as he kept laughing.

"What? I ain't tryin' to catch nobody. And anyway, I know I look good, don't hate, congratulate." I turned and walked back towards the kitchen and yelled with an attitude. "I ain't thinkin' about yaw'! Yaw' just wait there while I make sure Karina remembers to turn on the alarm while she's here by herself tonight!" I ran into the kitchen, wrote the note for Karina, and dashed back to the front door where they're still waiting. "Alright, ya'll ready?" I motioned for them to walk back out as all three of us left.

93

The ride to the Convention Center was rather long considering all the traffic we had to go through. I'm glad we finally made it though. The minute we walked in, there was an atmosphere of african fashion and live music. There's a band playing some familiar gospel music inside of the ballroom. Salva wants to go and check it out without much of a choice, Salvester and I followed. The minute we walked inside of the ballroom, their expression changed and my mouth dropped. It's Solomon singing with his gospel group. It feels like I just swallowed a brick. I mean, here's a man that I hurt very deeply and I didn't even know him. How could this be again? It's been about four years in counting. I thought I would never see him again. Kinda' like serendipity but leaving out the part about luck cause' I don't believe in luck, I believe in favor.

"Man it's been a long time since I talk to that boy. He didn't tell me that he was singin' down here tonight?" Salvester rushed towards the stage as Salva followed. I didn't wanna' be out of place so I followed too but at a slower pace. By the time I caught up with em', they had already went to the back of the stage to meet him. What do I do now? I thought. Do I go back there with them, or do I wait? He probably wouldn't receive me no way, and plus I'm not ready to face him yet. If ever, so I guess I'll just wait. I wanna' ask him for forgiveness but I don't think he'll receive it. I'm starting to look at him from a totally different perspective. Maybe he's not so bad? But why did he come at me like he did? Maybe he was just joking. I can't lie, deep down in the crevasses of my heart I kinda' liked the attention, and I could dig his plan of spontaneity. But the way it came out was a whole new experience in its entirety.

About 20-minutes later Salva and Salvester finally came from behind the stage without Solomon of course. We left from the ballroom, went and enjoyed the rest of the festivities.

We came back to my house. They stayed for about 15-minutes and left. The subject of Solomon never came up and I didn't bother asking. I'm sittin' in my lawn chair out on the beach enjoying the night's tides. I've got my legs crossed, my arms folded, and my eyes closed. I can dream out here forever. This' my world and I'm in it all by myself. No boundaries, no rules, no one to please, just me and my place called world.

"Ma'!" Karina yelled from the house.

I turned around to meet her voice. "What?"

"Telephone!"

"Bring it to me please!"

"Ma'! I'm too far away!"

"Karina just bring me the phone!"

"Yes mam'!" She ran down the sandy trail, gave me the phone and ran back towards the house.

"Hello?"

"Are you ok?"

"Who is this?"

"Salva silly. O' so you don' forgot my voice now?"

"Shut up!" We laughed. "What's up you called to chew me out?"

"For what?"

"I just thought you might because of ol' boy."

"What did I tell you about that? I thought we got that straight the other night?"

"We did but I'm askin' again." I kicked some sand towards the water.

"I ain't goin' back over that Miss. Barina. Anyway I just called to see if you were alright. I'll talk to you tomorrow."

"Ok, thanks for calling me." We both quickly hung up the phone. Now why she called me with nothing to talk about? I think she wanted something. Knowing her she'll ask me tomorrow. Salvester must've been sittin' next to her.

All I can think about is Solomon. I ask myself why am I feeling the way that I do? It's like I can feel him in my heart and in my soul. I now see visions of him in my sleep and thoughts of him when I'm awake. Could he be my husband? I never wanted to get married, felt it was a waste of time. But now I'm thinkin' about what Salva said about Karina needing a man figure in her life. I just don't wanna' get hurt nor do I wanna' hurt anybody. I'm enjoying my single life. I'm free to do whatever I wanna' do, go where ever I wanna' go, when I wanna' go, and not having to answer to anybody.

"Ma' Aunt Salva's here!" Karina yelled from the pool in the backyard.

What in the world is she doing here? "Ok! Send her down here!" I yelled back never turning around. About 30-seconds later this voice whispered in my ear,

"Many waters cannot quench love,
neither can floods drown it..." He
spoke softly.

I swung around, jumped to my feet, our eyes connected, and all I can say is Almighty God. "How did you get here? Who told you where...?"

"Shhhuuuuw', don't say a word." He whispered as he came and softly placed his finger over my mouth. "Just let me do the talking. I owe you an apology. What happened in the Bahamas was not your fault. It was mine. I came at you wrong. And when I saw you at the school, I freaked out because I was upset because I had to pay all that money to get out of jail. I thought about it later and I realized that if I were in your position, I would've done the same thing. Will you forgive me?"

"Of course I will." I said, barely able to speak. Salva was so right, this brotha' is so romantic even when he's just connecting simple sentences together. His proper accent is nothin' like the accent of the men I once dated. "Actually I owe you an apology, I didn't have to create a scene and I didn't have to lie and have them put you in jail either. I'm so sorry, I felt so bad and believe it or not, it has bothered me all these years. Can I ask you something?"

"Sure."

"How'd you get over here?"

"Your sister."

"Where is she?" He pointed up. I looked up only to see Salva standing up on the hill with her hands on her hips, grinning like a Cheshire Cat.

"Now I can leave!" She yelled turning and walking back into the house.

"I'm gon' get that girl. She didn't tell me anything."

"I didn't want her too." He came closer, but not close enough to invade my space.

"Why? I don't know you? Weren't you scared that I might do you like I did you the last time?"

"For some reason I wasn't worried this time."

"So are you tryin' to say that you have premonitions?"

"No I didn't feel that this was gon' happen but I was hoping, and it's turning out just the way I wanted." He smiled.

"That was a sweet poem you said to me earlier. I wasn't expecting that." He continued to stare into my eyes without saying a word. "Did you here me?" I looked up at him connecting my eyes with his...

> *"I adjure you... that you never stir*
> *up or awaken love until it pleases."*
> *He said.*
> (Song of Solomon 8:4)

I couldn't do nothin' but stare into his eyes until I finally got the nerve to say, "I'm touched by your romantic poems. It feels as if I've known you all my life."

"You have."

"What do you mean?"

"In the Spirit." He whispered. *"Set me like a seal upon your heart, like a seal upon your arm; for love is as strong as death..."* (Song of Solomon 8:6) He slightly grabbed my hand, bent down on one knee in the sand, and started singing,

> *"You are the bone of my bone...*
> *you are the flesh of my flesh...*
> *your soul is my soul... and I wanna'*
> *live with you for the rest of my life...*
> *Will you marry me?...."*

The sound of his romantic melodies echoed into the night's air.

"Ummm..." I sighed with my eyes closed as our souls connected. "Yes. Yes I will marry you." He got up and took me into his arms. The night's ocean tides are rushing towards us as if to swallow us both up. The fire works went off in our hearts and ignited in our Spirits. We gazed into each other's eyes without blinking for what seemed like forever.

Salva and Salvester finally came down and joined us out on the beach after Solomon proposed to me. We all went out to dinner and talked for over 3-hours. The four of us make a great four pair I must add.

Everybody gets along so well. Why didn't I say yes to this a long time ago? O' well I don't wanna' think about it right now.

Chapter Seven

Solomon and I are now planning for our wedding. Salva and Salvester are both more excited than we are. Salva couldn't wait to get the scoop and I couldn't wait to give it to her. We're supposed to be meeting for lunch to go over the wedding plans. She's picking me up and is late as usual. It's such a beautiful day. It's the kind of weather for surfing or jet skiing. I hear a horn honking outside it must be her. I walked to the window, looked outside, went back and grabbed my folder from the kitchen table, locked the door, and went and got in the truck.

"Hey Mrs. Solomon Pierre." She giggled as she backed out of the driveway and zoomed down the street.

There are so many hills and mountains out here in California. That's what I love about living here; it's so beautiful and free. "Girl you are so silly." I said, still looking out at the beautiful California life.

"I know. So tell me what happened? What did he say? How did he propose to you?" She asked, cheesing.

"I thought you were there?" I turned and looked at her.

"I was when he first came down the hill, but after that I went back in the house. I was afraid of what your response was gon' be, and I didn't wanna' see him look sad when you turned him down. But I see it turned out better than I thought. Now tell me what happened Miss. Thang?"

"Well girl it's so much to tell. I'll just say it like this, our souls connected. It was truly a bone of my bone connection. *(Genesis 2:23-*

99

24) I said yes without taking a second thought. It scares me to think back on it." I shivered as if to be cold and Salva laughed.

"Why girl?" She kept laughing.

"Salva, it all happened so fast. Did you and Salvester know that he was gon' propose to me?"

"Actually we did. When we went back stage he was shaking like he was nervous about somethin'. We asked him what was wrong and he said that he was scared because he had prayed that if God allowed him to see you again, it would confirm that you were his wife. And he said when we walked into the ballroom he didn't see us, all he saw was you. His heart fainted and he went to the back. When we got back there he said that he was going to propose to you that night. Salvester and I didn't know that all this was gon' happen. But we're glad it did."

"Hum', that's funny he didn't tell me that... Salva, I knew when I saw him again that he was the one. I can't tell you how, but I just knew."

"So are you gon' answer my question I asked earlier?"

"What question?"

"You know what I asked you knuckle head." We both laughed.

"Girl it was so romantic"

"I told you he was."

"Can I finish? Anyway, after he came down the trail, he whispered in my ear; *Many waters cannot quench love, neither can floods drown it...*" I screamed and Salva jumped. "Salva girl, he wouldn't let me speak at all! It was poem after poem. Even his simple words moved me—it was so romantic. I never would've imagined that my proposal would've happened the way it did. God is so full of surprises! I prayed and God answered me right away even though I didn't deserve it. Solomon apologized for how he approached me in the Bahamas and I apologized to him, and we left it at that. But that's not how it ended. I won't tell you that. That's none of your business." We both looked at each other and started laughing.

"Girl whatever, tell me please?"

"No mam'!"

"Well that's alright I don't wanna' know. Just make sure you're still pure and sanctified." We laughed again.

"Now you know I'm not talkin' about that, of course not. The next time that'll happen will be when I'm alone with my husband."

"And it better be Solomon."

"Of course. I wonder if he writes his poetry?"

"You know what, I don't know? You should ask him?"

"I will later I'm still tryin' to shake off what happened last night."

"Girl I ain't mad at cha'. Stay right there you dreamin', you dreamin' girl." She laughed as she turned into the Soups with Salad's parking lot. We decided to eat salads so we'll look sexy in our wedding dresses. Even though Salva don't have far to go cause' she's always been slim all of her life. It's me on the other hand, that have to watch what I eat so I won't gain unnecessary weight in places I don't want to. I smiled at the thought.

Salva and I stayed in the restaurant for over 2 ½ hours. We stayed in there so long that the waiter kept coming to the table asking if we were ready to check out. I know it was because they were ready for us to leave. I hope they knew that we weren't on their time, they were on our time as long as we were payin'? I smirked at the thought.

We're now on our way to the store to find my dress and the dresses for the bridesmaids. Salva just made a quick turn down Fifth Avenue where all the big time stores are. Solomon is the most romantic man I've ever met. The only flaw is, he doesn't have a lot of money. He doesn't have a 9 to 5, he just relies only on what he makes with his singing gigs, which isn't very much. The wedding'll basically be paid for by me. That's the only thing I don't like. Some may say I'm too picky and that they've love to have a man that truly loves them instead of a man with a lot of money that hates them. Well I want both. But since I didn't get that man, I'll just have to settle with what I got. "You know what Salva? I was just thinkin' bout' me having to pay for majority of my wedding. Don't get me wrong, I love Solomon but I'm just not pleased with having to be the bread-winner of the house. I mean it's not like he doesn't make any money, it's just not as much as me."

"He ain't got a lot of money so what? Look Barina, don't start gettin' too picky and start lookin' at the wrong things. O' and you gon' marry this man." She pointed her finger at me.

"You don't' have to worry about that, I don't have no problems marrying him. Just somethin' I thought out loud and you heard me." I smiled for her approval which she failed to give with her mouth, but blew me off with her hands.

"That's all it better be." She turned into the parking lot, we put on last minute make-up that rubbed off from our meals, got out, walked into the store, and now we're browsing around looking for my fantasy wedding dress.

A heavyset formal Caucasian woman who works at the store came over to us and asked, "Is there something I can help you two ladies with?"

"Salva answered like she's the one gettin' married. "Yes we're looking for the wedding dress of the century."

"Wait mam' she doesn't mean that." I turned and looked at Salva like she was crazy. "Salva I can't afford no dress like that?"

"Don't worry kid, this one's on me."

"You gon' pay for my wedding dress?"

"I guess I can considering all the things you've done for Salvester, Precious, and me. I figure this is the least I can do for you. Now I don't have enough for all the bridesmaids, but I do have enough for your dress. Salvester and I already discussed it so don't worry bout' what he'll say cause' he's already said yes."

"Thanks Salva. You know you don't have to do this? What I did for you and Salvester was not a give and take thing. I did it straight from my heart."

"I know Barina you're always tryin' to explain. If I don't know your heart by now, I'll never know it."

"Ok, well, in that case lets get ta' lookin'."

The woman asked right away as she started writing something on her invoice pad. "So will this be cash or charge?" You can tell this' a high priced store that's used to having big celebrities with big bucks because they don't waist no time taking your money.

"Wait a minute mam', we haven't found the dress we're looking for, so whether or not we have cash or a credit card really doesn't matter."

"Barina calm down, its ok mam' I'll be charging this." Salva frowned at me as the lady walked off.

"Well I'm just sayin'." I said as I walked off going towards the back of the store as Salva slowly followed.

Salva grabbed my arm and whispered, "You are so silly sometimes Barina. Sometimes I swear I feel like your mother instead of your friend."

"It's not good to swear. Stop being so bossy, I had to let her know. They need to slow down on the cash or charge thing. They make somebody not wanna' buy nothin'." I whispered back.

"Don't nobody have a problem with it but you Miss. El' Cheapo'." We both laughed. "And anyway, you forget you ain't paying."

I jerked my body around and pointed my finger in her face. "Look did we come in here to fuss or did we come in here to find my dress?"

Salva's trying to keep herself from bursting out laughing. She pointed her finger back in my face and said, "to find your dress Miss. El' Cheapo'." She added four more fingers with the one already pointed at me. "You know what? If I ever need a bodyguard I know where to find one."

"O' so you got jokes now?" I couldn't help but laugh. Salva can say the funniest things sometimes. "Come on act right before they kick us up out of here."

"That's you, don't lay that on me."

"Alright Salva you win. You always gotta' be right."

"That's because you know I'm always right."

"Not always, maybe majority of the time, but not always."

"Ok I'll give you that."

I walked over to the discount rack and saw this long white sheer dress with embroidered pearls and diamonds all over it. It has a low cut that cuts across the chest and it's sleeveless with a short train. I looked at the price tag. "All of this dress only cost $3,500? And that's with the discount. Salva can you believe this?" I showed her.

"Yea' that's nice you should go try it on?"

"O' you know I am." I rushed towards the dressing room not waiting for the lady to help me, squeezed my healthy body in the dress, and came out struttin' like it was the dress of my dreams.

"Barina I hate to tell you but you're burstin' out of that dress." We both looked at each other and laughed until tears fell from our eyes. "Hurry up and get out of it before I have to pay for two dresses. All them big thighs, baby got back, and big hips, we gon' need the jaws of life to get chu' out of it. Didn't you look at the size before you got off up in that? Look like you in a baby gap dress."

The lady broke in. "Ladies are you having some trouble?" She tried to keep from laughing as if she would get fired if she did.

"No." We kept on laughing. "No, we're fine." Salva could barely talk. "Barina you need to find you another one. I'm sure they're more to choose from?"

"But I want this one." I stuck my bottom lip out like a child.

"Look don't get baby fide on me. It doesn't fit so just simply get out of it and find you another one. Mam', can you help a sista' out?"

"What do you mean?" The lady looked confused.

"Can you help her find another dress?" Salva and I burst out laughing again.

"Sure, what size do you wear?" She asked.

"I wear between an 8, 9, and a 10."

"Now how you gon' wear all three of those?" Salva asked.

"Look, mind your own business. Now as I was saying, I wear between a 9, 10, or an 11."

"Will you just tell the woman what size you really wear?"

"Ok forget it, I wear a 12 but it just depends."

"Depends on what?" The lady asked. She's looking as if she's getting impatient.

"Depends on the color." This time we all burst out laughing. The lady laughed as she looked around to see if her manager was watching.

"You are so silly Barina. Mam' we don't mean to give you a hard time, we laugh like this all the time so please excuse us?"

"It's well ok. I'm enjoying watching you two have as much fun as you're having." She quickly pulled another dress from off the same rack. "What about this one?"

Salva tried to answer for me but I wouldn't let her. "No I don't like that, do you have another one in mind?"

"Yes I sure do but it's not on this rack it's on the rack over there." She pointed towards the $10-15,000 dollar rack.

"No we're not tryin' to go that route we'll stick with this rack—our best friend." I looked at Salva.

"Barina its ok let her show us what she has. You don't have to look out for me. Get whatever you want, I got this."

"Ok Salva you know me." I looked back at the women. "Can we see what you have? I want something with a train, strapless, and with diamonds all over it."

"That's not hard to find. In fact we have this one I think'll fit you just right." She grabbed this dress from the rack that took my breath away. I knew it was the dress from the moment she took it from the rack.

"This is the one. I don't even have to try it on I know it's the one."

"Girl go try that dress on and squeeze your way out of the one you got on." We laughed as I started walking towards the dressing room.

"I'll be right back." I disappeared behind the wall going back into the dressing room.

Salva and I stayed in the store for about another hour. The dress I tried on ended up being the dress of my dreams after all. After that we looked for the bridesmaid's dresses, and I'm so glad we found everything and now everybody should be happy. I can breathe now that we got that headache out of the way. We're finally on our way home. My whole entire wedding plans are complete. I know just how everything's ganna' go from the beginning to the end. The colors I want. The order I want, and who I want which will be Salva of course, Karina, Precious and one of Salvester's co-workers at work. Considering the fact that I don't have very many friends, she'll just stand in as another body. Things are quiet between us while the radio's doing the talking as we both are bobbin' our heads to the beat. All Salva listens to is Christian music. Which I think is the best choice in the world, keeps the mind free and peaceful. She has all the latest CD's, there's so many that I can't name em' all. Let me see if Salva's ganna' come with me to my next book signing I hope her schedule's free. "Hey are you gon' be able to help me at my next book signing?"

"Yea' where's it ganna' be?"

"At that huge Christian Bookstore by the house. O' yea' and remind me that we need to order some more books."

"Sure. What time does it start?"

"It's from 2-4pm."

"That's perfect. I'll still have time to make sure Precious'll be able to get home. You know those girls are growin' up so fast?"

"I know too fast. Sometime I can barely keep up with Karina. I don't know what I'm gon' do with that girl."

"I know what chu' gon' do, you gon' start disciplining her. Barina you don't get on her enough."

"I know I don't. You can't talk you do Precious the same way."

"No mam' there's a difference between rewarding your child and spoiling your child rotten. Precious gets rewarded for the things she does right and she gets disciplined for the things she does wrong. Can you say the same?" She never took her eyes off the road.

"Hopefully soon I can say that, Karina's got some lil' ol' boy callin' my house in the early hours of the morning. I done told her to stop them boys from callin' so late and when I say something to her, she got to come back with the last word. Sometimes I wonder if I'm even the mother anymore. I don't know what I'm gon' do with her."

"I know what chu' gon' do, you gon' take that phone away from her til' she do what you tell her to do." She turned the corner leading in my neighborhood.

"But I don't wanna' hurt her feelings Salva."

"What? You right she's the mama and you're the daughter. Barina are you crazy? You betta' start gettin' on her before she really gets out of control. I know what your problem is, you got her too spoiled. She is spoiled rotten. And see for a long time you thought that stuff was cute but now that she's older and runnin' all over you, you wanna' run somewhere and hide. That's what's wrong with kids today, they know how far to go with their parents. They only do what the parent let them do."

"But what about the one's who don't have parents?"

"That's a different story all together. Take yourself for example, look how lost and withdrawn you were. It took a long time for you to trust me. You thought everybody was your enemy."

"What's this gotta' do with my child?"

"Everything."

"Like what?"

"Well first of all I think the reason why you're so easy on Karina is because of how your parents abandoned you, and you don't want Karina to feel like you're abandoning her. All she's doing is taking advantage of your weakness. Also, your parents were hard on you and you had a problem with that so you feel that if you're easy on Karina, she won't rebel against you. But it's happening anyway because there's no discipline. You understand where I'm comin' from?"

"I can kinda' see that now. Ok so how do I come out of it Dr. Phil-lerette?"

"I'm serious Barina."

"Ok I'm listening." I chuckled.

106

"Well you start toughening up on her. Like I said earlier, you start threatening to take away all the things that she likes and the places that she likes to go like to the movies for one, and she'll straighten up real quick. I started doin' that to Precious and she like to had a fit at first but when she saw that I wasn't playing, it didn't take no time for her to get it together. But the key to it all is that you cannot go back on your word. If you take away her phone and stop her from goin' to the movies for how ever long, you gotta' hold to what you said you was gon' do. Because once they see that you're not for real, you might as well forget it. And I found with this you don't have to whip em' all the time." She turned down my street. "Just get those things they love and love to do, and that's just like whipping em'."

"Girl pray for me, I can do it, it's just that when I get on her about somethin' she gets this sad look on her face, runs to her room, and then I'll go up and apologize for hurting her feelings. I can't stand to see her sad Salva."

"See that's what's gotta' stop. She's playin' you Barina. And I can see her face too. No mam' she needs to be corrected, not babied. She's not a little baby anymore. She don't want you treatin' her like a lil' baby, then she don't need to act like one." She said as she pulled up in the driveway.

I scooted up in my seat with confidence. "Salva girl you got me pumped up now. I'm ready to tell her somethin'."

"Now don't start naggin' her about everything, just get on her for the things you know is not right. When you start naggin' her about every lil' thing, she's ganna' get used to it and then she's ganna' rebel even more."

"O' Lord I hope I remember all this stuff you tellin' me?"

"Trust me you will. When she work yo' last nerve, everything I said'll come back to your remembrance."

"Alright I'll take your word for it. Now what chu' gon' do for tomorrow? Are you rollin' or what?"

"I told you I would."

"I'll be by there to pick you up at 12:30pm. Salva please be ready, you know how slow you can be sometimes?"

"Ok I'll make sure I'm ready. What chu' wearing?"

"I'm wearing a pants suit. I ain't doin' the church dress thang'."

"I know that's right, we ain't gotta' wear our sanctified hats we wear with em' either." She started laughing.

"You so silly, I bet chu' gotta' matchin' hat to go with all your dresses? You probably sit on the front row like a first lady? Huh'?" I laughed. "Miss Missionary, you go girl." She looked at me and laughed again, then had the nerve to turn her head like girl shut up. I got out, opened the back door and grabbed my dress; all my bags, and closed the door behind me and started walking towards the house.

Salva let her window down as she slowly backed out of the driveway. "Don't tell yo' hubby what dress we bought! I'll pick up the bridesmaids dresses next week. I'll talk to you tomorrow, enjoyed you!"

"Bye girl!" I yelled waving my hand back and forth.

She raced down the street as if she was late to nowhere.

Immediately when I got in the house Karina told me that Solomon had called, my heart started palpitating—I'm in love with that man. I can't wait to call him back. I ran to the phone and he quickly answered on the first ring. "Hello?"

"Hey baby, how're you?" I asked, waiting to hear his voice.

He answered right away like he had been waiting on my call. "I'm fine. Did you guy's find everything ok at the store?"

"Yea'." My tone quickly changed to a softer tone. "It didn't take Salva and me long to find my wedding dress. What took long was finding the bridesmaid's dresses."

"Did you find em'?"

"Yea' we eventually did." I took the phone to my room and shut the door behind me. "So what did you do today?" I plopped down on my bed and started slowly gettin' out of my clothes.

"O' me and some of the fella's went lookin' for the tuxes. I got tired of being around them so I came home and called you."

"O' that's so sweet. Did you find your tux?"

"We did. Of course we didn't find em' as quick as you guys, but we eventually did."

"That's good." I said. I just have to close my eyes because I can't believe that I got an all-in-one package. This man has really got it goin' on. And he's about to be all mine. He's handsome, smart, intelligent, romantic, spiritual, caring, spontaneous, and got a job, well we'll work on a better one. What more can I ask for? I thought.

"What chu' doin' tonight?" He asked.

"Nothing. I hadn't planned anything. Why? What's up?"

"Wanna' go to the movies?"

"That sounds good. What time?"

"We can go to the 7 o' clock show, but I'm on my way over there right now."

"Ok come on, I'm about to cook some fish and fries."

"Cool. Hey let me ask you something and don't take this the wrong way…"

"What? Just say it." I said as I slipped into some casual slacks, a nice fitting blouse, then slid my feet into some matching heels, and dropped back down on my bed as if it was gon' catch me.

He hesitated before asking… "Is that all you know how to cook is fish and fries?"

"Of course not, you'll find all that out when it's all official."

"Should I be scared or overwhelmed with excitement?"

"Overwhelmed with excitement."

"Alright then, I'll take your word for it." He said. I can tell he's smiling, and I'm smiling too.

"Come on, I can't wait to see you. I haven't seen you all day."

"I'm on my way baby. Bye." We both hung up the phone.

Solomon lives about an hour away so I got time to go to the store and get the stuff. After he questioned me about my cookin', I sho' wasn't gon' tell him that I don't have no groceries in the house. Let me see if Karina wants to go with me. "Karina!" I opened up my door and yelled upstairs.

"Yea' mama?"

"I'm about to go to the store, Solomon's comin' over and I'm ganna' fry some fish and fries! You wanna' come?"

"Not really! But I guess I'll go cause' I need some shoes for this party comin' up at school!"

"Look Karina, I ain't got time to be runnin' you all around town lookin' for no shoes! I'll take you another day!"

"That's alright I'll stay here!" She slammed her room door.

I ran upstairs to her room as fast as I could and bammed on it. "Karina open up this door! You don't be slammin' no door in my face!" She opened it up before I could finish as I rushed in with my finger in her face. "Look I'm tired of the temper tantrums when you can't have yo' way! For now on if I see one curled up lip when I tell you to do somethin', you can forget about all your privileges! And furthermore, I gave you a choice to come with me, but now I'm tellin' you you're comin'!" I stormed off going back downstairs. Karina never said a word back to me I'm sure it's because I've never hollered at her before.

When I got back downstairs, I went and snatched my purse and went and got in the truck with Karina lagging behind.

As we drove down the street, Karina finally decides she wants to talk.

"Mama why did you holler at me? You've never hollered at me before? Does it have somethin' to do with you marrying Solomon?"

"No Karina it has nothing to do with me marrying Solomon. I'm just tired of your selfish ways. I do too much for you Karina for you to treat me the way you do. And now I'm gettin' on top of it, and again it has nothin' to do with me marrying Solomon."

"Mama why you ain't never tol' me about Solomon? I only met him one time, and that's when he proposed to you out on the beach. Are you ashamed of me?"

"I haven't known Solomon that long. In fact when you met him, that's almost when I met him."

"Why are you marrying a man you don't even know?" Her voice choked up as if she was about to cry.

"I do know him. You don't understand Karina."

"Make me understand. Mama you always tellin' me about not lettin' guys take advantage of me, and stayin' focused on my books and not on boys, but you're doin' the opposite of what you preach to me about. You're about to marry a man you hardly even know. And to top it all off, you're ashamed of your own daughter." She said with tears falling from her eyes. "You wouldn't even introduce him to me and I'm supposed to accept this stranger as my daddy? No, I don't think so." She curled her lips and turned her body towards her window.

"Karina I didn't know you were hurting like this? Look I'm sorry. I'm not ashamed of you. I'll never be ashamed of my baby. It all happened so fast for me. He's Heaven sent Karina and you just gotta' trust that I know what I'm talkin' about. And I do know him, I just can't explain it to you, just please trust your mother ok?"

She turned and looked at me with this dead stare. "Mama we don't need nobody else livin' with us. You don't need no husband, you got me and I'm all the attention you need. We can go shopping more, we can take trips together, and we can sit out on the beach and laugh. See?

You don't need him with all the attention you gotta' give to me your only baby?"

"Yes Karina and you'll always be mama's baby but I need a different kind of attention than what you're talking about. You and Solomon are two different people. You are my daughter, and he's about to be my husband. And the attention I give to you, I can't give him that same kind of attention so you oughta' feel special?"

"Special huh'? Yea' right I hear ya'." She folded her arms and sighed.

"Karina why are you talkin' like that?"

"Mama I'm just gon' go ahead and say it. I'm tired of being second best in your life. You put everything before me! Your books, your traveling, your conferences, you put em' all before me! Mama all I ever wanna' hear you say is that you love me! All I ever wanna' hear you say is that I'm beautiful instead of always talkin' about your career! All I ever wanna' hear you say is that I'm gon' be somebody in life instead of always worrin' about whether or not I'm gon' get pregnant! All you care about is what chu' need, than carin' about the simple things that I really need to hear! Like how was your day, or you're ganna' be successful in life! I can't wait til' your prom, your ganna' be so beautiful! I'm so proud of you! That's the kind of stuff I need to hear, not you always talkin' bout' where you about to travel too next and gettin' on me about some boy!" She screamed with tears flowing from her eyes. I can tell this is some deep rooted hurt that has built up from years back, but she just never said anything.

It was quiet for about 10-minutes. Then finally I had to say somethin'. "Karina, I'm sorry and I promise I'm ganna' do better. If you want me to stop my career I'll do it because you mean more to me than anything in this world."

"I don't want you to stop on the count of me. I just want you to love me like you're supposed too. And I don't need no new daddy to do it, I need you."

"I will work on loving you more but don't chu' think you're being a little selfish about me not gettin' married? You want me to be happy right?"

"No I'm not being selfish, and I do want you to be happy, just without a husband." She slumped down in her seat, folded her arms again, and looked back out of her window.

"Karina you are being selfish."

"Well call it what chu' wanna' call it," she yelled. "It's your fault you had me at an early age!"

My jaw dropped, and a sudden burst of anger just reared up inside of me. I couldn't keep my hand back from slapping her right in the face. She screamed like she was about to die and I was too because I had never in my life hit my child like that. The truck skidded to a complete stop right in the middle of the road with cars passing us honking and yelling out their windows. I yelled at Karina. "Don't chu' ever say that me again! You don't know how many years I struggled with you as a baby! You don't know the cost and the price I paid just to keep food in yo' mouth and clothes on yo' ungrateful back! All this big ol' mansion, money, and clothes didn't come from me havin' a silver spoon in my mouth, it came from struggle, hurt, pain, shame, disappointment, being talked about and rejected, and the list goes on! So much more that you're not ready for! So don't chu' ever fix yo' mouth to throw nothing like that in my face, because I've learned from my mistakes and I don't need you remindin' me of em'!" I slowly pulled the truck to the side of the road and sat there for a moment until I got my mind right. She didn't say anything, she just kept crying. She cried to the store.

Karina's in her room still crying from earlier. I feel like crying too but I'm so mad I can't. Let me call Salva.

Her phone rang about four times before she finally answered. "Salva speaking?"

"Salva hey girl, I got somethin' important I need to talk to you about."

"O' Lord what's wrong?"

"Me and Karina just got in to it." I put the food on, took my heels off, and walked out to the pool.

"You didn't kill her did you?"

"No but I almost did."

"What'll you mean almost?"

"I slapped her in the face."

"You did what?" She raised her voice. "Barina you have never hit that girl in your life."

"Look she made me do it. Talkin' bout' it's my fault I had her at an early age."

"Ok start from the very beginning because I don't understand what you're talkin' about?"

"Look, long story that I don't have time to go into because Solomon's on his way over here and I don't want him in this mess."

"He's already in it. You better prepare him so he won't be surprised. Don't worry about Karina, she's just goin' through some growing pains."

"I hear ya', but I will tell you this little bit, she doesn't want me to marry Solomon."

"Well she'll just have to get over it. Girl don't chu' let that girl ruin what God has blessed you with."

"It's more to the story I'll call you later when he leaves it might be late?"

"I don't care how late it is, call me anyway."

"Alright." I hung up the phone.

I had time to finish the food before Solomon knocked on the door. I ran through the house barefooted on the cold tile to the front door. "Who is it?" I yelled.

He whispered through the door. "It's me baby, your amour." I threw open the door and jumped into his arms like I hadn't seen him in years. "I'm so glad to see you." He said.

"I see." I said as he put me down. "Come on in the food's been ready. We can eat if you're ready?"

"Yea', I'm starving. I didn't eat because you said that you were cooking and I didn't wanna' loose my appetite. I'm excited about tasting your cooking." He smiled and grabbed me around my waist.

"You're so thoughtful." I pulled him closer to me. He's staring at me as if he can see right through me. "Why are you staring at me like that?"

"I'm just looking at you." He stepped back. "You look different."

"Like how?"

"Have you been crying?"

"Why?"

"Why? Because I'm concerned, now are you gon' tell me what's wrong with you?"

"I don't wanna' talk about it right now Solomon." I stepped back, then turned and walked to the kitchen as he followed me. He was so close on my bare heels I thought he was gon' step on the back of my feet.

113

"Ok fine we can talk about it later."

"I might not wanna' talk about it later." I said, pretending to turn the oven off and leaned against the center island. I threw a piece of apple I had cut up earlier in my mouth as if it was the only thing I had to eat all day.

"Ok we don't have to talk about it at all then." He leaned on the other side of the island with his 6' foot somethin' self, he's all the way on my side without trying.

"Fine… Solomon, why are you so understanding? I want you to disagree with me sometimes and stand your ground?" I walked out and sat at the patio table with him following behind me. We both sat down at the same time.

"Why disagree when there's no reason to disagree?" He asked.

"Because it's healthy." I said slipping my feet in some sandals I left underneath the table.

"No I think you got it backwards."

"Good! You finally disagree with me." I threw my hands up.

"What's your trip? Why're you worrying about petty things?"

"This' not petty, I think it's something that we need to talk about."

"About how to disagree?" He stood up and threw his hands up, and sat back down.

"Exactly."

"I'm not going to disagree with something I agree with?"

"I think this is cute." I smiled but he didn't. "We're having our first fight."

"You call this a fight?"

"And you don't?"

"Not at all. What kind of men are you used to dating?"

"Look now, don't start cause' I already had to put one in check, so don't make me have to put chu' in check."

"Why are you making something that's nothing out of something big?"

"Because you makin' me." I got up with my arms folded and walked to the edge of the pool.

"Ok let's just stop it right here." He came over and hugged me from behind. "Can I take you to a movie to get cho' mind off of whatever it is that's got you so up tight?"

114

"I thought we were already goin' to the movies?" I turned to face him. "That's the reason why you came over here?"

"What? So you didn't wanna' spend sometime with me?"

"Solomon of course I did."

"So what're you tryin' to say?"

"I'm not tryin' to say anything."

"Are you tryin' to tell me something that I don't wanna' hear?"

"What would give you that impression? You have to understand that we're ganna' have disagreements sometimes."

"I do understand that but not when something so petty makes you over react like this. That tells me that it's somethin' else that's bothering you Barina. And if you would be honest with yourself, you know I'm telling the truth. It doesn't take a rocket scientist to see that?"

"Ok Solomon whatever, you win ok? You win."

"Look Barina, it's not a game with me. I'm in this thing to win but I can't do it all by myself. I need you with me. I'm not all about games like all those other men you've had to put up with. I'm a one in a million man baby and you can't imagine how blessed I feel to have the most beautiful woman that's all mine standing in front of me right now. And soon it'll be confirmed with a ring around your finger, and a bond that no man can put asunder. Barina, one thing you gotta' remember is that it's God that's brought us together and it's God that'll keep us together. Nothin' and nobody'll ever be able to separate me from you. And you remember that—I love you baby."

I just stared at him thinking, I'm lost for words. Solomon has such a great way with words. I've tried to pick a fight with him and it didn't work, and I've tried to disagree but it didn't work. This' somethin' real special and I can't believe he's all mine. "Solomon I'm sorry for giving you such a hard time. I used to think that it takes forever for a man to find himself, but now since I've met you, I see that it's taking me just as long. I didn't realize that I had all these hidden insecurities that make me believe a lie instead of the truth. See, I've never had a God sent, God fearing, strong, and romantic man like you in my life and I really don't know how to receive you at times. I guess that's why I was acting the way I was. I'm sorry. But I just have to ask you, are you real? What are your intentions? Are you playin' me? Are you gon' lead me on, and then later drop me for another woman?" I asked. He looked at me with nothing to say, only his smile spoke, then softly planted a kiss on my forehead and I said to myself, "God this can't be real."

He waited and then said quietly. "Barina, like I said before, it was God who brought us together, and it's Him who will keep us together. And as long as we remember this, we gon' be alright. Now let's go to the movies." He walked away, then turned around and looked at me and spoke softly,

> *"...How beautiful are your feet in sandals,*
> *O' queenly maiden! Your rounded limbs*
> *are like jeweled chains, the work of a master*
> *hand."*
>
> *(Song of Solomon 7:1)Amplified*

He smiled with a look of pleasure, moved his hands in a coca-cola motion as if to say girl you fine, I then ran into his arms, we walked back in the house, ate the food I cooked, and left for the movies. The rest of the night was so much fun considering how the devil tried to destroy it earlier.

Chapter Eight

I picked Salva up on time; she was ready believe it or not, most of the time I have to wait an extra 20-minutes for her to get ready. Fortunately, we got to the book signing in plenty of time to set up.

Salva and I are sitting at a table they set up for us. We're doing our normal thing. Salva's taking care of the paraphernalia and making sure I have plenty books and supplies to sign, while I sign each book and give encouraging words. Salva's such a great help; I don't know what I would do without her. Most friends would be jealous, but she's not, she's just happy to be apart of all my accomplishments. I'm sure it has something to do with all the things we've been through. She was there when I didn't have anything and was still my friend. And now that I have a big mansion and a huge bank account, she's still there supporting me just like things never changed. It's awesome because Salvester's the same way even though he wasn't there in the beginning, but he still knows where I came from. I love em' both. I thought as I signed another book.

Salva just nudged me in my side. I looked up at her. "What?" I said as she pointed at the next person in line, and to my surprise its Wayne waiting to get his book signed.

He smiled and then said, "What's up girl long time no see? You all famous and thang's won't chu' sign my book?"

I didn't say a word. Unexpected anger and emotional feelings wouldn't allow me too. I signed his book and leaned around him to motion for the next person in line to come up to the table. I won't tell what I wrote in his book. I'll just put it this way, God wouldn't be pleased.

"O' so you just gon' blow me off like that?" He stepped to the side as the next person came up to the table as I took their book and begin to sign it. I never looked up at him, but I can see em' out of the corner of my eye look at Salva like he know her. "Now she gon' ignore me?" He kept looking at Salva, waiting for her response—which was nothing, and then looked back at me.

I still didn't say anything. In fact I didn't say anything until he left walking into the crowd. A local Christian radio station just came up to the table for me to do a quick interview. "So Miss. Barina Grant, we are so elated to have you on the air with us today. We heard about your book signing and we just had to come and see you for ourselves. So would you mind telling us a little bit about your new best seller?" She pointed the mic towards my mouth giving me the que to speak.

"First of all, I'd like to say thank God and thank you for having me. And I'd like to give a shout out to all my fans around the world. Stay encouraged and God's going to give you all the desires of your hearts." *(Psalms 37:4-5)* I looked up to see Wayne standing in the distance with conviction written all over his face. I guess he couldn't take it anymore, so he turned and quickly walked out the double glass doors. "...My book is about a man who stuggled with who he was as an actor on the big show biz scene. He was close to God before he made it big but allowed the enemy to come into his life and made him do things he thought he'd never do. He turned away from God and the thought of him ever coming back never crossed his mind. But eventually there was a little something left in his heart that pushed him back to God. And because God is merciful, He received him back, changed him, delivered him, from all those things he was battling with, and from then on he was never the same." She kept the mic up to my mouth as if she wanted me to say more, but I just smiled and said, "you'll just have to read the book to find out how he gave his life back to God."

I smiled, she smiled, and then she removed the mic from my mouth. "That was awesome I'm sure all those that are listening can't wait to get the book. I can't wait, in fact as soon as I finish with this interview, I'm ganna' get my copy and have it personally signed by the Miss. Barina Grant. So if you're listening you can beat me before I get my book and get your own by runnin' down here as quick as you can.

We're so excited to have Miss. Braina Grant as our guest author for the hour. We'll be getting back with you as the book signing goes on." She said. She kept talking into the mic as she turned and walked towards the crowd for their response. I went back to signing more books.

I signed over two hundred books, ended up doing more radio interviews, news paper interviews, and I don't know how many encouraging words I spoke to each person. My poor fingers are worn out.

Salva and I are cleaning up. Everybody has totally cleared out of the place. We're so tired we're not sayin' anything to each other, just tryin' to hurry up and get out of this place. Salva finally broke the silence.

"Girl I saw yo' face when Wayne showed up out of nowhere. How'd he know you were doing your book signing here?"

"Probably on the radio."

"You think?"

"I don't know." I snapped at her. "And I don't wanna' even think about it." I walked off with some empty boxes in my hands.

I can hear Salva puttin' her two cent in, "you ain't gotta' get no attitude with me I didn't tell em' to come." I could tell she was smiling by the tone of her voice. I didn't bother turning around I just went and threw the boxes in the trash and came back to the table.

"Girl I sho' do appreciate your help. Here's your blessing mam'." I said as I handed her a hand full of money. She took it with a smile.

"Hey this' way more than what you normally give me? Why?"

"Look do you want the money or do I have to take it back and give it to that trash can sittin' over there?" I started laughing.

She looked over towards the trash can and started laughing. "No that won't be necessary." It's a beat up trash can that looks way out of place for a nice big bookstore like this.

"That's what I thought. You know you deserve it because you always go the extra mile for me Salva, and I really appreciate you." I gave her a hug. "Now go buy your hubby some new shoes cause' I'm tired of seeing him in the same ones every time I see him." We both burst out laughing. "Girl those church shoes got em' sprung, he be wearin' em' with his basketball gear. He be sliddin' up and down the basketball court with his hands up talkin' bout' defense." Salva laughed so hard, she started crying. "Look like his feet's burstin' out of em'?"

119

"Girl you so silly." She kept laughing as if it was that funny. "Girl is his toes breaking through?"

"Yes mam' they're sayin', hello." I flashed a quick high five in the air. Salva bent over laughing with tears in her eyes as if her stomach was hurting. The manager just looked on laughing.

"You are so silly—just silly!" She rose up and leaned against the table.

"You make me act like this!"

We said our goodbyes with everybody still wanting hugs and more autographs. We finally made our way out of the bookstore going towards the truck.

"Barina you should've seen Wayne, he looked so jealous and convicted. Like a sick lil' ol' puppy. He stood there watching you for the longest until I guess he couldn't take it any more and left."

"O' well, he's the one who decided he didn't wanna' be in my life."

"Are you gon' tell Karina you seen him?"

"No mam', she don't need to know. It's not like he asked about her anyway." We walked a few steps and low and behold there was Wayne standing in the distance.

"Dawg' it took you a long time to come out." He walked up to us. "I went and put my book in the Hummer and had plenty of time to come back and wait on you to come out. What took you so long?"

Salva looked at me. "Girl you gon' be alright?"

"Yea'." I never looked at her, just kept looking at him.

"I'll be in the truck then." She stormed off to the truck upset.

I pointed my finger towards him. "First of all how dare you come up to me like you always been in my life. I'm not about no games Wayne and if that's what chu' all about then you need to step."

"Who said I was playin' games?"

"Look I could care less about cho' lil' so called famous football name. I got one too."

"I see ya' got the bling bling goin' on—I ain't mad at cha'!" He did a little dance and flashed his fingers towards me.

"Well you can keep on seeing it from a distance." I tried walking off but he grabbed my hand. I jerked it away and looked at him like I'll knock you out. "Don't chu' ever put cho' hands on me again!" I started walking away again.

He trotted behind me. "Barina, I'm not tryin' to cause' no scene here. I just wanna' see my lil' girl."

"She's not a little girl anymore, and besides she don't wanna' see you no way."

"How you know? Don't make my daughter suffer because things didn't work out for you and me."

"Work out?" I screamed not caring if all America heard me. "You were with me?" I pointed at him then at myself. "You never claimed me so you can get that part about things not working out with you and me out cho' crazy head!"

"Awh' come on Barina stop holdin' this guilt trip against me. Look I'm sorry if that'll make you feel better. I just couldn't mess up my career."

"Wayne, what chu' need to do is get out of my face. Go yo' way and I'm goin' mine before it gets real ugly out here, and I will not mess up my reputation because of you!" I ran up to the truck, got in, and sped off. If dirt were on the street it would've been all in his face, that's how fast I drove off.

"Girl what did you say to him?" Salva took a quick glance back at him and then back at me. "He's still standing there like he just lost his dog?" We both looked back and laughed at how he's still standing there pleading for me to come back.

"Salva I don't even feel sorry for him. How you think you just gon' come back into somebody life like you ain't never left and never done nothin' wrong?"

"I feel ya' girl."

"Girl I'm so mad I could just turn this truck around and run right over him." Salva didn't say anything. "Uww, I'm so mad I could drive this truck right off the road." *(Luke 3:14) (Deuteronomy 5:17)*

Salva hurry up and said, "now I know you outta' yo' mind. Now I wasn't gon' say nothin' but since you talkin' crazier I betta' let chu' know that you better calm down or drop me off first and then go drive off the road." I looked at her and then we both burst out laughing.

"Uwh' girl I just wanna' go back and get em'?"

"Barina you don't need to let him make you loose your joy."

"Salva I'm not tryin' to be spiritual right now. I'm talkin' about goin' and messin' him up."

"You better get spiritual before you do something stupid that you live to regret for the rest of your life. Now I'm tryin' to calm you down but if you don't wanna' calm down, then drop me off and go do yo' thang'."

"You're supposed to be supportive not bashing and threatening me."

"I am supporting you. I'm giving you reality and common-sense. Now how you choose to receive it is your business. God has brought you too far to let something like this mess your whole entire life up— now that's real."

"Yea' you right. I let him get me all rowed up. The devil will make you say anything won't he?"

"Yep, he sure will. Now let me ask you somethin' and please don't get offended."

"I won't go ahead."

"What's wrong with Wayne seeing Karina?"

"Look Salva, he hasn't been in her life all this time, why now when everything's peaches and cream?"

"Because that's her daddy."

"And so?"

"And so she needs to know her daddy. Look Barina just because he did you wrong years ago, and I admit it was wrong, doesn't mean you have to take it out on Karina not seeing him. Now after she sees him and decides that she doesn't want anything to do with him, it's on her and not on you anymore. But if you don't let her see him now, when she gets older and decides to find him for herself, she gon' resent you because you didn't tell her that he tried to find her."

Maybe Salva's right. Shoot that girl's always right. I can't come back to that if I wanted too. "I hear ya'."

"O' and another thing, you gotta' forgive and let go of the past. *(Ephesians 4:32)* He seems to be happy and enjoying his life while you're still holding grudges. I know it's easier said than done, but if you think about it you're the only one loosing sleep."

"Ok Salva I heard you, just pray for me this' not an easy thing to do especially when you've held a person for so long."

"Somehow or another I've heard this before, I hope it's different this time because I prayed the last time. See I can pray all day long for you but you've gotta' be willing to make a change for yourself?"

"I'm ready Salva. So what do you suggest I do first?"

"Me personally would talk to Karina about it first and if she wants to see him, let her see him, then go from there."

"I don't know how Karina's gon' receive me now, I'm sure she's still mad at me from slapping her."

"Girl I'm sure Karina done gotten over that, she loves you too much to hold that against you. When you get home just go and talk to her and I'm sure everything'll be alright."

"You know, I can remember when my parents threw me away like a rag doll and thought nothing of it. I just don't want Karina to ever feel like I'm throwing her away. And I don't want her to ever throw me away."

"See that's a stronghold. *(2 Corinthians 1: 9-10)* You have got to let your past go Barina. You've got to let what your parents did to you go, you've got to let what Wayne did to you go, and when you do this, I think you can love Karina better and appreciate Solomon for who he is."

"You think I don't appreciate him?"

"I don't think you know how to appreciate him because you really can't believe that God would send you an almost perfect man like him." She looked at me, reached down and opened her purse from between her legs and pulled out two pieces of gum. "Here I know you want one."

"Thanks." I took it from her. "Girl I really got some issues, I didn't think they were this bad though?"

"Don't start gettin' down on yourself; your issues ain't no greater than nobody else's. We all got issues. Just pray and fast about it Barina and I'm sure God'll give you what you need. *(Matthew 17:14-21)* I know you can do it because the bible says: "...greater is He that is in you, than he that is in the world. *(1 John 4:4)* He's greater than the situations that you're goin' through right now, and He's greater than your enemies that are against you. As much power as God's given you, trust me you can do it. The key is you gotta' do it."

"Thanks Salva, you're so encouraging." I smiled, threw the gum in my mouth, and turned into Salva's driveway. "I know we're done talking about my issues but I just have to say that I find it funny that you mentioned about me not being able to appreciate Solomon. We had our first fight yesterday."

"What happened?"

"I let my insecurities get the best of me, and I was also mad at Karina but I didn't know how to tell him that Karina doesn't want me to marry him. You know how jealous she gets?"

"So why couldn't you talk to him about it?"

"Because he probably wouldn't have taken it so well, and I didn't wanna' hurt his feelings. He's so perfect. I almost can't find not one ounce of wrong in him."

"Why're you tryin'? Look there's millions of women waitin' out there for a man like him. I suggest you get cho' act together before somebody shows him that they don't have no problems appreciating him." She squinted her eyes at me, gathered her things, and got out of the truck.

"Now you know I can do that, I ain't gon' let nobody take him from me and neither am I gon' leave him."

"I know that's right, you go girl. See that's what I'm talkin' bout'." We both laughed as she closed the door and started walking up the sidewalk. She turned around. "And don't worry about Miss. Karina, she'll be alright." She went on in the house as I backed out and left going home.

I'm thinkin' about what Salva said. That girl know she can counsel somebody, she need to open up a counseling business. I'm goin' home to talk to my baby; I hope she listens to me.

My cell phone rings. "Hello?"

"Hey to the most beautiful woman in the world."

"Hey to the most handsome man in the world." I smiled.

"I heard that." He waited. "So how'd things go today?"

"It went great." I can't tell him that I saw Wayne yet, I just can't. I'll tell em' later. "I made a lot of sales and got a lot of promotion deals and exposure."

"That's great Barina. I'm so proud of you baby. When I look at chu' in action at your book signings and everybody's comin' just to see you, makes me even more proud to be your man."

"You know? You are the sweetest man on this planet."

"No you're the sweetest woman on this planet."

"Thank you baby." I said cheesing.

"So what've you got up for tonight considering its Friday afternoon?"

"I'm on my way home from dropping Salva off and I'm goin' to talk to Karina about something."

"What's going on with her?"

"She and I are having a disagreement about something."

"O' must be one of those girly thangs."

"As a matter-of-fact no it has nothing to do with that."

"Then what is it? Is it that personal that you can't tell you're soon to be husband?"

"Of course not Solomon. It's just some concerns that Karina have about you and I gettin' married."

"What is it, she doesn't want you and I to get married?"

"No."

"Well maybe we all can sit down and talk about it?"

"We can try but she probably won't."

"Let's talk about this over dinner. Where are you right now?"

"I'm on Hollywood Drive."

"Great, meet me at Braidy's Landing."

"Wow that's the hottest and most expensive restaurant in this city?"

"Baby I wouldn't take you to no cheap restaurant. That would insult how much your worth."

"O' Solomon."

"I don't take a breath without taking one for you first." He sighed then slightly laughed like he was thinking about it. I almost ran off the road. "Come quickly I'll be waiting for you."

"But where do I meet...?" He hung up before I could finish.

It's amazing that nobody's coming and going in and out of the restaurant as popular as it is. I walked up to the door about to reach for the handle and a man looking like a butler pushed it open for me. Looking past him I noticed that there's not one person in the entire restaurant. I walked on in.

"Have a seat mam' you'll be served shortly." He smiled and walked away not giving me a chance to ask him why they're not any people in here.

I sat for about 5 minutes and to my surprise Solomon came around the corner grinning wearing a chef hat and carrying a tray of hot good smelling food. He put the tray down on the table, opened it as if to get my approval on what was cooked and pulled out a small piece of paper.

125

A man with a violin came from the back and started playing softly as Solomon began reading.

> *"...O' my love, how beautiful you*
> *are! There is no flaw in you... Come*
> *away with me... my promised bride...*
> *come with me... You have ravished*
> *my heart and given me courage...*
> *my promised bride: you have ravished*
> *my heart and given me courage with*
> *one look from your eyes, with one*
> *jewel of your necklace..."*

The music got a little louder as Solomon raised his voice to the music.

> *"...How beautiful is your love...my*
> *promised bride! How much better is*
> *love than wine! And the fragrance*
> *of your ointments than all spices!"*

The music lowered back down.

> *"...A garden enclosed and barred is*
> *my promised bride— a spring shut up,*
> *a fountain sealed... You are a fountain*
> *springing up in a garden, a well of*
> *living waters, and flowing streams..."*
> *(My Song of Solomon 4:7-10, 12, 15)*

He stopped reading, then waited for the music to stop and said, "I love you Barina. I wanted to bring you here to show you how much you mean to me." The violinist started back serenading me as Solomon came over and softly planted a kiss on my cheek, and hugged me like I was his teddy bear. He then sat down across from me, took a plate from off the table, put food on it until it was full, got up and came around to my side and put it in front of me and said, "I'm at your service. I will be your personal chef. I rented out the restaurant for the night so anything you want is yours I hope you like the food, I prepared it."

"I love it, I love everything. As always you know I'm lost for words. Solomon you are amazing, just amazing." A couple of tears slowly started running down my face. "You already know how I feel about you. Your poems are breath taking—you're breath taking. And yes I will go with you and be your promised bride." We hugged again, he sat back down, and we began eating. It was a romantic night filled with bloom in the restaurant.

I'm glad Solomon's following me home. We're almost there. I hope Karina's up so we all can talk. I pulled up in the driveway and Solomon pulled up on the side of me, got out, and came up to my truck and opened the door.

"O' how sweet, thank you darling."

"You're welcome." We walked in the house and went straight to the kitchen after turning on all the lights because apparently Karina forgot.

"I done told Karina over and over about having it dark when I come home." I put my 50 roses in a vase I got from the restaurant, and walked over to the counter and checked to see if I have any messages. Solomon sat at the table never taking his eyes off of me.

"Does she always do this?"

"Yes, and I'm tired of telling her over and over not too."

"Call her down here." He said.

"Hum'…where did this folded piece of paper come from by this phone? Karina must've left this up here." I opened it up and read it out loud. *"…You don't have to worry about me taking up anymore space, I'm gone to live with my soon to be husband. He's twice my age so he's more than able to take care of me. Don't worry about coming to find me because you won't…"* I threw the letter down and burst into tears, ran upstairs to Karina's room with Solomon right behind me, dropped down on the floor with my hands over my face, and cried. Solomon came over and held me, saying nothing.

"Solomon what am I gon' do? Should I call the police and report her missing? I shouldn't have ever slapped her!" I broke free from Solomon's arms, went and snatched her pillow from off her bed and started bamming it on the bed until my arms got too weak. Solomon just watched. "What did I do wrong? I tried to be the best mother that I could? Solomon I did the best that I could to raise that girl right, where did I go wrong?" He never answered me, he just continued to watch. "She's my pride and joy! She didn't want me to get married. I just

127

should've told her that I wouldn't if I'd a known that she would go and do something like this? And who is this ol' man she's stayin' with that's twice her age? You wait til' I get a hold of him, I'm a get em' for statutory rape!" I ran back downstairs back to the kitchen, grabbed a knife from the knife holder, just as I was about to do whatever with it, Solomon grabbed my arm and took the knife from me. I threw myself to the floor and screamed in tantrums. Still Solomon said nothing. "Why aren't chu' sayin' anything?" I yelled at him. "I need you right now! My child is out there with some sick ol' man and you sittin' there actin' like it ain't no big deal!" He still didn't say anything, he just closed his eyes. I couldn't take it anymore so I ran over to him, grabbed his shoulders, and tried to shake em' off his body. "Say somethin'! I need you to say somethin'!"

He looked up at me with a look of humility and said, "I'm praying." I stopped shaking him like God said it and laid down on the floor beside him. He stayed silent for about 15 or 20-minutes. I had no choice but to calm down. His prayer brought such an enormous amount of peace in the room to a point where I was too scared to move. God is totally in control. Solomon finally opened his eyes and said, "she'll be back tomorrow don't worry." I burst out crying again as he came over and picked me up from off the floor and carried me to my room. He took off my shoes and made me get in the bed. "I'll lock the door from the inside you'll be fine. Don't cry, everything's ganna' be alright." He turned the light off and left going out the door. His voice was so calm. Almost like an angel. He was a totally different person, that's how graceful he was. The peace was so strong in my room that it made me sleep all night on into the morning.

Chapter Nine

I was awakened by a door slam.

I ran to my door only to see Karina walking in just like Solomon said that she would. She went straight to the kitchen, got something to drink, and walked out to the pool. She never saw me watching her. I went back to the room, put my robe on, and walked out to the pool where she was.

Karina's sittin' on the side of the pool with her feet in the water. She never looked up as I went and sat down beside her. Things were quiet for about five minutes until I just had to say somethin'. "It's a beautiful day today huh'?" She never answered me so I asked again. "It's a beautiful day today huh'?" She still didn't say anything. "Karina you can talk to me I promise I won't hit you again."

She quickly turned and looked at me and said, "you right you'll never put cho' hands on me again. And just to let you know I'm gettin' married." She stood up. "You got all you need you don't need me no way. He's thirty-seven and he owns his own mechanic shop so he'll be able to take care of me. So much I can say for you." She started walking towards the patio doors.

I caught up with her. "Karina now you wait a minute." I jerked her around with a tight grip on her arm. "All I have done for you why are you actin' like this? I've taken good care of you. I always made sure you had before I did. I always respected how you felt about things..."

She jerked her arm from me. "Not this time. You don't even know this man!" She yelled. "He could be a serial killer for all you know? But you wouldn't care because he's all you care about. You wouldn't

129

even come lookin' for me last night, so I know you could care less about me! I'm oughta' here!" She ran back in the house on out through the front door and down the street.

I didn't even chase after her, felt it would've been a waste of time. She wouldn't have come back no way. I went back and got in the bed and went to sleep with another headache.

I slept for about another three hours.

I woke up to the sound of bird's chirping around my open window. The breeze from the wind is slightly pushing the sheer curtains towards me, and then pulling back out as if to take em' back. Umm' I love the smell of fresh evening spring air. I got up and went and made me some cappuccino, poured it in my favorite I love you mom mug Karina gave me for my birthday last year, grabbed the cordless phone, and went outside and sat down at the patio table.

That's weird, I haven't heard from Solomon. That's not like him. Let me call em' and thank him for what he did for me last night. I walked back into the kitchen while dialing his number; he finally picked it up after about five rings.

"Hello?"

"Hey, I thought chu' wasn't there. How you doin' today?"

"I'm fine and you?"

"I'm good. Solomon, thank you so much sweetie for what chu' did last night. I don't know what happened to me. Karina really threw me off, I'm glad you were here with me." I took a slow sip of my hot cappuccino. I can tell there's something bothering Solomon. I went and sat down at the kitchen table and waited for a second until I just had to ask him, "Is there something wrong?"

He hesitated for a quick moment. "As a matter of fact there is. Barina, I've been prayin' for you and the Lord revealed to me that you're not seeking Him enough. And I'm not pleased with that. Look Barina, I want a saved, sanctified, and Holy Ghost filled woman who's after God's own heart. I want a woman who can girt me up in the Spirit. Whose gon' be able to pray for me and hold me up when I'm weak, and who I can catch in the Spirit when she's weak. Who's sold out for God like I am. I want a woman who's submissive and loving, not screaming and argumentative with temper tantrums. And who don't have no problems readin' her word and bein' in love with the Lord just like I am. That's what kind of woman I'm lookin' for." Tears are

130

rolling down my face at the sound of disappointment in his voice. "I love you Barina I just expect more and what I'm expecting in you is not a bad thing. It's a good thing. And I want your expectations to be just as high for me. Look I could care less about your money. I care more about your heart and soul more than I care about how much money you got and how big yo' house is. I just want us to be right. We're about to go into this marriage and we've got to be one in the Spirit. We can't have other motives in mind. I take my vows seriously because I'm not just sayin' them to you I'm also sayin' them to God." He finally got quiet. I know he's waiting on my response.

"Solomon, I'm lost for words..." I said, barely able to speak. "Nobody's ever been able to touch me like you just did. I'm so convicted... convicted to do right. Solomon I don't wanna' loose you. I wanna' do whatever I need to do so that I can be all that you want me to be. I wanna' please you in every way..."

"See Barina that's one of things I'm talking about. God wants that from you. He wants you to say that to Him. Not to me first, you're not my wife yet. And even afterwards He still wants to be first in your life. Not me."

"How do I do that? How do I make Him first in my life? I mean, I gave my life to the Lord years ago with my mouth but I didn't do it with my heart. I played church and now I wanna' do it for real. And I do wanna' do it for the Lord. I need to get right Solomon, its way pass due."

"Barina you don't have to wait any longer. Do you want God to save you right now?"

"Yes I do."

"Ok all you have to do is repeat after me."

"Ok."

"Lord I know that I'm a sinner..." I repeated. "I have sinned against you... but today Lord I repent of my sins and now I ask you to come into my heart, my mind, my Spirit, and my soul." I repeated again. "And be my Lord and Savior and my Redeemer. I confess with my mouth and I truly believe in my heart." I repeated again. "That God raised Jesus from the dead and then He rose again just for me. By faith I do believe that I am saved. Thank you Lord for saving me!" He waited for me to respond.

I cried out to God as loud as I could without shame or guilt but with gratefulness. "Lord I thank you!... Lord I thank you! Thank you Lord for Your saving Power! Thank you Lord for giving me another chance! Thank you Lord! Hallelujah! Hallelujah!... Hallelujah!..." My praises lasted for over an hour under the presence of God.

I finally came too after being in God's presence. I didn't wanna' come out. It felt so good allowing God to touch me and fill me with His precious Holy Spirit. This' somethin' I have never experienced before. Out of all those years of growin' up in the church I had never been filled with His Holy Spirit. *(Acts 2:1-13)* I don't know when I got off the phone with Solomon. All I remember is coming back to myself and picking myself up off the kitchen floor, and that's where I'm at right now. I couldn't stop the tears from rolling down my face and the chills from stirrin' in my soul. I have never wept like that before, and I grew up in the church. This was a whole new experience for me. Now that I'm thinkin' about it, I've never had a man to lead me to the Lord. In fact I've never met a man who loved the Lord as much as he does. I mean, this man is saved for real I just wish I knew how to receive him. It's hard when a person's been hurt so many times to open up and trust somebody new. After a while you wonder if anybody's real anymore. It's even harder when a person's pouring out nothin' but love and trust, especially when you know they've been sent from God. Most men could care less whether or not you're saved. All they want is the goods and don't care how they get em'. And if you don't watch em', they'll sweet talk your clothes right off of you. And when it's all over with, you'll be wonderin' how in the world did I allow that to happen? I can't just pick on the brotha's; I know they're women out there that are just like that too. But I can only speak from a woman's perspective because I'm a female. I thought smiling to myself, snapping back from a daydream.

The phone rings twice. I picked it up.

"Hello?"

"How are you?" He asked.

"I'm fine. It's good to hear your voice."

"Well it's good to hear your voice too. How you feel?"

"I feel like a whole new person."

"You are a new person." *(2Corinthians 5:17)*

"O' Solomon, I can't describe what I'm feelin' right now."

"I know you can't baby. I'm so proud of you. And I'm proud of what God did in you. I'll never forget it. Now you can go to church with me tomorrow?"

"You ain't said nothin' but-a-word. I'm too ready to go."

"Good, I'll be by there in the morning between 8:30 and 9. Be ready."

"I will. What's the dress attire?"

"Wear what chu' have my Pastor doesn't look at all that. He cares about your soul not your outer appearance."

"That's good he's like that. He'll draw a lot more people that way. I'll wear a dress anyway."

"Ok go get chu' some rest and I'll see you in the morning."

"Ok, bye." We both hung up the phone.

"Now let me see what I'm gon' wear. Should I wear my ruffled burgundy dress suit, or should I wear my long peach dress suit with the beaded pearls hanging down the sleeve? O' well I'll see in the morning." I said out loud as if somebody was in the kitchen with me.

Still sittin' at the kitchen table the phone ranged. I answered it like it was my million-dollar call. "Hello?"

"What's up Miss. Thang'?" She asked. I can tell she's cheesing.

"What's up sis?"

"You got it."

"No you tha' one who got it."

"No mam' you got it. Tell me what's goin' on?"

"Girl you wouldn't believe me if I told you three times what happened to me earlier."

"What happened? You dumped Solomon for an old flame?" She laughed.

"Old flame? You so silly Salva. No it's not about an ol' flame. It's what happened between Solomon and me. Girl do you know he lead me to Christ?"

She screamed. "He did what?"

"He led me to Christ."

"How did this come about? Well I mean I know how it came about because I had been prayin' for you for a long time and now God has heard my prayers!"

"Salva I feel so different. I'm not ignoring you. Thank you for all your prayers. And no they weren't in vain. God did hear you. And not only did He save me, but He filled me with His precious Holy Spirit."

133

"Not tha' Holy Ghost too?" She screamed again and then called Salvester.

"Look now don't be callin' everybody. I don't want everybody in my business."

"Salvester's a part of yo' business mam'."

"But still."

"Anyway." She got off the phone. "Salvester guess who just got saved?" I can hear him ask who. "Yo' sista'-in-law!" I can hear him in the background say, "Say what?" She got back on the phone. They both are shouting. "Barina we're just too excited over here!"

"Good I'm glad you two are. So…" She cut me off.

"So how did it all happen? Was he there with you? Where were you two?"

"We were on the phone." She cut me off again.

"So come on tell me in detail."

"I'm tryin' to if somebody would stop cuttin' me off."

"Ok I'm sorry. I'm just excited. Go ahead."

"Ok so as I was sayin' before I was interrupted." We both laughed. "I noticed that Solomon hadn't called me and I knew that wasn't like him so I called him and girl the phone must've ringed about five times. He finally answered it and was soundin' real dry and quiet. I asked him what was wrong and do you know what he told me?"

"What?"

"He told me that he had been prayin' for me and the Lord revealed to him that I wasn't seeking God enough…" She cut me off again.

"What chu' say?"

"And then he started sayin' all the things that he wants in a woman and how he wasn't satisfied at how my Spiritual life was going. Then he was like he couldn't take that and that he wasn't accepting no woman who don't go to church and who's is not saved. Salva ain't no man ever made me feel bad about how I was livin'. I was too through. And he didn't stop there. He asked me did I want God to save me. And all I could say as the tears just ran from my eyes is yes. I was so convicted."

"That's weird how God knows who to use to change a person's life. He couldn't do it through me even though He used me to lead you to the Lord years ago but you backslide since then. *(Jeremiah 3:22)* So

He knew who to use to help you come back to Him. Remember you left Him, but He's been there all along."

"Yea' you right."

"Barina I need to share somethin' with you, now you need to get all up in that Bible and pray. Because just when you get saved the devil's gon' come with his tricks, and you don't wanna' go back out there talkin' and actin' the way you used too." *(Hosea 14:4)*

"I hear ya'."

"I hope you do cause' I'm not playin'. That thing's real, I don't care how strong you think you are. " Her tone was serious.

"I do." I said, reinforcing that I understood.

"What I called to ask you before somebody came at me with all this good news was if I could borrow your cookie pan. I'm bakin' some cookies for Precious she's gotta' take some to her Sunday school class in the mornin'."

"Sure you can, when you gon' come get em'?"

"I'll come a little later before it gets too late."

"Alright then."

"I'll call you before I come."

"No just come I ain't gon' be doin' nothin' but reading my bible."

"I definitely don't wanna' disturb that."

"You won't. By the time you get here I'll be done."

"Are you sure?"

"I'm sure."

"Ok then I'll see you later." She said ok and we both hung up the phone.

Not a minute later the phone ranged again. "Hello?"

"Yes is this Barina Grant?"

"Yes it is, may I help you?"

"Yes you can. I'm Wayne Matthew's lawyer and I'm calling to find out some information about his little girl. He wanted me to call and ask you if he could make an agreement with you."

"What kind of agreement?"

"Well he really feels bad about how he hasn't been a part of his daughter's life for all these years so he wants to make you a personal settlement offer."

"No sir. You tell him his daughter is not for sale."

"He's not trying to buy his daughter; he's just trying to give back to you everything that is due to you for all the years of taking care of his child."

"She's not a child anymore."

"I'm sorry I mean his daughter."

I waited for moment and said, "How much is he talkin'?"

He quickly said, "$600,000 dollars."

"Come on now, I don't have time for games."

"This is not a game. Trust me I have better things to do than to do silly things like this." The phone got quiet. $600,000 dollars just flashed before my eyes.

"Ok are you sure he said $600,000 dollars?"

"Yes mam'."

It didn't take long to think about it. "Ok that'll be fine. How will I get my money?"

"I'll get with him and we'll come up with a day when we can meet. Maybe over lunch?"

"I can agree to that I just need to know ahead of time. And you be sure to remind him that this ain't takin' the place of all those years he hasn't been there for his daughter."

"Yes mam', I'll be sure to tell em'."

"Ok well goodbye."

"I'll be in touch with you Miss. Grant."

"That'll be fine." We both hung up the phone.

$600,000 dollars is all that's runnin' through my head right now. I could use $600,000 dollars right about now. I mean I'm not strugglin' but I can always use more to bless somebody else.

Hours have passed and night has taken its course.

I love the way this Jacuzzi feels after a long day. I closed my eyes, laid my head back into the water with the back of my head floating, and my face breathing up the coolness of the night's air. The water's massaging my scalp as the warm pressure thrust against the back of my head. I'm thinkin', when I get that check in my hand is when I'll believe it. I smiled at the thought.

Let me get out of this Jacuzzi before I fall asleep and drown, God forbid. I laughed out loud like somebody was with me. I grabbed the towel I had resting on the back of the patio chair, went into the house, grabbed a DVD from the movie chest, set it on the big flat screen tv, turned off all the lights except the lamp standing in the corner of the living room, lit a couple of candles Salva gave me, went to my room, and changed into my baggy pj's. I'm puttin' em' on thinking, it ain't like I gotta' be romantic cause' ain't nobody here to romance me no way. I know I shouldn't have thought that but O' well I did. I giggled.

There's a knock at the door, must be Salva. I quickly grabbed my housecoat and let the doorbell rang about five times before I made my way to the door. "Who is it?" I screamed from behind the door.

They waited and then answered, "Wayne."

"Wayne?" I quickly grabbed the straps on my housecoat and strapped it closed as if he could see me.

"Are you gon' let me in?"

"What're you doin' here? And how did you know where I live?"

"If you let me come in I'll explain everything."

"Wayne look…"

"Come on Barina, I promise I won't be long."

I waited and then slowly cracked opened the door. "Wayne what do you want?"

"I wanna' talk to you, is that ok?"

"Of course not, it's late at night so what chu' gotta' say to me that's so important that you couldn't wait til' some other time?"

He pushed the door all the way open and walked passed me like he owned the place. I turned my head with my mouth open and followed him to the living room. I'm shocked that he would just walk in my house without permission, but I'm not shocked at how fine he looks. Just one look at him brings back so many memories. A flash back just flashed before my eyes that I'm far from proud of. He and I, alone, and the rest is history. Not to mention the atmosphere is already set with the lights off and nothin' but sweet smellin' candles burnin'. Lord have mercy. I see right now he can't stay long. I'm about to be a married woman and this can't be happening. I don't know why I'm thinkin' this way, I didn't feel like this the other day.

"You have a nice lil' ol' pad here." He looked around scopin' out the entire downstairs area. "I gotta' give it to you, you do have good taste." He smiled. Then walked over to the open floor modeled windows and looked out into the dark sky line of the beaches horizon. He put his hands in his pockets, which gives me a perfect view of his entire frame. All I see is this towered silhouette of a 6'9, tight fittin' tan

137

shirt wearin', thick broad shouldered, blue jean wearin' long legged body that's well put together. I don't know what they been feedin' him but it sure did do the body good. All the chubbiness he once had has turned into nothin' but muscle. His full lips and short black dreds and thick eyebrows that have no style to em' can put a model to shame. I can't shake these thoughts that's cluttering up my mind. *(1 Corinthians 10:6)* I turned my head hoping that that would take the ungodly thoughts away. But it didn't. I love Solomon and that's all I'm gon' think about. He came back and sat down across from me on the leather recliner. I shook my head tryin' to shake the thoughts again. The thoughts of what we used to do keep coming back up in my mind. *(2 Corinthians 10:5)* I'm remembering what Salva said earlier about gettin' in my bible because now that I'm saved, the devil's gon' try and come with his tricks. Well he sure don't waste no time. I better say somethin' before I forget why he came. "Are you ready to say what chu' gotta' say." I looked at him pretending like I could care less but my flesh is about to go crazy, my palms are sweaty, and my bodies dripping with passion. My flesh is saying leave Solomon right away and have it all night long with Wayne, but my Spirit is saying don't make the wrong mistake and loose something special from God. I closed my eyes at the thought for a split moment.

"Hum', yea' I'm ready to say what I gotta' say... Barina I know you know the reason why I came over here an...?" He asked.

I cut him off. "No I don't know. But first of all tell me how you found out where I live? Then tell me why you came over here?"

"You forget that I'm a multi-millionaire? I can find out anything I want too. You just gotta' have the right contacts. I was about to tell you why I came over here but you cut me off. Look I came to see my child."

"I keep tellin' you she's not a child anymore."

"You know what I mean." He looked at me and frowned. "My lawyer called you earlier about makin' an agreement with you."

"I already know that."

"Are you gon' let me finish or are you gon' keep giving me a hard time?"

"Look, just say what chu' gotta' say."

"Naw', what I wanna' know first is where is my lil' girl?" He got up and looked up towards the upstairs balcony. "Before we go any further that's what I wanna' know." He sat back down.

"To be honest with you I haven't seen your daughter in a while. We had a disagreement, she walked out callin' her self runnin' away with some dirty ol' thirty seven year old man that owns his own mechanic shop, and you can put the rest together yourself."

"How long she been gone?"

"A while and that's all I'm gon' say."

"Come on now, you owe me a better explanation than that."

"No I don't. You do good comin' over my house in the middle of the night tryin' to act like you such a concerned daddy." I yelled across the living room.

He jumped up. "This' is crazy. I see now I'm just wastin' my time." He started walking towards the front door and I got up and ran to shut the door behind him but he stopped and turned around and said, "I'm gon' find my lil' girl." He started pacing and massaging the back of his hair with his hand. Then he brushed passed me again like he did earlier and went and sat back down on the sofa.

"What's really goin' on?"

"I need to be honest with you Barina." He waited. "I'm crazy about you. I know I did you wrong years ago but I don't wanna' go back to the past. I know you still crazy about me but you just don't wanna' admit it, look at cha', probably been sittin' there daydreamin' about the times we spent together." He stared at me daring me to look away and I lifted one eyebrow daring my mouth not to open up and tell the truth. "When I saw you at that bookstore and how beautiful you looked, I was sorry I ever treated you the way that I did."

"Look Wayne I don't have time for some tied ol' lines."

"Call it what chu' wanna' call it, you know you're still in love with me."

"Wayne you are so much history it's pitiful. And anyway I'm about to get married."

"Married?"

"Yep, married. And about to be happily married." He stared at the floor.

"I guess there's no need for me to keep wastin' yo' time then." He got up and walked to the front door as I followed and then turned around to face me. "I'll see you later." He waited. "Can I have a hug?"

139

Not waiting for my response, he reached out and pulled me into his arms and slowly kissed me right on the mouth. His hug is like this strong tower that just took away all of my fears. It's like I'm reuniting with him all over again. Not with my soul, but undoubtedly with my heart. Mixed feelings? That's to be true. I'm shaking em' as best as I can. His lips are soft and moist, so soft that my mind doesn't want to release him.   I broke away from him. "Are you crazy?" I wiped my mouth repeatedly hoping that this is all a dream and I'm about to wake up at any moment.

"Barina I know you still love me, I can see it all in yo' eyes. If you just be honest with yourself. This dude you bout' to marry don't mean nothin' to me, you do. If you give me a chance I'll show you how much happier I can make you. I know he ain't makin' as much money as me? And I know you like a man that's financially stable. And furthermore, Karina needs her biological daddy in her life not somebody that can't relate to her. Even though I haven't been there, she still got my seed and that's enough to relate too. They always say it's better for the biological daddy to raise their child than for some tied ol' step daddy too. Let me gone get oughta' here, you ain't tryin' to hear me." He turned and walked out on the front porch, then turned back around and said, "O' I almost forgot, here's our agreement." He slightly grabbed my hand as I reached for the check; he then walked to his truck and drove away.

How could I've let some thing like this happen? I walked to the kitchen, put my head down on the counter, and hoped that my thoughts would erase what just happened. But they were interrupted by a knock at the door.

I slowly walked back to the door hoping that it wasn't Wayne again. I looked through the side glass window and saw that it was Salva and let her in.

"Girl what took you so long to open the door? Solomon ain't up in here is he?"

If she only knew. "Girl naw' he ain't up in here. What's up?"

"What's up? You forgot that I was comin' to get the cookie pan?"

"O' yea' let me go get it." I tried to run to the kitchen and get the cookie pan so she could get it and go without noticing that something is wrong. But it didn't work, she followed me to the kitchen and the

140

first thing that came out of her mouth was what's wrong? "Salva you know I'm always honest with you right?"

"Right."

"Well something just happened and I can't seem to shake it."

"O' Lord what happened?"

"Wayne came over here."

"What Wayne? How'd he find out where you live?"

"Long story. But anyway, he came over here wanting to make a settlement with me for Karina."

"Did you tell em' she's not for sale?"

"I did but listen, first his lawyer called me on the phone right after I got off the phone with you and said that Wayne wanted to make an agreement with me. He proceeded to say that he hasn't been in Karina's life all these years, so he wanted to make up for all that he didn't do for her so he offered me, are you ready for this?"

"Yea' girl come on tell me."

"$600,000 dollars."

"What?"

"You heard me right."

"Girl if he offered me that much Solomon would be history." She laughed but I didn't. When she saw I wasn't laughing she stopped.

"I'm sorry, but girl that's a lot of money? Did he give it to you?"

"O' he gave it to me alright."

"What chu' mean by that?"

"I mean he not only gave me the check, but he gave me a hug and a kiss that I can't seem to get off my mind."

"What in the world? Barina what got into you? You just got saved and I told you to get all off in that Word cause' the devil's gon' try and come with his tricks. Didn't I?" She pointed her finger like a mother.

"You did."

"He not only came with a hug and kiss, but he used all this money to do it. Barina you can't get caught up in this money thing. Just because he got a lot of money don't mean he's better for you than a man who don't. At least Solomon has something that's better than what Wayne can give and that Man's name is Jesus. Why would you let a man who's not saved and probably don't desire to be, come in yo' life—better yet into yo' house and turn mind tricks on you?... Huh?...Lord please have mercy on this woman... Look, just repent and ask the Lord to forgive you and move on."

"Salva I appreciate you're preached words but I don't need you to preach to me right now, I need you to listen and just pray for me later. I don't know what's about to happen. I just need some time to think." I sat at the table and put my head down.

"Think about what?"

I raised my head up and looked up at her. "Think about my future, my daughter's future, and my happiness."

"Future? You're about to have a wonderful blessed future with a fine wholesome man who loves you. Do you hear me?" She came over and shook my shoulders. "Do you hear me Barina? You better not mess this up. I don't care if Wayne is the biological father, that don't mean nothin'... I'm gon' leave you on that note. Just remember these words, ain't no man's money gon' make you happy without Jesus." She walked out the house with the cookie sheet in one hand, and an attitude in the other.

Why do I feel as though my life is about to go down a different road?

Chapter Ten

I woke up out of a dream in a huge ring of sweat. It was about Wayne and me. I tossed and turned tryin' to go back to sleep afterwards but couldn't so I went downstairs, made me some fresh cappuccino, sat at the table, and thought about how that dream shook me.

All I could see in the dream was Wayne and I with fire all around us in a room full of darkness. Then I saw Solomon in the corner of the room looking at us with an overwhelmingly sad expression on his face. It was one that I'll never forget. I could feel the pain of his hurt in the dream, even after I woke up. That's how real it was. I can never tell Solomon what I allowed to happen last night with Wayne. I just can't.

Solomon was not a minute early and not a minute too late, he was right on time as he rang the doorbell. I had just enough time to throw on one of my solid bright red dress suit's and my red and black leopard strap-over high heals I have in my walk in closet.

He rang the doorbell again. I quickly ran and opened it without hesitation.

"Good morning sweetheart." He reached to hug me.

"Good morning. How you feel?" I said, noticing that I looked at him differently but he didn't notice.

"I feel great; you look breath taking as usual, and you smell good too." He sniffed the perfume I sprayed on my wrist and neck.

"Thank you."

"Let me turn on the alarm stay right there." I ran to the hall closet and as I was just about to set the alarm, the phone ranged.

143

"Hey, baby the phone is ringing!" He yelled from the front door.

I came out of the closet trying to ignore it. But Solomon wouldn't let me. The phone ranged again. "Barina you don't hear your phone ringing?"

"I hear it but we gotta' go, church'll be startin' soon and I know you don't wanna' be late?"

"Barina go answer the phone." He pointed towards the kitchen where the phone is.

I went and answered the phone without looking at the caller ID. "Hello?"

"Hey beautiful."

"Who is this? No thank you I won't be buying it…" I slammed the phone down with Solomon looking straight at me. "Lord those teller marketer's get on my nerves. They don't care when they call. They'll call you on a Sunday mornin' and know they need to be at church somewhere." I tried smiling but for some reason I think Solomon saw the big lie I just told. I tried walking passed him but he stood in the way.

"Who was that?"

"I told you it was a teller marketer." I brushed passed him and walked to the front door. He stood in the hallway staring at me. Never saying a word he followed me to the truck, got in without opening up my side first, and drove us on to church.

Church service was one that I'll never forget. I was convicted the entire time. I couldn't stay still in my seat. Everything the Pastor said applied to me. He talked about the lust of the flesh, the lust of the eyes, and the pride of life. *(I John 2:16)* I mean he broke it all the way down to real life situations. He said that right when the Lord's about to bless you, the devil will come with his counterfeits, meaning unreal blessings. Then he talked about loving the things of the world and if any man loves the things of the world, then the Father (God) is not in him. *(I John 2:15)* All I could think about was Wayne. I know he's probably not the one for me but I have to do what's best for Karina. I gotta' get my child back. She means the world to me. But I love Solomon and I do want to be his wife and live happily ever after. But I don't know if that's ganna' happen.

144

Things were pretty quiet on the way home. Out of nowhere Solomon says, "So are you ready to tell me what's goin' on with you?"

"Nothin."

"That's all you ganna' say?"

"What do you want me to say?"

"I want you to say what's on your mind." He pulled up in the driveway and shut the motor off.

"Solomon, I have a lot on my mind. But I don't wanna' talk about it right now."

"See this' the kind of things we gotta' get passed. We gotta' be able to work out anything that comes our way." He turned the music all the way down. "Barina can I ask you something?" I didn't answer I just looked at him. "Do you still want to marry me?"

"Why're you jumpin' to conclusions? All I said is that I don't wanna' talk right now?" I opened the door and got out leaving the door open.

"Ok. Fine. I'll leave it alone. Just know that I love you Barina and I want you to be my wife. And yes you are the wife that God has for me so don't be confused." I shut the door as he started up the truck, watched me walk to the front door, and pulled out of the drive way and drove off down the street.

I couldn't wait for him to get out of sight before the tears came streaming down my face. Why does life have to be so difficult? Why do I have to make these detrimental decisions? I feel like that's the last time Solomon'll ever be over my house.

As soon as I got in the house the phone was ringing off the hook. I ran and answered it. "Hello?"

"What's up Barina? Why you hung up in my face this mornin'? You couldn't tell yo' man the truth?"

"Wayne I'm not fixin' to stay on this phone and let you talk crazy to me."

"Wait! I'm just messin' with chu' woman." He laughed. "Look we're leavin' tonight to go to Chicago to play the big boys. I got some extra time and I'm not too far from yo' house so I was wonderin' if I can take you to get chu' a bite to eat? I know yo' man ain't fed you cause' if he did, you wouldn't be there right now. And if he was there with you I know you wouldn't have answered the phone—so talk to me?"

Why is he all up in this house? That is so true. I am hungry, and Solomon didn't offer to stop and feed me so... "I guess I can do that."

"Cool. I'll be there in about five minutes."

"Alright. Look don't get cho' hopes up. I'm still with Solomon and I still love him."

"That's cool. I ain't doin' the talkin' you are."

"Bye Wayne." We both hung up the phone.

It was less than five minutes and Wayne was knocking at my double glass front door. I opened it, we went and got in the truck, and drove off.

"So where can a brotha' get chu' some substance?" He asked never looking in my direction.

"I want some lobster."

"Dawg' woman you are expensive. I like that in a woman who knows what she wants."

"What did I tell you about them tied ol' lines?" I looked at him crazy.

"Tied? I ain't tied. I've always been a mac daddy." He smiled with confidence.

"I hate to burst yo' bubble, but you ain't all that."

"I hear ya', I hear ya'. So what chu' gon' do with that big fat check I just gave you?" He quickly looked over at me and then back at the road.

"Umph'."

"Not that you need it and all. Girl you got mo' money than me and my grandma' put together." He laughed at himself like what he said was really funny.

"Don't worry bout' what I'm gon' do, you just worry bout' what chu' gon' say to your daughter."

"I know right?"

"Yes sir."

"And you say you don't know where she is?"

"Everything I told you is all I know." We got quiet.

"That's messed up. I don't understand how you gon' just let yo' daughter go just like that?"

"I'm not lettin' her go nowhere. She wanna' be grown, I'm gon' let her get out there and see how grown she is."

"I don't think that's the right way to do it."

"Right now your opinion don't count, invisible daddy."

"Ok, ok you can cool out with the comments. Look Barina like I said before, I know I ain't been there all these years but at least I'm tryin' right now? And look, I just wrote you a fat check. That's more than what any brotha' would do."

I opened my purse that's sittin' between my legs, pulled out a comb, and started combing what lil' curls I got left. I did a lot of sweatin' at church especially when the Pastor was steppin' all on my toes. And I gotta' do something to ignore what Wayne just said so I won't get mad all over again. But I'm thinkin' maybe he's right, I do have to forgive him and give em' another chance because God gave me another chance. *(Luke 17:3-4)*

We turned into the restaurant's parking lot.

"This' a nice restaurant what chu' know about this?" I said laughing as I slapped him on the shoulder.

"Girl you violent, did you take boxing lessons or somethin'?"

"As a matter of fact I didn't. It just comes natural."

"I heard that, I like a strong woman like that." He smiled devilishly.

"Wayne whatever, let's change the subject I was only playing with you."

"That's cool we can do that." He whipped in a parking space so fast I thought he was gon' hit both of the cars beside us.

"You know you... you drive too fast." I said as I got out and started fixing my clothes.

"You don't need to fix yourself up you already look beautiful." He tried to grab my hand to lead us towards the restaurant but I jerked it back.

"Don't touch me. I don't want nobody to see you holding my hand. And anyway I don't want you to hold my hand no way."

I started walking ahead of him like he wasn't with me. He stood there for a moment and then trotted to catch up with me. It's so crowded at the restaurant we had to park almost a mile away. As we got closer, there were some fans who noticed who Wayne was and asked for his autograph. I wasn't left out because right when they spotted him, a group of women came up and asked me for my autograph. So we both were signing autographs together. I thought that was kind of special even though we're not together. Hopefully the

147

thought'll never cross my mind again. I wonder what Solomon's doin'?"

Wayne and I signed our last autograph, went in and got a table before about thirty couples. I guess it pays to be famous. Or should I say it's a blessing. I smiled thinking to myself.

The waiter greeted us and asked us what we were having, we told him, and he left to make the order. Wayne's such a big guy that he can be very intimidating if you don't know him. And I think the waiter was, somewhat.

"So what'll you think about the joint?"

"It's nice. I've been to better places though." I just lied. I know it but I couldn't give him the satisfaction of satisfying his ego cause' it's already too big as it is.

"You know you always got somethin' smart to say. Why can't chu' just relax? Can I enjoy this evening with you or not?"

"Yep, you sure can. Look Wayne I'm not tryin' to be rude or anything but you knew what you were gettin' yo' self into when you asked me out to eat. Better yet when you so called came back into my life."

"I realize that Barina but how can I get chu' past all that?"

"You can't."

"What chu' mean I can't?"

"Just what I said, you can't." I grabbed the glass of ice water from off the table the waiter just brought and took a sip. "Only God can."

"O' Lord here we go with the Jesus stuff."

"You act like that hurt you when I said that?"

"It didn't hurt, it's just not somethin' I wanna' talk about."

"Well you just called His name?"

"When?"

"Just a second ago."

"What did I say?"

"You just said Lord."

"No I didn't."

"Yes you did."

"Ok whatever." He waved his hand at me and started gulping down his ice water.

"I'm ganna' refresh your memory. You said, O' Lord here we go with the Jesus stuff. Did you not just say that?"

"Whatever you got me. I see you're the type of person who just gotta' be right all the time."

"No I'm far from that. You're the type of person who love to use the Lord's Name in vain and then don't wanna' serve Him."

"I do serve the Lord."

"Wayne where do you serve the Lord?"

He waited like it was a hard question. "I serve the Lord right out there on the football field." He laughed so loud people next to us turned and looked.

"See that's what I'm talkin' about. How do you serve Him just out on the football field?"

"When I make a touchdown I point towards the sky."

"And that means what?"

"That means thank you Jesus." He laughed again like I was going to join him but I didn't, I just looked at em'.

"That's not funny. You know there're a lot of people who say the name Jesus or God but don't believe in Him? So they use His Name in vain. Like O' my God, they're really not calling on God, there just using the phrase because it's a familiar phrase.

"Since when did you become a preacher?"

"Look I'm not tryin' to preach I'm just statin' the facts. But I see you can't handle it so I'm a change the subject."

"Good. So where yo' man at?"

"Where did that come from?"

"From my mouth." He smiled. "Na' I'm just playin'. I'm curious to know why you decided to go out to eat with me?"

"Why you always gotta' get so personal? Just enjoy the moment for the moment because there might not be another time." I said.

"Cool, I'm a leave that alone. So when did you start writing books?"

"I started when I was still in high school."

"Hum' I never knew that. So what made you wanna' start writing?"

"I can't explain it. All I can say is that it's a gift. One thing I will say is I would write when things got real hard for Karina and me. You know I used to be homeless?"

"I kind of thought you were, some people around school would say lil' thangs, and you said it yo' self when you came over my house that day."

I broke in. "Ok let's talk about somethin' else, me and that subject don't get along."

"Alright then." Things got quiet. "Barina I just wanna' let chu' know you're the strongest woman I've ever met. And I don't mean that in a bad way."

"Well thank you Wayne that was real nice of you. For a minute there I didn't think you had it in you." We both laughed as the waiter finally brought out our food. We started eating as soon as he placed the plates on the table. Wayne's such a big guy, his rack of ribs was gone in a matter of seconds. What's so funny about it is that's not all he ordered. Now he's on his chicken fettuccini.

It was complete silence as we ate.

Wayne finally spoke up and said, "We gotta' hard game tomorrow. Man we gotta' win this game in order to make it to the play-offs." He put one elbow on the table and threw some fettuccini he had on a fork in his mouth. "Coach said we got the game if we come hard in the beginning."

"So what're you think?"

"I think we can pull it off." He said throwing his napkin on his plate.

As we were talking I didn't notice that a group of men just walked in. And one of em' is oh' my God, Solomon. Before I could hide my face, he turned and saw Wayne and me. He rushed over to the table so fast I didn't have time to warn Wayne.

"So is this how you tell me you don't want to marry me?"

I stood up. "No Solomon please let me explain." I reached to hug him but he pulled away.

All of a sudden Wayne stood up and stuck his hand out and said, "What's up man I'm Barina's baby's daddy."

Before Wayne could get the words out of his mouth good, Solomon punched him right in the mouth. Blood flew on the table. Wayne quickly retrieved himself and they started wrestling on the floor, on the tables, picking up chairs and throwing plates that were on the tables. People are screaming and running towards the front entrance.

I started yelling. "Somebody stop em'! Don't just look, stop em'! Somebody stop em'!" I yelled so loud. And I kept yelling until some of Solomon's friends jumped in and pulled them apart. Solomon's friends dragged him out while he was still going back and forth with Wayne with words. The owner ran out from the back and told Wayne he was going to call the police. Wayne ran back to the back with the owner and that's where he is now.

I never would have imagined in my wildest dreams that something like this would happen. I can forget about a wedding. I just lost the love of my life. I know Solomon don't wanna' be with me anymore now. Kinda' made me mad because it's like he didn't even trust me. He just saw us together and over reacted. Wayne finally came from the back, grabbed my arm, and pulled me out of the restaurant like a daddy pulls his child out of church when they're actin' up. I didn't resist because I knew he was mad and I wanted to make sure I had a ride home. It's way too far to walk.

Wayne's running lights, tailgating cars, and cursing out every car he passes up. I can see anger written all over his face. I dare not say a word.

We made it to my house in seconds. He pulled in the driveway going as fast as he was driving. I quickly threw open the door and just as I was about to get out he put his hand on my thigh and said, "Wait." I turned and pulled my leg back in the truck, leaving the door open. "I just wanna' apologize for what I did in the restaurant." He tried wiping the dry blood from his mouth but it wouldn't come off. "I would never do anything to embarrass you Barina. He came at me first."

"I understand Wayne. And you right he did hit you first. So it's not your fault."

"If he wasn't cho' man, I'd a killed em'."

"Somehow or another I believe you."

"Yep I sure would have." He nodded his head like he was assuring himself. "I just hope I didn't ruin things with you and him?" He turned and looked at me.

"You didn't. If it's ruined it's between me and him." I got out of the truck and closed the door.

He let the window down. "Alright then, hey you mind if I come in and wash this dry blood off my face, I promise that's all I'm gon' do?"

"Come on."

We both walked in the house and I led him to the front bathroom. He washed his mouth and left just like he said he would.

My life has just made a turn for the worse. I never realized that choices could become so detrimental. If you make one wrong decision

151

you can loose it all. It's a trip because a person can have all the money in the world and still be unhappy. And right now I feel just like that person—horrible. I lost my baby, I just lost my one and only love, and now it feels like I'm loosing my mind. Where do I go? Who do I turn too? I guess that's why a person should never play with fire because it'll turn around and burn you. I should've never gone out with Wayne. I entertained the devil and when God made a way of escape, I didn't take it. *(1 Corinthians 10:13)* And now I know I got a lot of time to think about it because I know Solomon don't want nothin' else to do with me. I wouldn't dare call and tell Salva what happen. She wouldn't understand no way. This Christian walk is so hard, but can't nobody take the blame for it but me. I'm making it hard. I allowed this man I haven't seen in years come back into my life and bring past feelings and emotions back to my heart, and made me turn from the man I was destined to be with. Solomon was perfect—just perfect. I should call em'? He probably would hang up in my face. All I can think about is what's best for Karina. I love my daughter and I really want her to come home. Whatever it takes that's what I gotta' do. It seem like nobody understands that but me. Not Salva, not Salvester, not Precious, not Wayne and surely not Solomon, even though I never had the nerve to tell him the truth.

Chapter Eleven

*I*t's goin' on five years now and my life has made a 360-degree turn for the worse. All I can do is lie in this bed, eat me a big ol' bag of cheetos, and think about how this sad love story went sour.

After the day Solomon and Wayne had that fight, Wayne and I started dating and three month's later he asked me to marry him. I said yes without hesitation. Solomon went back and told Salva and Salvester what happened at the restaurant and I am assuming that that's why they haven't spoken to me since then. I tried calling her but she refused to talk to me. All she ask me was, why did I hurt Solomon. After a while I got tired of tryin' so I just gave up. This is the first time Salva and I have ever been apart since from the time we first became friends. All this is over some man, how crazy does that sound? It's been just that long since I seen Karina. She just kind of disappeared from off the face of the earth. I'll find her one day.

Wayne made so many promises before he put this huge million dollar diamond rock on my finger that he's failed to keep. One of em' was that he was gon' find Karina which was one of the reason's why I married em' in the first place. And another one was that he would never hurt me, which was another lie. That's all he's been doing. If he's not hittin' on me, he's out all night with some other woman. He's a totally different person from when he first came back into my life. He was nice, patient, and considerate. But now he's a demon from Hell. After Wayne's games he goes straight to the bar. He never calls to say when he's back in town; I have to see it on the news. Sometimes I sit up all night long waiting for him to come home. And when he finally

153

does, questioning him is out of the question because a backhand follows if I try. I'm so stupid, how could I have ever thought that choosin' the baby's daddy was the best choice over a single, no kid's, never been married, saved, sanctified, and Holy Ghost filled man who was madly in love with God and me? It was Satan. He had me looking at the money and the biological daddy thing and not at what God said. Solomon was my soul-mate and I knew it, I wish I could turn back the hands of time but I can't. I didn't realize that I had all these hidden demons from my past that was haunting me day and night. When Solomon came into my life I couldn't believe that he could help erase all of them. Now I'm thinking, maybe we moved too fast? I don't know. I thought, as I let my imagination run wild.

The phone rang. I answered it on the first ring. "Hello?"

"Hello? Is Wayne there?"

It sounds like a young lady's voice. I can't tell who it is though. "Who is this?" She hung up the phone. I wonder who that was, probably one of his women?

Wayne finally came in after being gone for I don't know how long. He took off his clothes and dropped em' right in the middle of the floor like I'm supposed to pick em' up right behind him. He hasn't spoken to me yet. He went in the bathroom and took a shower that lasted about an hour. He just came out and still not saying nothin' like a big ol' kid. The way he's actin' they must've lost and probably not goin' to the play-offs? Inside I'm happy. He don't deserve good things to happen for him especially when he's doin' bad things to me. I smirked to myself. He walked in the walk-in closet, changed into some goin' out clothes, walked over to my bed and tried to kiss me goodbye but I turned my cheek and said, "Where are you goin'?"

"What I tell you about askin' me that?"

"Forget it Wayne I don't feel like fightin' with you just go."

"Oh' I'm goin' anyway. You ain't runnin' nothin' but cho' mouth." He walked to the door and turned around. "By the way, I found yo' daughter." He tried walking out of the room but I ran and almost tackled him on the floor.

"You found Karina? Where? Please tell me Wayne!"

"If you get off me I will." I moved back. "I saw her and her husband at this club I was at last night. I remembered how she looked on the

154

picture you had hangin' up in yo' house a long time ago. I introduced myself; she introduced herself and her husband to me..."

I broke in. "So how did she know it was really you?"

"Who don't know me?" He pointed to himself. "She saw me on one of your pictures you hand in yo' photo album a long time ago. She didn't quite know who I was, all she knew was that I was a professional football player. But last night it didn't take her long to receive her daddy." He smiled. "That's a shame I had to find my own daughter after all these years." He walked downstairs and yelled back up to me as I stood upstairs looking down from the balcony. "I got her phone number too..."

"You what?" I ran downstairs. "Give it to me Wayne."

"Look I'm gon' call her first. You'll see her when she comes over here. And don't get cho' hopes up cause' she still don't know you're here."

"I'm not worried about all that. Just get my daughter over here."

"Yea' well whatever you just gon' have to wait." He said walking out of the house and closing the front door behind him.

I ran back upstairs and tore the room up lookin' for her phone number. I didn't think about it but that may have been her who called earlier. Let me go look on the caller ID.

I ran and looked on the cordless phone for the number. But it showed up unlisted, so much for that. I went and got back in the bed in tears hoping that she would call again but she didn't.

Yesterday came and went. The days seem to be going by so fast. I can't tell what day it is. I'm sure it has to do with the fact that I'm depressed. I think I'm wailing in a state of depression. I've lost who I am and who I used to be. In the past there was no way a man would ever be able to control and dominate me. It's like I ain't got no more fight in me. He's torn my self-esteem down to the lowest. I don't have confidence in myself anymore, I'm not assertive like I used to be, my faith is zero, and I feel like a scared lil' ol' puppy that's being controlled by its over-bearing master. I don't go nowhere, all I do is sit around here and wait on him to get home so I can have his food cooked and ready—like some kinda' slave. I'm livin' in a house that I didn't even decorate. If I move the furniture or the flowers around, he goes into a burning rage and starts hittin' on me. He's very abusive. He beats on me like I'm some kind of rag doll. He would beat me naked. There are times when

I come out of the shower; he would be standing there waiting on me with his fist balled up, like some mad monster. All because he would be mad at one of his mistresses and he would find something to beat on me about. I'm dead in my own house. I'm glad I went and got on birth control without him knowing it because I don't wanna' have a child by him. This is not what I imagined a marriage to be. I thought it was supposed to be a two-way thing? I thought it was supposed to work both ways? She plays a part and sho' nuff' he plays a part too? But that's not the case here. He don't do nothin'. He never encourages me on my past successes, and getting pampered with flowers and gifts are totally out of the question. He's stopped all of my plans and dreams; all he does is talk about his career and what he wants, and who did what to him. He don't want me goin' out with nobody. If I start hangin' with some friends, he gets mad and tells me to cut the friendship. And I do it just to keep peace. It's one thing to have a man whose head of the house and makes wise Godly decisions for the house, than to have a controlling, abusive, jealous, insecure, immature, dominating, and manipulating man as a husband. *(Proverbs 6:34)* And he is all the above. I thought.

Wayne just walked in. I just heard the front door slam.

He called me from downstairs.

"Wayne, you called me?"

As I started running down the curving stairs without hesitation, all I could see is this silhouette of a young girl standing beside him looking up at me. My first thoughts are I know he's not messin' with young girls too, and my next thought is, he got the audacity to bring home a woman and introduce her to me in my own house? Hopefully he gon' tell me that he don't want me no more, that way I could get oughta' here today without delay. But when I got down there, it was a whole different story. We all just looked at each other as if to say what's next? I finally reached to hug Karina. I can feel her slightly pull away. After all this time she still hasn't forgiven me. Wayne walked off going towards the movie room. I motioned for Karina to follow me to the living room but she refused, said she wanted to stay where she was because she wouldn't be long.

"Do you wanna' stay for dinner?"

"No that won't be necessary." She walked to the door and grabbed the doorknob.

I walked up to her and put my hand on her hand. She looked down at it. "Karina are you sure you don't wanna' stay and talk, I haven't seen nor heard from you in years? I missed you?"

"I gotta' go can you go get my daddy?"

My lips wouldn't say another word especially after she said the words my daddy. Out of all these years of him never being in her life, she calls him daddy. And I've taken care of her even with my own life. And from a little slap, she don't have two words to say to me. "Wait right here." I went and got him and walked off going back to my room. I could hear her say somethin' like what is she doin' here? And I need some money. I can't believe my own child has totally disowned me. She acts like I never gave birth to her. Her and Wayne are still talking and that's the way I left em'. This room has become my sanctuary. As big as this mansion is I don't wanna' go nowhere else in it but right in here.

Wayne finally came up to the room after about forty-five minutes. I guess him and Karina had been talking that long.   "Why did you act like that with Karina? Now she's all mad and she said she ain't comin' back over here? I can't count on you to do nothin' right. I tried to get cho' daughter back and you just threw her away again. You ain't nothin' but an unfit motha'." He yelled as he pointed his finger in my face and pushed my forehead backwards. Of course as usual I didn't do nothin' just took whatever he said and hid it in my heart.

That day came and went with Wayne goin' out again and coming back home drunk. He's still sleep with a hang over. I dare not wake him up. I love it when he's sleep cause' then he ain't torturing me. I went and put dinner on and started washing clothes.

The phone ranged. The caller ID said unlisted. I better answer it before it wakes Wayne up and I gotta' hear his mouth.

"Hello?"

"Is Wayne there?"

"Who's speaking?"

They waited for a minute before answering. "This is Karina." She said sounding like she had been crying.

"What's wrong? Are you ok?"

"Can you just put my daddy on the phone?" She yelled.

I'm not gon' even contest to that. I went upstairs and told Wayne to pick up the other phone. I walked back downstairs, hung up the phone and finished doing what I was doing before she called. I'm not gon' beg for her love, I'll just wait til' she's ready to give it to me—if ever.

"I'll be back." Wayne ran by me, grabbed some cookies from the cookie jar and ran out of the house. I didn't even ask him where he was goin' I just kept mopping the kitchen floor.

Three hours later Wayne and Karina came back in with bags and suitcases in their hands, and what look like this three-year-old baby girl came slowly walking in right behind her. I just watched from the balcony. They never looked up until all of their bags were inside.

The little girl looks around as if to be lost. I just went back to my room with my head down. I can't understand if Karina needed a place to stay why didn't she ask me on the phone, I am her mother? This' really hurting me and I don't know what to do.

Wayne came running upstairs like he had been out on the field working out. "Why you not downstairs? Don't chu' wanna' see yo' daughter and grandchild?" He smirked then walked back downstairs and started playing with the little girl.

I walked downstairs without a grin on my face. "So who's the lil' girl?" I asked, undoubtedly nobody said nothin' so I asked again. "So who's the lil' girl?" Nobody still said nothin', then all of a sudden the little girl walked over to me like she knew I was her grandmother. I hugged her while looking at Karina and Wayne. They both stared at each other without an expression.

The little baby asked, "Who are you?"

"I'm your grandmother."

"Grandmama?"

"Yea' I'm yo' mama's mama."

Karina came running over and grabbed her out of my arms, which I'm not surprised. Wayne just sat there grinnin' the whole time. I think he likes the fact that there's division between Karina and I with his evil self. He gets off on it every chance he gets, as if to say now take that after all these years.

Karina and the baby have been stayin' here for about two days now. Our conversation hasn't gotten better at all. I stay to myself and she stays to hers. Wayne's the only one she'll talk too. The house is big enough to where we can go days without seeing each other if we wanted too.

I'm vacuuming the upstairs balcony area. Wayne and Karina just ran to the front window and looked out. Somebody just threw and huge rock through it. I stopped vacuuming and just stood there and looked down at em'. Wayne took off running after the car but he couldn't catch em'. Karina ran out to the front yard and watched.

Wayne came back with Karina behind saying, "I knew he would find me! I can't hide from him cause' he's gon' find me every where I try to go." She's hysterical.

"Look calm down. Ain't nobody gon' do nothin' to you. That dude ain't bold enough to mess with this."

"Look like it to me, he just threw this." She picked up the rock from off the floor. "Trust me you don't wanna' mess with this man, he's crazy."

"I'm crazy too." He said. Ain't that the truth I said to myself.

"I mean it daddy." Karina insisted.

"I mean it too. The only reason why he was able to throw that rock through my window is because I left the front gate open."

"He followed us I know he did." She plopped down on the couch, pushed her hands in her face, and started crying.

"Karina you ain't got time to be no big baby about this. He ain't gon' hurt chu'."

She jumped up and threw her hands up. "You don't understand what I've been goin' through, I've already been through so much with him! I know it's because I got an abortion while we were married! *(Revelation 9:21) (Matthew 15:19)* He beats me, he stalks me, and he's even molesting my lil' girl!" She dropped back down on the couch and put her head in her lap.

Wayne looked up at me. My heart sank right in my chest. My own life just flashed before me. That sounds just like what I'm goin' through. I'm sure that's why Wayne looked up at me because he knows how bad he's treatin' me. It's funny how you can be blind to your own problems, but open to other people's problems. I wanna' hear what he gotta' say to that.

"Well I don't know what to tell you. You need to leave that no good fa' nothin' fool alone. He's too old for you anyway Karina. You can do better than that."

She looked up at him. "It's easy for you to say you big time football player. You ain't gotta' worry in the world. You got everything here, the house, the cars, the good family life, and it looks like you and her are gettin' along?" She jumped to her feet and yelled. "You don't understand my situation I need this man! My baby needs this man! I don't have no job, no money, and no place to stay! And I ain't stayin' here forever!" She waited. "This man's crazy and he will kill you daddy if you cross him wrong. I'm just lettin' you know."

"Look I ain't scared of nobody. I'm yo' daddy and I'm here to protect you. You got that?" He looked up at me again; I rolled my eyes, looked away, left the vacuum sittin' there and went back in the room.

They talked for about another hour or so. I fell asleep. When I woke up and went downstairs, him, Karina, and the baby was lookin' at TV.

I haven't cooked yet and I can already feel him about to fuss.

"Say it's about time you woke up! We been sittin' down here hungry and you act like we don't even exist!" He rushed over and slapped me right in the face. The force threw me against the wall. I shook my head to shake away the stars that's floating right before my eyes. It took Karina and the baby by surprise. They jumped like he just hit them too, their eyes widened and a little smirk came across Karina's face.

"Wayne stop I'm tired of you hittin' on me!" I screamed, as I tried to run towards the kitchen.

"Naw' umh' umh' come back here!" He grabbed me by my hair and slung me around. "You ain't tired cause' you keep on doin' the same things over and over!" He backhanded me right in the face. The force of his punch threw me to the floor. Blood seeped out of the corner of my mouth. Karina didn't say a word she just kept on watching. "See Karina yo' no good fa' nothin' mama make me do this to her! Wit' her dirty self! Now go upstairs and clean yo' self up! Stupid just stupid…" He walked off and went outside. Karina and the baby's eyes followed me until I vanished around the upstairs wall to my bedroom.

I cried on into the next morning.

My mind is made up. I'm gon' leave Wayne. I've gotta' get oughta' here. If I stay here another day either I'm gon' kill him, or I'm gon' kill myself. But for some small reason I still love him. If only he would just act right we could have the world. O' but what a dream that is. I thought looking out of the window at my next door neighbor. She's an elderly white lady with long blondish black hair down to her waist, gray eyes, and freckles. She looks to be real pleasant and nice. But Looks can be deceiving though; unfortunately I found this out the hard way. My face is still a little swollen from his punches. She's watering her garden. I guess I could go water his ol' tied weeds I ain't tryin' to get it lookin' like hers I just need somethin' to do. I thought as I left going downstairs and out to the backyard.

She did her thing and I did mine. As long as I've been livin' here I haven't ever talked to my neighbors let alone gotten to know em'. They probably wouldn't talk to me no way. I'm sure my conversation wouldn't amuse her anyway. At this point in my life I wouldn't be good conversation for anybody. She looks like she has way too much wisdom for me. She wouldn't wanna' fool with somebody so young and way out of her league.

Out of nowhere she yelled, "Hey how ya' doin'? Wanna' come help me water my garden?" Her yells squeezed through the open burglar bars that are separating her yard from ours.

I didn't answer the first time so she repeated. It's not that I don't wanna' talk to her, I'm just shocked and tryin' to find the right words to say. It's been awhile since I had a conversation with somebody let alone an intelligent elderly white woman. She probably feels sorry for me by the looks of Wayne's weed garden. I finally got the nerve to speak up. "Ah' yes mam' I'm fine!" I yelled back as she walked up to her burglar bared fence. "I really don't know anything about watering a garden so I'm sure you wouldn't want my help!" I picked at the weeds.

"Awh' come on, you're the perfect helper." She put her hands on the fence. "I have plenty of gloves so you won't cut your hands up, I know you wanna' keep em' nice and soft for your hubby?"

I'm thinkin', hubby? Yea' right, not at all. "O' ok um', I well, I really don't think so."

"Ah' come on you're too young to be so indecisive."

Man that's a big word. I haven't ever used that in any of my books. I thought walking over towards the fence. "Ok since you put it like that, I guess I can help you out." I said, hoping she'd change her mind, but she didn't.

161

We ended up working on her entire garden and then she came and redid Wayne's entire weed garden. We worked from sun up to almost sun down. I'm surprised that she never asked me why my face was so swollen. I'm glad Wayne had football games out of town and won't be back til' about a week. Thank God. I know he would've had a problem with me being out there that long.

Ms. Mattie's her name. She ended up being what I thought she was a nice, pleasant, and sweet spirited lady. It's funny because she was tryin' to witness to me on the cool.

(Isaiah 55:4) She invited me to church but I declined because I knew Wayne would disagree. And just maybe I'm not ready yet. I mean, I know I need to go but I really don't think I'm ready to commit myself considering the circumstances I'm in right now. One thing that the old lady said that really stuck in my mind was that God is soon to come and to make sure that I'm ready when He comes back for His people. And I realize that tomorrow's not promised I can be here today and gone the next... But I just can't right now, I just can't. *(Matthew 24)* But for some reason I feel this strong urgency to get right deep down in the crevices of my stomach, and I can hear God's still small voice sayin', *"Hear my voice. I'm standing at the door, all you have to do is knock... and I'll come in..." (Revelation 3:20)*

Karina's on the sofa with her head down, which isn't anything abnormal. She's always walkin' around here in her pity parties and sleepin' all day. But it's somethin' about today that seems different though. I don't know what it is. I just got this eerie feeling for some reason. I went out to the mailbox and came back in and sat on one of the ottomans and kept thumbing through the mail thinking....

I see my books haven't been selling by the looks of my sales report. The mortgage company's been houndin' me about my mortgage payments. I haven't been able to make a payment since I first moved in with Wayne. The mortgage company said if I miss another payment, they gon' take my mansion from me. That's all I got left besides the clothes on my back. I sold my truck when I got late on my payments a while ago. The sad thing about it is that he won't give me the money to pay off my house. Said that I don't need another home, everything belongs to him. This huge mansion, all seven cars sittin' outside, and all the pension plans 401k's, the stocks, Karina, and ain't no tellin' whatever else. He tricked me into signing off my name on it all by asking me to sign a bunch of papers after he had his way with me in the bed. It had been a long time since we even touched one another so I was worn out afterwards and he figured that was the right time to do it. Well it worked. I didn't even read em' because I trusted him and was caught up in the moment. After all he is my husband and shouldn't nothin' be wrong with that. If I don't remember nothin' else about what the bible says, I do remember it saying when you are married the bed is undefiled. *(Hebrews 13:4)* But it's when your not married is when it's a sin because then its fornication. (Sex before marriage) *(Galatians 5:19) (1 Thessalonians 4:3)* I went and sat down on the sofa across from Karina.

I love my mansion. It was my first home, and a perfect dream home at that. It's all I got left and I feel as though I'm about to loose it. I was doin' the apartment thang' up until out of nowhere the Lord allowed my books to become bestsellers and the money started rollin' in. And I mean that literally. The first thing I bought was my truck, then my house, pampered Karina with gifts and money, and then I bought Salva and Salvester a home and a car. If I loose my home, I'll loose my mind and go crazy.

Karina and I suddenly jumped up off the sofa and ran towards the kitchen to somebody bamming on the front door—Sayin' not a word, just bammin' like somebody loosing their mind. They bammed again then stopped. Karina's husband's been stalking her every move, I wouldn't be surprised if it's him. Karina ran to the back of the house to lock the patio door but it was too late. He came rushing through the patio door and grabbed Karina around the neck yelling, "where's my child? I tol' you you ain't gon' never get away from me! I own you! Do you hear me? I own you! I'll kill you before I let chu' leave me!"

All I could do is watch with fear and call on the Name of Jesus, which I hadn't done in a long time. He threw her down on the floor, pulled out a knife, and tried to stab her but she kicked him in the face throwing him on the kitchen table and breaking it. He laid there as if he was unconscious as we both ran upstairs, grabbed the baby, and went and hid in the workout room closet like our lives depended on it. As we hid, the sounds of sirens in the distance cluttered the air. For some reason I knew then that he was gone.

We stayed in the closet for what seemed like forever. Neither one of us said a word, which wasn't nothin' new. The police got here fast. Its weird cause' neither one of us called em'. I wonder who did? I asked myself. The police asked Karina and me a bunch of questions after they made us come outside. Some were important and some weren't. The police said that when they got here, he was nowhere to be found. It could be that after she kicked him on the table, he heard the sirens and took off.

Karina asked him. "How did you know we needed help?"

"Somebody called from this address and we came right out mam'." My jaw dropped. They looked at each other and we did too, even though we still don't talk to each other. In my heart I know it had to be God, He's the only one who can work miracles like this. *(Galatians 3:5)*. Its amazing cause' all I did was call His name and He answered me in an instant despite how I've been livin'. *(Romans 10:13)* It's funny how a person can call on the Name Jesus when they're in a desperate situation.

Karina told the police that she was scared of him and scared for her life. She couldn't get a restraining order because her address is still with him. So they said that they would do extra patrolling around the house and the neighborhood. It was good to hear that they were ganna' also tighten up on security at the check in station before anybody can drive in the neighborhood. Karina seemed relieved but she was still shaking from the trauma and I was too.

"Are you ok?" One of the police asked.

"Yea' I'm fine I'm just still shaken up. I'm more shaken up because he only used to beat me up, but now he's using knives and talkin' about killing me." She sat down on the ground and placed the baby between her legs.

"Mam' you have nothing to worry about, we're going to do everything in our power to protect you and your family."

"I wish my daddy was here."

I walked back in the house after hearing that.

After all the police and fire trucks cleared out, Karina came back in and went upstairs to bed. And I went and sat out on the patio and said in my heart that I would give my life back to the Lord if He finds me a church home.

I can't believe I was too scared to help my own child insomuch that I would watch an outrageously gruesome, contentious man that was so full of false vengeance and rage, try to hurt her. I know in my heart that it didn't have anything to do with the fact that she and I still aren't talkin'. At this point in my life I've learned that you never know what you would do until you're faced with the situation. So many things run through your mind at one time. All bodily functions shut down and you're only survivin' off of adrenalin. If a person's never believed in God, in the mist of what just happened, trust me somewhere during all that they'd call on Him quick—I did.

Ms. Mattie just came out and walked towards the fence. "Do you mind if I come over?" She yelled.

Still a bit shaken up I tried yelling back to her. "No I just wanna' be alone!"

"I understand."

She slowly started walking back towards her house. But for some reason she stopped as if to wait for me to change my mind. So I did. "Ms. Mattie! How long will it take for you to get over here?"

"Not long with my runnin' shoes." She said as we both laughed. She came quicker than I thought she would. She came through the unlocked gate that was left open from Karina's husband. "Hi ya' doin'?" She sat in the patio chair across from me.

"Fine." I said, still shaken up from what happened earlier with Karina's husband.

"I'm not going to keep you long. I just wanted to come over and check on you and to personally apologize to you for asking you to come to church with me the other day. I realized that my timing wasn't the best choice and I'm sure that's what startled you."

"Thanks for checkin' on me, and no it didn't startle me. As a matter of fact you didn't have to come and apologize. I believe you were supposed to ask me that. God wants everybody to be saved and to live for Him." *(Romans 10:9) (Colossians 3:3)*

"You're such a gifted young lady. I'm an old woman now and I look at you, you have a chance to let God use you. When I first saw you I knew that you were a nice person. It was somethin' different about you. Are you a minister?"

"No mam'."

My attention is straight on her.

"God is definitely with you. You are a very gifted young lady."

"How can God be with me out of all that I'm going through?"

"Are you dead?"

"What? Of course not. You talkin' to me aren't you?"

"I'm serious."

"I don't mean to sound disrespectful, but I'm serious too."

"God has so much in store for you. And it's better than the evidence that's written all over your face." I just looked at her. "Come to church with me. I believe in your heart you really want too."

"Hum...you right."

"So how bout' Sunday morning?"

"That's fine. I'll be ready." We stood up.

"Ok, what's your phone number so I will not have to put on my running shoes even though I don't run?" She laughed like her joke was funny but it wasn't.

"My number is 621-8654."

"She grabbed a piece of paper and a pen from off the table and wrote the number down. "Ok I have it and I'll call you. Stay encouraged." She walked off going back across the yard to her house.

This woman has so much grace about her I couldn't tell her no if I wanted too. Her asking me about being a minister didn't come as a surprise. I remember years ago when Salva first met me she asked me the same thing. I know God has somethin' for me to do and it's left up to me to do it. I didn't hesitate saying yes that I would go to church with her because Wayne's still out of town and I probably won't see him until Monday. I don't know what'll happen after that.

The week went by fast. Karina took the baby and left that same night that all that went down. I haven't seen her since. I didn't ask her where she was goin' and she didn't offer. Wayne never calls when he's out of town so he still doesn't know what happened and with Karina up and leavin'. I noticed before she left her stomach seemed a little pudgy. I hope she's not pregnant. I'm so glad to have the house all to myself I just wish I knew where she went for the sake of the baby.

It seems like Sunday was just yesterday. Ms. Mattie called me bright and early this mornin'. She was so excited that she had some loud church music goin' in the background that made it hard for me to hear her. She told me to meet her in the front of my house. She was gon' drive around and pick me up.

Now she's rollin' up in a crimson-cream, four-door 2004 Cadillac. Old women always get these kinds of cars. It fits em' well though. They're just satisfied with their 55 miles per hour on the freeways, and

20 miles per hour on the streets. I laughed to myself. Well I take that back. All elderly women don't roll like that because I saw one in a mustang with a roarin' v8 engine. We were at a stoplight. She was already roarin' her engine daring me to take off first. When the light turned green, she spun out kickin' dust all over my windshield. It was so funny. Mama wasn't playin'. I laughed at the thought.

Ms. Mattie's church is about fifteen minutes away, in fact right down the street from our neighborhood. I'm surprised I never seen it because I'm well aware of my surroundings. I was shocked when I walked in the church. I mean I'm not tryin' to judge or anything, but Ms. Mattie didn't strike me as a lady who knows how to get her groove on for the Lord. Like the ol' folks used to say—cut a rug. I laughed quietly. She strikes me as a lady who rocks in her rocking chair all day reading the bible. Dancin' in the Spirit was the last thing on my mind. I can't stop laughing. She was all over that church and everybody else was too. I can't talk because somehow or another it transferred on me and I couldn't stop dancin' and praising the Lord either. I've never experienced that in my life, not even in my old church. Or should I say my parent's old church. And they were some floor stompin', tambourine playin', and some sangin' sangin' sangin' folks. I can remember the sounds of soulful spiritual melodies floating through the atmosphere, and even outside of the church as everybody walked up wearing their Sunday hats, with beautiful bright colored designer dresses and suits. The sounds made you wanna' go in, fall out on the altar, and beg God for forgiveness. That's how awesome and convicting the praises were. Well, that church don't have nothin' on this church. Not only does this church have the presence of God there, but it also has His love. It was all in the people. They were all so loving and they reached out to me. And because of it, I was able to break through and break out of all the bondage and baggage that was weighin' me down for years. I gave my life back to God. I strayed away from Him in the past but this time I gave Him my whole heart, mind, Spirit, and soul. *(St. Mark 12:30)* The bible says that love covers the multitude of sins. *(1 Peter 4:8)* That's why it pays to love. Because you can save somebody's life just by showin' em' that you love them, and that you care. That's all people want. L-o-v-e. But the world don't show nothin' but hate, and that's why there's so much murder and crime. I'm not just talkin' about God's people lovin' God's people and hating those that are not of God. But we should love everybody because when Jesus was here on this earth, He loved everybody even His enemies. *(Mark 14:43-52) (Luke 23:34)* He didn't just love those who looked good, dressed good, or even those who smelled good, but He loved everybody. And this is what brings people to Christ. People don't wanna' know about religion, they wanna' know who Jesus really is and how much He loves them no matter what they've done in their past—without condemning them, because God doesn't come to condemn us. *(Romans 8:1)* It's funny because I remember reading in the bible where the woman was caught in adultery and everybody was about to stone her because of what she had done, but Jesus wrote in the sand and said, "...He that is without sin among you, let him cast the first stone." And because everybody there had sinned, they couldn't stone her nor could they judge her. So they dropped their stones and left. *(John 8:1-11)* God doesn't judge us about our sins after we have repented; He convicts us to get right and to stay right. *(Romans 8:1)* And this is what He just did for me. I strayed away from God since the last time Solomon lead me to the Lord. Actually that happened right before Wayne and I got married. I never expected to come here and give my life back to the Lord, nor did I expect to release everything and everybody I had been holding in my heart all my life. Wayne was one of them. Salva was another. Then Karina, and last but truly not least, my parents even though they're dead now. I had to release the anger, the bitterness, how they all disappointed me in their own ways, how I disappointed myself, the hurt, the shame, the pain, and all the fear that I had accumulated while being married to Wayne. Somehow or another, I still feel that God's not through delivering me. I still have a lot more trials and tribulations to go through in order to make me stronger that I might get to the place that He wants me to be. *(Romans 5:3-5, 12:12)* I thought still crying from what just happened to me at the altar. The more I try to go to church with Ms. Mattie, the more the devil in Wayne tries to stop me. Time I start gettin' dressed, he comes and rips off my outfit, forces himself on me for hours, and then starts tryin' to pick a fight afterwards. Talkin' about I'm sneakin' off because I must have another man. He talks about the church and about Ms. Mattie. Saying that they're taking all of my money and the preacher ain't no good, he's sleepin' with all of the members including men, and Ms. Mattie's an ol' nosey old hag. But Ms. Mattie's a prayer warrior and I know she ain't scared of him. She's prayin' for my courage to stand up for myself and to trust God for His will to be done in my life—I can appreciate somebody like her.

We're sittin' out on Ms. Mattie's porch drinkin' cappuccino. While things are quiet, I'm remembering how I used to drink it out on my patio and down on the beachfront before I lost my mansion. That was one of the first largest blessings that the Lord's ever given to me and I appreciated it like it was the only thing He was gon' give to me. When they called for the last time to say that they were seizing my home, I wasn't even shocked. I was num, but not shocked. At this point in my life I'm like what else can happen? I'm so used to wrong and everything goin' wrong that I've gotten a don't care attitude. But since I've been goin' to church whenever Wayne goes out of town, I've gotten better. At least I don't wanna' kill myself anymore. But there's so much more that needs to come out of me though. But I've got to get a way from him in order for God to do it cause' if I stay here any longer, somebody ain't gon' make it.

Wayne's in the house sleep. I just fixed his food, he ate, and now he's sleepin' before he goes out and get drunk. I hate to see em' get drunk, but I love it when he's gone so I can breathe and enjoy my space.

"Wayne's in the house?" Ms. Mattie asked, taking a sip of her cappuccino.

"Yea'."

"You mean he let you come over here?"

"He's sleep."

"I figured it had to be something like that."

Things got quiet for a while then I said never looking her way and as if to be out of breathe. "Ms. Mattie, I'm tired. Tired of gettin' beat." Her eyes widened but she said nothing. "Tired of him verbally degrading me, tired of hiding my bruises and covering up my shame and pain at church."

She looked at me strange. "Barina he's that bad?"

"Yes mam'. You didn't know?" I looked up at her.

"Well no I sure didn't. I thought he was only verbally abusing you, not hitting on you?" A tear started running from her right eye.

"I just knew you knew. When I first met you Ms. Mattie, you looked like you could see right through me, and I just knew that you knew and didn't say anything. In fact he had just jumped on me the day before and bruised my face before you asked me to come help you with your garden."

"I remember seeing the bruises, but I thought it was from something else. But I did know that he was abusing you in some sort of way. I just didn't know to what extreme."

"Ms. Mattie, I thank God for you. When I look at you, you don't look like you've ever hurt anybody nor does it look like you've ever made anybody feel less of a person. You know? You're like the mother I never had. Mine never did spend time with me like this."

She got up and walked to the edge of the porch. "Barina I have to be honest with you... I haven't always had a personal relationship with the Lord like I do now. I used to be a very bad person. In fact I used to be evil and didn't know why I was evil. I never wanted to be evil." She turned and looked at me and I looked at her waiting to hear what she had to say next. "I used to have a husband I knew I could run all over, and I could get anything out of at any time. And if he didn't give me my way, I had a way of scaring him into giving it to me. When we first met he shared that he was thrown away as a child. His parents gave him away and because of that he had a problem with being unloved and rejected—he had to deal with this all of his life. I used his weakness against him, which made him much weaker until I got him under my total control and my every command. I knew it was wrong but I couldn't stop. I didn't wanna' stop. And changing was out of the question because then I would loose control. It's called manipulation. I manipulated his heart, his mind, and his soul. I was operating in witchcraft as the bible talks about it in *(1 Samuel 15:23, Acts 16:16, Deuteronomy 18:10-12).* Back then I didn't know, I was blind because I was rejected, I was controlled by my parents, I was manipulated and molested by my step father. *(Isaiah 42:7)* So I thought I was doing right by protecting myself, but I was deceiving myself the whole time. *(Romans 7:11, 7:1-25)* But now I can see, and my life has never been the same since I surrendered it and the life style I was living to the Lord."

"Wow... So how did God deliver you?"

"Well... honey I'm not done yet... I used to beat my husband unconscious." My eyes got wider and my jaws flew open. "Yes me... Yes me a woman, beatin' him a man. My ex-husband. I used to physically abuse him. When I first saw the fear, I took advantage of it.

I knew he was too afraid to fight back so I took advantage of him. He never told anybody because, well now, that's something that most men just don't admit to for the fear of being talked about and for the fear of being called weak or a softy. And I knew that. There were times when I would dare him to go and tell because I knew he was too scared to do it. I was operating in a Jezebel Spirit. I wanted total control like she had with her husband and everybody else that was around her. *(1 Kings 16:31-34, 17-22)* I wanted my way and I got my way. And if I didn't get it, I would do whatever I had to do to get it. I wasn't gon' be told no. No way, form, or fashion. And that's how Jezebel was. She ran her husband. She controlled him, she manipulated him, and she dominated him and everybody around her. The difference between she and I was that she was murdered, and I found the Lord. I died to an evil heart, and resurrected to new life, love, compassion, and to a humble heart." *(Isaiah 57:15) (I Peter 3:8)* She sat back down.

"So how did you get saved?"

"Wait, I'm still not done youngin'." We laughed.

Ms. Mattie's so funny she would make a great storyteller.

She slowly started talking again. "Out of all the ten years we were married, he has never tried to hit me back. But one day all that changed. I used to make him clean up if I was gon' cook. And one day he didn't clean up and I went at him knowin' that he couldn't over power me because he had never tried to fight me back. Well all of a sudden after I had hit him, he jumped back up and hit me so hard, he knocked me completely out. And he kept hitting me even though I was still out. My life flashed before me. I thought I was dead. And the Lord spoke to me as clear as day and said. *"If you do not change, you will be dead before this day is over."* *(Romans 6:23)* Then God began to call my name sayin', *"Come to me… I will save you… and I will deliver you and give you new life… I love you despite what you have done. All you have to do is surrender your will to Me…"* *(Matthew 11:28-30)* And I began to weep. I began to cry out to God. My husband looked at me, gathered his stuff, and moved out. I haven't seen or heard from him since, and that's been over fifteen years ago. But after that day I have never been the same. Later on I met a friend that went through almost the same thing I went through. She helped me to release a lot more things I had been holding, and she took me to the church that I'm a member of right now. My Pastor took me in and began to be a spiritual father to me. Not controlling me, but spiritually guiding me as Christ guides him."

"Ms. Mattie by looking at you I would've never thought you used to be the way you were."

"Whom the Son sets free is free indeed." *(John 8:36)*

"You're so funny Ms. Mattie. Every time you laugh, your nostrils flare up."

"That means my discerning antenna's are up and don't start no stuff." We laughed.

"See there they go." I pointed at her.

"Don't let me get after your hinny lil' girl. You know you're my adopted daughter now?"

"How that's gon' look a young black woman with an old white woman talkin' bout' that's my mama?"

"Easy, I'll say I loved to eat chocolate when I was pregnant with you and you came out as my milk chocolate little girl."

"Yea' right, ain't nobody gon' buy that."

"Yea' you're right but I could care less because there's no color in Jesus. He sees us all the same. He's no respect of persons." *(Romans 2:11)*

"And I'm so glad."

"Me too."

Things got quiet for a moment.

"Barina you don't have to put up with nothing from the devil. You just began to pray and believe God to change your situation around, I guarantee you He will. Don't take it upon yourself to handle it, or to change it, because you're just ganna' get in the way and create a mess, and it'll be worse than it is now. But if you wait on the Lord, He will make everything all right."

Chapter Twelve

I did just the opposite of what Ms. Mattie told me to do. It's goin' on seven months and Wayne's gotten worse. All he does is hit on me. He doesn't care if he hits me in front of Karina and the baby either. He beats on me and all she does is laughs. It's like she never was this sweet, caring, considerate child I once knew and birthed. I know Wayne's upset because Karina's pregnant again with a brand new baby boy from a guy she had a one-night stand with. Now she got two small babies to raise. I had a feeling she was pregnant before she and the baby girl left unannounced after the incident happened with her and her husband. She didn't stay gone long though. Guess she found out the street life was way too much for her to handle with a baby and one on the way. She'll never be able to understand how I made it being homeless with her and still finished school and then went on to finish college. If she did, she wouldn't be treatin' me the way she does.

This is why I believe Wayne's taking it all out on me. He was furious when he came back in town and found out that Karina's husband had come over here and did what he did. He has totally stopped me from goin' to church and he's stopped me from seeing Ms. Mattie too. I miss her so much. She was calling me every Sunday morning to go to church and we started spending time almost everyday. But it all ended when Wayne answered the phone and threatened her life so she never called back. Well, he didn't scare her she's just not calling to protect me. One thing I do know is that she's a prayer warrior and she's praying for me, and right about now I need all the prayers I can get. Now I can't even go outside anymore because he watches my every move. All I do is stay stuck up in this house. He's here everyday since football season is over. Every now and then he'll go out of town or somewhere for a couple of days. I still don't go nowhere because I'm scared he'll find out that I left and come back home and beat me. God is nowhere in the picture. I have totally strayed away from Him—again.

I'm tired of cleaning blood off my face and doctoring on all these cuts and bruises from his blows. God where are you in this? You said if we cry out to You, You would hear us! *(Exodus 22:23) (Luke 18:7-8)* I'm crying out to You Lord. I can't take any more of this. My body can't take any more of this. Lord I miss You so much but I don't know how to come back to You. They could care less about you. This is a mansion of Hell and Satan is the head of it. I promise if he hits me again I don't know what I'm gon' do. I'm so tired. My mind and my body are tired. Tired of being a punching bag, and I'm tired of gettin' stabbed in the heart by his words.

Sure as to test what I said earlier, he came in and started fussing for nothin'. Said he was tired of looking at me, and he wished he'd never married me. He ran over and knocked me on the bed. Somethin' jumped on the inside of me and I flew off the bed before I realized it, and punched him right in the mouth. As big as he is he flew back against the dresser, bucked his eyes, and grabbed his mouth. He couldn't believe that I got the courage to finally hit him back. I ran out of the room and on out of the house. Karina and the baby followed me for some reason. When I turned around they were gettin' in the truck with me. I'm surprised. I just looked and didn't say anything. Wayne never came runnin' after me and I never looked back to wait on him. We drove for about thirty minutes until finally I pulled over on the side of the road and burst out crying. Karina didn't say a word, and the baby didn't either. Most of the time when babies see drama goin' on they'll start crying but she didn't. She just reached for me. And Karina let her come. I pulled her over on my side and she laid her head on my shoulder as if I was her own mother. I can't believe it. Karina started sniffing and then a burst of tears started wailing up and then fell from her eyes. Even though I had the baby in my arms, I reached to hug Karina as she met me with her hug. I guess it's true if you cry out to God He will turn your situation around in an instant. I'm a believer now because He just did it for me. Even with Karina communicating with me like this.

"I'm so sorry Mama. I had so much bitterness and hate towards you. And I took daddy's side thinkin' that he was the good guy. But when I constantly watched him beat on you, I felt bad because I was wrong all this time. It reminded me of how my husband would beat on me. I felt sorry for you. I'm so sorry mama I'll never treat you the way I have for so long."

She cried for what seem like forever. And I cried with her....

Karina finally spoke up and asked, "Where we gon' go?"

"I don't know we can't go back to our old house. They took that."

"You know daddy's gon' try and find us?"

"I know, we gon' be alright... I wonder if we could go over Ms. Mattie's house?" I turned and looked at her.

"Who the old white lady that lives next door?"

"Yea'."

"Do you know her number?"

"Yea' as a matter of fact I still do remember it."

Karina pointed towards this bar that's right up the street. "Drive to that bar and I'll go in and call her. I know somebody who'll let me make a free phone call."

"No mam' I don't want you back in there anymore. We can't take that chance cause' Wayne may come up there. Remember, that's the bar you guys met at and always go too?"

"Yea' that's true. Then where we gon' go?"

"Let me think for a minute." I pushed my hands in my pockets and pulled out the pocket liner with some loose threads in between my fingers. "This is so sad, I ain't even got a penny in my pocket. I left my purse and everything at the house. He's probably goin' through it right about now."

"Hey mama, look in the ash-tray. There may be some change in there. I've seen em' throw some in there when I was ridin' with him."

I'm sayin' to myself, now why didn't I think of that? When I looked, sure as day there were a bunch of change just sittin' there. We drove to a pay phone and called Ms. Mattie. She answered the phone on one ring.

"Hello Ms. Mattie?"

"Yes this' Ms. Mattie."

"How you doin'? This is Barina."

"Barina? O' my Lord, where are you?"

"I'm, well, we're at a pay phone." I'm tryin' not to cry.

"Whatcha' doin' at a pay phone, and with who?"

"Long story. Ms. Mattie we need a place to stay."

"You can come on over here?"

"See it doesn't work like that. I'm in Wayne's truck and with Karina and the baby."

"What's goin' on?"

"I'll explain it all to you later. Can you come and pick us up right now?"

She quickly answered. "Sure honey, no problem, whatever I can do. I hope nobody tries to rob you because…"

I cut her off. "What? Ms. Mattie I'm not tryin' to think like that right now I just wanna' get somewhere safe."

"Ok, where are you? I'm sorry I'm on my way."

"I'm on Broadway and Cavalcade St."

"I know exactly where you guys are. I'm on my way. Stay right there."

Not a minute later the police showed up with every siren blowing and lights flashing daring us to drive off. They pulled up in the parking lot surrounding us. I feel like I'm a fugitive on the run and my time is about to be up.

The police yelled into the car speaker. "Please get out of the truck with your hands up and face the opposite direction."

We got out and did exactly what the police said to do. The baby's crying and grabbing a hold of Karina for dear life.

"Now lay on the ground!"

"I can't!" Karina yelled back. "I'm pregnant!"

"Then sit down and face the opposite direction!"

We both did the same thing. They quickly ran up to us and tried to restrain us but I lost control of the anger inside of me and picked up a piece of glass and started stabbing one of the cops in the neck. The cop is yelling and clinching his neck while the blood's profusely pouring from his wound. Karina and the babies screaming in disbelief, Karina's yelling at me to stop. But I can't, I think I've just lost my mind. The thought of me goin' to jail after all these years of gettin' beat by somebody who never loved me in the first place, I can't imagine it and I won't. Nobody's gon' make me go I'll kill myself before I let them take me. I picked up a piece of glass and started slicing my wrist. About eight police came up and rushed me like a man. They tackled me, handcuffed me not caring about the huge gash on my wrist. Blood is goin' everywhere. They wouldn't let Karina and the baby come near me. They put em' in another car. Karina's crying uncontrollably and I am too. I truly think I've just lost my mind. Our screams are like a song that's about to end...

Instead of puttin' me in jail, the judge put me in a mental institution. Said I had a mental problem and that I was crazy—insane is the word I'm lookin' for. They doped me up so bad I don't know whether I'm comin' or goin'. I'm in such a deep depression that I don't know who I am anymore. I can't talk, can't walk, can't feed myself, nor can I use the bathroom on my own. I'm wearin' a diaper and they have this huge urine sack hanging behind my wheelchair. The drugs they give me have made me a vegetable. They drug me day and night because they're afraid that if I sober up, I'm gon' tare up my hospital room like I did before. It took em' almost twenty minutes to restrain me. I know the medicine is just to calm me down but it has totally drained my bodily functions and now I'm totally addicted to the drugs. If I don't get em', I'll go into convulsions and start shaking and sweating. My stare is a stare of death and hopelessness. It's not worth living anymore. *(Acts 17:28)* I'm in bad shape. My new home is an empty hospital room with one bed, one thin sheet, one thin pillow, one chair with one small night stand, not that I need it, one huge light in the center of the ceiling, and one door to walk through. I never expected my life to turn this way again.

Nobody comes to see me. Karina came to see me a few times until she went back to her husband—they moved clear across the earth to Germany. I haven't seen nor heard from her since. I'm sure he moved her far away from me so she couldn't have any more contact with me. She told me before she left that Wayne moved out, divorced me, and married some professional cheerleader, of course he didn't need my signature to sign off. I'm sure they felt like a crazy woman like me don't have no say so about nothin'. And I'm almost positive that money was a big plus for him. Ever since Karina's been gone, I've been wobbling in loneliness and deep depression. I can't talk. All I do is think, think, think. I don't even pray anymore cause' it ain't worth it. God ain't tryin' to help me up in here. I'm goin' through all this drama because I made the wrong choice. If I had of listened to what I knew God was tellin' me at first, none of this would've ever happened. I try so hard to do what's right, but wrong is always chasing after me. And it's been chasin' me for a long time. (Romans 7:7-25, 7:14-21 focusing scriptures)

They just wheeled me outside in the courtyard where everybody else is which ain't nothin' new. I'm slumped over in my wheelchair, looking down at the grass as the sun's broilin' down on the back of my neck.

Someone just tapped me on my shoulder, I didn't move nor did I look up. They tapped me again this time saying, "hi Barina." I know this voice anywhere. It's Ms. Mattie. She finally came to see me after six months of being in here. I thought she gave up on me like everybody else did. "Hi Barina, it's me. Ms. Mattie. Look up so you can see me." She tried lifting my head up by my chin but it just dropped back down to my chest. She walked over to one of the doctor's and asked, "What's wrong with her, why can't she hold her head up? What have you done to her?"

"Mam' I suggest you calm down. If you are not the immediate family or her relative, we cannot give you any information."

"Whata' you mean you can't give me any information?"

"One more word out of you and I'm going to have to ask you to leave."

"Why are you so mean?"

"Ok that's it, let's go." He started pushing her towards the entrance. I couldn't say a word. I wanted so badly to talk to her but my mouth would not open for nothin' in this world.

All I could do is watch her leave without accomplishing the mission that she had come to do. I could feel that somethin' special was going to happen, even though I still feel as though God doesn't want anything to do with me anymore. *(Hebrews 13:5)* I had the man of my dreams and I chose to go with a man with a cheap thrill and a smooth tongue. And now I'm a vegetable in this wheelchair. The drool from my mouth forms a pool in my lap everyday, all day. I'll never walk, talk, or live again and I really don't want too. I'll die in this place. I fought so hard to get my daughter back, only to loose her again all because of wrong choices and decisions. If I haven't learned anything else in this, I've learned that the choices we make are real and they can be very detrimental. That's why it's important to make the right choices and to live right, *(Romans 14:8)* that way drama like this won't be an issue.

But it's all too late now. I don't know when Ms. Mattie'll be able to come back. Hopefully they'll let her come back tomorrow or on another visiting day. Now thinkin' about it, it doesn't matter if Ms. Mattie comes back cause' there's nothin' that she can do to make everything better. I've given up on life and I've given up on people. They all can't do nothin' for me but come in my life and then leave.

Today is as hot as yesterday. No sign of Ms. Mattie yet. Probably won't be comin' back again. They may have stopped her from visiting which is crazy. Some people are so evil. My next door neighbor screams all night long everyday and every night. It's crazier in here than it is out on the streets. One guy constantly talks to himself. His wife shot and killed herself right in front of him and it's gone to his mind. They were supposed to had been married twenty somethin' years. Everybody up in here got mental problems, I guess that's why they call it a psych. ward; and I've come to accept the fact that I'm just as crazy as they all are. My mind don't even function the same especially with all the drugs packed up inside of me. Some may say all we need is deliverance, and that may be true, but I certainly can't deliver myself. *(Daniel 3:17, 2 Timothy 4:18)* I need help, but help can't do nothin' for me.

"Let's go. We're goin' outside."

The nurse comes in quite frequently. She baths me, changes my thin white robe, and leaves just the way she came in. These people have no compassion. I might as well get used to it cause' don't look like I'm gettin' outta' here no time soon. Another nurse just came in and wheeled me outside to the same courtyard as the other day. This is an everyday routine for me. I'm wobbling in depression, oppression, and no sign of rationalism. *(Psalms 9:9-10)* I have no sense of reasoning, no sense of belief, and no sense of knowledge. All I have is my self-conscious mind to keep me company.

The sun's beatin' down on my head as the clouds make their way towards me. Look like storm clouds, hopefully they're just passing through.

"Ms. Barina, are you ok? Do you want me to move you out of the sun?" She didn't wait for my answer because she knew she wasn't gon' get no answer out of me. She moved me under the patio in the shade. Feels better already, I hope it doesn't storm cause' it seems like the people up in here gets crazier when the Lord's doin' His work. I can remember when mama used to tell me to get somewhere and sit down and be still while the thunder and lightening was going forth. She used to say that the Lord was doin' His work and He didn't need me interfering. It's funny because I didn't always obey, and on this particular day I was singin' and dancin' in front of the mirror—that's when I thought I was cute. I smiled inside. And as I was prancing around, the light from the lightening blasted through my room window and I threw myself under the bed. She didn't have to tell me twice after that... I kinda' miss my parents. People should cherish their parent's while they're still living because when they're gone, they're gone. Too bad I didn't get a chance to make it right, nor did I get a chance to cherish them, nor did I get the chance to love them inside of my heart. It took me a long time just to forgive them and after I forgave em', I had to release em' because I had been holding them and holding the hurt for so long. But in order for God to deliver me, I had to release the hurt, the pain, and the disappointment. *(Matthew 18:21-22)* Salva showed me in the bible when I hadn't known her for long, that when you don't have a mother and a father or when your mother and father forsakes you, God will be your mother and father. *(Psalms 27:10)* And he has had to be ever since then.

Now at this point in my life I can't feel God anywhere near me. My life is so at a lost—a lost for hope and a lost for a successful future. It's a shame how you can have riches, fame, and fortune one minute, and be broke the next with a crazy mind in a mental institution. Never thought this would ever be me, but now I'll never say never. Because I've learned that sin will make you do anything. It made me have sex before I got married and the result was a baby at fourteen years old. It made me pick a man that I was never meant to be with. It made me not appreciate the riches that God gave me because I wouldn't get up and serve Him—I'd give anything to get my life back. All that stuff don't mean nothin' to me anymore. Just give me Jesus. It's an awful thing to gain the whole world and loose your soul. *(Matthew 16:26)* I've gained the whole world and now my soul is lost. God if You still love me, You'll come and save me. You'll give me back my mind, my love, my joy, my peace, my freedom, my dignity, and most of all my life...

I have deteriorated in the past four years. I've lost so much weight. My wheelchair is swallowing me up. They had to put pads in my chair and straps around my waist and chest just to keep my back from slumping over and me from falling out of my chair. I don't know what writing is anymore. I can't define what I am and the confidence I used to have in myself. I haven't picked up a pen in over four years. All I've ever known was writing. Writing is what helped me get through all the rough times with a baby at fourteen and homeless. Writing is what changed my life forever. It made Barina, Barina. Most people would say that God made Barina, Barina. But I beg to differ because if He did I wouldn't be in this crazy house nor would my mind be in the condition that it's in right now. *(I Corinthians 10:31)* I haven't seen or heard from Ms. Mattie. She just kinda' disappeared from off the face of the earth. I hope she hasn't died. That woman has helped me so much spiritually she's truly a real woman of God and she'll always have a special place in heart.

This room is always so cold. And this thin sheet they give us can't keep a newborn baby warm. Everything in this place is white. White sheets, white pillows, white curtains, white walls, white floors, white door, the nurses wear white uniforms. I guess they have it like this to help promote peace and purity. It would really be awful if everything was the color black. I'm already in enough bondage, I don't need nothin' to add to it. I was just thinkin', it's not fair to get beat and tortured by a man and he still go forth and prosper. I can't understand that. Wayne's still out there goin' strong on the football field, got a new wife, new home, and I'm sure he's got a bigger football deal, which means more money. I ask myself how can this be? Everyday, over and over and over again and I still don't have an answer. My mouth still won't open up. I don't have the courage to speak. Nobody wants to hear what I have to say. My voice means nothin'. Nothin' to me, and nothin' to this world.

The nurse came through the door.

"Ms. Barina, you have a visitor." She reached behind her and directed the person behind the door to come in. "Right this way." After a moment the door closed. There's complete silence.

She finally speaks softly as her voice trembled. "Hey Barina, this' your sista' Salva. Remember me?" She waited like she was between being scared of my reaction and whether or not I was gon' talk back to her. She spoke again but this time her voice shook more extensively. "Barina, can you hear me? Maybe I should come back some other time?" She took two steps towards the door, but turned around and came right back.

I still can't say a word, and I can't look up at her even though I want too so bad. I can't believe it's really Salva. She came to see me. It's been almost ten years since I've seen or heard from her. I wonder how she knew that I was in up here? I'm shocked, I thought to myself.

"Barina it's so good to see you. Girl it's been almost ten years, can you believe it?" I still said nothin'. My lips will not speak, just my thoughts and only my mind. "I guess you're wondering how I found out that you were up in here...? Well I ran into Wayne. Girl you'll never guess where I saw him and what happened to him? He's as broke as a bum on the streets. And I do mean that literally. I saw him downtown panhandling. When I walked up to him he had this solemnly sad look on his face. Trust me pride and arrogance was far from his vocabulary. He didn't know who I was. He begged me for money. But before I gave it to him, I made him remember who I was. Then girl shame was written all over is face. He sat on the curb and broke down, I kinda' felt sorry for him. Said that he got hurt, something about he tore his ACL, which ended his career. Got hooked on coc', sold all of his stuff and what he didn't sale, he lost. His wife left him and left him with nothin' but the clothes on is back." She got quiet and looked at me with this deep stare.

I'm thinkin', I have no remorse for him. Actually I'm happy. I know I shouldn't be but I am. That man took me through too much. He stole my mind, my peace, my love, my joy, my inner values, and most of all my freedom and my dignity. And he left me with poverty and a hopeless life—a life full of hopelessness conditions. I'm just happy to hear that the devil didn't win. He got what he deserves. I realize that I didn't hit a home run myself. I'm reaping what I sowed. I sowed the biggest mistake of my life and now I have to suffer the consequences. But somehow I believe that there's still some mercy left for me. *(Galatians 6:7) (Hebrews 4:16)*

After a moment of silence she finally said. "Yea' girl he went on to tell me that he divorced you about four years ago, he took everything you had because you were playin' over him. And he said that they threw you in a crazy house because you tried to kill yourself—

somethin' about you being insane. I didn't know what to believe. It's been so long since I've seen you. He wouldn't tell me what institute they had you in so I went and looked you up on the Internet, made some phone calls, and took out on my way to come and see you." I can hear the tears in her heart the more she speaks. And I know they're real. More real than a sister's love for her own blood sister. "I'm sure you can't receive me right now because of how things ended between us. It was so hard on me Barina because we haven't been apart from each other for this long. It's my fault I got so wrapped up with Solomon, that I failed to look at your feelings too. Actually none of it was my business anyway. Your life is your life. Who you chose as your man is who you chose as your man. I guess I was tryin' to be your sista' instead of being the friend that you really needed. I'm sorry." More tears fell from her eyes. "I'm here now and I ain't goin' nowhere."

My mouth still will not bulge. I can tell that Salva thinks I've had a stroke because of the uncontrollable drool that's flowing from my mouth, and from the enormous amount of weight loss. She's leaning over my wheelchair with her arms around me like a mother comforting her child. I missed this girl. I just need help receiving her again. I'm careful because I haven't been delivered from rejection. So my guards are up cause' I don't know if she'll get mad and disappear on me again.

"Well, I'm sure you're too over-whelmed right now to talk so I'll just let you rest. I know where you're at now and I guarantee you that I'll be coming back until you're oughta' here." She stood up, looked at me with tears streaming down her face, walked to the door, looked back at me one last time, and vanished silently out of the door closing it behind her. I broke down. Not because I'm sad, but because a little hope has finally come my way. I'm encouraged but not confident.

Chapter Thirteen

Salva kept her word and came back just like she said that she would. The nurse walked her in.

"Hey Miss. Thang how you feelin'? Brought chu' some sweet homemade lemonade just the way you like it." She went and set the cooler-cup on the night stand next to my bed, grabbed a plastic cup from off the stand, and poured some in the cup. "Girl they tried to give me a hard time at first about bringing this cooler but they couldn't stand up to all this favor God placed on my life." She said laughing as she came over and kneeled down in front of my wheelchair and put the cup up to my mouth as if to feed me. "I'm sorry I didn't get the chance to come yesterday. Precious sang her first solo at our church revival and I couldn't miss it. She sends her love. She's such a young woman now. You wouldn't know her if you seen her." She waited, watched the tears cloud my eyes and the drool fall from my mouth, then she put her head down as the tears began to fall from hers.

All I can think about is how close Karina and Precious used to be. Where is my baby? I wonder. Will I ever see her again? I can't help but think back on how much fun we all used to have years ago.

"Precious said to tell my auntie hello and that I love her. And I promised her that I would. Barina, girl she was out there so bad for a while. And I just prayed and believed God that He would bring her back and one day she just popped up on my doorstep from out of nowhere, battered, bruised, and broken, just broken girl. All I could do was hold her, not saying one word. A week later, she walked up and rededicated her life back to God during church one Sunday. Girl now

185

you know I was all over that church." She giggled to herself. "I couldn't stop shoutin'. God had answered my prayers and brought my baby back to me." We both began to cry again. "You look like you feel better?" She turned her head as if to make herself believe what she said was true. She got up and walked outside the door leaving the door cracked. I can hear her whispering to the nurse.

"Hey excuse me, nurse can I ask you somethin'? Why isn't she talking back to me?"

"She hasn't talked in four years now. She's in a deep depression. We don't know what's going to bring her out of it? I don't think she'll ever come out it if you ask me. We've tried every medication on the market and nothing's worked. And we've tried all kinds of therapy and not one of em' has helped her. She's a lost hope and a vegetable waiting to die up in here just like everybody else. So mam' we suggest that you not get wrapped up into her because it'll be a waste of your time and ours."

"I totally disagree. She's not a lost hope and you may have tried what you think was everything but you didn't try one thing I know will work—Jesus. He never fails. I've learned that prayer changes things, people, and situations." *(James 5:16)*

"Well, whatever mam'. We don't believe in doing that here. I mean look around, don't you see all these crazy loonies? They'll never come back to their right minds again; they'll never be normal people again. That's why they were placed up in here to die. Look down there do you see that lady?" She pointed down the hall. "She can't hold her bowels. We have to clean her all day everyday. Nobody wants to be around her because she stinks all the time. And..."

Salva cut her off. "Ok, enough. I didn't come all the way up here to hear all this negative, non-believing nonsense. I'm findin' out that you guys are just as bad off as the people are up in here. You're supposed to lift them up and help them get their lives back, not tare them down? I refuse to see my sista' go down up in here. I'm ganna' help her get her life back and get her out of here with or without your help."

Salva must've walked off from her because right after she said that she quickly walked back in and closed the door behind her, walked over and grabbed a chair from beside the bed, came and set the chair beside my wheelchair, leaned over and grabbed my hands and began to pray silently. I wanna' say something but the evil spirits inside of me won't let me. I'm being tormented and I don't know how to come out of it. *(Ephesians 6:12-13)* I'm sure that's why she's here. I heard her heart while she was outside the door. I could hold a grudge against her for lettin' a man come between us, but my heart won't let me. She's the only family I have left.

After she prayed silently, she got up and laid both of her hands on my head, one on each side, and began to pray out loud. *"Matthews 16:19* tells me... whatsoever I shall bind on earth, shall be bound in Heaven; and whatsoever I shall loose on earth, shall be loosed in Heaven. And right now I bind the spirit of depression and oppression; I bind the spirit of bondage in the Name of Jesus! And I loose healing, liberty, freedom, love, joy, a peace of mind, and the Spirit of the living God to flow freely through you! In the Name of Jesus! In the Name of Jesus!" She declared as she kept on praying. I'm a little scared because she hasn't ever prayed for me like this. She has never put her hands on my forehead. At first I thought she was checking my temperature, but I quickly figured out that that wasn't what she was doing. Even though I can't open up my mouth, I can still feel all these spirits lifting and all that she's praying against stirring up inside of me and right now they're about to come out. It feels like I have to throw up. Not because of bad food, but because of deliverance. She then laid her hands on my stomach and began to pray. I can feel healing and deliverance stirring up inside of my stomach. I know that God is doing something through her and it's all about to come up and out. And that it did right on the floor. Salva thanked God and kept praying for me. A wave of a cool breeze came across my face and my body, captured by a chill of sweat that's resting on the pores of my skin. I know God just delivered me from depression and oppression and everything else I was strugglin' with. I felt those spirits and the sickness leave my body. There was this enormous amount of heat building up inside of me—the heat of healing and deliverance and all I can do is weep and thank God...

I can now look up but I still can't talk. She asked me a question and when I didn't answer her, she quietly said to herself, "What did I leave out? I guess I have more prayin' to do. I gotta' bind the strong man of a Dumb and Deaf Spirit. *(Mark 9: 14-32) (Matthew 12:29).* She cleaned up the floor and left without saying bye.

The day came and went as if it was fast forwarded into fast motion. I couldn't complain about Salva's visits if I wanted too. She's so different, God really did somethin' in her in these past ten years. Another maturity level has found her. Even her demeanor is different. She has a whole new look on life. I can hear it in her voice, and I can feel it in her touch as she prayed for me. She has always been like a sister to me even though I'm a little older than she is. Sort of like a watchmen over my soul. I thought that I would never see her again considering our last conversation. I remember the last thing she said to me was, ain't no man's money gon' make me happy without Jesus. At that time it didn't register that I was headed down the road to Hell. The only thing that was on my mind was gettin' my daughter back and doing what was best for her. I did not realize that that choice was the worst choice that I could have ever made in my life. I lost who I was as a woman and as a human being. I lost apart of myself, apart of my innocence. Life? Integrity? Love? Dignity? Pride? Power? Self-worthiness? I couldn't find anywhere. They were all thrown in a dark closet never to be taken out again. The thought of what I did to that cop is unbearable. An insane maniac is what I was and I'm still not far from it now. My mind went berserk; I turned into an animal. I was determined not to let another man put his hands on me, and I was determined not to let them put me in prison. Now I wish that they had because this is worst than any prison. This mental institution is what it says it is—Mental. Everybody here have mental deficiencies. When you walk in here there's a dark creepy fear. It's like a tingling evil presence that surrounds you as soon as you walk through the double doors. It's a demonic fear that has captivated my mind from the first time they brought me up in here. They're having conversations with only people they can see. There's nothin' but screams in the night hours along with the banging of what sounds like somebody bamin' a board against the wall, but it ends up being the woman basin' her head against the wall shouting 1,2,3… on up into the thousands. It's a mad war house up in here. And me? I'm drooling uncontrollably all day and all night because of the strong medication.

Salva's clutching a piece of tissue in her hands and slowly wiping her nose and eyes. I want so badly to open up my mouth and tell her thank you for coming to see about me and for praying for me the other day. I know God did somethin' mighty within me.

188

She's sittin' in the chair next to me, thinking... All of a sudden she just got up and left out of the room. I can hear her talking to the nurse again. "Look, do not give her anymore drugs, they're not doin' nothin' for her but only makin' her worst."

"Mam' like I told you before, she's a lost cause. You're wasting your time. We have to give her those drugs in order to keep her under control."

"Under control of what? Satan?"

"Satan? Are you some kind of witch?" She smiled like it was funny.

"Witch? Are you crazy? I'm not with the sorcerers or the soothsayers, *(Micah 5:12)* I'm with Jesus Christ the Son of God. Do you know Him?"

"Look mam' I don't have time for church games, the drugs are only used to sedate her, not to poison her. What you see coming from her are not from the drugs."

"Don't worry about it, God'll take care of her." As Salva walked back in the room, I could hear the nurse say that she wasn't worried. And I believe every word too. They're not worried about any of us. Salva appears to be very grieved. She threw herself down in the chair, shook her head, and mumbled as if to be still talking to the nurse. She's determined to help me. I know she is. And I'm going to try to cooperate with her as best as I can. Since the last time she prayed for me, I've gotten a little better. I'm still drooling but not as much. I can now look at her. But that's not enough for Salva, and believe it or not, it isn't enough for me either. She noticed me looking at her and she started smiling and said. "Thank God, I know this' not gon' be a long journey, I just know it's not."

Salva was right about it not being a long journey. From the time the doctor said that there was no hope for me, Salva got even more consistent. She came everyday for about two week's, read my books and the bible to me, prayed, and anointed my head with anointing oil. She continued to rebuke the spirits that were trapped inside of me which was causing me to be bound. It wasn't long before I could see clear, stopped drooling, and somehow she got me to eat as my appetite came back. It's amazing what God can do through a person if they would just yield themselves to Him. *(Hebrews 12:11)* She yielded herself to Him. I yielded myself to Him. I had no choice, He sent his angel to help me. Now I can truly say that God is a healer. *(1 Peter*

2:24) He healed my body from sickness and disease. When I couldn't see, He gave me my sight back, when I gave up hope, He gave me my hope back. When I needed help and He sent help, but first I had to be honest. And a person can get help when they're honest and real with themselves. Like right now I'm honest about not being where I need to be in Jesus. I'm honest about my mind still being in the condition that it's in. And because I'm honest with God, I know He's ganna' continue to help me. And He's not gon' let me down.

Salva broke in my thoughts and said. "Ok, mam', time to eat." She took the plate from off the tray that's sittin' on the stand, walked over, and started feeding me. "Barina, you don't know how proud I am of you. You have made such a miraculous progress in just weeks. Now you know that ain't nothin' but God." I slightly smiled letting her know that I agree. "Girl, Precious is a trip she's just goin' on in the Lord. She's so active in church. She's in the young adults ministry, in the choir, and look like she's tryin' to start up a gospel singin' group. Did you know she could sing?" She kept on talking as if I responded. "I didn't know she could either." She giggled to herself.

Somehow a bulge is starting to build up in my throat. There's this strong desire to say somethin'. I'm pushing and pushing. Salva thinks I'm choking so she went over to the night stand and got the cup of water and brought it to me. "No." I slowly forced the word from my lips.

Salva's eyes widened. She ran and threw the cup back down on the tray, ran over to my wheel chair, and started crying out to God. "Thank you Lord! Thank you Lord! I speak total healing in the Name of Jesus!" She kept shouting and praying for about another minute or so.

Another bulge came to my throat and I said. "Sa-al-va." She cried even louder. Surprisingly the nurses aren't running in. "I... ca-n... t-al-k."

"That's right! You can talk Barina! Take your time God is healing you! He's giving you back your voice!" She's jumping all over the room. Running up to my wheel chair, backing away, and coming back towards me like a child that's excited about receiving a piece of candy. She ran and threw the food off the tray and ran over and placed the tray in front of me and asked. "What's this Barina? What's this?"

"Tw-way."

"That's right! Can you say tr-ay?"

"Tra-ay."

"Yes! Thank you Jesus! Ok, ok, ok." She ran back over to the stand and got the cup and ran back over and brought it to me and asked. "Now what's this?"

"Cu-up."

"Yes Lord yes! Now say it fast."

"Cup."

"Hallelujah! Barina do you know you're healed? You're healed Barina!" I smiled and shook my head yes.

Before it was all over with, I was talking in sentences fluently. By the end of the day I had my voice back and believing in miracles. God is so amazing! He's just amazing! Salva went and got the nurse she had been talking off and on too. They just came back in. Salva turned to the nurse and said. "See, look, she can look up now, she's not drooling, and she's talking back to me. See? Listen." She reached and grabbed the tray from off the table and placed it in front of me and said. "Barina what is this?"

"It's a-a-a tway."

"Can you say it faster?"

"It's a twray."

"Good. Now what's this?" She grabbed the cup from off the table.

"It's a-a cup."

"Very good B'." She looked at the nurse who had her nose stuck up in the air.

"And, that doesn't mean anything." She turned and walked back towards the door and turned around. "She's still a lost cause. Look at her, she's still stuttering." She flinched a crooked smile.

Salva walked up to her and said. "How crazy can you be? Can't chu' see that this brave woman has made miraculous progress within a day's time? There's no way that I could've possibly done something like this. Don't you believe?"

"Believe in what?"

"Believe in God?"

"I believe in God but I don't believe that God can work miracles like that." *(Mark 9:24)*

"Then you don't believe. You don't believe because you don't wanna' believe. All the evidence is here. It's obvious that God is in total control. There's no way that I could've done all this in one day?"

191

"O' it's possible."

"How?"

"Because she probably was faking from the beginning. Look there's no way that you're ganna' make me believe." She quickly walked out not giving Salva a chance to respond.

Salva looked at me. "That's alright, she'll believe before it's all over with, or she'll go to Hell." *(Isaiah 5:14-16, James 3, 3:6)*

I shook my head yes in agreement and said. "She-e'll be-believe o-one da'day."

"Yea' hopefully Barina. I'm ready to get you oughta' here. They're so hateful up in here."

I cut her off. "Da' don't worry."

"What? Girl you're talkin' better and better. I just can't get over this." She started gathering up her things to leave. "It's almost time for visiting hours to be over with so I guess..."

"Sa' Savesta'."

She quickly turned around in shock that I had asked that question.

"Um, um well he's at his house."

"Is house?"

"Yea' his house, I didn't wanna' tell you because I know how much you love him. But we separated two and a half years ago." I put my head down and she put her purse down on the bed. "We're still friends though. In fact he doesn't even know that you're up in here. Actually he doesn't know that I'm talking to you again."

She waited for my response; I didn't say a word. I'm too hurt to say anything. I didn't expect for her to say that. Thinkin' back, I don't ever remember her mentioning Salvester's name—just Precious. They were the perfect couple, nothin' could keep em' a part. It's crazy because they both loved the Lord; they both had good incomes, and a loving family. Salvester was the sweetest man I've ever met. I used to want a man just like him loving, romantic, and sincere. Until Solomon came into my life and I found that there was a man that was better than Salvester. Maybe if I'd a' went on and married Solomon like I was suppose too, Salva and Salvester wouldn't have ever broken up? I don't know. I really don't wanna' think about it, it's too painful.

She kept waiting til' she got tired. "I'm ganna' go ahead and leave." She started walking towards the door again.

"Go ba' backk." I looked at her with tears in my eyes.

She turned around. "Hum'?"

"Go baack ta' to him."

Salva looked at me and left without saying goodbye.

I cried off and on for the rest of the night, on into the morning.

Salva made her usual entrance after not showing up for three whole days.

"Hey what's up my girl, how you feelin'?" She came in with a chipper attitude and put the cooler of lemonade on the night stand. "Sorry I didn't come for the past three days. I was tied up... No let me stop. I wasn't tied up, I've just been thinkin' about what chu' said to me about Salvester." She pulled up her usual chair and set it beside my wheelchair. "Actually it was my fault. Somewhere and somehow I started not being able to trust him. I accused him so much that he got tired and left me. It was so much drama. Barina I just knew he was cheatin' on me and I didn't know why? Turned out, he wasn't and I couldn't forgive myself. Precious tried to get us back together but he wasn't havin' it. The drama was still new. A year after that I saw Salvester at a restaurant with some old friends and he wanted to get back together then but I didn't. I just couldn't let the past go. I couldn't forgive myself for the drama that I had caused him and for the trauma that I had put Precious through. She was devastated which was the main reason why she had run off and stay gone for as long as she did. It's been a year and a half since I've seen or talked to Salvester. I miss him so much. He probably got somebody else by now.

"Maybe not."

"Yea' you may be right. What do you think I should do?"

"Go back ta' to him."

"But how?"

"Call hii' him."

"His number has been changed."

"Go up ta' his school."

"You know what? I didn't think about that, that's what I'm gon' do. Thanks B'. You know this is new? Most of our lives I've always been the one with all the answers and advice, now you counseling me."

I smiled. "That's wha' what friends are for." We both laughed.

"Girl I'm just talkin' and laughin' with you and I didn't notice that you're talking so freely? God is healing you by the minute. Look at cha', you can laugh now."

I smiled like I just won a million dollars. "Salva, thank yoo' you for all dat' you ha' have done. I'll ne'never forget it." I slowly reached for her hand as hers met mind.

"I know you won't. But you do know that it wasn't me? I give God all His props, even though I know you already know this. Hey, now that God has given you back your voice, lets see if He's given you your strength to walk?" She stood up in front of my wheel chair with her hands reaching towards me. "Come on Barina, get up real slow, real slow now."

I placed my hands on each armrest, slowly scooted up towards the edge of my seat, shaking from lack of strength and fear. I rose up enough to get on my feet. But when I went to take a step, I fell towards Salva. She picked me up and made me do it again. So I did. The first step was the hardest but with Salva's encouragement, I was able to overcome it.

I ended up walking again little by little. We laughed and celebrated at what God was doing. She helped me sit back down and asked. "Hey, you were never in an accident, how did you get stuck in this ol' wheelchair?" She pointed at the wheelchair.

"Deep de' depression."

"To make you not wanna' walk again?"

"Yes."

"That's some deep sadness?"

"Yea'. My entire body sh'shut down and the me' medicine didn't help a' any."

"Oh' Barina. I'm so sorry I wasn't there for you. This crazy stuff wouldn't have ever happened if I was here... So how did you get put up in here?"

"Long story."

"Please tell me, I wanna' know." She sat back down in her chair.

I'm thinkin' to myself that the more I talk, the more I'm claiming my healing. Can't nobody be healed without faith. *(Hebrews 11:6)* "Well, you know I went on and ma' married Wayne. He was perfect wh'when we first got married, but it didn't take long for the re' real Wayne to come out. He started beating me, terrorizing me, stalking me, and possessing and controlling me. I...I was a slave in his house. He took everything from me. He tricked me into signing everything over to him after having sex with him. I was caught up in the moment. You would th' thi' think that a husband wouldn't do somethin' like that. But he did, and without any conviction. I wa' was truly mistaken. I knew after I had married Wayne I had made the greatest mistake of my life. He stole everything from me. My life, my possessions, my mind, my heart, and anything else he could think of. I lost my mansion. They took it before I got the courage to leave. I believe wh' wh' when a person get sick and tired of being sick and tired, they gon' leave. And when I left it wasn't cute. He came in fussin' about nothin' as usual. Came and knocked me on the bed for the last time, I jumped up and hit em' so hard it knocked him into the dresser and I ran for my life. Karina and the ba' baby came too. That's another story within itself. Wayne never came after me, he just called the cops and they picked us up. Salva, I don't know what happened to me. I went berserk. I picked up a piece of glass and stabbed the cop right in the neck and started slicing my own wrist with it. That's how I got put up in here. The judge said that I was too insane for prison. When I got here I was down to my last, so I began to shut down. I was tired of the world and the devil winning. So I was gon' give em' somethin' else to celebrate about. My entire body, mind, and soul shut down. My legs wouldn't move and after a while I just accepted the fact that I was never ganna' walk again. My bodily functions shut down. Everything shut down but my self-conscious mind. And everyday the devil was speaking to me telling me that I would never walk nor talk again because I had done too much wrong. But while he was speaking, I still had some God left up in me, He gave me another chance even though I talked against Him and gave up on Him. I can say that He never gave up on me. *(Hebrews 13:5)*

The door opened while Salva was crying and a nurse came in. "Hello, I'm here to give you your medication and to take you out for recreation."

Salva jumped up and said. "Who are you? And where's the other nurse?"

"She's no longer working here. I'm the new nurse now." Her smile lit up the entire room.

"What happened to her?" Salva smiled.

"I'm not for sure. I try not to get in other folks business. But somehow I feel it had something to with somebody praying?" She put the tray of medicine down on the night stand.

"What a' you mean?"

"I'm a strong believer in God, and I could feel the presence of the Lord the moment I stepped into this room. I just gotta' feelin' that somebody's been prayin'. Is that true?"

"Actually you're right. I've been praying and I'm not surprised that she's gone. I'm so happy because God answered my prayers." Salva clapped and then threw her hands up in relief. "She was a terrible person. She was an unbeliever. She didn't care about the patient's at all. And Barina is one of em'. When I first started coming to see Barina." She turned and looked at me. "Barina you don't mind me being honest do you?" I nodded my head no. "Well Barina looked like a lost cause. She looked like there was no hope and that she would never be the same Barina that I once knew. Healing was out of the question. And I talked to the nurse about why Barina wasn't talking back to me; and that if they would take her off the medication because the medication was making her worse. And that's when she implied that Barina would never make it and that I was wasting my time. I rebuked her and told her that Jesus would heal Barina. And so I began to intercede. I began to pray and pray and pray, and lay hands and lay hands, and cry out to God, and lay hands, and cry out to God, and pray and pray and pray until God moved. Barina's not drooling anymore, she's not drooping over in her chair anymore, she's got most of her weight back, she can use the restroom on her own now, she can look up at me and communicate back with me. The pigment of her skin is even lighter. So what you see here is what God did in weeks."

"Wow, God is a miracle worker! There's really no reason for her to be up in here anymore." She smiled, picked up the tray of medicine, and walked back to the door.

"Are you leaving?" I asked.

"Yes I am, there's no reason for me to stay any longer."

Salva jumped in and said. "Well aren't chu' gon' give her her medicine?" She smiled.

"That won't be necessary anymore." She waited. "One thing will be necessary is that you take her out and get her some beautiful sun light, it's beautiful out there today. And when you guy's come back, get her prepared." She started walking out of the door as her coal dark skin, coal dark eyes, and coal black hair shinned as the light layed down on them.

"Prepared for what?"

196

She never answered as she walked on out of the door.

Salva helped me get fixed up to go outside. The courtyard is beautiful. I forgot how beautiful it could be. When I would come out here before, it never soothed me like it's soothing me now. I'm sure it's because I have a better out look on life, and a new hope in Jesus. He showed me who He was and that He's never given up on me. He came through for me and He used Salva to do it. I'm rubbing my toes through the freshly cut grass, and Salva's sittin' on the round concrete table right behind my wheelchair. "Hey Salva, help me up I wanna' walk through the grass."

She came and helped me up, then let me go and stood back and watched. I weaved back and forth at first but God gave me strength as I began to take every step until I could walk on my own. I'm walking now but I'm walking slow and careful. I'm walking, talking, eating, and starting to feel like I can live my life again. I have a new determination, a new outlook on life, and a whole new perspective on who God is. I didn't realize how special He is, and how He can work so many amazing miracles in such a short notice. *(Acts 2:22)* My life will never be the same....

When we got back to the room, the nurse was there waiting on us with some papers in her hand. She had already taken the sheets and the pillowcase off the bed and prepared it as if for someone new.

Salva spoke up first because she's so out spoken. "What's goin' on?" I'm looking at Salva's expression. It's already saying that we're about to hear some good news.

"These are for you." The nurse turned and handed me the papers. I looked at em', looked back at the nurse, at Salva, and then began to read what each of the three papers said. As I read every word, my smile grew wider and wider until I was cheesing from ear to ear. "I'm being released! O' my God Salva, I'm being released!" We all celebrated and cried for about thirty minutes and then I gathered my things, slowly walked towards the discharge station with Salva right beside me. The nurse was leading the way, or should I say an angel. She's an angel in disguise. *(Hebrews 13:2)* God sent her here for such a time as this. *(Esther 4:14)* All I can think about is how my condition was when I first got put up in here. I was as low as a person can go but I thank God that as I look back, I can say that I'm lookin' back on darkness and I'm walking towards new light—the light that only Jesus can give.... *(Luke 1:79)* I'll see where it takes me from here...

I'm walking out to the same truck I bought Salva when I first hit it big. Our words were few and full of imagination and excitement. Salva started the truck up and sped off like we had a destination to reach. I'm thinking. Where do I go from here? What do I do first? I didn't think about it but where am I gon' stay? I asked myself.

"Barina I know you're probably wondering where you gon' stay?" She took the words right out of my mind. "But I've already made plans for you to stay with me and Precious."

"Thanks Salva. It was definitely somethin' that my mind had questioned. But I'm glad that you answered it." We both laughed like old times. "So what's up with you and Salvester?" All laughing stopped.

She turned and looked me up side my head. "What chu' mean what's up?"

"Just like I said, did I stutter?" We burst out laughing again.

"Barina, I just don't know. What do I do?" She looked at me, then back at the road.

"Call em' Salva, that's all you have to do."

"That's easy said than done. It's been over a year now I mean he probably has somebody else?"

"You don't know that, just call em'."

"O' Barina why are you so straight forward?"

"How do you want me to be? You want me to give in to this pity party you got goin' on? Look Salva, Salvester is a good man. And I don't want you to make the same mistake I made with the man of my dreams. I lost him because I didn't appreciate what God gave me. Instead I chose somebody who couldn't and wouldn't ever make me happy—I really miss Solomon…"

"I hear ya'. I miss Salvester…" We were quiet for about fifteen minutes as we thought about the times we spent with them. Salva finally broke the ice and said. "I'll call him when we get home."

"Cool."

The ride to the house lasted over an hour. I didn't know Salva traveled all this way almost everyday to see me. Some friends are for a season, but this friendship is for a lifetime.

Salva pulled up in the driveway like an Indy 500 driver just like she used to do years ago. It's amazing how God works things back around. You can see a person ten to fifteen years ago and depart from them for whatever reason, and then years later they just pop back up in your life again. And its better knowing them than it was before. This I can say for Salva and me. I thought I'd never see my sista' again. Actually I didn't think I'd see anybody again cause' either I was gon' kill Wayne, or he was gon' kill me if I hadn't of left when I did.

"Ok mam' we're here." Salva said as she got out and grabbed what little bags I had in the back seat, waited for me, then we both walked in the house. "Wait here while I turn off the alarm and turn on some lights." She did it and came back to get the bags left by the door. "Come on girl. I'm a put on some cappuccino. I know you want some. Betcha' you ain't had none in a long time?"

"You right I haven't." I said following her into the kitchen.

"Girl, so how does it feel being a free woman?"

"It feels great. I can't describe what I'm feelin' right now."

"You know God didn't let you out for nothin' right? Now it's time to share your testimony and get to work for God." She went over and grabbed the coffee pot from off the counter and started making the cappuccino.

"I know Salva, I know." I smiled. I know she's glad that I didn't disagree.

When the cappuccino was ready, she brought two coffee cups over and set em' on the table. I grabbed mine like it was a piece of candy. It's been so long since I've had me some good ol' cappuccino. That's all I used to drink when I had my own house.

She blew her coffee as the steam and aroma rose into her nose. Then she took a quick sip and said. "So what's on your mind chick? I know you're ready to unwind?"

"No actually I'm thinkin' about my baby. I don't know where she is. Last time I heard she was in Germany. I don't know where she is now." I took a sip of my cappuccino and sighed with sadness. "I've gotta' find her Salva. I've just got too."

"You will. I'll see to it." We sipped our cappuccino until it was all gone. "You want some more?"

"Naw', girl this is already startin' to do somethin' crazy to my stomach." We giggled. "I'm a take five in a minute."

"Well before you take five, I want you to know that I'm about to call ya' boy."

"Who?"

"Salvester silly."

"O' go for it. I'm takin' five." I ran out of the kitchen and went straight to the front bathroom.

When I came out Salva was already on the phone talking. I looked at the clock and hadn't realized that I had been in the bathroom for almost forty-five minutes. Salva's goin' strong with all smiles. Hopefully Salvester has something to do with that.

"Sure I can do that." Salva said with a glow on her face. "When?... Tomorrow?... Well, Barina's here with me and she may need to take care of some business. How bout' the next day?... Ok, well I can't wait to see you... O' how sweet, thank you... I have one question for you... What is your girlfriend gon' say about this?... You don't have one?" She turned, looked at me, and winked. Her heart was sinking right in that seat. "That's even better. Ok well I'll see you tomorrow night at seven thirty... Do you remember where I live?..." She laughed and I'm sure he did too. "Have a peaceful night... Bye." AHHHHHH!!!! She screamed so loud the inside of my ear-drum rang. She ran over and hugged me so tight, I thought all the air was sucked out of my body. "Ah' girl! Now you know you're a genius? You my girl! Girl he's single, he never got with anybody else! He said that he's been waiting for me!" She screamed and danced all over the kitchen, and I watched. I think I'm more excited than she is or excited that I dropped that big load. I don't know, they're both good. I laughed to myself.

"So what did he say?"

She sat down at the table out of breath. "Whew', let me rest... I called him as soon as you went to the bathroom. He answered the phone on one ring. We talked about ol' times and I apologized even though he wouldn't let me. I told him that I loved him and he told me that he loved me too and that he had been waiting for me. He said if it had been ten more years later he'd a still been waiting. We're supposed to go out to dinner tomorrow night. That's ok with you right?"

"O' sure I ain't cho' mama."

"I know silly, but you just got out and I know you have a lot to do?"

"That is true but for somethin' like this, trust me it can wait. And besides, it ain't like I

have a date. And I'm not gon' be runnin' errand's that late either so..."

"Alright then I guess it's a go then. Barina, chi' thank you so much. If it had not been for you, Salvester and I would still not be talking.

Thank you mam'!" She walked off into the living room and yelled. "I'm about to get your room ready for you. I know you're tired!"
"Yes mam' I am!" I yelled back.
"Ok. I'll be right back make yourself at home!"
"I know what to do you just do yo' thang!"
"Alright don't get smart you know who's the oldest!"
"Yea' yea' yea' whatever!"
I had to sit back down at the table and think. I'm happy for Salva but yet I can feel a little jealousy rising. I guess because my life is still not yet fully complete. If her and Salvester gets back together which they will, I know I won't hardly see her because they'll be mending, so that leaves me by myself again. And then I'm thinkin' about Solomon. Will I ever see em' again? I don't want nobody else but him. And if I can't have him, I'll just stay single for the rest of my life. Then I'm thinkin' about my child, where she is and will I ever see her again? Only God and time can answer this question.
Salva finally came back down and said Precious is spending the night at one of the sister's house from church. So I'll see her tomorrow. She doesn't know that I'm here. I looked at my wrist, rubbed the scare from the knife wound, and thanked God that He didn't allow me to kill myself because Hell is just too hot. What was I thinkin' anyway? Sin will make you do anything.
"What's wrong?" Salva asked as she came over to the table.
"Nothin'."
"Come on now, you know I know you? Now what's wrong?"
"I'm just missin' you know who."
"Who? O' Karina?"
I looked at her and said yes. I won't even mention that it's Solomon who I'm thinkin' about. I'll just leave that subject alone. "I really need to find Karina."
"You'll find her. Where did you say she was again?"
"Germany, last time I heard."
"Wow, that's far away."
"Yea', it is pretty far. But I know that nothing's too hard for God." *(Genesis 18:14)*
"Now see, you don' said somethin' right there." We both threw up our hands and laughed in faith.
I'm laughing on the outside, but on the inside I doubt whether or not I'll ever see her again. *(Matthew 21:21, Romans 14:23)* I realize that if

201

I doubt, then I'm not trusting God, but if I believe and have faith, I know God will hear me and answer my prayers.

Chapter Fourteen

I had a chance to try and contact Ms. Mattie after all these years of being in the nut house. The bad news hit my heart like a sharp bow-and-arrow. It was a hurting thing to hear that Ms. Mattie died of a heart attack two years ago. One of her relatives answered her old phone number she gave me. I'm sad because I really didn't get a chance to get to know her like I wanted too, considering the circumstances that I was in at that time. I miss her with my whole heart. She had become my mother—my confidant. I never got the chance to tell her how much I appreciated her and how grateful I was for her taking me to church. O' God it's hard for me to think about it because the pain is still fresh in my heart. I know Ms. Mattie's in Heaven routing me on, I just know she is....

Salva should've been a detective. She's so awesome with finding people. After my first night of being free, she went to work at finding Karina. It helps that she knows that Internet. She can find anything and anybody on that thing, that's how she found me. She found out that Karina's in a crack house in New Orleans. Now how she got way out there, I don't know. And how did Salva find out that Karina was in a crack house? I know they don't have a website for that? That's nonsense. Probably made some phone calls that lead up to it. When she surprised me by telling me that she found Karina, I didn't even ask how, I was just glad that God answered my prayers. Now I see what a little faith will do. It'll go a long way. All God requires is that we have faith the size of a little grain of mustard seed. *(Matthew 17:20)* And I

203

must've had that cause' we're gettin' ready to take a trip to New Orleans to get my one and only daughter back. I'm cheesing.

"Girl, are you packed? Our plane leaves in an hour. We need to go cause' you know how the traffic is out there?" Salva asked.

"Yea' and I know how you drive too."

"Whatever, I've gotten better." She laughed at herself as if to make her self believe what she said was right. And I laughed too cause' it was funny.

"You may've gotten better, but you still got a long ways to go." We laughed again.

We jumped in the truck headed for the airport that's not too far away. Traffic's movin' along pretty good considering how early it is.

"So what's on yo' mind? You're kinda' quiet?" She turned and asked, then looked back at the road.

I looked back at her and barely said, "I just wanna' get my baby back." Then I looked back out of the window at the cars passing us by.

"I know that. But what's really goin' on with you?"

Salva has a way of looking at a person that'll make em' fess up and say whatever's wrong, but somehow I still can't. "I told you." I said trying to look like I just told the truth.

"Barina now you know I know you by now?"

"Ok I might as well say it because you ain't gon' leave it alone if I don't."

"Good."

"Well, you know I'm really happy for you and Salvester gettin' back together right?"

"Right."

"Well, I have to admit that I'm a little jealous for two reasons. One reason is that I'll hardly ever see you and not be able to hang out with you. We've been apart for over ten years and there's so many things that we need to catch up on, and so much to fill one another in on. And now with you about to give Salvester all of your time, that won't be possible. You're all I have besides God now that mama and daddy are both dead now. You're the only sista' I've ever known and will ever have." I got quiet for a moment to catch the tears. "And two, when I look at you and Salvester gettin' back together it makes me jealous and

I don't wanna' be, but it does because every time I think of you two gettin' back together, it makes me think of..."

She cut me off. "Solomon."

"Don't cut me off Salva. And how'd you know that?"

"Didn't I tell you earlier that I know you? You gon' believe me one day. Anyway, I knew that when I first told you what happened on the phone. Barina I fully understand. Well since you're confessing, I need to confess somethin' too. First of all I want to apologize for leaving you in the past the way I did. I was jealous of you and Solomon." My eyes widened as if I just seen a ghost. "Yea' that's right. I'm being honest and real. I saw in you and Solomon what I wanted in Salvester's and my relationship. It was the devil that made me feel that way. You two looked so good together. It's like you two were made for each other. That's when you know somethin' or someone is God sent. I adored Solomon, and for a while my emotions got the best of me. I mean it was crazy Barina. He started turning me on when he would sing. Then it got worse, I started having sexual dreams about me and him, then I started wanting him while I was in his presence and I started sweating in places I dare not mention. And that's why when Salvester would go to visit him or to go hear him sing, I wouldn't go because I was fighting my true feelings and mixed emotions. I was fighting what I didn't want to accept. I didn't want to accept that I had a problem and I needed to be real with myself and God so that He could solve it. *(I John 1:9)* And Salvester was good to me. Our marriage was good. Our life together was good and nothin' at that time could keep it from being wrong, except for what was going on in my mind, in my thoughts, in my imaginations, and in my dreams. Most of these feelings happened after you two broke up and I hadn't seen you in a while. But some of it was there before you and I separated and I was fighting it because I didn't want to feel the way I was feeling. And I wanted you and him to work out because I wanted to see you happy even though you were makin' a sista' mad at how bad you were treatin' the brotha'." She smiled but I didn't. "See these are the kinds of things that people think and will never expose for the fear of people not seeing them the same again, or for the fear that their friendships or relationships would be broken, separated, or severed. And in our case it was separated, but not severed. It took ten years for God to do a work in us. And now look at us, we're back together again." She turned, grabbed my hand, and smiled.

I'm thinking, I can't squeeze her hand in agreement because maybe I'm a little ticked off at what she just revealed to me. I'm glad she didn't expose this years ago because she's right about friendships being severed. I would've written her off and never talked to her again. "You know Salva, I kinda' had a little feelin' that somethin' extra was in you with Solomon because you used to take up for him way too much. And the way you looked at him, it was like you were lookin' at Salvester. You had a twinkle in your eyes. I didn't say anything though. But I'm glad that you told me this, now I love you even more just for being honest. Everybody can't be honest, especially with something like this."

"You know what Barina, I made up in my mind that I'm gon' be honest even if I have to loose some folks in the process of doing it. I figure honesty is the best way... I don't have those feelings nor the thoughts or the dreams anymore for Solomon. I wanted to be delivered from those adulterous thoughts. *(2Corinthians 10: 3-5, Galatians 5:1, Romans 12:2)*... and God delivered me years ago. He delivered me by His word, by fasting, and by cleansing me. And how He delivered me was after I was honest with Him, myself, and Salvester." *(Romans 12:17)*

"Salvester?" I said as I just looked at her.

"Yea' girl Salvester. I probably didn't have to go so far as to be honest with him, but I wanted nothin' but honesty in our marriage. And if I wanted him to be honest with me about everything, I had to be honest with him. You may not agree." She looked at me for my answer but I didn't give her one. "But I loved my husband and wanted the unethical feelings that I never asked for to be gone. I came to the realization that it was Satan tormenting me and trying to bring division between Salvester and me, then you and me. It ended up working for a while but not for long because God had His Hand in it. When you're destined to be with somebody or destined to be friends with somebody, can't no devil, no demon, or nobody stop it. They may hinder it for a while, but they can't stop it. Now look at God. You're back in my life, Precious is back in my life, and Salvester's back in my life." She turned into the parking garage at the airport. "Now my life is complete. And I promise you Barina that I will not go down the same road that I came from." She pulled up to the ticket machine, pulled a ticket, waited for the lever to go up, and drove through. I'm still quiet, listening to every word she's saying. "Girl I want all of what God has for me. You know what I'm sayin'?"

I nodded my head yes, still kinda' upset but not letting her know. I would never tell Salva that I'm upset because she was honest. "Yea', I'm just glad all that drama is over and now we can start a new."

She parked and quickly jumped out. I opened my door and we grabbed our bags and started walking towards the airport entrance. "So, you're missing Solomon huh'?"

"To be honest with you, yes I really am. I've been for a long time now."

"I know. Maybe you'll get a chance to see him again one day?"

"No I don't think so Salva, he's probably married now with kids?"

"You don't know that, I guess you don' forgot about all the advice you gave me concerning Salvester the other day? Now look at chu'? Look, if a man's your soul-mate, do you actually think God'll allow him to marry somebody else and have a bunch of kids? I don't think so. He's saving him just for you, who ever he is just in case it's not Solomon."

"What?"

"I'm just kidding. I just wanted to see if you were listening." She laughed out loud.

"Girl don't play with me right about now." I looked at her sternly. "You know this' a sensitive subject for me." I said, hunching over from the weight of the bags.

"Ok ok ok, I'm sorry." She held her suitcase in one hand and patted my back with the other one as we kept walking.

"I'm not playin', I think about him everyday. I really did this brotha' bad and now I'm hurtin' for it."

"I feel your pain. I felt just like that wit' cho' boy." She said. We finally made it to the ticket counter, got our tickets from the clerk, went and put our bags on the bag belt, and headed for our terminal. "I hurt Salvester bad too. At first I hated that I was ever honest with him. Because for a while he was so distant, then he started throwing it in my face, then he started actin' a little funny with Solomon like him and I had slept together. We were already goin' through because he felt like I didn't trust him, which for some reason I didn't. So when I broke down and was honest with him, he took it and ran away with it making me hate that I ever told him."

"Ok, let's talk about somethin' else this' vexing me."

"Yea', it is a drag."

"Yea', and it's pullin' all the energy out of me. Let's leave the past in the past. You forgave him, he forgave you, and now he's back in your life so make the best of it... You know you somethin' else, I saw that new computer and printer you bought me. Thank you so much Salva. Now I just gotta' find the feelin' for writing again. You know it's been years?"

"I know but you can do it. I'm so glad you saw it. I was waitin' on you to say somethin'. At first I thought you didn't see it. Barina God gave you that awesome gift and He didn't give it to you for no reason. He wants you to use it. He healed your body, your mind, and brought you from behind the prison gates so that He may use you. Now it's time for you to get back to work. You have a whole new story to tell and a great big ol' world to share it with. You can probably write about your own life and change the whole world, cause' you know you don' been through so much?"

"Don't I know it."

"So what cha' waitin' for?"

"Nothin'."

"So get to work. I miss goin' to all the book signing's with you and traveling to every city in the world. You kept money in a sista's pockets. Girl you were really well known? Now you gotta' tell the world what happened and that you're not a failure, but an overcomer. O' Hallelujah! You gon' make me start shoutin' up in here!" We laughed as she started doing the Holy Ghost dance right in the middle of the airport.

"Salva you are so crazy. You know you should've been a minister."

"Well I'm workin' on that, pray for me."

"I'll pray for you alright, you boot-leg preacher." We laughed even louder and some of the people around us laughed too.

The receptionist broke in and said. "Right this way. May I see your ticket's please? She looked at em'. "Ok walk right through there." She pointed towards the open terminal. "Enjoy your trip on our air lines ladies." She smiled generously.

"Thank you." Salva and I both said at the same time.

We boarded the plane surrounded by about a hundred more people doing the same thing.

208

I wrote all the way to New Orleans. None stop. Salva boosted my confidence, which caused me to get my desire for writing back. I haven't decided whether or not I'll write about my life yet. I realize that young girls and young women, well people period need to know that abstinence is the best and only way. They don't have to give their bodies to a brotha' just to keep em', and brotha's don't have to give theirs up to a sista' so they won't be looked at as being gay. I would encourage them not to have sex until they're married. *(1 Corinthians 6:13, 6:18)* Wait on God to send them the right man or woman who will love them and himself or herself, life, and the Lord. There are so many diseases out there. I didn't wait for the Lord, and this is why I had a baby at fourteen and out of wedlock. I'm not proud of it, but one thing I didn't do, I didn't give up. I asked God to forgive me, I forgave myself, had my baby and took care of her with all that I had, and I pressed on. And I didn't stop there, I made somethin' out of myself and I would let them know that they can too. Abortion is not the answer. *(Deuteronomy 5:17)* They will have to answer to God and live with it for the rest of their lives. *(Revelation 9:21)* We all have a great responsibility to keep our bodies clean before God. *(Romans 12:1)* A lot of times people use pregnancy as a style whether they're married or not. When a married couple gets an abortion, they're just as wrong as a person who's not married getting pregnant. It's all sin in the eye-sight of God. And we all will have to give an account for every wrong that we all have done on this earth. But the good news is that we can ask God to forgive us with Godly sorrow, I do believe He will. *(1 John 1:9)*

The cab just dropped us off at the hotel in the ever growin' city of New Orleans. The plane ride for the most part was good. A bit bumpy at times, but mainly smooth.

Salva's now walking towards me after checking us in. She's got two sets of keys in her hand. "Here's your key. We're on the fourth floor. The man said that the elevators are around the corner." She pointed in the direction and I followed without any questions.

When we got to the room it was already nice and cool. Most of the time you have to wait forever for it to get cool, but not in this case. I'm sure it has somethin' to do with the fact that Salva got us in one of the most expensive hotels in the city. "So whata' we do first?" I asked. I threw my luggage on my bed and looked at Salva.

"We wait."

"Wait? How long?"

"Barina calm down. We gon' wait til night when all the action is goin' on. I think we'll find her easier this way. Don't start that worrin', we'll be here for three whole days. That's enough time to find her."

"Hopefully she's still here."

"Look don't start doubting."

"I'm not doubting I'm just being real."

"Do you want your daughter back?"

"Salva you know I do." I said as I walked in the bathroom and started playing in my hair.

"Well stop thinkin' like that and start thinkin' like you've already found her. Cause' I'm a' tell you somethin'. I didn't come all the way out here for nothin'. I already had vacation time. I came to work. I'm tired of watchin' Satan do his thang. I'm ready to see the Lord do His thang. And if we believe, God will do just that."

What she just said brought me out of the restroom, I dropped on the bed and started crying.

"Barina don't cry. Karina needs you to be strong." She walked over to the window and opened up the curtains as the sunlight blinded my eyes for a moment.

"I hear you Salva but it's hard. Put Precious in Karina's position."

"I have, that's why I'm here and ready to work. Not wimping out." I gave her a sharp look. I could pop her in her mouth for callin' me a wimp. "Karina's like my daughter too. Now get up and go wash your face cause' in a couple of hours we gon' get oughta' here and I'm a call for a cab."

I got up just like she told me too. I trust Salva, I know she knows what she's doing, and I know she knows how to hear from God. And it's gon' take every bit of God to pull my baby out of the crack house. Lord I hope she's alright...

Chapter Fifteen

*O*ur journey began earlier today with walkin' up and down the big busy Bourbon Street without a destination to reach, or any leads. We asked every drug user, every drug pusher, every pimp, and every prostitute. Nobody knew or had ever heard of Karina. One of em' asked me for another name she goes by. And I got mad because all I've ever called my baby is by her name. I can't imagine anybody callin' her out of her name. Salva calmed me down.

Not too long ago we came back to the room with no leads and no hope. But Salva has assured me that we're ganna' find her because God showed her in a vision while she was praying. Now why didn't He show me considering that I'm the real mother? I thought to myself, I hope I see that vision come to past.

It's the second day. I woke up to Salva throwing open the curtains and the thrust of the early morning light's bursting down through the window next to my bed.

"Come on Barina, it's time to get up and go to work." She grabbed the toothpaste from her suitcase and walked into the restroom with her serious war face on.

I'm gettin' up discouraged in my heart. It's the second day and no sign of Karina. We only have one more day, so if we gon' find her, it must be done today.

Salva came in and walked over to my bed as I was makin' it up and said. "The Lord told me to tell you to have faith. You must have faith

Barina." *(Hebrews 11:6)* She turned and walked away. I'm tryin' with everything within me to keep from bursting out crying. "Hurry up we gotta' go before the sun comes out." She said rushing towards the door.

I quickly went and brushed my teeth and then put on my clothes and thought, Lord this is my baby we talkin' about. You know how it is.

Salva rushed back over to me. "Come on let's pray before we leave." She grabbed both of my hands and began to pray. "Lord, in the Name of Jesus, we come as humble as we know how. First of all thanking You for allowing us to get here safely, and for waking us up this morning. Now God we come in Your Name, asking that You would go before us and tare down the walls of the devil. Stop the hand of the enemy in Karina's life; pull down every stronghold and evil imagination, even in us as we go forth in battle today. Whatever the devil has planned for us today, Lord we pray that You would destroy it and not let it prosper. We thank You, and that it is so, and done, and that the victory shall be ours, and Karina will come back home safe and sound... Thank you now Lord in Jesus Name, amen."

Salva hugged me after she prayed and it made my knees shake. The power of God is all over her. I know she's ready to conquer anything that'll come her way. I want that same power.

We set out at the crack of dawn.

It's now noon and we haven't had any leads. The sun's burnin' down on us non-stop. We're so dehydrated we've already drank about ten soda's a piece. I'm frustrated. Salva's sweating. Her hair is soaking wet and both of our clothes are drenched. But she's still encouraged and going strong. I ask myself how I know this, because she's still encouraging me even though I continue to speak doubtful words. I don't know if I can do this any longer. I don't know if I'll be able to be strong if I see her in one of those nasty places. I'm thinking, what will she look like? What condition will she be in? Will she still look like my little girl? I don't know if I can make it. I'm a tell Salva to go by herself tomorrow, I don't think I can do this. A tear escaped from the corner of my eye.

Salva's asking this guy about Karina, who's playing his harp on the curb of the street. She showed him the picture, he took it and looked at it for a minute, and then said yes he seen her. But he said that the girl he seen was white and not black. So that was a lost cause. Salva turned and looked at me and said. "Barina don't you dare give up." She walked off and I followed.

There's this abandoned building in the distance and I already got the feelin' that Salva's ganna' say come on let's go in that building. "Hey Barina, do you see that abandoned building over there?"

"Yea' I see it." Barely able to walk because of dehydration.

"Come on let's go, this may be our break through."

She sped up walking like Karina's life depended upon it. When we got to the building it was boarded up. Salva walked around the side and found an opening.

"Come on Barina!" She yelled.

"I'm comin'." Even though I didn't want too.

When I walked around there, Salva was already inside the building. So I squeezed my way inside, looked around, and wanted to run out of there because the smell was unbearable. Trash is all over the place, old mold and urine-smelling furniture is scattered all around the place with holes in them, feces is splattered all over the walls and floors. I'm literally holding my nose. Somebody sprayed and painted nasty words of graffiti all over the floors, walls, and the ceiling. Salva's nowhere insight. I can hear footsteps walking upstairs I hope that's her. Let me go up stairs. I think we're wastin' our time, ain't nobody up in here.

"Hey you wake up!" Salva yelled from upstairs as I ran to see if she had found Karina

"Who are you? Leave me alone."

When I got upstairs, Salva was talking to this woman who's high on heroin. "Have you seen this young woman?" Salva showed her the picture, but she pushed it away.

"You betta' get oughta' my house befo' my friends come back and kill you!"

"This ain't no house, it's an abandoned apartment building that don't have your name nowhere on it! Now are you gon' tell me if you've seen her?"

"Get oughta' here!" She yelled, waving her hand as she tried to push the picture away.

"Not until you answer me!" Salva grabbed her and shook her.

"My friend's gon' kill you, let me go you crazy _____!"

"I ain't scared of yo' friends!"

I tried pullin' Salva away from the woman as I yelled all at the same time. "Come on, don't worry about it! We don't know who her friends are! Come on Salva forget it, let's get out of here!" I tried pulling her towards the stairs but couldn't.

She yelled. "You gon' tell me!" Salva pointed her finger and went back over to the woman and shook her again.

The woman finally spoke up. "Stop you sick woman! Ok ok ok I seen her about a month ago and that's all I remember. Now go!"

My heart dropped. My baby was actually in this filthy, nasty, dirty place. Salva was satisfied with the information so we left going to more places. By night's fall, I was drained spiritually, emotionally, and physically. I believe Salva was too, even though she never said it.

We're back in the hotel. Salva's taking her bath and I'm eating some take out food we got on our way back. A hamburger taste like a steak when a person ain't ate all day.

My heart bleeds just thinkin' about Karina being in that place. A vision of the place flashes before me constantly, and constantly it burns in my heart. We have one more day to find her, meaning one last chance.

The night came and went like the hours ran by the seconds.

It's morning and the sun's fighting its way through the cracks of the plain orange colored curtains. Salva didn't open em' all the way this time. I tossed and turned all night long. There were times through the night I could hear Salva praying in her bed. I couldn't understand every word but I do remember one thing she said, something to the fact that the number three being the number of change. Today is day three, let's see if there's ganna' be a change. *(Esther 4:16)*

We left a little later than yesterday morning. We've been walking, catching cabs, riding buses, walking in homeless shelters, calling hospitals, mental institutions, half way houses, everywhere and no sign of Karina. Salva finally showed her frustration and started kickin' the wall of this abandoned building when she found out that Karina wasn't there. We've had nothin' but false leads, leads where Karina was there but not anymore, just a bunch of time wasted. Salva insisted that it wasn't time wasted and that there's still hope. We haven't left the city yet. I want so badly to believe her. I really do but somehow in the back of my mind I don't.

Another day without any signs of finding Karina and any leads that would take us to her. I remember in the bible where it says, "...faith is the substance of things hoped for, and the evidence of things not seen..." *(Hebrews 11:1)* I said softly to myself. If I don't do nothin' else Lord, I take You at this scripture. And because I know Your Word to be true, I'm going to trust You.

We came back to the hotel. Salva apologized for the blank trip but quickly said that there's still hope. I guess she can see that I'm discouraged so she's tryin' to encourage me. "Barina sometimes it's not what we see, it's what we don't see."

"You know Salva that's amazing because I just said that to God and He gave me the scripture about faith being the substance of things hoped for and the evidence of things not seen. So that's confirmation."

"That's good Barina. Well we gon' hope on that." She said as she picked up the phone and called Precious to check up on her.

"Hello, Precious? Hello? Can you hear me? How's everything going?... You had fun?... Ok don't forget to do what I asked you to do... Aunt Barina's sittin' over there on her bed. You wanna' talk to her?... Hold on... She wanna' to talk to you." She came and handed me the phone.

"Hey my favorite niece! It's so good to hear your voice again. I've heard nothin' but great things. I heard that you're doing great things for yourself? You know ya' mama's very happy?... Well auntie's gon' talk to you when we get back, pray for our safe return ok?... I love you too. Bye, bye." I handed the phone back to Salva. She took it and walked away. They talked for about another twenty minutes and then she hung up.

Night came and went as fast as it did on yesterday. We caught the first cab available. The streets are crowded as usual. We checked out at 9am this morning. Both of us feel like failures. Salva felt like she had failed God and me. But I reassured her that I'm not upset and that I'm very proud of her.

The Hispanic cab driver is taking advantage of the long road and sites leading to the airport. He slowly drove with a long cigar hangin' out the corner of his mouth and with a very nonchalant attitude. We're passing through a low poverty area that looks like where gangsta's and drug pushers do their thing. Salva and I already came through here so now we're quite impatient, and at this point we're just ready to jump on the plane and get back home.

As we're slowing down to a stoplight, I have a chance to see the different types of low poverty, urban businesses and sites. Clicks of people are gathered around each another smoking and drinking. Some are fussing with one another while others are walking in and out of the stores, and walking up and down the streets. This particular convenient store to my right has a lot of people sittin' and standin' around the walls like they ain't got nowhere to go. When the light turned green, the cab driver took off. My eye just met the face of a woman standing in the crowd but leaning against the wall. My breath is taken away. O' my God! It's Karina! I yelled so loud, the cab driver slammed on his breaks as if he had hit something. "Turn around, turn around! I just seen my baby!" I yelled and Salva screamed.

He screamed back tryin' to hide the fact that we had scared him. "Al'right! Al'right lady hol' joe' horses!" He said with a slight Hispanic accent. He swerved around like a cop after a thief. He went back and dashed into the parking lot and standing there as clear as day is Karina—dirty but alive. Salva said nothin', only her tears did the talking.

I jumped out of the car with Salva following me and ran up to her callin' her name. She dropped to the ground, covered her face, and started crying uncontrollably. Then Salva and I dropped down and we all held each other and cried and cried and cried. "We've been here for three whole days lookin' for you! Are you alright?" I asked. She has this raunchy smell, but I could care less.

"Yea' I'm alright. I'm so glad to see you." She said, shaking with fear.

"We're glad to see you too." Salva said.

I looked up to the sky as the tears clouded my eyes, and thanked God for answering my prayers; for keeping His promise, and for sending me a miracle. "Come on you're comin' with us." She came with us without puttin' up a fight.

We took her to a nearby store and bought her some new clothes, some food, and then took her to a nearby hotel and cleaned her up. After that we took the first plane back to Cali.

The plane ride was more exciting than comin'. It was a quicker ride I guess because Karina and I had a chance to talk all the way back. We only talked about general things like how she became homeless in the first place. I never asked her about the kids and she never offered, probably because there were people sitting next to us. Some looked at us when Karina talked about surviving out on the streets. She was saying how she sold her body just to get food and drugs, how she went weeks without taking a bath, and how she and her friends used to shoot up together and get stone high, at times forgetting who they were. This was like a dagger in my heart. My daughter ain't never did drugs, nor have she ever sold her body, or even ever smoked a cigarette. And the part about her havin' sex with all these different men, even women in order to survive, I hated hearing that. I asked her was she a lesbian, her response was real. She said no but that she had to do what she had to do. Inside I thanked God and rebuked that homosexual spirit anyway. *(Romans 1:25-32)*

Salva had to sit behind us because of her ticket number. There was so much to talk about and Salva made sure she wasn't left out she sat up and listened for a while, then laid back and went to sleep. I know she was tired she stayed up all night long praying and pushing me not to give up. So I know God is giving her back everything that she poured out.

We're all back in Cali and now we're walking to the truck with our luggage and bags in our hands. Karina didn't have any luggage so she's carrying some of Salva's and some of mine. I still can't believe she's coming home. Her entire look is different. She looks older, experienced, and have lost a lot of weight. Some may ask how could I recognize her because she look so different, and I would tell em' that a mother knows her child. I knew right off that that was Karina standing in front of that corner store. She was so filthy when we found her. Salva said while Karina was in the shower that she believes she was on her last limb. If we had not found her when we did, she probably would've been dead the next day. That's how bad she looked.

Salva and Karina had time to jell as Salva raced us back to the house weaving in and out of the evening traffic. Salva asked her a lot of questions. Some she answered and some she didn't. They got along great just like ol' times. The weather's beautiful! Not a cloud in the sky. Mountains are in the horizon and the city life is all around us. I love Cali. Thin air and cool nights who wouldn't wanna' live here.

I finally feel like I'm gettin' my life back. Everything seems to be falling back in place. I'm restored, my life is restored, my freedom is restored, my health is restored, and my daughter and I are restored back together again. My life has been one that I never expected to turn this way but I believe this happens to everybody. There is no life that's perfect. We all make mistakes but we don't wobble in them, we get back up and try again until we conquer that what we're strugglin' with. And if a person can't get up on their own like I couldn't, all they have to do is pray and ask God to help them and He will send someone who He knows can get that person back up and back goin' again. In my case He sent Salva because He knew that I would eventually get over my anger and bitterness towards her, and forgive her, and then listen and allow her to help me as God directed her. God knows when we're just too weak to help ourselves. And this is why the bible tells us to "...bear one another's burdens..." *(Galatians 6:2)*

We drove up in the driveway on into the garage as Salva used her remote to let up the doors. She sped inside like a pro. We all got out, got all of our luggage, and is now headin' towards the inside door leading into the utility room. Just as Salva opened the door, Precious dashed out and tackled Karina and I on the floor. Salva jumped in like we're all on the football field. Luggage and bags are everywhere. We all laughed and cried for what seemed like forever.

Precious screamed. "What's up cuz'? Man it's so good to see you! And you too Auntie!" She looked us up and down. "Ya'll look great!" She reached to hug us both at the same time. "I missed ya'll so much! I thank God He brought us all back together again. We ain't gon' let nothin' tare us apart again. Never!" She started crying again.

We all eventually walked in and dropped our bags in the living room, dropped on the couch and love sofa, and started talking about ol' times. Karina started first.

"So this' the same house I used to come to as a young girl?"

Salva jumped in. "It sure is."

"Wow." Karina looked up and around, amazed. Things got quiet for a moment and out of nowhere Karina started crying and said. "I need to find my kids ya'll... They took em' away from me when I finally got the nerve to leave my husband. The court ruled in his favor after I got hooked on drugs, became homeless, and I couldn't care for em' so social workers came and took em'. That was years ago and I want em' back." She cried out loud. "I'm still a drug addict and I need help! I feel myself feigning for heroin right now! We used to sniff everyday and sometimes all night long. Weed wasn't strong enough... I hate to spoil the mood."

"No that's alright, take your time." I said as I got up and started rubbing her back. Precious ran and got some tissue from the bathroom and brought it back. Salva just kept saying Lord Jesus, Lord Jesus.

"I can't stay here long. If I stay here, I'm a pawn everything up in here. I really need help. So if ya'll wanna' help me, you can help me by gettin' me some help as soon as possible." She looked down at the coffee table.

"Karina if you want help, why don't chu' pray and ask God to deliver you?" Precious asked.

"I did, that's why I'm not shocked that I'm here. Before I would shoot up and sniff up, I would ask God to forgive me and not let me overdose. And believe it or not, He wouldn't. He's kept me in my sin even when I didn't wanna' be kept. *(John 17:12)* I prayed in my mind and asked God to help me and He sent me help. Mama and Aunt Salva came out of nowhere and got me from off the streets. It don't take a rocket scientist to know that. And this' why I'm askin' God to give me a mind to serve Him. I'm askin' Him to clean me up. And I can't stay here while He do it. Cause' if I stay here, I'm a take all yo' stuff and get what I need and I don't wanna' do you like that auntie."

I can't take it I broke in. "Look Karina, baby, we're just happy that you're home. Why don't you go take a shower and get chu' some rest, we'll talk about all that tomorrow ok?"

"Ok mama." She stood up and turned around to face us. "Hey I really need my kids back. That's really been pressin' on my heart. Even when I was out on the streets I thought about it."

"Like I said, go take a shower and we'll talk tomorrow ok? And don't worry about the kids, God's gon' take care of that." I got up and kissed her on the forehead as Precious took her upstairs and helped her get settled.

Salva and I look at each other silently until Karina and Precious was totally out of sight and then we burst out crying. "Salva girl I'm so grateful. We thought God had forgotten about us *(Hebrews 13:5)* but He didn't. He came right on time and He did it unexpectedly." We smiled as the tears fell.

"You know you're absolutely right. I had gotten to a point where I thought God would do it another way. But He came through just in time and right before we got on that plane." She laughed. "God is so awesome. You know what, God didn't lead us to her during those three days because He wanted us to trust Him. *(2 Corinthians 1:9)* He knew all the time that He was gon' bless us to find her before we left, that's why He led us there. But He wanted us to trust and to have faith in what we couldn't see, yet have it in what we hoped and prayed for." *(Hebrews 11:1)*

"It's a trip girl cause' we didn't know that our blessing was that close, we didn't know that God was about to bless us with what we had asked Him for. Just like before you came and started visiting me in the crazy house, I prayed for help and just that quick God sent me help. I didn't have to look for it, He sent you to me."

"Ain't that somethin'?" Salva jumped in.

"You know it is."

"Now what are we gon' do?" Salva said again.

"What God's gon' do."

"Yea' that's right."

"We gotta' find her some help, you heard what she said?"

"Barina I ain't worried about Karina. What we need to be worrying about is when she starts really feigning for more drugs."

"Now didn't you just say that you wasn't worried?"

"Ok your right, I just know how a drug addict does when they want their drugs."

"We'll deal with that when or if it comes. Come on now you're the one that's always sayin' God will take care of it." I said.

"I know Barina. I'm sorry. How're you feelin'?"

"...I'm fine. To be honest I'm happy but sad all at the same time."

"Why do you say that?"

"Because I'm happy to be free and to have my daughter back in my life. But I'm sad because of how she looks. She's lost so much weight. And I'm sad because of all the things that she got involved in. If I had just made the right decision in the first place all this drama would not have ever happened. Karina would not have ever gotten involved in all that she got involved in and me either.

"Barina, that's the past. You gotta' get over what you didn't do, what bad choices you made, what you didn't do as a mother. You did the best you could at that time and now I want you to move on. You got your new computer, now keep using it. Write all the books you can and get cho' confidence back. Ok? Do you have plans tomorrow?"

"Not to my knowledge." I answered.

"Let's go ridin' then."

"That's cool. What time?"

"About noon or when we get the girls together. They may go out somewhere by themselves."

"That's fine. Girl I got cramps like it ain't no tomorrow. They hittin' like I'm in labor?" Salva laughed as Precious came back downstairs without Karina.

Salva asked. "Where's Karina?"

"After she took her shower, she crashed. She's knocked out in the guest room. And I'm about to crash myself. I'll see ya'll in the mornin'." She came over and hugged and kissed both of us, walked back towards the stairs, turned around and said. "O' by the way, I'm so glad you're here Aunt Barina, I love you so much." She blew me a kiss and went upstairs.

"Girl I think I'm gon' go get in the bed myself, I'm beat." Salva said.

"So am I." We both got up and Salva started turning off the lights as we both started walking to our separate rooms.

"Good night." I said walking up the stairs never looking back at Salva.

"Night." She went into her master bedroom downstairs.

I'm so glad that Salva has four bedrooms. It's plenty of room for all of us.

Chapter Sixteen

*I*t's the early hours of the morning.

I woke up to screaming and yelling. I ran down the hall only to find Karina on the floor next to the bed shaking, sweating, and screaming. "Stop the pain, stop the pain! I need a fix! I need it, I'm not gon' make it! I'm not gon' make it!" She's huggin' herself, rolling and knocking over things in the room while I'm trying to restrain her. I jumped on her and started holding her. Precious and Salva just ran in. Salva threw herself down on the floor and started praying as Precious just watched.

This went on for a little over an hour. Salva's praying worked. We didn't give Karina drugs, I rocked her and rocked her as Salva and Precious prayed out loud. She finally went back to sleep. Her sheets were soaking wet, I'd rather have em' wet than to have given her drugs or let her tare up the house.

It's goin' on twelve noon. I didn't realize that we all had slept that long. Karina and Precious are still asleep. Salva and I are in the kitchen sittin' at the table drinking my favorite cappuccino.

Salva said. "Precious wanna' take Karina to a revival service with her tonight what a' you think?"

"It's fine with me. What about you?"

"Well you know I'm not her mother even though she's grown. I think it would be a great thing for her she may even get delivered. Who knows?"

223

"That would be awesome because last night was somethin' else. I mean somethin' else. I can't go through that every night we gotta' do somethin'."

"We ain't gon' do nothin' but watch God move." She said smiling.

"I hear ya'." I smiled back. Salva got up and walked over to the counter, brought the hot coffee pot over to the table, poured us some fresh hot cappuccino in our cups, and then took it back. She leaned her back against the counter as if to be hiding the coffee maker, folded her arms and said. "Never know what God's gon' do?" She walked back, sat back down, and took a slow sip of her cappuccino.

"You know I know."

"Hey let's go ridin'."

"Right now?"

"Yea' girl before traffic gets heavy. It's after noon?"

"Let me go get some clothes on and grab my shoes."

"I'm a do the same, see ya' in five." We both laughed as we departed to go put our clothes on.

Fifteen minutes passed.

I'm waitin' on Salva with her slow self. She finally came back in the living room. "Girl I've been waitin'on you for fifteen whole minutes, you said five?" I looked at her and rolled my eyes and snickered to myself.

"Now you know me by now." She said as we walked out to the garage where the truck was, got in, backed out, and zoomed on down the street headed to nowhere, so I thought, knowin' her, she probably got somethin' up her sleeve.

"Where are we goin'?" I just had to ask.

"Just sit back and ride."

We made turn after turn. Hit what seem like every freeway in Cali. Finally we're in a familiar neighborhood, sittin' in front of a familiar mansion. "It's my mansion!" I yelled. "I can't believe it! And it's still for sale?" I jumped out and went to the front door, grabbed the door handle like it was unlocked; then looked through the window with my hands squeezed between my face and the glass. "Salva you knew this?"

"Of course I did. Actually we should've been here. I just took you way out of the way so you wouldn't know what I was doin'."

224

"Girl you are somethin' else!" I went and shoved her in the shoulder.

"Awch' girl that hurt!" We burst out laughing as she grabbed her shoulder.

"Now you know I ain't got no money for this great big ol' mansion?"

"Barina what did I tell you about that doubtin'? Don't chu' know that God can do the impossible?" *(Luke 1:37) (Mark 9:23) (Matthew 19:26)*

"I hear ya'. So what do I do first?"

"You take down the number on the for sale sign."

I wrote it down as we went and jumped back in the truck. "Salva girl, I can hear the sound of the ocean waves. You know I used to love that sound." I closed my eyes as if to imagine it.

"I remember." She dialed the number on her cell phone, put it in the air so that I could hear, and sped out of the driveway on down the street.

"Summer Creek Estates?" The representative answered.

"Hi, I'm inquiring about a mansion you have for sale on 8803 Pebbles Coast? Can you tell me how much you're selling it for?"

"Sure hold please?"

"Ok."

She left Salva holding for about fifteen seconds and came back and said, "Its $895,000.00. But we're takin' the best offer. Would you be interested? Someone can meet you there if you like?"

Salva looked at me and I nodded my head yes. "Um', yes that'll be fine."

"Give us about ten minutes?"

"Ok that's fine see you there?"

"Yes."

"Hey can I ask you a quick question?"

"Sure."

"Why did the previous owner sale the home?"

"Actually they didn't sale it, they lost it. The house got seized. We got some offers but none ever went through, so it's been vacant ever since."

"Ok I'll see you soon."

"That'll be great. Bye." Salva pushed the button on her cell phone and smiled.

We turned around and went back and waited about fifteen minutes, which didn't seem long because I'm sittin' here admiring what I once had.

"Salva I can't believe that nobody's ever bought this place?" I said as we lifted up the unlocked gate and walked towards the backyard.

"What's for you Barina is for you."

"You think God saved this mansion just for me?"

"I believe He did."

"So that means He's gon' have to give me $895,000.00 real quick." I bent down and dipped my finger in the clean chlorine smellin' pool water.

"What did I tell you earlier Barina?"

"I know, I know. God can do the impossible."

"Now believe it."

"Ok I believe it. Its gon' take a miracle though."

"He's a miracle working God."

"And that He is."

No sooner as I said that, the realtor came from the front of the mansion and met us.

"Hi I'm Cindy." She reached out her hand with a friendly smile and a chipper personality. She looks to be a rich white woman with blonde hair and black streaks. A size five does justice for her. She looks like she makes sales all the time. Kinda'cocky if you ask me.

"Hi I'm Barina and this' Salva." We reached and shook her hand.

"Hi."

"So can we look inside?" Salva asked.

"Sure let me get the key."

We all walked back to the front, then she walked back to her shinny black convertible Mercedes, got the key, and walked back and unlocked the door as we all walked inside.

"Wow, I thought I would never see this place again." I looked around with my mouth open.

"O' you've been in here before?"

"Yea', actually I'm the lady who lost it."

"Really? That hardly happens. Are you trying to get it back?"

"If I can." Salva elbowed me in the side. "O' um', I mean yes I wanna' buy it."

226

"Great, so there's no need for us to look around because you already know what it looks like?"

"You're right. Let's talk business." We walked back outside to the front yard.

"Great, so you know how much this house is right?"

"Right."

"Ok we ask for $15,000 down. And whatever extra you have after that you take up with your lender. I'm sure you know all that already?" I nodded my head yes. "Do you have $15,000?" She looked at me then at Salva.

I hesitated and then said. "Uumm, well actually..."

A yellow convertible Porsche quickly pulled up and an older lookin' white man that looks to be in his late sixties, with a head full of gray hair, a bushy beard, worn jeans, and a plain navy blue t-shirt jumped out and walked up to us.

Cindy quickly said. "Hi, good to see you again." She smiled and he smiled back as they shook hands. Salva and I looked at each other like who's this and what's going on?

"Yes well I don't know why I'm here but it seems like I need to be here for some reason."

Salva and I kept on lookin' at each other.

Cindy introduced us. "This is Barina and Salva right?"

"Yes Salva." Salva answered as he shook both of our hands.

"Well Mr. Gary's my name, nice to meet you two ladies."

"Nice to meet you too." We both said.

"So Mr. Gary, are you thinking about buying this home right now? Salva asked.

"No."

"Then why are you here?" Salva asked again.

"Like I said I don't know. And no I don't wanna' buy this house. Got too many of em' as it is." He smiled and looked at us as we both made the smile mutual. "So are you ladies gon' buy this nice place?"

"Actually I'm tryin' to buy it." I broke in and said.

"Nice isn't it?"

"Yes, it's real nice. I used to own it a long time ago, but I got caught up in a horrible situation and lost it. It's truly a long story that I choose not to elaborate on."

"I understand. That's great that you can come back and buy your old house back?" He said.

227

"Yes it is."

Cindy cut in. "Mr. Gary volunteers with our company at times. Don't mind him. So do you have your down payment today?"

"To be honest with you, I don't. I'm just gettin' back on my feet and I don't have close to the amount needed. But I do have faith." Salva smiled but Cindy didn't. Mr. Gary walked off and went inside the house.

"Is there someone who you can borrow from or your bank?"

"No I'm really not in the position to be borrowing money from anybody."

Mr. Gary came back out of the house and Cindy walked over to him. They talked for a moment about business, then he waved goodbye and got in his car and left.

Cindy walked back over to us and apologized for the distraction and asked us again about borrowing the money.

"Like I said earlier, I don't have the money and I'm not in the position to borrow the money from anyone, not even from the bank."

"Hum, ok." She started writing on her clipboard. "What's your full name? You know there are some people that might have a program that may be able to help you. Would you be interested in trying that?"

"Sure, is it ganna' cost me anything?"

"Not a dime."

"Ok what do I need to do first?"

She handed me her clipboard and said. "Just sign in the blank space right there." She pointed on the paper.

Just as I was about to sign on the blank line, I'm shocked to see that it's a check for $895,000.00. I looked up at her as my mouth flew open and pulled the clipboard closer to my face to see if the check was real.

She smiled and said. "It's real and it's yours. Say hello to your brand new home again." She pointed towards the house as her smile grew into a laugh showing all of her teeth.

My mouth flew open again, and Salva snatched the clipboard out of my hand and said. "Is this really what we think it is?"

"It sure is. And trust me the check is good." She quickly answered.

"Why did you do this for me?" I asked with tears in my eyes.

"I didn't Mr. Gary did."

"What? When did he do this?"

228

"When he went in the house he wrote it out in there. Mr. Gary does things like this. He's a tycoon. He has so much money he doesn't know what to do with it so he volunteers at our company and when, so he says a little angel moves in him, he will come out to the site and write a particular client a check for the full amount of the house. So in other words he will buy their home for them. And they don't have to put a dime on the house. Just like you."

"$895,000.00 isn't enough along with taxes?" I said as Salva looked at me crazy.

"Yes it is. The taxes are included. We're selling it as is. Mr. Gary knew this before he came out here. He was there when you called. His little angel chose you today." She smiled with confidence.

"Yea' and angel's are sent from God." Salva broke in.

"I believe that." She agreed with Salva as they both laughed.

I looked at Salva, back at Cindy, signed the check, handed the clipboard back to her, fell down on my knees in the grass, and broke down crying right in the middle of the front yard. Salva was right along with me. Cindy started for a moment but dabbed her eyes, and started writing on the clipboard as if to keep her composure.

When we finally got up, Cindy hugged us and said. "Now I need you to come to the office so that I can give you your papers, sign some more papers, and get your keys and all that good stuff." We all laughed as the tears kept falling from Salva's eyes and mine.

"And don't worry about the insurance right now until you get on your feet. It was part of our special. You get one year free. So that gives you plenty of time to get your stuff together. Also this is going to blow your mind so Salva you may need to sit her down on the grass." Salva didn't hesitate; she sat me down on the grass and held my hand as I started shaking. "Are you ready for this? You do not have to worry about furniture because Davis Furniture Gallery is going to fully furnish this home tax free."

"O' my God. Is this really real God?" I looked up and reached my hands towards the sky as if I could touch it, laid back in the grass and started screaming and crying with tears of joy.

"O' it's really real." Cindy said excited as I jumped up on my feet.

"Salva did you hear that?" I grabbed her by the shoulders.

"Yes mam', I told you that God can do the impossible!" Salva said as she gave me a hard high five.

"You said it, yes you sho' did! O' my God! O' my God!" I started dancing and screaming with joy and admiration as Salva started dancing with me. I know Cindy thinks we're crazy but she doesn't know where I came from. I've been through so much and God didn't turn His back on me! He kept His word. And He showed me so much mercy and still rewarded me! *(Psalms 103:10) (Psalms 57:2) (Psalms 86:10) (1 Corinthians 2:9)*

Salva asked Cindy. "So you knew what Mr. Gary was doin' all along didn't you?"

"Yes I sure did. He doesn't do it for every customer, only when his little angel speaks to him."

"We don't know what to say but thank God. All the glory belongs to Him!" Salva said.

"I'm right with you. Are you guys ready to go to the office and finalize this contract?" She started walking towards her car. "We need to go ahead and do this so that you can pick out your furniture and have it delivered as soon as tomorrow. We're ganna' do a rush job."

"Yes mam' I'm too ready." Salva and I shouted all the way to the truck and to the office. "God is a miracle worker!" *(Exodus 4)*

It took two days to actually get all the paper work done and get all the brand new furniture in place just like I like it. They even gave me extra patio furniture. That wasn't even in the deal, only inside furniture. Favor is just on my side. *(Job 10:12)*

Now I'm back in my own home again. God showed mercy towards me and gave me back my mansion. I'm comin' out better this time, I had to pay for this house and buy my own furniture the first time, but this time I didn't have to pay anything. I set my furniture up differently because I don't wanna' remember nothin' about my past.

Salva helped me get my phone and lights on. My new book is almost done so I know I should have royalties comin' from that. I'm not worried I'll survive. Salva also bought me a pantry full of food—enough to last Karina and me for a couple of months.

It's funny because whatever God did for Karina at that church service, changed her life forever. I believe He totally delivered her from heroin. I mean she doesn't scream and shake at night anymore. And her countenance has totally changed even though it's only been three days; I know she's been delivered.

The phone ranged as I ran from the patio to the kitchen to answer it. "Hello?"

"Hey Miss. Thang! Girl this' like ol' times! I gotta' get use to this!" Salva yelled in my ear as she always does when she's excited about somethin'.

"And you know it!" I yelled back into the phone.

"Where are you?"

"What chu' mean where am I?"

"Where are you?"

"I'm in my house."

"No silly, I know you're in your house but where are you in your house?"

"Oh' I'm in my, do you hear me? Kitchen Miss. Thang!"

"Yea' I hear ya'. Hey go outside and get your newspaper and bring it back to the phone I wanna' show you somethin' in it."

"I don't get no newspaper?"

"Are you sure? Go look anyway I thought I saw one the other day?"

"Ok so you wanna' waste a sista's time?"

"Look hardhead just go and look, you know I love lookin' in my newspaper for everything."

"Alright, hold on." I walked to the front door, opened it, screamed, and ran back to the phone. "Girl there's a..."

"I know, I know, I know."

"Well can I say it?"

"Go ahead."

"There's a spankin' brand new Infiniti truck sittin' in my driveway with a huge bow around it!"

"Go start it up."

"Start it up? How, I don't have no keys?"

"Look on the top of the left front tire."

I ran back out there and did exactly what Salva told me to do, and sure nuff' the keys are right there.

I jumped in and Karina ran out and jumped in the passenger seat sniffing and said. "I love the smell of new vehicles."

"I love new vehicles period!" I yelled, looking all around as if to be looking for somethin'.

Salva and Precious pulled up and parked beside us. We all jumped out and hugged each other. "Girl where ya'll came from? And who's is this?"

"I was on my cell phone right down the street." She pointed down the street. "You askin' who's is this? It's yours!"

"Mine?"

"Yes yours." She nodded her head yes.

"All mine?"

"All yours."

"Ok now wait, where did you get this from? I know you ain't got that much money?"

"How you know?"

"I know all yo' business my sista'." Karina and Precious looked at each other and burst out laughing.

Precious said. "Well this time your wrong. Mama's been saving' this money for years. Even before her and daddy broke up. She was savin' it for hers and daddy's wedding, but she said that she would rather use it to buy you a new truck. She was ganna' use it to help put a down payment on your new house but God used that ol' man to buy it instead."

"Wow, for me Salva?"

"This is the least I can do for you Barina after all you've done for us? Remember you bought my house and me and Salvester's truck so I'm just returning some of the favor. I realize that I can't return all of it back, but here's some of it."

"Salva what can I say?"

"Nothin' but get cho' lil' self in there so we can go crusin' around town."

We all started talking to each other at the same time as I went and locked the front door, and we jumped in the Infiniti and stayed gone all day and all night.

Chapter Seventeen

Karina's been goin' to church with Precious every Sunday for about five month's now. Salva and Salvester are now engaged. He proposed to her the other night. She was so excited and said that they're expecting a huge wedding. It's funny because I can remember when Salva was helping me look for my wedding dress, and now I'm helping her look for hers. I've learned through life experiences that you never know what the future will bring so you just have to live it like it's your last, and to do good to all men. I'll tell anybody my testimony after goin' through what I've been through—you better know Jesus. *(Romans 10:9)* I thought I could live without Him with a bunch of pride, and it got me put up in the crazy house. Now that I'm not a fool anymore, I'm sittin' large again and this time I appreciate it more and I didn't have to work hard at it. All I had to do is receive it.

It's a little before 10:00am and Precious and Karina have decided to try to go get Karina's kids back. It's been over a year since she's seen em'. Karina called some of her husband's kinfolks and they told her where they were and gave the phone number to where he is now. She supposedly talked to him and he agreed to let her see the kids but he said that she couldn't keep em', nor could they ever come back and stay with her.

Karina just walked in the living room where I'm sittin'. "Mama, we're about to leave, I'll be back in about a week."   "That long? Karina, I really don't think you and Precious should go up there. What if he starts actin' crazy again? What chu' gon' do?"

233

"Mama I'm a grown, saved, and delivered woman now. Trust me I do know how to take care of myself, and so does Precious. You and Aunt Salva gotta' stop tryin' to treat us like babies. We ain't babies no more."

"I realize that Karina, but you and I have been through so much and I don't want nothin' to happen to you guys."

"Mama do you trust God?"

"Yes I do Karina. And your point is?"

"My point is, then trust that He's ganna' take care of us." The horn blew outside. "That's Precious I'm gone." She quickly planted a kiss on my cheek. "I'll call you when we get there!" She yelled going out the door not waiting for me to follow her. I walked up to the double glass doors and looked out. Precious waved at me as Karina threw her suitcase in the trunk, got in, Precious backed out, and they left speeding down the street. Lord please don't let nothin' happen to my child. She's the only one You gave me...

I haven't had to get a job at all. God's been taking care of my every need. I'm still preparing my book. Somehow or another I can't seem to finish it. Somethin' about it seems incomplete, and at this point I don't know when I'll complete it.

There's a knock at the door. I went and looked through the double glass doors. It's Salva and Salvester.

I opened it. "Hey Mr. and Mrs. Salvester." They laughed and came in. "Girl yo' daughter's just left."

"I know, we started followin' Precious on the way here but Salvester stopped at the store to get some coals. We're que'in at the house, you wanna' come and hang out with us?" Salva asked as if she knew I was gon' say no.

"That's sounds good, about what time?"

They looked at each other and smiled. "In about a couple of hours..."

Salvester cut Salva off. "I gotta' get my fire started real good, you know how I used to do it?"

"Of course I remember I'm the one that tol' you you should've been opened up your own restaurant."

"That's right you sure did my sista'. I appreciate chu'. I'm lookin' around in this big ol' free mansion and thinkin' it's amazing how God brought everything back around for you. But this time even better with some learning experience."

"We all have learning experiences." I quickly said, letting him know he ain't perfect.

Salva looked at Salvester crazy and quickly broke in. "Auh' um', well B' we gon' see you in about an hour ok?" She started pushing Salvester towards the front door.

"Why ya'll rushin' off? I ain't thinkin' bout' Salvester." I followed them. "I haven't forgotten that chu' play too much, and that cho' big mouth always get chu' in trouble." Salva and I laughed while he just smirked his lips, which I could care less.

"Now Barina girl you know I just be playin' with chu'? It's all good though. But I do wanna' let you know that I'm very proud of you. And you're a strong woman. And if we wanna' talk about life experiences, I can't talk about nobody but myself... and my soon to be wife." He looked at her, she looked at him and smiled, he slightly grabbed her hand and they walked on out to the truck, we said our goodbyes, and they got in and left.

Let me go try and write a little in this book. I grabbed a towel, my shades, paper, pen, clip board, and put my sandals on and walked on down the old sandy trail leading to the beach. I forgot my lawn chair so I went back and got it and then came back and began writing. It feels good being able to listen to the ocean as the waves roll back and forward at a repetitious pace. There's a cool calm breeze out today. Boats are in the far distance and my neighbor's are out doin' their thang, some are wading through the water while others are walking up and down the sandy beach.

After over ten years I never thought I'd be sittin' out here again, let alone me livin' in this huge house again. My very first home, wow. God is so amazing. Just when I thought my life was over, God said different. I actually thought either I was gon' kill Wayne or he was gon' kill me. Our marriage ended the best way it could. I don't ever wanna' make a terrible mistake like that again, I'd rather stay single. I'd probably do better like this anyway. Keeps me out of a whole lota' unnecessary mess.

I can actually close my eyes again and dream. The thought of me being able to dream again never crossed my mind because I felt that it would never happen again. Well time, reality, and God proved me wrong. I squeezed my eyes tighter, sighed, and leaned back further in my chair and went to sleep.

When I woke up, a couple of hours had passed. I know Salva and Salvester's wonderin' where I am. I jumped up, went back up to the house, changed my clothes, and drove over there.

Salva met me at the front door looking down at her watch. "Girl where have you been?" She looked up at me. "It's been over two hours, we thought chu' weren't comin'. We don' played about twenty games of dominos waitin' on you."

"I fell asleep and then I stopped to get some gas." We walked in. "I got this pound cake from the store." I handed it to her and we walked straight to the backyard. "Why it ain't nobody else here? Who else did you invite?"

"You're our main guess, don't chu' feel special?" Salvester had to put his two cents in.

"Don't chu' look special?" I said as we all started laughing.

"Alright that ain't nice saint of God." Salvester yelled from the barbeque pit as he took the long pitchfork and turned the meat over.

"I already asked God to forgive me."

"When? I didn't see your mouth move?"

"It didn't. I did it in my heart." We all laughed again.

"Paugh', yea' right!" He put his hand over his mouth.

"Boy, will you lay off me? Salva get cho' soon to be husband."

"Girl I ain't gon' touch that, I'll let you two have that one." She went and sat down at the patio table. And I went and grabbed me a soda from the cooler and sat at the table with her.

Salva has a huge backyard with a rectangular cemented covered patio. She also has two patio sofas, a patio table with three chairs, which used to be four but Salvester sat down on it and broke it, and they also have an open bar grill area that Salvester's standing at now. I gotta' give it to her, that girl's a great decorator. Kinda' reminds me of an outside living room.

Salvester burst out laughing and said. "So Barina what's up? You ain't gotta' man yet?"

I stood up and hit the table like a man as the domino's jumped off the table and landed everywhere. "What's up Salvester, you got beef with me?"

"Naw' girl I'm just messin' with chu'. Look like I struck a nerve."

"Yea', well, you did, you messin' too much. I'm not in the mood for all your non funny jokes!" I sat back down and took a sip of my soda.

Salva looked at me and got up and started picking up the dominos from off the ground. "So what's on your mind mam'?"

"So I guess you wanna' mess with me now huh'?"

"I'm not messin' with you I'm askin' a serious question." She sat back down.

"Nothin's on my mind. The question is what's on ya'll mind?" I leaned over and whispered. "Don't get big shot cause' you back with him and I'm still single." I went and threw myself down on one of the sofas. Salva followed and sat down right beside me.

"So that's what's wrong with you. You're lonely."

I shoved her in the shoulder. "I'm not lonely, where'd you get that from?"

She smiled. "I'm just lookin'." She whispered to me. "Your prince and shinning armor will come one day don't worry."

"Salva I'm not worried. Why are you tryin' to make somethin' wrong with me?"

"Because it is. Look, don't act like I don't know you. I know when somethin's wrong or is bothering you."

"Ok well then just pray for a sista'."

"I already have."

"You know you're a trip?" I said.

"I know all that tell me somethin' new?" She got up and walked over and took a piece of sausage from off the tray beside the pit.

I'm thinkin', I'm not mad at Salvester, he just wanna' play at the wrong time. Maybe if he hadn't of mention about me not havin' a man, I'd a been alright. Of course he doesn't know that that's a sensitive side of me because the man of my dreams is still not in my life. When I think about him it hurts. It hurts with passion. But it's not the passion of God it's the passion of my flesh. *(Ephesians 2:3)* And I can't control it one way or the other. I've tried so hard to forget about him, felt that it was best because I knew that there was no way on this green earth that I was gon' see em' again. But my feelings still haven't changed. I'm longing for him, for his company, for his affection, and for his spiritual guidance. I realize that all that's a fantasy now and I need God to deliver me. Most of my mind is him, Most of my thoughts is him, most of my imaginations is him, and much more I'm not proud of.

237

Solomon was so loving, caring, and considerate. But most of all he loved the Lord and a woman can't beat that.

"So what's up you gon' eat?" She walked back over to me and then walked back over to the barbeque pit where Salvester's standing.

I followed her. "So what's on the menu?"

"What cha' want sis'?" He asked as he jabbed at the meat with the fork.

A little bit of everything." I said as I grabbed a plastic plate and fork.

"Alright."

He put a barbequed chicken leg and breast on my plate. Threw some wieners on the side and took some barbeque sauce and spread it all over the meat. Salva made some potato salad and barbeque beans. She just ran in the house and came back out with em' and scooped some out on my plate. Salvester dropped two pieces of light bread on top of my beans and potato salad. I'm thinkin' to myself, this' gon' be messy, but it's gon' be good. Finger lickin' good. I smiled.

Salva asked. "Girl what chu' smilin' at? You act like it's the best barbeque you ever had?" Salvester laughed and threw some of Salva's potato salad in his mouth, then licked his fingers.

"Somethin' like that."

We all sat down and ate for about twenty minutes without a sound.

The phone rang, breaking the silence.

Salva got up, ran in the house, and answered it after three rings. "Hello?" She yelled from inside the house. "Precious is that you? I can barely hear you?" She yelled. "He what? Ok... ok... Where's Karina?... What time?... Alright... Umm, good... We'll be waiting... Be careful... I love you... Ok bye." She came back out slower than she went in. "That was Precious. She and Karina are on their way back."

"Where's Karina? Why she didn't get on the phone?" I said.

"Because she was talkin' to her husband."

"You mean the babies daddy?"

"There you go, you know what I mean."

"What time are they comin' back?"

"I said they're on their way."

"O' I didn't hear you."

"Barina don't start gettin' worried."

"I'm not. I'll just be glad when they get here that's all."

"They'll be ok."

"I know." I said finishing off all the barbeque meat Salvester gave me. "Umm, now that was good. That stuck right to my ribs." I got up and threw my plate in the plastic garbage bag that's sittin' by the patio door.

"I'm glad you liked it sis'." Salvester said, cheesing.

"Well I'm bout' to get out of here, Salva are you comin' over later?" She looked at Salvester for his approval. He didn't say anything and she didn't either. "That's alright I'll talk to you later." I walked out and got in my truck.

Salva ran up to my window. "Barina please don't be mad at me. You'll understand when your prince comes." I just looked at her and didn't say a word, just thinkin' that I will not be controlled by no man. "Well aren't chu' gon' say somethin'?" I still didn't say anything. "Look, I'm not gon' beg you Barina."

I started slowly backing the truck back. "You don't have to Salva. Just remember one thing, men come and go, but your sister will always be there." I started backing out faster.

"Wait!" She held on to the window as she backed up with the truck. "Barina I know you're here for me! But this is somethin' that I gotta' do, it ain't got nothin' to do with you…" I backed on out into the street. "You don't understand!" She yelled as I drove off. "You don't under…" Her voice faded as I got further and further away. I looked in my rear view mirror and saw Salvester standing in the front yard hugging Salva. I would feel bad about my actions but I don't. Cause' it's been too long since Salva and I have been apart and we have yet to make up for all the time wasted. And no selfish man's gon' come in between that. Maybe I'm wrong but maybe I just might be right. Salvester doesn't act the same as he used too anyway. He used to be quiet and sweet, but now he's a smart-allick and he talks way too much. He gets on my nerves. Maybe she's right about me being lonely. And that may be true, but one thing I do know is that I'm not desperate.

I got home fairly quick. Traffic wasn't bad at all actually I'm wondering where everybody is during this late evening?

As soon as I stepped foot in the house, my body said I'm so glad to be home. I threw my keys on the hall table, went to the kitchen and checked for messages. "I got two messages I wonder who those are?" I looked at the caller ID. The numbers show unlisted. "Let me listen to these messages before I get situated."

First message. "...Mama! This is Karina. I'm just lettin' you know we made it and we alright. I'll call you later..."

Second message. "...Where are you? It's four hours later. You must be over Aunt Salva's or you had a book signing and didn't tell me?... Call Precious cell phone...604-528-3221... Bye!..." Click.

I would call her back but the second message was three hours ago. I better call anyway Salva never said that I was there. I dialed the number.

The answering machine quickly came on. "...Yo' what's up? This Precious voice mail. Yea' yea' yea' you missed me so leave that number and I'll call ya' back... Hope Heaven's smilin' down on you?..." I left a message and hung up; made me some cappuccino, poured it in my favorite coffee mug, walked down to the beach, sat in my chair, and started watching the rough tides roll in and out. The tides in the ocean is a little heavy considering the fact that it's somewhat windy and all. Looking out into the early night's atmosphere brings a chill over me. I closed my eyes and started imagining the last time I was out here this late; Solomon came and took my breath away. He took it a way with his charm, with his surprise, with his charisma, and with his romantic smooth assertiveness.

"Mama, I'm home!" Karina broke into my imaginations as she yelled from inside the house. "Mama where are you?"

I ran up the trail going back to the house. "Karina, I'm out here by the pool!" I yelled running around the pool to get to the patio door. Just before I got to the patio, out came running two little human beings. One is a little girl, and the other is a handsome little boy. Karina came out after them smiling.

I ran up to them as they met me with a hug. "O' my grand babies! Hey, come here and give granny a big ol' hug!" They ran up and hugged me tight around my neck as they fought each other for my love. "O' Karina, they're beautiful, they look just like you girl!"

Precious came from around the corner of the patio door and said, "No Auntie, they look just like you."

"Yea' mama, they do look just like you."

Precious walked up and grabbed the kids by the hands. "Here let me take em' and give em' a bath so you two can talk. Come on ya'll so I can bath ya'll and put ya'll to bed. Are ya'll sleepy?" Precious voice faded around the corner until she got upstairs.

"So how'd you get em' back?" I asked as we sat down at the patio table.

"Believe it or not, he let me take em'. Said he didn't want em' anymore. I think it's because he gotta' new wife and she got five kids. So you know how my babies looked when I got there?"

"How?"

"Crazy. Just crazy."

"Hum'."

"Hum' is right mama. He didn't even put up a fuss. He just said take em' and go. So we left with the quickness." We both laughed.

"I bet you two did."

"Her kids were all over the place tareing up the house. And the house was so nasty, pure nastiness, looked like they ain't cleaned up in years. He just got oughta' jail. I'm figurin' that he probably met her while he was up in there."

"Do you still care for him?"

"Mama are you serious? Lord no."

"I'm just checkin' cause' I don't want you runnin' behind him like you used too. And now that you have the kids means he's gon' know where you live, and I don't want him thinkin' that he can come back down here clownin' like he used too and tare up the house the Lord gave back to me."

"Mama don't be worrin' about all that. He ain't gon' be no problem, I guarantee you. Just be happy for me right now please?"

"Ok, I'll be happy. But remember what I said... I can't get over how cute they are?"

Karina chuckled as if she thought about what I just said as Precious came back outside.

"What're ya'll talkin' about?" Precious asked as she plopped down on one of the black leather Barcelona chairs sittin' across from us.

"You." Karina answered.

"Me? For what?" Precious sat up.

"I'm just kiddin', mama's still talking about how cute the kids are."

"Yea' they are cute. I'm so glad you finally got your babies back." Precious said as she came over and sat at the table with us. "Now we can take em' to church and groom em' up the right way." *(Proverbs 22:6)*

"I know that's right." I said as me and Precious high-fived each other. "You two remind me so much of me and yo' mama, Precious. I tell you if you ain't just like yo' mama girl. Feisty, bold, and confident." I said.

"Yes mam'." Precious said, smiling as if to be proud at what I just said.

"You have helped Karina so much and I just wanna' tell you thank you. It's so good to have somebody like you in Karina's life. Don't ya'll ever depart like your mother and I did at one time over a man." Karina and Precious looked at each other and then back at me. "If a man can't accept one or the other, then you don't need em'. And don't ever settle for anything. Take your time and save yourselves for the right one. Even though you two aren't virgins anymore, you can become virgins all over again in the Lord. Marry Jesus and He'll become your lovers." They listened intensively. Only the ocean tides are speaking.

"Thank you Aunt Barina. I really needed to hear that because I was thinkin' hard about whether or not to do it with this guy I'm dating. But he's pressuring me so much. Most of our conversation is about sex. So I don't know. I'm tryin' so hard to go somewhere in God and I don't have time to be side tracked. I'm wonderin' what should I do?"

"Precious by the sound of it, you already know what to do." I said.

"Why you say that?"

"Because you just said most of your conversation is about sex and that you're not tryin' to get side tracked. Don't chu' think that if you have sex with him that you would get side tracked?"

"Yes mam' I would." She looked at Karina as Karina started snickering underneath her breath.

"Karina don't laugh this goes for you too." I said as Precious started laughing. "Any guy that don't ask you do you have a personal relationship with God, do you go to church, do you have a job, how your day was, and what are your goals, you need to leave em' alone. Especially if they ain't got no job and ain't tryin' to go to work nowhere." We all laughed. "You want somebody who's not gon' be all about themselves. Somebody who's gon' love and respect you first as a human being, then as a woman; then as a woman of God. You two deserve nothin' but the best. Tell God what kind of man you want, and

He will give you the desires of your heart. *(Psalms 37:4)* And be specific."

Karina asked. "He'll give us exactly what we want?"

"Yes mam' as long as it's to edify Him and not for some ungodly reason."

"Wow that's alright. I didn't know that." Karina said.

Our conversation lasted about two hours. Ending with Precious saying that she was leaving the guy she's dating alone. The whole while we all were talking, he was constantly blowing up her cell phone.

"See I missed out on my good thang from God. He was just what I wanted and just what I needed. He was the man of my dreams and I messed it up thinkin' that I would make it better with Karina's daddy than I would with who God had sent me. I thought that because he was Karina's daddy, that would help bring Karina back and we would be a family again."

"Awh' mama you did? I didn't know that?" Karina said.

"You weren't there you were in your rebellious stage."

"I know mama please don't remind me." She lowered her head in shame.

"But anyway it ended up being the worst mistake of my life. And I paid for it. That's why I'm just now comin' out of the Hell I went through with him. So I can tell you what to do and what not to do."

"Yes mam'." They both said at the same time.

"Do you think you'll ever see em' again?" Precious asked.

"I don't think so. I had my chance and lost it."

Karina broke in. "I almost feel like it's all my fault cause' if I hadn't of ran away, tryin' to be jealous, all the drama you went through wouldn't have ever happened." She put her head down between her arms and rested them on the table.

"No mam'. One thing you must understand Karina, mama makes her own choices and decisions. I made the choice to do what I thought at that time was the right thing. One thing you two will learn in this life is that somethings are supposed to happen and somethings we can bring on ourselves, and unfortunately this' somethin' that I brought on myself. But now it's all over, and I have moved on with my life. And I've left my past back where it is. Karina pick your head up, you ain't got nothin' to feel bad about." She picked her head up. "I'm alright, you're alright, and now everything's alright. And there ain't nothin' to feel bad about. Now you have your kids back. God gave em' back to you. Now do what chu' suppose to do with em' and move on. Ok?"

"Yes mam'."

"Come on let's see what we got sweet in there to eat, I gotta' sweet tooth." We all got up talking at once.

"No I'm hungry I want some food." Precious said.

"Mama did you cook?" Karina asked as she followed.

We kept walking and talking until our voices faded going into the house.

Chapter Eighteen

The babies are getting so big considering the fact that they were so small when I saw them again. Malnutrition was written all over their little bitty bodies. But now there's some meat on their bones and I've made Karina give em' vitamins everyday.

Salva just knocked on the door. I opened it and she dashed towards me with a big grandma' hug. "What's up my lil' sista'?"

"Girl if you don't get cho' hands off me?" We laughed.

"Awe' come on now you ain't got no love for your big sista' no mo'?" She kept trying to hug me.

"Big sista'? Whatever shut up and come on in." She let me go as we started walking towards the kitchen.

"So where's everybody?"

"They're upstairs."

We walked in the kitchen where I have eggs and bacon on the fire. Salva hunched over the island while I started stirrin' and chopping at the eggs and the bacon at the same time. The aroma flooded my nostrils sending chills through my body. That's how good it smells.

"Girl how're you gon' cook eggs and bacon at the same time?"

"You see me doin' it don't chu'?"

"I see ya' alright. Burnin' the kitchen up." She laughed.

"Whatever don't be jealous."

"Jealous? Trust me it never crossed my mind." We both laughed.

"So where's your hubby?" I asked peaking back at her.

"He's not my hubby yet."

"Well almost."

"Yea', almost but not yet."

245

"Why you soundin' like that?"

"Cause' he made me mad. After you left I finally confronted him about his mouth and his controlling ways. He got smart and I had to tell em' off."

"You got smart? Not you?" I smiled.

"Yea' me, so what." She got up and went and sat at the kitchen table. "Look Barina I refuse to go down the same ol' tied path with Salvester again." She looked at me and I didn't say a word, just kept stirrin' the food.

"But I thought you were the one that was wrong?" I turned and looked at her, then back at the food.

"I was with most of it, but not all of it."

"Look Salva ain't nobody perfect. You used to be the main one gettin' on me when I was so hard on men, now look at you? So you mean to tell me you're havin' second thoughts about marrying him because of one lil' ol' argument?"

"I never said I'm havin' second thoughts, I'm just not gon' put up with his controlling and smart-allick ways anymore."

"Now I can agree to that." I went and placed the huge plates of bacon and scrambled eggs on the table, went and started buttering some toast, and put it in the oven.

Salva watched me and then rested her head on the table. "You know? Men can be so difficult sometimes."

"They sure can be but you don't have to let em' be controlling. A man will do only what you allow him to do. If he try ta' take off your blouse on the first date, you better leave em' alone cause' you already know what he's about to do next, or if he curses you out for no apparent reason on the first date, you better leave em' alone cause' he may be a sike-o-manic." Salva raised her head up and burst out laughing.

"Girl you are so crazy!"

"It's true."

"I know it's true." She put her head back down.

I took the toast out of the oven and sat it on the island to cool off.

Salva asked, "so what chu' got goin' on for today?"

"Not too much."

"What about later on tonight?"

"Nothin'. Why what's up?"

246

"Just asked."

"Why you just asked nosey?" I put the toast on the table next to the bacon and eggs.

"No reason, just askin'. Uwh' somebody's so defensive?" She took a piece of toast, parted it with her fingers, and took the biggest bite she could out of one half.

"I'm not being defensive. I'm just wonderin'. Normally when you ask me a question like that. Either one or two things are goin' on with you. One, you think I'm lonely and depressed or two, you wanna' go do somethin'."

"That's it. I think you're lonely and depressed."

"You lyin' Salva. You know it's a sin to lie?" *(Colossians 3:9)*

"I know but I ain't lyin', you are lonely right?"

"Possibly." We burst out laughing.

"Well you are depressed right?"

"Maybe."

"So now there you have it. I wasn't lyin'."

"Whatever shut-up. You always tryin' to get the mote out of my eye, when you need to get the beam out of your own eye." *(Matthew 7:1-6)* I sat at the table and looked at her like now take that.

"Don't try to get religious on me."

"The Word is the Word." I jumped up, went to the stairs and yelled for Karina, the kids, and Precious to come eat.

Karina yelled back instantly. "We're on our way mama!"

I walked back to the kitchen and sat down at the kitchen table.

They all trampled down the stairs talking and laughing with one another.

Karina yelled first. "Mama what cha' cook?" They all came in the kitchen and went straight to the kitchen table. Precious went and hugged Salva before sitting down. Karina made sure the kids were seated first then she sat down.

"Looks and smells good." Precious put her two cents in as she fixed her plate and started eating. Karina got up and fixed the kids plates and then sat down and started eating. I looked at Salva's lips and I knew that she was about to say somethin'.

"It's so good to see your babies Karina." She pointed. "That baby boy looks just like yo' mama." She looked at me and smiled.

"You need to quit Salva. You know them kids don't look nothin' like me." I said.

Precious burst in. "Yes they do Aunt Barina. Look at em'." We all looked as the two of em' started smiling and blushing.

"Yea' I can see it now since ya'll pointed it out."

Breakfast was a blast. Kinda' like a reunion. It's so amazing how God'll take people out of your life in order to place them back years later totally different. I smiled as the waves rushed and roared as they fought each other towards me.

They all decided to go out to the mall and to the movies. Salva begged me to come but I couldn't because God said no. He wanted me to get in His Word and finish writing and taking care of my business. Now that I have a personal relationship with God, He makes me do that at times. I don't even wanna' talk about gettin' up early in the mornings. I don't mind because there's so many rewards behind being obedient. *(I Samuel 15:22)* I can always go to the movies and to the mall, but I just chose this intimate time with God and I'm lovin' it. I sniffed the fresh smell of the beach water as the cool slight shower of the waves tapped against my face. God speaks to me through this water; I can hear His voice so clear. "O' how I love Him..." I said, making my feelings a reality.

Evening came quick I guess because I hadn't been payin' attention to the time. No sign of everybody, they must be havin' a great time. I gotta' taste for my favorite cappuccino. I walked the sandy trail back up to the house, made me a fresh cup, and turned the volume up on the TV Something just caught my eye. I was just about to go back down to the beach but I gotta' stop and hear what this preacher on Christian television is talkin' about. He's talkin' about lovin' man more than lovin' God. He's sayin' that you can actually love your husband, wife, kids, and or your friends more than you love God. You do this when your mind is constantly on them and not on God, and when you try to fix every one of their problem's instead of allowing God to fix it for them; also when you spend more time with them than you do with the Lord. God is a jealous God. *(Exodus 20:5)* He wants your time. And last, how we can serve them and put them first instead of God. Seeking man's approval and help instead of God's. Now that I've started Watchin' Christian television, it has really helped my spiritual growth and has helped open my eyes. It has allowed me to see that I was puttin' my family and friends first. I was seekin' their advice instead of seeking the Lord's advice. I was actually holding Karina in my heart and in my spirit and didn't realize it. I was afraid that somebody would come along and take her away from me and that they would wreck our relationship again. I never had a real relationship with my mother so I guess I was tryin' to get what I didn't have in Karina. So I held her close to my heart so that she would never leave my life and heart, but this' what God wanted from me. All the love, time, and attention that I was seeking from her, God was longing that from me. I'm finally seeing this thing. It's all about God and not about me. Not about what I want and when I want it. It's all about the Father in Heaven and what He wants. I finally got this thing together and now He's giving me the desires of my heart. *(Jeremiah 42:1)*

I walked back down towards the beach with these questions running through my mind. Does my Spirit crave the Devine Holy God, even in the presence of the best that the world has to offer me? Do I take the time to meet the Great I Am each day, lettin' Him talk to me and tell me of His intimated love? Do I have a constant sense of my Savior's presence regardless of what I'm goin' through? Do I realize that my voice lifted in praise and adoration is sweet to His ears, or do I hold back for fear or with no conviction? I stood and looked into the scattered sky filled with white smooth clouds. I closed my eyes to the thought of these questions, strugglin' to keep em' closed as the sun's beaming light lit up the inside cover of my eye lid's. I dropped down in my beach chair and continued to think about these questions that continue to pop up in my head. What is my greatest concern, the thing that I need God to help me with the most? When He asks to hear my voice, what do I tell Him? Am I willing to go through adversary, if it will better me for His presence and His companionship? In my weariness from the cares of this world do I hesitate to answer when God knocks at my door, which is the door of my heart and turn from Him? Is my Savior unquestionably the One altogether lovely, the One above all others most kind and precious to me? Can I tell how and why Christ is more to me than any human being or than all my earthly possessions? It took a long time for me to allow God to open up my eyes. And now I can truly say that I can hear and see without deception.

My thoughts carried me right on into my dreams and on into the night.

249

I'm too over whelmed to dwell on what just happened to me right on this sandy beach. That preacher on Christian television ushered me right on into God's presence and into His anointed glory. Just the thought of God brings a sensation through my body and a comforting smile to my face. "You didn't have to do it." I whispered to myself but talking to God. "But You did... And I love You for it." I whispered again, this time with my eyes closed as if God was standing right in front of me.

"I love you too..." A voice suddenly met mine. I quickly jumped to my feet and made eye contact with the one I thought would never come back into my life.

"How... how'd you get here?" I asked as he stood over me like a tower.

"Shuuuww..." He put his finger over my mouth. "...Many waters cannot quench love, neither can floods drown it... The love that I have for you is much more than just physical pleasure and intimacy, but a depth of feeling, love, power, and commitment. Barina, true love never fades with the changes we had brought by time, but is merely stronger even than life and death. Waters of time, nor the countless disappointments in our lives, nor the tragedy of loosing you before, can wash away the love I have for you. I know you're standing here lookin' beautiful and thangs, maybe chosen to be somebody else's lady. But I figured I still have a chance since you still don't have a ring on your finger. Barina I love you and I never stopped loving you. I prayed to God that He would bring you back into my life. There were times when I felt like it was impossible for God to do that. But when He constantly kept showing me you in the Spirit, in my dreams: bringing your lovely face before my face in your beautiful wedding dress, and when the physical situation changed and began to present itself I jumped on it. And I'm standing here today hopefully for the last time as your long time ex, but about to be your long-time man forever... Can we do this for the last time?... I need you. Not another second, not another minute, but I need you right here and right now." He pointed towards the sand. I stared in tears, mesmerized, and shaking as he got down on one knee, took my shaky hand, stared solemnly into my eyes, and softly asked. "Will you be my lady?... Will you do me the honor of being my wife for eternity?"

I quickly answered as both of our hands shook together. "Yes! O' my God yes! Yes! I will be your wife for eternity!" We hugged tightly, then he spun me around in his arms and we laughed and cried for what seemed like forever.

I looked up towards the house as the tears continued to cloud my eyes to see that everybody's cheering, crying, and looking on. They all ran down with champagne glasses in their hands. The kids beat everybody down. Karina, Salva, Salvester, Precious, and the kids swarmed us with hugs and kisses. Karina turned to me and said. "Mama you're right, he is Heaven sent." I agreed and kissed her on the cheek remembering that I had said that a long time ago.

Salva had to get her two cents in as she came up and pointed her finger in my face and said, "You betta' not mess this up again." I pushed her finger away and hugged her while Salvester and Solomon hugged, snickered, and laughed with each other.

Feels like the 4th of July. Spiritual fire works are exploding into the distant sky over the ocean sea as we all embraced, drank some grape juice with the champagne glasses, tipping glasses together, and finally finding our way back up to the house. The kids went and played games upstairs while us grown folks turned up the music and kept on celebrating. I couldn't stop huggin' Solomon; he held me so tight and so close as if to say you're not gettin' away from me this time.

And this time I didn't... We danced the night away...

Salva was right when she prophesied years ago that we would have a double wedding. And that we did. It was off the chain. Solomon sang to me and I wanted to faint. It was breath taking and beautiful. Everything turned out perfect. It couldn't have been any better. I thought from the way my life has went that I would never see him again, nor would I ever find love again. But now I'm a strong believer that *"...many waters cannot quench love, neither can floods drown it."* And I'm a strong believer that nor life, nor death, nor height—nothin' cannot separate me from who and what God has for me. Nor can it separate me from the love that God has for me either. *(Romans 8:38-39)* He is the rose of Solomon and the lily of my valley.

We all went on our honeymoons together. I wanted our rooms down the hall from each other. Privacy was very important to me. I smiled at the thought. The first night Solomon was so gentle and romantic. He had a picnic candle light dinner set up on the floor surrounded by what seemed like a thousand red rose pedals. After we ate he caressed my head, he rubbed my back, he massaged my feet, then he ran my bath water and I won't tell what happened after that. It's a honeymoon thang', just me and my baby...

The morning fell fast.

Salva and Salvester are bamming on the door for us to go out shopping and sight seeing.

Salvester yelled through the door. "Ya'll love birds come oughta' there! It's way too much to see out here in big ol' Jamaica!"

I yelled back. "Just hold your horses we comin'. I put the finishing touches on my braided ponytail and ran to open the door.

"That's what I'm talkin' bout'!" Salva came rushing in. "What's goin' on up in here? Ya'll act like ya'll ain't never been married before?" She couldn't talk from laughing.

"Girl shut up and get chu' some business." I walked past them and on out the door as they followed. Solomon turned to make sure the door was locked.

Solomon looks better than he did years ago. He's much more mature now, not that he wasn't then, but I can tell that God's done a lot more work in him. I've learned that time, wisdom, and just plain ol' goin' through will mature a person too. I can't help but admire what Solomon's wearing. He's wearing some khaki cream shorts, a cream button down with soft designs in it, some masculine brown sandals, and a brown twisted belt to match. Our plans to match each other worked out really well I must say. I'm wearing some cream shorts, a lil' tighter than his, a bikini top with a see through sleeveless over short, and yes I'm still saved. I giggled to myself. I have a brown twisted belt with everything tucked in so neatly, and brown sandals with a slight heel. Salva and Salvester's tryin' to copy us. They have on the same outfit but different colored shirts. I laughed to myself as we left going out.

We all had so much fun after a long day of swimming, shopping, sight seeing, and just plain ol' runnin' the streets. More fun that I've ever had insomuch that I never wanna' leave this place. Palm trees are everywhere! With the big beautiful clear blue water rushing towards the white sand as tourists were wading, resting on their towels tryin' to get a tan, some were jet skiing and surfing all over the place, while children were splashing the hollow waters on the banks, and I can't leave out the perfectly sunny vacation honeymoon atmosphere we had all day. It was breath taking. Even the air smelled fresh and clean, I inhaled it as if to keep it. Solomon couldn't have chosen a better place.

We're all back in our rooms gettin' changed before we all go and get a bite to eat down at one of the most expensive restaurants. I didn't have to ask myself where all the money came from to pay for all this. Solomon went back to school and got his degree in architectural engineering. Now he works for one of the largest chemical plants in the city. He's makin' big bank, added to my bank. I smiled at the thought. He paid for the entire wedding, reception, and honeymoon, Salva and Salvester included. Salvester's hookin' us up every chance he gets. I'm sure it's because he's appreciative of all of what Solomon paid for and he don't wanna' feel any less of a man. Solomon's so sweet he's not fighting with him either he's allowing his manhood to be relieved.

I love my life now. God gave everything and everybody back to me considering how I did Him. He's so merciful and kind... I thought as I stood in the bathroom mirror putting on last minute make-up.

Solomon broke in my thoughts as he came and stood in the doorway. "Hey baby we have yet to catch up on the time we missed apart?"

"Yea' I know. I'm sure tonight'll be a good night if you don't find me too pleasing?" We giggled as he came over and...

"Now see now, you didn't have to go there." He tightly held me. "Baby you're more beautiful than you've ever been. I can't thank God enough of how He brought us back together. I guess that's why we can't ever give up. I never gave up on you. God used to show me in my dreams that you and I would find our love again. I just didn't know when. So I just prayed, fasted for you, and believed that God would keep His promise. You know what it wasn't too long ago that I felt you so strong in my spirit, so I began to pray for you. I don't know if you were in trouble, if you were sick, or if you were dealin' with somethin' that you couldn't come out of? But I prayed and cried out to God for you and when I broke through, I had a peace in knowin' that you were ganna' be alright." He held me tighter. "I wasn't gon' let nobody take my baby before I could get chu' back." He stared down into my eyes as I stretched my neck to look up at his beautiful caramel hazel eyes overshadowed by his thick eyelashes. He swinted his eyes as if he couldn't see but is actually absorbing my every move, reaction, and being.

I can't believe this is really true. I just wanna' pinch him to see if he's real or am I still dreaming. It all happened so fast. I can say that my blessing over-took me all at once. Beginning with Salva coming back in my life, then with Karina and I being restored back together, then with God givin' me back my mansion—costing me nothin', my books becoming bestsellers again, and last with the man of my dreams comin' back in my life and now as my husband. Life itself is so surreal. It's like an irrational dream that I cannot put into words.... I ponder about it everyday.

Salva and Salvester just came beatin' on the door shoutin' let's go. Solomon and I are still in each other's arms not saying a word. They knocked for about five minutes before we snapped out of our love connection and opened the door.

She burst in. "I guess the love birds are at it again." She looked at Salvester as they both laughed. "Look it's way too early to settle in if you know what I mean?" She smiled. "There's way too much food to eat and too many places to go, so snap out of it."

"Salva stop hatin'." I said playfully.

"Hatin'? Who's hatin'?" She stepped up to me.

"You." I pushed her forehead with my finger as her head slightly went back.

"I got way too much love sittin' right here to be hatin'." She pointed at Salvester.

"Well love on that and stop hatin' on mine." I pointed at him as she and I laughed and ran out the door. Solomon and Salvester looked at each other like that's your wife, not mine and followed behind us.

The night was far spent with all of us enjoying Jamaica's nightlife and festivities. Salva and Salvester turned in early because Salvester had a headache. I guess everything was too overwhelming for him and he had to go lay it down.

After I called to check up on Karina and the kids, I joined Solomon out on the terrace as the head of the orange sun hid behind the water's horizon with the dark blue night clouds resting behind the water. I walked up behind him and wrapped my arms around his waist and pushed the side of my face in his upper back. "It's beautiful out here isn't it?"

I stepped back as he turned around. "Yea' makes you never wanna' leave this setting... Come here." He held out his hand and I went into his arms without hesitation. "I thank God for my blessing—you. You're my beauty. My prize. My sanctuary. My queen. My everything. My long song. God is the true lover of my soul, He's singing to me the greatest and most beautiful love song of all." He started singing softly as if to whisper. My knees are shaking and my heart is playin' strong drums.

> *"...You are God's treasured one...*
> *You are His beloved, chosen one...*
> *And He delights in you just like...*
> *I delight in you, and He in us...*
> *...My darling, He showed His*
> *wonderful love to me, and now I'm*
> *showing my wonderful love to*
> *you..."* He sang louder.
> *You are like a sweet aroma*
> *of perfume that Makes everything*
> *in my world smell good..."*

The more he repeated the song, the more the tears ran from my eyes with passion. I'm thinking, God as much as I love this man, I love You more. I'm now complete. I sighed. I don't ever want this to get away from me again.

He got down on his knees and helped me down on mine. "Close your eyes and repeat after me..." I did just as he requested. "Lord You have placed us as a sealed covenant over Your heart. And we have sealed our hearts to You. Neither death nor life, neither angels nor demons, neither the present nor the future, nor any powers, neither height nor depth, nor anything else in this world will be able to separate us from Your love... *(Romans 8:38-39)*

We had sweet communion with the Lord and with one another for the rest of the night on the terrace...

Chapter Nineteen

*T*hree month's have past.

Our trip back to the city was somewhat disappointing. Even though Solomon made me feel better I'm still a little disappointed. It was a whole different world up there. I had an experience with God and Solomon that I've never had in my life. It's too awesome to explain. I realize that I can't compare the two, so separation is justified. Now I'm on my way to a book signing at this big time prayer breakfast. Solomon agreed to move in with me and let Precious, Karina, and the kids move in his two-story, four bedrooms, three and half bath, and game room home. They all have plenty of room. So now my, oops, I mean our mansion has peace and quiet.

The married life is takin' some getting used too. I'm so used to going like I want too. But now I have somebody I have to answer to and take care of. At first it was a little challenging for the both of us with wanting our own space, but we worked it out. And now it's much easier. I love it. Some people may say that they regret it, but I totally disagree because I got the right man. And this man loves God and the things of God and that plays a huge role in our respect, compromise, and love for one another.

My cell phone just rang. "Hello?"

"Barina! Barina! You gotta' come home quick! Salvester pasted out at work and they rushed him to the hospital!" Solomon yelled. "Salva just called hysterical and all in shock!"

"Ok, ok, ok calm down, let me call Cal and tell him I'm gon' have to cancel my book signing and I'm on my way back right now!" I hung

257

up the phone and called Cal as I skidded the truck around, sped back to pick up Solomon, and sped to the hospital running a few traffic lights but we made it.

When we got to the ICU, Salva ran and hugged us screaming in shock. A group of doctors are standing around us watching.

"He's dead! He's dead! God why?" She dropped to her knees and looked up as if she could see God Himself. "You gave this man back to me to take em' away? No! I won't accept it!" She laid out on the floor like a baby wanting its way. Precious just came from around the corner, ran up to her mama, and cried with her. We all are crying and hugging one another as Karina and the kids joined us. The kids didn't know what was goin' on but they were crying because we were crying.

The funeral was quick and straight to the point. Solomon sang and it wasn't a dry eye in the entire place including mine. I thank God that he was saved. Now he's in Heaven shinning down on all of us. I didn't realize that he was so popular. Almost the entire school district came and paid their respects, along with Salva, Precious, and their church family. His mother over-dosed years ago off of cocaine, we wasn't expecting his daddy because he never knew em', and four of his sisters and brothers out of we think twelve who are still alive came, they were distant though, I guess because he never had a relationship with em'. I never saw a tear fall from their eyes. This was my first time meeting them, I just hate that it had to be during a time like this. I couldn't gather myself to go up and see em' in the casket, but Solomon said that he looked like an angel. The glory of the Lord was all over his still countenance. The doctor's said that he died from and aneurysm in the brain. I don't know how that could've been? He seemed so worry free. I've learned from this that we don't know when it's our time to go, so we gotta' be ready at all times. This is why it's so important to be saved (to have a personal relationship with the Lord), live right, and treat and love your neighbor like you love yourself. These scriptures come to my mind. *(2 Corinthians 4:12-18, 5:8-10) (18)…We look not at the things which are seen, but at the things which are not seen: for the things which are not seen are eternal. (5:8) We are confident, I say, and willing rather to be absent from the body, and to be present with the Lord. (9) Wherefore we labour that, whether present or absent, we may be accepted of him. (10) For we must all appear before the judgment seat of Christ; that every one may receive the things done in his body, according to that he hath done, whether it be good or bad.* This is why I'm not taking my life lightly anymore. I'm goin' all the way with the Lord. It may get hard sometimes and I may have to cry, and I may loose some friends along the way, but I'm still goin' all the way with the Lord. It may get rough and I can't see my way through, but God will lead and direct me as I go. *(Psalms 37:3)* My trust is in Him...

I'm on my way to check on Salva. I've had to watch her closely because she wasn't safe being alone. I was afraid that she would do somethin' crazy, but she didn't. She's better now that time has taken its course. It's been three weeks and her mourning has become lighter with the help of her Pastor, church family, his friends, and all of us.

"I pulled up in her drive-way, got out, and went and knocked on the door. Precious came to the door and opened it. She reached out to hug me. It's been hard on her too.

"Hey baby, how you feelin'?"

"I'm ok Auntie, come on in she's sittin' out on the patio."

I walked straight to the backyard. She stood up when she saw me and I went and hugged her. It's taking every muscle in my face not to burst out crying. I have to be strong for her and Precious.

"Sit down. I'm so glad to see you." She pointed towards the chair opposite of her.

"I just came to check on you."

"Thank you so much B', you've been such a big help to me and Precious." She reached out her hands and I met hers with mine.

"Awh' you don't have to thank me." I smiled. "I'm yo' sista' did you forget?" She forced a smile from her lips.

"No mam' I'll never forget. We've been through too much." She let my hands go. "You know? I've learned not to question God and to just accept His decisions. I've had to be strong through many things, but this has been the most challenging. I loved that man Barina. Nothin' and no one could keep me from em'. And just when we get back together, share our love, and start a new, he disappears from my life again. But this time forever."

"You'll see em' again Salva."

"I know Barina but I miss him so much right now." She started choking up as if to cry.

"I understand."

"I don't ever wanna' marry again. They'll never be another man that'll ever be able to take his place. He was a one-of-a-kind human being." She stared across the grass as if to be in a daze.

"You don't think you'll ever wanna' date either?"

"No, never. And I'm not thinkin' about that right now anyway."

"I know I'm sorry."

"No, its ok you're just being real. It's just ganna' be me and my baby. She's all I need right now. She's not takin' it so good. She's slept with me since he's been gone, really I wanted her too. I didn't want to be alone. She said mama, I'm here for you now that daddy's gone. That touched my heart. You know?"

"O' yea' I know. She's your only child and you cherish her like yourself." I said.

"You got that right." She stared towards the back-woodened fence.

Things got quiet for a moment. "So have you guy's eaten?" I broke the silence.

"No, I'm not hungry. I really don't have an appetite."

"I know Salva but you gotta' eat somethin'." I got up. "Let me cook you and Precious somethin'?"

"No you sit down, I'm fine. If you're hungry you can go fix you somethin?"

"I'm not, let me go see if Precious is." I went in and saw that Karina and the kids were here. She's fixing them all something to eat so I'll go back out with Salva.

She quickly asked me a question as I came through the patio door. "So where's Mr. Solomon? That man is incredible Barina. He's sent me a vase of flowers everyday since the day of the funeral. That is a good man, don't chu' ever mess that up." She looked at me.

"He is a very good man, and no I won't ever mess that up again. I've truly learned my lesson."

"I bet chu' have." She said as we both giggled.

"You so silly."

Chapter Twenty

A year has past.

Solomon's been worrin' me about introducing one of his single co-workers to Salva. I told him that I'm very cautious about that considering it's only been a year. He insisted that this would help her to move on. And that he's not tryin' to find her a husband, but merely a friend or companion. I agreed. I called her and she didn't say yes right away but I talked her into givin' the brotha' a chance. She may enjoy his conversation. She finally agreed. She's coming over here. I haven't met him so I think I'm more inquisitive and anxious to see what he looks like than she is. I'm sittin' in the front yard on the porch. Solomon just came out and said that Kalvin called and said that he's on his way. Then fifteen minutes later, Salva called and said that she was on her way.

Thirty minutes have past and Kalvin's now pulling up in the driveway in a fully loaded, all black Yukon. His rims are shinnin' bright as the sun's reflecting off em'. He got out with a yellow rose in one hand and what looks like a card in the other. I thought, humm, what a fine lookin' bachelor. He looks better than what Solomon described him. A man can't describe how another man looks for some macho reason. They think it makes em' look soft. But anyway he looks to be about six feet, that's enough for Salva. She's like me about height. I laughed to myself. No offense on the short men but a tall, smooth, fine, good lookin', good smellin', fit just right brotha' will turn my head any day. Kalvin has all of these qualities. He's wearing some light shaded polo shades; some fitted blue jeans and a nice tight

261

blue button down short-sleeved shirt. His steel-toed boots clacked with every step he took as he walked on the sidewalk towards me. I'm smilin' like I know Salva'll be pleased.

I stood up and spoke before he could. "How are you?" I reached to shake his hand.

"I'm fine and yourself?"

"I'm good. I've heard so much about you."

"That Solomon does talk too much." We both laughed as I rebuked what he said on the inside. My baby doesn't talk too much. I smiled with him.

Solomon came out and greeted Kalvin with a hand shake on into a quick hug. "So I see you found your way alright?"

"Yea' man, the ride was pretty smooth." He looked out towards his truck as Salva pulled in beside his truck.

I ran out to greet her. "There she is."

She got out and gave me a hug. I'm glad she kinda' dressed up and wore somethin' to show her figure. I informed her through Solomon that the brother was pretty conservative. I'm lookin' at her as we're walking towards them. Kalvin and her sort of look alike, only difference is, he is a dark chocolate color and she's not. He has an ok grade of hair considering that it's cut real low and tapered on the sides. He has a thick goatee that's neatly trimmed around his full lips.

They caught eyes as we got closer. He smiled but Salva didn't at first. I kinda' thought she knew him. I looked at Solomon like I hope she don't dis' this nice lookin' brotha'. He stared back as if to agree with me.

As we got almost to them, Kalvin walked out and greeted her himself, then handed her the single rose and card he had in his hands. She said thank you and accepted them without hesitation.

"It's good to meet you. You're beautiful just like Solomon said."

"What? Humm', I look alright." She looked at me and curled her lips. Lord I hope she do not ruin this good thing and make me wish that I never should've told her.

We all walked in the house and sat in the living room. Things were quiet for a moment, and then Solomon motioned for us to leave them by themselves. I got up and said. "Hey we're ganna' walk out to the beach so you guys can get acquainted." Kalvin shook his head yes and smiled at Salva but Salva wasn't smiling at all.

Before we walked out the house, I could hear him ask her if she wanted to play a game of chest. The next thing I heard was the front door slamming. Solomon and I ran back inside and Salva was nowhere to be found. "What's up man? What happened?" Solomon asked as Kalvin quickly stood up.

"I don't know, all I asked her was did she wanna' play chest? And that I love the game of chest?" Kalvin said.

"Chest?" Solomon asked.

"Yea' that game you have sittin' on your ottoman." Kalvin pointed at it as we looked.

"Don't worry about it." I slightly brushed Solomon as I walked up to Kalvin. "Its ganna' take her some time. She's still a little sensitive. Maybe we can re-schedule?"

He walked towards the front door. "Naw' I don't think so. Seem like she didn't dig me from jump."

"She likes you just give her some time? She's not a mean person at all." We all walked out to his truck as he got in and let down the window.

Solomon said. "I'll call you later bro."

"Alright man, check you later." He let up his window, backed out and zoomed down the street as if he wasn't ever coming back.

I looked at Solomon. "I'm sorry it didn't work out like you wanted it to baby."

"It's cool. I don't think he wants to deal with her again." We walked back inside and went and put our feet in the Jacuzzi.

The phone rang.

I ran inside and grabbed the cordless and looked at the caller ID as I walked back out and put my feet back in the water. Solomon helped me down.

"Hello?" I answered.

"Barina why did you and Solomon do me like that?"

"Do you like what?"

"Allow me to meet a dirty man like that?"

"He's not dirty." I looked at Solomon and he turned and looked at me. "What are you talkin' about?"

"He said somethin' about my chest."

"Salva were you listening to him? He asked you to play a game of chest."

"That's what I'm talkin' about. He was tryin' to be funny."

263

"No he wasn't Salva. That man isn't like that. Now if I did somethin' like that, you would've chewed me out. Now look at you? You gotta' stop being so sensitive."

"I'm not sensitive?"

"Yes you are. Salva it's been a year and you gotta' move on." She got quiet. Solomon tapped my leg and whispered for me not to go there. But I am anyway. "Salva, move on with your life. Salvester would've wanted you too and you know this." She's still quiet, listening to every word I'm sayin'. "That man came over here excited about meeting you. He brought chu' flowers and I'm sure a beautiful friendly card. He wasn't tryin' to see what you looked like underneath your clothes, or for that matter tryin' to be your husband; he just wanted to have a good time with you by playing a game of chest. The game is sittin' on my ottoman. It was right in front of you."

"Well I'm sorry. I miss understood him. Barina I don't have time for no foolishness."

"Who said he was being foolish?"

"Nobody but I can't be hurt again."

"Look Salva you're readin' too much into this."

"I guess I am. Where is he?"

"He left right after you did."

"Was he mad?"

"I'm sure he was disappointed because he didn't know why you were treatin' him like you were. I have to say that I'm disappointed in you right now too."

"Don't be Barina you gotta' understand where I'm comin' from?"

"You right I do, that's why I'm sayin' from this day forward, move on with your life."

"Can he come back over there?"

"When?" I looked at Solomon, he looked at me.

"Now."

"Let me ask Solomon. Hold on." I pushed the mute button. "Solomon she wants to know if you can call him back over here?"

"I'll see what I can do. Tell her you'll call her back."

I pushed the mute button. "Salva."

"Huh?"

"Solomon's ganna' call him, I'll call you back. Where are you cause' I know you're on your cell phone?"

"I'm parked in a shopping center parking lot."

"Ok stay there we'll call you right back."

"Alright bye." We both hung up the phone.

Solomon's dialing Kalvin's cell phone as he put it on speaker. "Yo' man what's up? Where are you?"

"I'm up at this fast food joint gettin' me somethin' to eat. Why what's up?"

"I want chu' to come back over here."

"What? Look man I got some things I need to do. I already seen you and your wife I don't need to come back over there."

"You're not comin' back for us?"

"Well who am I comin' back for?"

"Salva."

"Salva? O' no way man look I've already got rejected once, I don't plan on gettin' rejected twice."

"Look you won't get rejected again. I'll see to it."

Kalvin got quiet. "Alright but this time you guys stay in the same room just in case she go into one of her tantrums again."

"Cool we can do that. Are you on your way right now?" Solomon asked.

"As soon as I get my food."

"Don't worry bout' your food we got plenty here."

"Alright then I'm on my way."

"How far away are you?"

"I'm about fifteen minutes away. I stopped in this shoppin' center up here at this fast food joint. I'll be there shortly.

"Ok hurry up man."

"Why, she already there?"

"No I just want you to hurry up."

"Alright then chief." They hung up together. He handed me the phone to call her back.

I dialed her number. "Salva, come back he's on his way back."

"Ok."

"How far away are you?"

"About fifteen minutes."

I'm saying to myself, that's the same amount of minutes he's away. I wonder if they're at the same shoppin' center? "Alright then, come on."

"Ok bye." She hung up before I did.

I turned, looked at Solomon and smiled. He smiled back and winked his right eye.

"Solomon I think they were at the same shoppin' center and didn't even know it. They seem so compatible?"

"Yea' they do but we'll see."

We got up, dried our feet off with a towel, and went back into the kitchen. Solomon's about to fry some fish and fries.

There's a knock at the door. I ran and opened it. It's Salva. I told her to come in and have a seat in the kitchen with us.

She asked. "Where's what's his name?"

"Salva don't start again."

"No I'm serious, I forgot his name."

Solomon broke in. "Kalvin's his name." The grease from the fish is popping all over his clothes.

"Kalvin. Ok now I know." She turned and smiled at me.

There's another knock at the door. Solomon said that he would get it and for me to watch the fish.

After a minute they came walking through the kitchen door. He and Salva quickly made eye contact. This time it's not so much tension in the air.

Solomon's talking to Kalvin as Kalvin went and sat at the island on one of the bar stools.

Salva and I aren't sayin' anything but watching them. It's kinda' like he's ignoring her now so I'm a break the ice. "Hey Kalvin, I heard you have an important position down at the chemical plant?"

"As a-matter-of-fact I do. I have to over-see about thirty employees and make sure they do their job and take care of business."

"How long have you been working there?" I asked.

"For fifteen years. I got the job straight out of college. I did a lot of interning with em."

"That's good Kalvin. So what else do you like to do besides work?"

"Not too much, I love to volunteer my time down at the elderly center. I go read poetry and the Word of God to them."

"Really?" I took a quick glance at Salva then back at him.

Solomon stopped turning the fish and looked at me then at him. "Hey man you didn't tell me that?"

"Well now you know." He smiled. "I read my bible day and night since the Lord called me into the ministry."

266

"O' that's good Kalvin." I won't even look at Salva anymore. I can imagine what her facial expressions like right about now.

"Say man I gotta' ask you about those scriptures you gave me the other day, they were powerful." Solomon said.

"That's cool, we can do that. God gave em' to me right after you and I talked that day."

Salva all of a sudden broke in. "So would you like to play chest?" We all turned and looked at her with amazement. "I love me a good game of chest." She smiled at him and he smiled back as if to forgive her.

"That's fine." They both got up and started walking towards the living room.

"So how long have you been playing chest?"

There voices faded as they vanished around the corner. Solomon and I looked at each other, smiled, and said at the same time: *"Many waters cannot quench love, neither can floods drown it..."*

Message from the Author to the Youth and Young Adults

You may be a teenager or a young person that has made many mistakes and you feel as though God will never forgive you. But I'm here to let you know that God will. Barina made some terrible choices—one she thought she would never come out of. She became a young, single, fourteen year old mother and homeless. After she repented and gave her life back to God, He began to restore her and bless her with things she never thought she could ever have. He showed His great favor and miraculous blessings toward her, and because she had positive friends around her, they received them too.

Yes she did succeed despite he circumstances, yes she did over-come her demons and the confusion that was so evident in her mind, all because she didn't give up. She hung in there with all the strength and power that she had and she made it. And I want you to know that you can too. We all have made mistakes, some we thought that God would never forgive us and we held our heads down because of shame and guilt. I'm here to tell you to pick your head up and get your life back. You can still be successful. It's not too late. If Barina can do it, you can too! If Salva can do it, you can too! If Karina can do it, you can too! If Solomon can do it, you can too! Look at their lives. It's a perfect example of another we fall down, but we don't stay there, we get back up and keep on going...

God is a forgiving God. Once you have repented and asked Him for forgiveness, and accepted Him in your heart, He will then begin to turn your life around and make you brand new.

God has a purpose and a plan for your life so don't you give up and miss out on what He has in store for you. You are special to God, and you are special to me...

269

Prayer of Salvation

If you are not saved or unsure of your salvation, just say this prayer out loud believing in your heart that what you are saying is true:

Lord, I know that I'm a sinner, I have sinned against you, but today Lord I'm repenting of my sins and I ask you to come into my heart, my mind, my spirit, and my soul, and be my Lord and Savoir and my Redeemer. I confess with my mouth and I truly believe in my heart that God raised Jesus from the dead. By faith I believe that I am saved and I'll never be the same! Amen. (Romans 10:9)

Praise God! Now your Name is recorded in the Book of Life. *(Revelation 13:8)* God has wiped your past clean! He is not going to remember what you have done anymore! *(Hebrews 8:12) (Jeremiah 31:34)*
Now that you are saved, don't walk in condemnation or unbelief. If you believe what you have just said out loud, know from this day forward that you are saved and that you are a new creature (person) in Christ. Old things are passed away, behold all things have become new. *(2 Corinthians 5:17)*

The Author's Special Prayer for this Book

My prayer for this book is that lives will be changed through God's salvation, healing, deliverance, restoration, His favor, His prosperity, His love, joy, and peace. I pray that God will restore families, relationships, and friendships back together and that you will never be the same after reading this novel. I prophesy and decree this prayer done in Jesus Name, Amen.

Remember if God has promised you something, don't give up on it, it will come to past all you have to do is **STAND ON HIS WORD** and **BELIEVE** that He will bring it to past. *(Number 23:19-20, Habakkuk 2:2-3)*

My mission while on this earth is to try to do the will of God and to finish it. Through this, there is not one thing I cannot accomplish. *(Philippians 4:13)* I look forward to seeing lives change through this novel and that God will do A NEW THING in His people.

"...my meat is to do the will of Him that sent me, and to finish this work." *(John 4:34)*

Recommended Reading and Prayer

Salvation:

Romans 10:9- "That if thou shalt confess with thy mouth the Lord Jesus, and believe in thine heart that God hath raised him from the dead, thou shalt be saved."

Romans 10:13- "For whatsoever shall call upon the name of the Lord shall be saved."

Deliverance From:

Unforgiveness- *Matthew 6: 14-15-* "For if ye forgive men their trespasses, your heavenly Father will also forgive you:"

6:15- "But if ye forgive not men their trespasses, neither will your Father forgive your trespasses."

Loneliness- *Psalm 4:8-* "I will both lay me down in peace, and sleep: for thou, Lord, only makest me dwell in safety."

Isaiah 54:10- "...my kindness shall not depart from thee, neither shall the covenant of my peace be removed, saith the Lord that hath mercy on thee."

John 14:18- "I will not leave you comfortless: I will come to you."

Fear- *Isaiah 41:10-* "Fear thou not; for I am with thee: be not dismayed; for I am thy God: I will strengthen thee; yea, I will help thee; yea, I will uphold thee with the right hand of my righteousness."

Psalms 112:7- "He shall not be afraid of evil tidings: his heart is fixed, trusting in the Lord."

Sexual Sins- *Romans 1:24-32- (fornication, pornography, homosexuality, adultery)*

1:24- "Wherefore God also gave them up to uncleanness through the lusts of their own hearts, to dishonour their own bodies between themselves."

1:25- "Who changed the truth of God into a lie, and worshipped and served the creature more than the Creator, who is blessed forever. Amen.

272

1:26- "For this cause God gave them up unto vile affection: for even their women did change the natural use into that which is against nature:

1:27- "And likewise also the men, leaving the natural use of the woman, burned in their lust one toward another; men with men working that which is unseemly, and receiving in themselves that recompense of their error which was meet.   *1:28-*   "And even as they did not like to retain God in their knowledge, God gave them over to a reprobate mind, to do those things which are not convenient;

1:29- "Being filled with all unrighteousness, fornication, debate, deceit, malignity; whispers,

1:30- "Backbiters, haters of God, despiteful, proud, boasters, inventors of evil things, disobedient to parents,

1:31- "Without understanding, covenantbreakers, without natural affection, implacable, unmerciful:

1:32- "Who knowing the judgment of God, that they which commit such things are worthy of death, not only do the same, but have pleasure in them that do them."

1 Corinthians 6:13-18- "...Now the body is not for fornication, but for the Lord; and the Lord for the body."

6:18- "Flee fornication. Every sin that a man doeth is without the body; but he that committeth fornication sinneth against his own body."

Matthew 5: 27-28- "Ye have heard that it was said by them of old time, Thou shalt not commit adultery:

5:28- "But I say unto you, that whosoever looketh on a woman to lust after her hath committed adultery with her already in his heart."

Genesis 19- (The Lord destroyed Sodom and Gomorrah because of the sexual sin. (Fornication and Homosexuality, Adultery)

Jealousy- *James 3:14, 16-* "If you have bitter envying and strife in your hearts, glory not, and lie not against the truth."

3:16- "For where envying and strife is, there is confusion and every evil work."

Worry- *Isaiah 26:3-* "Thou wilt keep him in perfect peace, whose mind is stayed on thee: because he trusteth in thee."

1 Peter 5:7- "Casting all your care upon him; for he careth for you."

273

Feeling Unloved- Isaiah 40:31- "But they that will upon the Lord shall renew their strength; they shall mount up with wings as eagles; they shall run, and not be weary; and they shall walk, and not faint."

Matthew 11:28-30- "Come unto me, all ye that labour and are heavy laden, and I will give you rest."

11:29- "Take my yoke upon you, and learn of me; for I am meek and lowly in heart: and ye shall find rest unto your souls."

11:30- "For my yoke is easy, and my burden is light."

1 John 4:16- "And we have known and believed the Love that God hath to us, God is love; and he that dwelleth in love dwelleth in God, and God in him.

Low Self Esteem- Romans 8:37- "Nay, in all these things we are more than conquerors through him that loved us."

Murder- Deuteronomy 5:17- "Thou shalt not kill."

Abuse- Luke 3:14- "...Do violence to no man, neither accuse any falsely; and be content with your wages."

Friendship- Proverbs 18:24- "A man that hath friends must show himself friendly; and there is a friend that sticketh closer than a brother."

Temptation- 1 Corinthians 10:13- "There hath no temptation taken you but such as is common to man: but God is faithful, who will not suffer you to be tempted above that ye are able; but will with the temptation also make a way to escape, that ye may be able to bear it."

From your tongue- Psalms 39:1, 45:1, 34:14- "I said, I will take heed to my ways, that I sin not with my tongue: I will keep my mouth with a bridle, while the wicked is before me."

39: 9- "I was dumb, I opened not my mouth; because thou didst it."

45:1- "My heart is inditing a good matter: I speak of the things which I have made touching the king: my tongue is the pen of a ready writer."

34:14- "Keep thy tongue from evil, and thy lips from speaking guile."

Gluttony/ Obesity (Excessive eating) - Proverbs 23:21- "For the drunkard and the glutton shall come to poverty: and drowsiness shall clothe a man with rags."

Rape- Isaiah 54:17- "No weapon that is formed against thee shall prosper..."

Witchcraft- Micah 5:12- "And I will cut off witchcrafts out of thine hand; and thou shalt have no more soothsayers:"

Confidence in yourself and in God- *Philippians 4:13-* "I can do all things through Christ which strengthens me."

Hebrews 13:6- "So that we may boldly say, The Lord is my helper, and I will not fear what man shall do unto me."

Hebrews 10:35-36- "Cast not away therefore your confidence, which hath great recompence of reward.

10:36- "For ye have need of patience, that, after ye have done the will of God, ye might receive the promise."

Philippians 1:6- "Being confident in this very thing, that he which hath begun a good work in you will perform it until the day of Jesus Christ:"

1 John 5:14-15- "And this is the confidence that we have in him, that, if we ask any thing according to his will, he heareth us:

5:15- "And if we know that he hear us, whatsoever we ask, we know that we have the petitions that we desired of him."

Habakkuk 3:19- "The Lord God is my strength, and he will make my feet like hinds' feet, and he will make me to walk upon mine high places. To the chief singer on my stringed instruments."

Proverbs 3: 25-26- "Be not afraid of sudden fear, neither of the desolation of the wicked, when it cometh."

3:26- For the Lord shall be thy confidence, and shall keep thy foot from being taken."

Romans 8:37- "Nay, in all these things we are more than conquerors through him that loved us."

Prosperity (finances)- *Ephesians 3:20-* "Now unto him that is able to do exceeding abundantly above all that we ask or think, according to the power that worketh I us."

III John 2- "Beloved, I wish above all things that thou mayest prosper and be in health, even as thy soul prospereth."

Psalms 34: 10- "The young lions do lack, and suffer hunger: but they that seek the Lord shall not want any good thing."

Deuteronomy 28: 2-8, 11-13- "And these blessings shall come on thee, and overtake thee, if thou shalt hearken unto the voice of the Lord thy God."

275

28: 3- "Blessed shalt thou be in the city, and blessed shalt thou be in the field."

28: 4- "Blessed shall be the fruit of thy body, and the fruit of thy ground, and the fruit of thy cattle, the increase of thy kine, and the flocks of thy sheep."

28: 5- "Blessed shall be thy basket and thy store."

28: 6- "Blessed shalt thou be when thou comest in, and blessed shalt thou be when thou goest out."

28: 7- "The Lord shall cause thine enemies that rise up against thee to be smitten before thy face: they shall come out against thee one way, and flee before thee seven ways."

28:8- "The Lord shall command the blessing upon thee in thy storehouses, and in all that thou settest thine hand unto; and he shall bless thee in the land which the Lord thy God giveth thee."

28:11- "And the Lord shall make thee plenteous in goods, in the fruit of thy body,
and in the fruit of thy cattle, and in the fruit of thy ground, in the land which the Lord thy God sware unto thy fathers to give thee."

28:12- "The Lord shall open unto thee his good treasure, the heaven to give the rain unto thy land in his season, and to bless all the work of thine hand: and thou shalt lend unto many nations, and thou shalt not borrow."

28:13- "And the Lord shall make thee the head, and not the tail; and thou shalt be above only, and thou shalt not be beneath; if that thou hearken unto the commandments of the Lord thy God, which I command thee this day, to observe and to do them:"

Psalms 37:25- "I have been young, and now I'm old; yet have I not seen the righteous forsaken, nor his seed begging bread."

Luke 6:38- "Give, and it shall be given unto you; good measure, pressed down, shaken together, and running over, shall men give into your bosom. For with the same measure that ye mete withal it shall be measured to you again."

II Corinthians 9:6-8- "But this I say, He which soweth sparingly shall reap also sparingly; and he which soweth bountifully shall reap also bountifully."

9:7- "Every man according as he purposeth in his heart, so let him give; not grudgingly, or of necessity: for God loveth a cheerful giver."

9:8- "And God is able to make all grace abound toward you; that ye always having all sufficiency in all things, may abound to every good works:"

Proverbs 13:22- "A good man leaveth an inheritance to his children's children: and the wealth of the sinner is laid up for the just."

Proverbs 10: 22- "The blessings of the Lord, it maketh rich, and he addeth no sorrow with it."

Psalms 62:10-11 "Trust not in oppression, and become not vain in robbery: if riches increase, set not your heart upon them."

62:11- "God has spoken once; twice have I heard this; that power belongeth unto God."

Psalms 37:4- "Delight thyself also in the Lord; and he shall give thee the desires of thine heart."

Deuteronomy 8:18- "But thou shalt remember the Lord thy God: for it is he that giveth thee power to get wealth, that he may establish his covenant which he sware unto thy fathers, as it is this day."

Proverbs 3:27- "Withhold not good from them to whom it is due, when it is in the power of thine hand to do it."

Philippians 4:19- "But my God shall supply all your need according to his riches in glory by Christ Jesus."

Joshua 1:8- "This book of the law shall not depart out of thy mouth; but thou shalt meditate therein day and night, that thou mayest observe to do according to all that is written therein: for then thou shalt make thy way prosperous, and then thou shalt have good success."

Deliverance from Creditors- *Deuteronomy 15: 1-2* "At the end of every seven years you shall grant a release."

15:2- "And this is the manner of the release: every creditor shall release that which he has lent to his neighbor; he shall not exact it of his neighbor, his brother, for the Lord's release is proclaimed."

When you are without an earthly mother and father or when your earthly mother and father forsake you- "When my father and my mother forsake me, then the Lord will take me up." (Adopt me as his child)

Psalms 22:10- I was cast upon thee from the womb: thou art my God from my mother's belly."

Patience- *Psalms 27:14-* Wait upon the Lord: be of good courage, and he shall strengthen thine heart: wait, I say, on the Lord."

Psalms 37: 7- "Rest in the Lord, and wait patiently for him: fret not thyself because of him who prospereth in his way, because of the man who bringeth wicked devices to pass.

Deliverance from your Enemies- *Psalms 37: 8-9-* "Cease from anger, and forsake wrath: fret not thyself in any wide to do evil."

37:9- "For evildoers shall be cut off: but those that wait upon the Lord, they shall inherit the earth."

Psalms 41: 11- "By this I know that thou favourest me, because mine enemy doth not triumph over me."

A New Heart- *Ezekiel 36: 23-30-* "And I will sanctify my great name, which was profaned among the heathen, which ye have profaned in the midst of them; and the heathen shall know that I am the Lord, saith the Lord God, when I shall be sanctified in you before their eyes.

36:24- "For I will take you from among the heathen, and gather you out of all countries, and will bring you into your own land."

36:25- "Then will I sprinkle clean water upon you, and ye shall be clean: from all your filthiness, and from all your idols, will I cleanse you."

36:26- "A new heart also will I give you, and a new spirit will I put within you: and I will take away the stony heart out of your flesh, and I will give you a heart of flesh."

36:27- "And I will put my spirit within you, and cause you to walk in my statues, and ye shall keep my judgments, and do them."

36:28- "And ye shall dwell in the land that I gave to your fathers; and ye shall be my people, and I will be your God."

36:29- "I will also save you from all your uncleannesses: and I will call for the corn, and will increase it, and lay no famine upon you."

36:30- "And I will multiply the fruit of the tree, and the increase of the field, that ye shall receive no more reproach of famine among the heathen."

Grieving over a loved one- *Psalms 30:5, 11-* "…weeping may endure for a night, but joy cometh in the morning."

30:11- "Thou hast turned for me my mourning into dancing: thou hast put off my sackcloth, and girded me with gladness."

Peace of mind- *Psalms 37:11-* "But the meek shall inherit the earth; and shall delight themselves in the abundance of peace."

Ephesians 2:14- "For he is our peace, who hath made both one, and hath broken down the middle wall of partition between us."

Philippians 4:7-8- "And the peace of God, which passeth all understanding, shall keep your hearts and minds through Christ Jesus."

4:8- "Finally, brethren, whatsoever things are true, whatsoever things are honest, whatsoever things are just, whatsoever things are pure, whatsoever things are lovely, whatsoever things are of good report, if there be any virtue, and if there be any praise, think on these things."

Being Content with what you have- *Philippians 4:11-12-* "Not that I speak in respect of want: for I have learned, in whatsoever state I am, therewith to be content."

4:12- I know both how to be abased, and I know how to abound: every where and in all things I am instructed both to be full and to be hungry, both to abound and to suffer need."

Trusting in the Lord- *Psalms 37:15-* "Commit thy ways unto the Lord; trust also in him; and he shall bring it to pass."

Proverbs 3:5-6- "Trust in the Lord with all thine heart; and lean not unto thine own understanding."

3:6- "In all thy ways acknowledge him, and he shall direct thy paths."

Protection- *Proverbs 3: 23-24-* "Then shalt thou walk in thy way safely, and thy foot shall not stumble."

3:24- "When thou liest down, thou shalt not be afraid: yea, thou shalt lie down, and thy sleep shall be sweet."

Bitterness- *Ephesians 4:30-31-* "And grieve not the holy Spirit of God, whereby ye are sealed unto the day of redemption.

4:31- "Let all bitterness, and wrath, and anger, and clamour, and evil speaking, be put away from you, with all malice:"

Shame & Guilt- *Hebrews 12: 1-2* "Wherefore seeing we also are compassed about with so great a cloud of witnesses, let us lay aside every weight, and the sin which doth so easily beset us, and let us run with patience the race that is set before us."

12:2- "Looking unto Jesus the author and finisher of our faith; who for the joy that was set before him endured the cross, despising the *shame*, and is set down at the right hand of the throne of God."

Romans 8:1- "There is therefore now no condemnation to them which are in Christ Jesus, who walk not after the flesh, but after the Spirit."

279

Healing From:

Healing from your mind- *Romans 12:2-* "And be not conformed to this world: but be ye transformed by the renewing of your mind, that ye may prove what is that good, and acceptable, and perfect, will of God."

Romans 8:6-7- "For to be carnally minded is death; but to be spiritually minded is life and peace."

8:7- "Because the carnal mind is enmity against God; for it is not subject to the law of God, neither indeed can be."

Healing in your body- *Isaiah 53:5-* "But he was wounded for our transgressions, he was bruised for our iniquities: the chastisement of our peace was upon him; and with his stripes we are healed."

3 John 1:2- "Beloved, I wish above all things that thou mayest prosper and be in health, even as thy soul prospereth."

Healing from the flesh- *1 Corinthians 1:29-* "That no flesh should glory in his presence."

Romans 8:1- "There is therefore now no condemnation to them which are in Christ Jesus, who walk not after the flesh, but after the Spirit."

Receiving the Holy Spirit- *Acts 2: 1-4-* "And when the day of Pentecost was fully come, they were all with one accord in one place."

2:2- "And suddenly there came a sound from heaven as a rushing mighty wind, and it filled all the house where they were sitting."

2:3- "And there appeared unto them cloven tongues like as of fire, and it sat upon each of them."

2:4- "And they were filled with the Holy Ghost, and began to speak with other tongues, as the Spirit gave them utterance."

More Scriptures:

Tithing- *Malachi 3:8-10-* "Will a man rob God? Yet ye have robbed me. But ye say, Wherein have ye robbed thee? In tithes and offerings."

3:9- "Ye are cursed with a curse: for ye have robbed me, even this whole nation."

3:10- "Bring ye all the tithes into the storehouse, that there may be meat in mine house, and prove me now herewith, saith the Lord of hosts, if I will not open you the windows of heaven, and pour you out a blessing, that there shall not be room enough to receive it."

Strength- *Isaiah 40:31-* "But they that wait upon the Lord shall renew their strength; they shall mount up with wings as eagles; they shall run, and not be weary; and they shall walk, and not faint."

Discouragement- *Deuteronomy 31:6-* "Be strong and of good courage, fear not, nor be afraid of them: for the Lord thy God, he it is that doth go with thee; he will not fail thee; nor forsake thee."

Pride- *Proverbs 16:18-* "Pride goeth before destruction, and an haughty spirit before a fall."

Suicide- *Psalms 118:17-* "I shall not die, but live, and declare the works of the Lord."

Alcohol- *Proverbs 20:1-* "Wine is a mocker, strong drink is raging: and whosoever is deceived thereby is not wise."

Drugs- *Galatians 5:21-* "Envyings, murders, drunkenness, revellings, and such like: of the which I tell you before, as I have also told you in time past, that they which do such things shall not inherit the Kingdom of God."

Women and Men in Prisons- *Psalms 142:6-7-* "Attend unto my cry; for I am brought very low: deliver me from my persecutors; for they are stronger than I."

142:7- "Bring my soul out of prison, that I may praise thy name: the righteous shall compass me about; for thou shalt deal bountifully with me."

Backslider (When you have strayed away from God)- *Jeremiah 3:22-* "Return, ye backsliding children, and I will heal your backslidings. Behold, we come unto thee; for thou art the Lord our God."

Marital Problems- *Genesis 2:24-* "Therefore shall a man leave his father and his mother, and shall cleave unto his wife: and they shall be *one flesh*."

Ephesians 5:21- "Submitting yourselves one to another in the fear of God."

5:22- "Wives, submit yourselves unto your own husbands, as unto the Lord."

5:23- "Therefore as the church is subject unto Christ, so let the wives be to their own husbands in every thing."

5:24- "Husbands, love your wives, even as Christ also loved the church, and gave himself for it;"

5:25- "That he might sanctify and cleanse it with the washing of water by the word."

5:27- "So ought men to love their wives as their own bodies. He that loveth his wife loveth himself."

5:33- "Nevertheless let everyone of you in particular so love his wife even as himself; and the wife see that she reverence her husband."

Scriptures from the Book by Chapters

August 1989- Reagon High:
Philippians 4:7
1 Thessalonians 4:3
Romans 1:29-32

November 1989:
Galatians 5:21

May 1990:
1 John 1:9
Romans 10:9
Galatians 6:7
Romans 10:9
Proverbs 22:6

September 1990:
Matthew 12:1-44
1 Kings 4:29-34

July 1996:
Proverbs 18:16

Chapter 2:
2 Corinthians 9:6-7
Psalms 118:17
Isaiah 53:5
3 John 2
Isaiah 55:11
Isaiah 43:26

Chapter 3:
St. John 11:1-45
Ecclesiastes 12:13
Deuteronomy 28:1-14
Psalms 105:15

Scriptures from the Book by Chapters

Chapter 4:
Galatians 5:19
Romans 8:1
Song of Solomon 7:7-9 *amplified*
Matthew 25:1-11
Galatians 6:7

Chapter 5:
Psalms 8:2

Chapter 6:
Song of Solomon 8:7
Song of Solomon 8:4

Chapter 7:
Genesis 2:23-24
Song of Solomon 7:1

Chapter 8:
Psalms 37 :4-5
Luke 3:14
Deuteronomy 5:17
Ephesians 4:32
2 Corinthians 1:9-10
Matthew 17:14-21
1 John 4:4
Song of Solomon 4:7-10
Song of Solomon 4:12
Song of Solomon 4:15

Chapter 9:
Acts 2:1-13
2 Corinthians 5:17
Jeremiah 3:22
Hosea 14:4

Scriptures from the Book by Chapters

1 Corinthians 10:6
2 Corinthians 10:5

Chapter 10:
1 John 2:16
1 John 2:15
Luke 17:3-4
1 Corinthians 10:13

Chapter 11:
Proverbs 6:34
Revelation 9:21
Matthew 15:19
Isaiah 55:4
Matthew 24
Revelation 3:20
Hebrews 13:4
Galatians 5:19
1 Thessalonians 4:3
Galatians 3:5
Romans 10:13
Romans 10:9
Colossians 3:3
Mark 12:30
1 Peter 4:8
Mark 14:43-52
Luke 23:34
Romans 8:1
John 8:1-11
Romans 8:1
Romans 5:3-5
Romans 12:12
1 Samuel 15:23
Acts 16:16
Deuteronomy 18:10-12

285

Scriptures from the Book by Chapters

Isaiah 42:7
Romans 7:11
Romans7:1-25
1 Kings 16:31-34
1 Kings 16:17-22
Isaiah 57:15
1 Peter 3:8
St. John 8:36
Romans 2:11
Romans 6:23
Matthew 11:28-30
Exodus 22:23
Luke 18:7-8

Chapter 12:
Acts 17:28
Romans 7:7-25
Romans 7:14-21
Hebrews 13:5
Romans 14:8
Daniel 3:17
2 Timothy 4:18
Psalms 9:9-10
Psalms 27:10
Matthew 16:26
1 Corinthians 10:31
Galatians 6:7
Hebrews 4:16

Chapter 13:
James 5:16
Ephesians 6:12-13
Matthew 16:19
Matthew 12:19
Mark 9:14-32

Scriptures from the Book by Chapters

Matthew 12:29
Micah 5:12
Hebrews 12:11
1 Peter 2:24
Mark 9:24
Isaiah 5:14-16
James 3
James 3:6
Hebrews 11:6
Acts 2:22
Esther 4:14
Luke 1:79
Genesis 18:14
Matthew 21:21
Romans 14:23
Hebrews 13:5
Hebrews 13:2

Chapter 14:
Matthew 17:20
1 John 1:9
2 Corinthians 10:3-5
Galatians 5:1
Romans 12:2
Romans 12:17
1 Corinthians 6:13
1 Corinthians 6:18
Deuteronomy 5:17
Revelation 9:21
Romans 12:1
1 John 1:9

Chapter 15:
Hebrews 11:6
Hebrews 11:1
Romans 1:25-32

Scriptures from the Book by Chapters

Galatians 6:2
St. John 17:12
Hebrews 13:5
2 Corinthians 1:9
Hebrews 11:1
Esther 4:16

Chapter 16:
Luke 1:37
Mark 9:23
Matthew 19:26
Job 10:12
Exodus 4
Psalms 103:10
Psalms 57:2
Psalms 86:10
1 Corinthians 2:9

Chapter 17:
Romans 10:9
Ephesians 2:3
Proverbs 22:6
Psalms 37:4

Chapter 18:
Colossians 3:9
Matthew 7:1-9
1 Samuel 15:22
Exodus 20:5
Jeremiah 42:1
Romans 8:38-39

Chapter 19:
2 Corinthians 4:12-18
2 Corinthians 5:8-10, Psalms 37:3

Put Your Prayers into Action

My Goals-

_____

_____

_____

My Dreams-

_____

_____

_____

What I need to be delivered from-

_____

_____

_____

Secret sins-

_____

_____

_____

What I need from the Lord-

_____

_____

_____

I will encourage myself-

_____

_____

_____

Things that have changed after reading this Book-

_____

_____

_____

291

My Song of Solomon Prayer Journal

My Song of Solomon Prayer Journal

"Be careful for nothing; but in everything by prayer and supplication with thanksgiving let your request be made known unto God."

Philippians 4:6

My Song of Solomon Prayer Journal is filled with daily scriptures of love, healing, and deliverance with plenty of space to write your daily notes. This journal will take you from day to day as you travel on your journey of life. It will help you to receive back that part of your life from that which was lost. It is also filled with subjects such as: *How to give and find love again, healing from past hurts, making your own confession of faith, my faith walk (testing of your faith—did you pass?)*, and so much more.

$12.00 *plus S&H*
To order or order in bulk call or write to:

Heavenly Realm Publishing Company
P.O. Box 547
Houston, Texas 77001-0547
713-742-3405
 www.stephaniefranklin.org

I Believe God! ***Prayer Journal,*** *Write Your Own Profession of Faith*
$12.00 *plus S&H*

292

Contact & Order Page

Please send your testimonies, comments, and/or to set up book signings and speaking engagements to:

Address: Heavenly Realm Publishing Company
Stephanie Franklin *(CEO & Owner)*
P.O. Box 547
Houston, Texas 77001-0547

Email: stephanie2fr7@aol.com
www.stephaniefranklin.org
713- 742-3405

<u>To re-order:</u>

My Song of Solomon
Call: 713-742-3405 or visit: www.stephaniefranklin.org
P.O. Box 547, Houston, Texas 77001-0547

<u>To Order:</u>

When Ramona Got Her Groove Back From God
Visit: www.stephaniefranklin.org, or you may call
713-742-3405.

My Song of Solomon Prayer Journal **Call:** 713-742-3405 or write to:
P.O. Box 547, Houston, Texas 77001-0547.

About the Author

She's the best-selling author of *"When Ramona Got Her Groove Back From God"*. Stephanie is letting her multi-talents shine, but within all of these talents she's quick to give God all the glory. She is an author, playwright, director, producer, poet, designer, illustrator, motivational speaker, minister, entrepreneur, and educator. Evangelist Stephanie Franklin is all of these things and more. She speaks to the hearts of those who are in need of a life transformation and an up-lifting spiritual and mental move. God has called, anointed, and appointed her to be a Prophetess and to evangelize the world. She is very humble in allowing God to use her spiritual gifts in prophecy, healing, and deliverance. As a result, many people have been uplifted, healed, and delivered under her powerful prophetic ministry.

Her books have so many twists and turns that will keep you on the edge of your seat and your eyes flowing through every line. Her spiritual realism, dazzling—heart turning and soul moving novels will make you want to change your life at a heart beat. Her work ministers to the hearts of millions all over the world, inspiring them to change, and challenging them to love and to live a new and wholesome life.